Dance of Blades
Rage of The B
By Eve R

Table of Contents

Chapter 1

Tusk trudged through the snow, the weight upon his back dragging him down. His tan skin and long black hair were barely visible beneath his hood, made from goat skin and lined with wolf fur. At each of his hips was a small axe, one with a blade of stone, and the other raw iron, each affixed to a short but thick shaft carved from a tree branch. The pack he wore on his back was made of leather straps, clutching tight to a human body wrapped in wool sheets.

Around him began to appear stray spears, each with a humanoid skeleton impaled upon it. As he passed the first spear, its skeleton turned to look at him, the long dead jaws opening as if to speak. He ignored it and continued onwards. A raven began to circle as the spears fell into a more uniform arrangement, the skeletons all reaching out as though Tusk could free them from their fate.

The man came to a stop in a circular clearing amidst the spears where a small den resided, with a door made of animal bones and skin greeting him. This in of itself wasn't much of a concern, you make use of whatever you had if you wanted to survive. But it was the chatting of gumless teeth and pleading motions of the skeletal frame that made his heart scream with panic.

Mustering his nerves, Tusk called out in a booming voice, "DEAD WOMAN! WHERE ARE YOU!?" and waited. The raven circled. The skeletons grasped at air. "I KNOW YOU'RE HERE! Please, I need you..."

Then she stood before him, her skin as pale as the snow. She dressed only in a black cloak made of several different materials, with black feathers jutting out of the shoulders and brim. It did little to hide her naked form, something which disturbed her guest. Her face though was concealed by her hood, only a set of otherworldly green eyes peering out from the darkness. The dead woman raised her arm to her belly and bowed, a gesture that Tusk did not understand.

"You are bolder than your tribe, barbarian," she addressed him with a young but raspy voice.

"I need your help," Tusk explained. "You are the only one that can do this."

The dead woman peered beyond him, taking in the sight of the body. "Your wife?" She asked though it wasn't truly a question.

"No," Tusk replied simply.

"Hm. Present her to me," she ordered.

Tusk complied, gently dropping the pack to the ground. Then he picked the corpse up in his arms before placing it in front of the woman. He carefully undid the laces that kept the sheets bound around the body's head and pulled them apart to reveal his mate's face. Her grain yellow hair spilled onto the snow, her face just as pale as the woman's, her eyes closed and her lips blue.

The woman reached forward, grasping the sheet, before roughly yanking it back despite Tusk's look of outrage. She gazed upon the body's blood-stained thighs and asked, "Did the child survive?"

"Yes," Tusk simply replied.

"And is it yours?" She asked, pressing him for information.

"No matter whose she may be, she is my daughter," Tusk answered.

"I cannot help you," the woman abruptly said, the smallest hint of remorse in her voice.

"Why not?" Tusk growled, his anger beginning to overpower his sorrow.

"The curse that has touched your tribe, it would be difficult to work around, but not impossible," she spoke of Tusk's hidden fear despite knowing none of his people had ever told her. "But even greater than a curse is destiny. It pools around that child, and the circumstances of its birth prevent me from recalling her soul. No, the most I could do is reanimate the flesh. It would not be your lover, but a corpse given motion. Would you like that?"

"No," Tusk said softly, his anger falling into grief once more.

"What will you do with the body?" The woman asked, tracing her eyes over the corpse's porcelain skin.

"It will be buried on our lands," Tusk answered. "Away from you."

"Very well," she politely stated, though she had wished it was an offering instead.

"One more thing, dead woman," Tusk spoke. "Her soul. Did she reach the plains?"

"What was her name, her true name?" She asked.

"Silk," Tusk told her in earnest.

The woman reached out her hands, pressing the tip of her left middle finger to the body's brow and the tip of her right middle finger to the center of its chest. After a moment she answered, "She has now."

Tusk looked at the thing before him, the monster dressed almost like a person, and then at the body of his fallen mate. Then he wept, for it was all he could do now. "Thank you," he said between tears.

"She would have made it without me," the woman spoke. "I merely helped her along."

Tusk looked up at her and opened his mouth to speak once more.

***

The Granny looked up at Tusk as he entered, pity held in her wrinkled brow. Her body obscured his view, taking up most of the space not already occupied by strange herbs and alchemical ingredients in her small tent. She hobbled towards Tusk, reaching up to grasp the man's face. He had to lean down for her tender hands to wrap around his cheeks, taking in the feeling of his remorse.

"I warned you," she told him.

"I know, Granny," Tusk grimly replied.

"The child has fallen asleep," she stated. "Doe will nurse her."

"That is kind of her," he signed.

"Let me finish, boy," she scolded. "She will nurse her until her own daughter is old enough. But no longer. You will need to find a way for her to live."

Tusk thought for several moments then said, "The Dwarves. They keep goats. I will go to them, and bring one back."

"And if they don't give it to you?" She asked.

"Then I will take it from them," he said, and truer words had never been spoken. "Now let me see my daughter."

"We performed the test-" she began before Tusk cut her off.

He simply said, "I don't care."

He pushed the Granny out of his way and moved to the end of the tent. There was a cot that Doe sat at, a half-orc with light green skin and red hair. She herself was asleep, gently holding a small bundle in her arms. Tusk quietly approached and looked down, taking in the sight of his daughter in his kin's arms. Her skin was tan like his, though, beyond that, he could see a resemblance neither to himself nor her mother.

"Have you thought of a name?" The Granny asked, stepping behind him.

"Silk did before she passed on," he quietly said.

"That's what you will call her?" She asked with judgment in her voice.

"It's what she wanted," he replied. "Wolf."

***

Tusk's feet ached and stung as he trudged up the mountain path, pebbles sliding beneath his every step. He did not know how the path could be so clear of snow, especially not when the rest of the mountain seemed to wear it like a cloak, but the dwarves had many secrets. They were a strange people, distrustful of magic, and yet seemed to hoard magic that the barbarians had never seen anywhere else.

As he reached the end of the path, a small cave seemed to open up a few dozen meters ahead. The opening was no taller than he was, leading deep into the mountain. It was dark inside, far too dark for human eyes to see in. Tusk cautiously approached the cave, hoping he wouldn't have to journey while blind. He had nothing on him to start a fire, and the only things he could burn were his clothes.

Before he could get close, five strange spears with shafts made of wood and metal appeared from the dark. Each of them was flat-tipped, with a hole in the end. From beyond one of the spears, a gruff voice declared, "Hold yer self, human!"

"I mean you no harm," Tusk replied, showing his empty palms to them.

"What do you want?" The voice asked again.

"I need a goat," he answered. "A female, for milk."

"Ye don' look like ye got anything to trade," the dwarf responded.

"I will do whatever you need," Tusk responded. "Be it with my axe or hands. I need a goat."

"Anything?" The dwarf asked. "Even if it may kills ye?"

"It won't," Tusk firmly stated. "I can't die now."

The dwarf let out a laugh, and then one by one the spears disappeared. "Come on in, lad. We have a job for ye."

Tusk slowly approached the cavern entrance, bending down a few inches so he could fit inside. His eyes began to adjust, and almost instantly he could tell some strange dwarven magic was at work. Within a few steps, the darkness had been replaced by the soft light of a thousand amethyst crystals. The room he now stood in was over three meters tall and stretched to nearly seven meters in either direction. It was perfectly square, carved from stone and flint, with crystals suspended from the ceiling by a golden thread.

Around Tusk were five dwarves, each coming up just barely to his stomach. Their beards were thick and wild, either black or brown, and took up half their bodies. Their skin colors consisted of black, brown, and white between the five, with two white dwarves looking like brothers. Each one wore hide suits used for working the mines, with various tools tucked into pockets. In their hands, they held their strange spears, while pickaxes and hammers were strapped to their backs.

The one Tusk assumed to be the leader, who wore a silvery iron helmet with fierce eye holes, spoke in his gruff voice. "Ye ain't scared u' spiders, are ye lad?"

"No," Tusk simply answered.

"Heh, good," the dwarf chuckled. "Come with me then, I'll show you where it nests. Just don' touch anything. Ye don't want to be cursed, do ye?"

The dwarf led Tusk into a hall just as perfectly carved as the entrance room, and then through a dozen more rooms and halls. Each one was sculpted and shaped with precision, unlike anything the human had ever seen. In some places, the rock type changed, and in others, jewels and crystals were growing from the walls like fruit from a tree. In one room there was some strange fungus growing from some old logs that a few young dwarves seemed to be cultivating. In the distance, Tusk could hear the bleating of goats bouncing off the walls but had no idea if they were within a short walk or hours away. The dwarven cavern was impossibly large, and making sense of it was impossible for him.

Eventually, the pair came to a ravine made entirely of amethyst, beautiful purple gems, and crystals filling up the walls for hundreds of feet into an abyss lit by the glow of the crystals themselves. Near the place they walked, there was a large wooden platform with iron chains connected to it, stretching from a wooden crane down to the ground below. Atop the platform were several empty chests and a mine cart filled with pickaxes.

The Dwarf waddled towards the platform and said, "C'mon lad. It's down 'ere. Just don' take nothin. Ye wouldn't want a curse now, would ye?"

"I know," Tusk answered as he followed.

"Good," he seemed to smile beneath his beard. "Ye folk always seem to touch when they shouldn't. Always ruinin everything."

After the pair had their feet firmly planted on the platform, the dwarf pulled a lever, and the chain began to lower them down. Tusk risked a glance down below, quickly regretting the decision. He took a step back and waited as they rapidly approached the bottom. When the platform came to its sudden stop he would have leaped off it, were it not for the jolt that nearly knocked him off his feet as the chain snapped taught. While Tusk got his footing once more, the dwarf laughed at him and began to trot along.

There were many tunnels carved into the crystals, some of them several meters high with wooden ladders leading up to them. As they reached the end of the ravine, the pair turned into one of the tunnels and began to travel down it. After a few minutes, the crystals were replaced with stone and gold ore, much of which had clearly been mined already. Then suddenly a hole opened up, so wretchedly non-uniform like everything else Tusk had seen so far. It was as though the mountain had been stabbed through by some great god, leaving it with an unnatural wound.

"What happened?" Tusk asked as he gazed into the hole, seeing true and terrible darkness.

"Thas' what happens when we let a 'uman in," the dwarf grunted. "No offense."

"A man did this?" he asked in disbelief.

"Not quite, but he's responsible," he explained. "Dwarves ain't greedy, not on their own. But when a man brings his greed, it spreads. There was a wanderer a few months back, wanted to make a deal with us. The ol' chief agreed, and let him inspect our mine. He pulled out a light crystal and called it an "amy this," whatever that is. Says they 'are worth a lot of gold in his home, which I suppose is also worth a lot. Asks us to start mining them so he can sell them, instead of mining them for home and light. Then this happened."

"What's inside?" Tusk asked.

"Spiders," the dwarf shrugged. "It killed the merchant. Took the old chief, and some of the tribesmen. We want to fill it, but if we do, it might come after it. So we want it dead. But yer not gettin' a dwarf to go in there."

"I'll go," Tusk sighed. "Do you have a light?"

The dwarf trifled through his pocket before producing an amethyst crystal with a thin chain soldered onto it. He held it up for Tusk and said, "Wear this and it will keep you lit. Not much, but it's better than nothin."

"Thank you," Tusk nodded as he took it.

The barbarian pulled the necklace over his head and pulled his axes from his sides, before gazing once more into the darkness. Then he stepped forward into the unknown, blackness consuming him. Almost instantly the odor filled his nostrils, a rotten and putrid smell that made him want to vomit. Then there came the chilling cold, biting at even the parts of him wrapped under layers of fur and hide. Were it not for the crystal, he wouldn't be able to see anything at all, but by its dim light, it was enough to make out his surroundings. Stalagmites and stalactites grew from the floor and ceiling of this immense and dreadful chamber, while thick layers of webbing marked the walls and bound stone pillars together.

Tusk pulled his collar over his nose and carried on, though it did little to protect him from the cold or the smell. The suffocation was nearly overwhelming, but he fought passed it, marching deeper into the cavern. Soon, lumps began to appear on the walls, sickly-shaped things bound heavily in the web. From some, a viscous black substance leaked to the ground below. In others, small creatures seemed to be moving around, desperate for escape. The lumps only grew larger the deeper into the cavern that Tusk went, the webs growing denser but with more signs of travel.

When at last Tusk came upon the monster, he couldn't believe his eyes. It was nearly as tall as he was and far wider. Its abdomen was a cold grey color, similar to the stone, with black hair lining it. Each of its eight legs seemed to possess the blades of scythes, sharp enough to cut through a man with little effort. Upon its head were five eyes, two black orbs arranged vertically on either side of its head, and one centered between them that glowed with a familiar ethereal green. Attached to the back of its abdomen was a massive sack that Tusk wagered was responsible for leaving the webs he had traveled through.

The monster moved forward without noticing him, clearly not expecting an intruder inside its lair. Tusk silently crept forward, crouching down behind a boulder to watch the spider. It stopped at a large lump on the wall and leaned forward, sinking white fangs into it. After a few moments, the spider pulled away, and that black fluid spilled out. As Tusk watched, he couldn't help but notice that the lump seemed to be smaller. The spider crawled away, moving back towards the center of the chamber, before settling down once more.

Tusk stood up and moved forward a few paces, before moving himself into a running stance as he raised his stone axe overhead. The barbarian threw the weapon, hitting the spider in its side. Within the blink of an eye, he was running forward with a battle cry. Blue blood seeped out from the spider's wound, but it seemed not to notice any pain as it turned to meet its enemy. It waved one of its arms, nearly slicing Tusk in two before he managed to slide underneath it. Tusk quickly drove his axe into the monster's arm, spilling blue blood onto his face as he slid past, ripping the blade out behind him.

The spider opened its mandibles to roar at the human, a strange yet terrifying sound, only for Tusk to roar back. He took his axe and brought it down over the beast's head, but was knocked away by its uninjured front arm before the blow could land. Tusk collided with a brittle wall, web-covered rocks falling over him while the spider climbed forward, keeping its injured limb off the ground. It raised its arm back as he grabbed hold of a loose stone, then drove it towards his chest. Just in time, Tusk managed to block the attack with the stone, shattering it in his grip but avoiding the lethal blow. He counterattacked with another strike to its injured limb, driving the axe in deep. The spider attempted to retreat, but Tusk ripped the blade out before slamming it down again, severing the limb entirely.

The beast cried out in pain, blue blood squirting over the human and its web, but it wasn't done. Neither was Tusk. It turned to unleash a blast of webbing, but Tusk rolled out of the way and ran forward. He delivered a slash across each of the legs on its right side, tilting the monster towards him, before tearing his stone axe out of its abdomen. It turned, hoping to deliver one last blow, but it was already too late for that. The barbarian delivered strike after strike to the monster's face and shoulders, tearing into it with his axes. Even after it fell to the ground and went limp and its legs curled up, Tusk continued to slash it apart, only stopping after there were no traces of fangs or eyes left.

The barbarian turned, marching away from the spider's corpse. He didn't release his axe, because he knew that this cavern held more monsters than just this one. He passed by the dead and dying creatures he had seen when he first entered, leaving them entombed for it was not his place to free whatever monsters they may be themselves. Eventually, a familiar purple glow greeted him, and Tusk approached the entrance to the dwarven keep.

"I don' believe it," the dwarf gasped as Tusk emerged, drenched in blue blood.

"The spider is dead," he declared as he returned his axes to their holders.

"I can see 'at," the dwarf said. "An' look at you! Not even a scratch on ye!"

"The goat," Tusk stated. "I need it."

"Of course," the dwarf said as he turned for Tusk to follow. "We keep 'em back up top. Use 'em to sniff out salt." As they rode the lift back up he ventured to ask, "Why do ye need a mere goat so bad, lad?"

"For my daughter," he explained. "She will die without it."

"I see," the dwarf murmured. "Yer a good lad, for a human. The name's Colstone."

"Tusk," the human replied.

"Ye know, Tusk, if ye ever need to do trade er anythin, our keep is open to you," Colstone said.

"Thanks," Tusk nonchalantly replied as he prepared himself for the trek back.

***

The journey back was considerably easier, though Tusk found himself frequently pulling upon the leash that Colstone had provided him. The goat, a piebald thing with a thick coat and unnerving yellow eyes, seemed to enjoy stopping every few minutes and eating a mouthful of snow. Each time that Tusk pulled the leash to urge it after him, it would yell at him before trotting along. The creature was annoying, but it would have to do.

Once they had reached the camp, Tusk hitched the goat's leash to a pole outside the granny's tent and entered. Once again he found the old woman surrounded by her herbs and ingredients, though this time he could see her mixing some dried leaves with the spit in a small bowl. Behind the granny was Doe, two babes suckling from her. One was his newborn daughter, and the other was a larger child with grey-green skin and reddish-brown hair. The orc woman looked up at him and nodded, a gesture that he returned.

"I've come back with a goat," Tusk stated to the two of them.

"Of course you have," the granny said as she pulled a garlic bulb from a hook and began to crush it between her withered fingers.

"Is there anything else I need to do?" he asked, his gaze switching between the two women.

The granny crackled and asked, "If you want to care for that child, boy, there's a lot you need to do."

"Like what?" Tusk asked, humbling himself before her.

"First, you best start paying attention to the women folk," she explained, stepping towards Doe to smear some of the paste she had made onto Doe's forehead. "You don't have a lick of mothering in you, but most of them do. Pay attention to how they treat their young'uns, what they do to keep them safe and happy."

"I'll do anything I can," he said.

The granny turned back to him, and planted a sharp nail against his chest, poking him even through his hide shirt. She said,

"You best find a wife while you're at it, too. Maybe one of the widows with kids of her own. They will do a better job than you ever could."

***

"Wolf!" Tusk yelled out, releasing an arrow from his bow.

The girl leaped down from above, landing upon a squealing boar that already had an arrow in its rump. A bundle of thick black hair and hide, the girl clung on for dear life, a heavy stone knife held firmly in her right hand. The boar attempted to shake her off, but she wrapped her legs tight around its torso and gripped one of its tusks with her left hand. As her father ran forward, Wolf began to stab the beast in its throat, rapidly ripping the rough blade out and forcing it back in. The boar's squeals began to grow more gargled, but still, it fought her, finally succeeding in throwing the young girl off of it.

She hit a tree hard, knocking the air out of her before landing on the ground. Tusk looked on in horror, still running to catch up, and pulled another bone-tipped arrow from his quiver. Wolf rose to her feet, barely able to breathe, and looked the boar dead in its eye as it began to charge at her. Tusk pulled the arrow back as she grabbed a heavy-looking rock from the ground, the stone half the size of her arm. She let out a roar as the pig ran at her, and Tusk released his arrow. It hit the boar in its side moments before it would have collided with Wolf, throwing it off balance. A heartbeat later, his daughter struck the beast in the side of the head, knocking it to the ground.

Tusk approached her as he placed his bow over his back, then looked down at the bloody pig, still breathing. "Your kill," he told her. "Finish it."

Wolf raised the stone overhead and brought it down over the boar's skull, sending a sickening crunch throughout the woods. She looked up at her father, brown eyes gleaming with pride. "Did I do good, papa?" she asked him.

"You did," he smiled. "Though you need to work on throwing your weapons instead of tackling the beasts. We'll practice at home."

The past ten years had been kind to Tusk, though he knew he was aging, he found himself just as capable as he was a decade before. The thin lines of grey in his hair and occasional wrinkles in his skin were almost unnoticeable as well. The time with Wolf had been more peaceful than he could have expected, with only a handful of small conflicts arriving over the years. His tribe had once again gone to war with the orc encampment a few kilometers away, but it had ended with only a handful of deaths two days later. The occasional troll or wyrm tended to pop up, but with some effort, they were quickly brought down. All in all, Tusk found himself enjoying this peaceful existence.

Wolf was growing fast, and he could tell that one day she might even be as tall as him. The girl was a ravenous eater, outpacing even adults as she tore through meat and fruit by the handful. She was far more wild than her older peers, a trait that Tusk appreciated, though found himself struggling to control at times. However, she had also proved herself capable with a hand axe, though Tusk never let her practice in the open.

Together they gathered up the boar's carcass and Tusk slung it over his shoulder. They walked side by side, enjoying the summer breeze. The mountains rarely got this warm, just enough that they had no need to wear fur or more than one layer of hide. It would soon be over, the second mud season coming within a month, then the long winter setting in. While it lasted though, they would be foolish not to enjoy it.

After reaching camp, Tusk sent Wolf off to play while he gutted the boar. He placed it on a table near the center of the tribe's village, close to the communal fire that would be lit after sunset. Nearby, two of the tribeswomen gossiped and exchanged glances at him. Tusk did his best to ignore it, focusing on his work. Still, it wasn't long before one of the women approached him.

Her name was Spring, a woman Tusk had known his entire life. She was six years his senior and had been showing more and more interest in him after her husband had died. Her skin was a dark brown, with eyes to match, and flowing brown hair. Like most of the women there, she was dressed in a hide tunic and fur cowl that wrapped around her shoulders. A water gourd hung from her hip, bouncing with each step she took.

"You look well, Tusk," she smiled at him, stepping close to his side.

"Thanks," he grumbled as he continued his work.

"You know," she began. "It's been several months since Hoof died."

"I know," Tusk said as he peeled back the boar's skin.

"My bedroll has been so lonely," she sighed.

"I can imagine," he simply replied.

The woman narrowed her eyes, before pushing herself against his shoulder. She quietly said, "I could use your company, and your daughter needs a mother."

Anger flared across Tusk's face for a moment, but quickly passed. Instead, he only said, "She has a mother."

Shock sprang across Spring's face before quick realization set in. She quickly apologized, "I didn't mean it like that. Only that she needs a woman to learn from."

Tusk finished with the boar, wiping his hands across his shirt before turning to her. "You want company?" He asked her, though his tone was melancholic.

Spring smiled at him, then grabbed his wrist and began to pull him away. "More than anything," she said, licking her lips.

***

Wolf was never at peace with the other children in the tribe. There were only about two dozen she ever interacted with, thirteen girls from ages six to fourteen and eleven boys who were all fourteen or fifteen. Most of the girls had started just as wild as she, but even as a young child, she could see how they were treated differently. The girls only a couple of years earlier acted like entirely different people than they did now, accepting their future in the tribe and practicing for when they came of age. It made Wolf sick, especially since half the time the girls undercooked the meat.

The boys were even worse though. Since there weren't any younger boys, they had all formed their own strange hierarchy. At the bottom was the most timid boy, Splitter, who still ranked above any girl. They were constantly roughhousing, wrestling, and fighting with one another. When they weren't, they would be throwing axes or practicing with their fathers' bows. If any of the girls would watch them, the boys would either attempt to one-up each other or mock them. Today was one of the latter cases.

The biggest boy, Shank, dragged Splitter under his armpit towards the several girls that sat on a fallen log watching them, while Wolf sat on a stump several meters away from them. The boy was nearly six feet tall despite only being fourteen, a quarter orcish with a slight green tint to his skin and large canines that he liked to bear for all to see. His head was shaved, and like most of the boys there, he carried with him a wooden hand axe. Like most of the boys' weapons, it was stained with blood from sparring, a proud symbol of their strange little pecking order.

"What are you looking at?" He barked at the girls, causing one of them, Leaf-Dew, to fall back and scramble away.

"We wanted to watch you fight," another one, Bright-Stone, meekly offered.

"You jealous?" He smugly asked, tightening his grip on Splitter's neck while the other boys began to gather around.

"We just wanted to watch," she murmured, looking down at her feet.

"You girls need to stick to sewing," Shank growled. "You ruin the wrestle just by being here!"

Splitter began to tap on Shank's elbow, attempting to gasp out a handful of words. Wolf took note of the boy and began to quietly creep over, watching him attempt to get the bigger boy's attention. Shank was too focused on the girls though, spitting on them and laughing as they ran off. Bright-Stone made a rude gesture at the boy, a simple hand gesture where she kept her middle and ring finger on her palm while curving the rest of her fingers. It was the sign of the Serpent, calling Shank both evil and a coward.

"You little bitch!" He called after her. "If you weren't a girl, I would kick your ass!"

"Let him go," Wolf said from behind him, earning the gazes from every boy there, including the now blue-faced Splitter.

"What'd you say to me?" Shank asked, turning to face the small girl before him.

"Let him go," she simply repeated.

Shank finally took note of the breathless boy under his arm and released, dropping Splitter gasping to the grass. Shank marched forward as he said, "Don't tell me what to do, you stupid little bi-"

Wolf punched the boy square in the nose, feeling the sensation of his cartilage breaking beneath her knuckles while blood squirted out onto her fist. A chorus of gasps erupted as Wolf looked at her blood-stained hand in surprise. Shank had fallen back from the unexpected blow, unable to comprehend what had just happened. But that moment quickly faded as he wiped the blood from his nose and stared at the ten-year-old who had just given him a wound that his friends never managed to dish out.

"Bitch," he growled before charging at her.

Wolf dodged his charge and kicked him in the back, though it didn't seem to do much beyond make him lose his balance for a second. He quickly turned and grabbed hold of Wolf's wrist before punching her across the cheek. He brought his other fist back to strike her again, but this time Wolf delivered a knee to his groin. Shank squealed in pain, while Wolf punched him in the side of the head twice. That's all the time she had though, before Shank grabbed her by the throat and lifted her into the air. He began to strangle the girl as she dug her nails into his wrist, growling in pain.

At last, the boy dropped her, then looked around at his companions and shouted, "The hell are you waiting for!? Beat her!"

The surrounding boys complied quickly, encircling Wolf and delivering kicks across her body. The only one who didn't was Splitter, who had squirmed away the moment he got the chance. Each strike sent a wave of pain throughout Wolf's body. She would have cried out in pain, had the air not been knocked from her lungs. Instead, she gasped for breath, writhing atop the dirt as she was bludgeoned over and over. It would be nearly two minutes of this before the boys began to stop, one by one, until they stood staring down at the bruised girl.

"How does that feel, little bitch?" Shank asked with a chuckle.

Wolf didn't respond and instead reached into her pocket. Shank stepped closer, prepared for a kick, and then screeched in pain as Wolf stabbed into his standing ankle with her knife. She ripped the blade out and he fell to his knees, blood gushing from his wound. She slashed across his face, leaving a deep scar that would brand him for life. Then she dug the blade into his shoulder and ripped it out, a terrible smile on her face. With a kick to his chest, Wolf knocked Shank onto his back. For a moment she was triumphant. But it was just a moment.

The others reacted slowly, but there were enough of them that it made little difference. Wolf dodged and weaved as best as she could, but she was still pummeled by fists. As that realization set in, she began to ignore the pain and lashed out blindly with her hunting knife. A slashed wrist here, a severed finger there, it wasn't much but it was enough to cause them to retreat. One of the boys dragged Shank back to give the others more space as they tested Wolf. One would step forward while another came from behind, trying to catch her off guard. She cut the first boy to try this across the back and stabbed the next through his knee.

She stood surrounded by them, panting, yet full of excitement. One of them let out a battle cry and charged, followed by three more. She cut the first across his hip and the second on his chest, while the third avoided an attack. She spun on him as he attempted to tackle her, and stabbed him square in his gut. The girl yanked the blade out as the boy stumbled back, before falling to the ground. One of the boys whose fingers she had cut off picked up a large rock, catching her eye amidst the crowd. As he prepared to throw it, she retaliated with a throw of her knife towards his head. The blade sliced clean through his ear, scraping against his skull, then embedded in a tree behind him. After several seconds of stunned silence, he began to scream in pain and dropped the rock to the ground.

The boy she cut on the chest grabbed her at that moment, holding her left wrist as he began to choke her in a headlock. Wolf brought her hand over his face and began to apply as much pressure as she could, sinking nails under his skin. Then her thumb found its way to his eye, and he began to scream louder than any boy there. She didn't stop until he let go, and by that point, his eye was nothing more than a bloody mush. His friends pulled him away, leaving Wolf standing alone. Her skin was badly bruised and her hands were covered in blood. She was a menacing thing, a primal growl emanating from her throat as she cast her gaze across each of the boys.

But then she realized that it wasn't just the boys who stood there. Some adults had gathered, watching in a mix of shock and excitement. How long they had been standing there she had no idea, but they had clearly seen enough. A large hand roughly grabbed her wrist and Wolf went limp, unsure of what to do or how to act. Besides, the adrenaline had already worn off, and she was filled with tiredness that smothered her consciousness state.

By the time Tusk had made it to the chieftain's hut, it was far too late to make any sort of argument. Fang took one look at Tusk, haphazardly dressed in his tunic and weaponless, and his mind was settled. Tusk's own gaze flickered from his father, old yet more imposing than any other man, and his daughter in the back of the tent. Each of her arms was held by a tribesman who clutched an axe and spear respectfully. She seemed barely aware of her surroundings and was coated in a thin layer of blood that was not her own.

Fang asked a simple question that carried with it the weight of a thousand worlds. "Did you teach her our ways?"

The fear in Tusk quickly transformed into anger, "The tribe is dying!" He growled.

"It will last," Fang said adamantly. "It is not right to teach a girl such things."

"And you would rather no one know?" He asked, his eyes boring into his father's. "No boy will ever be born to us again. We either teach the girls, or we die."

"Then we die," Fang retorted. "Better to die than to corrupt our ideals. You and that bastard are disgraces to this tribe."

The words cut through Tusk better than any knife ever could. The only words he could muster were, "Is that what you think of her?"

"You are no longer a part of the tribe," Fang replied without answering. "You are banished to the wilds, where the world may either consume you, or you it. Never shall you stand upon Frost Lion lands again."

The guards roughly shoved Wolf forward and she fell into Tusk's arms, giving them a hiss of her teeth as she glared back at them. Tusk held her tight, holding back tears as he tried to think of something to say. But there was nothing. All he had now was her, and enough sorrow to crush mountains. But he would not cry, not in front of his father, or the tribesmen, and never Wolf.

Fang said simply, "Go."

So they left.

***

The winters would come and go in the blink of an eye. Wolf grew remarkably fast, rivaling Tusk's size in what felt like no time. Her ferociousness was fearsome, and not something it seemed he could tame. Neither of them spoke much, and sometimes he wondered if that's why she behaved like she did. More in growls and grunts than speech. But the near animal-like behavior she exhibited when hunting was otherworldly, seemingly both a gift and a curse. Thanks to it, they often had enough meat when the land frosted, but it tore at Tusk's heart how carelessly she gazed upon other people. As though they were no more than future threats to be faced in the midst of a terrible storm.

There was easily enough reason he could see in this. During a bad winter when she was thirteen, a lost traveler stumbled upon their burrow. He had been hungry, and so they fed him and offered him shelter until the storm passed. Late into the night, the traveler attacked Tusk and stabbed him in the leg. Within seconds Tusk had driven his hunting knife into the man's throat, and though his own wound bled fiercely, it was mended within the hour. Yet it seemed as though Wolf never recovered after that. She stood behind Tusk in all his meetings with the dwarves, glaring at them with an intensity you would give your most bitter rival. On the rare occasions, someone came across their camp she would drive them off, usually by roars of fury, but more than a few liters of human blood marked their border.

He did his best to help her adapt to people, their time with the dwarves went from trade expeditions to frequent work in their mines. Still, even after helping them build many strange devices and elevators, the girl never really spoke to them. Colstone once joked that she got along better with the goats, but soon that joke became reality. He and Tusk would often arrive at the goat chamber late at night and find her there. Sometimes she slept amongst them, other times she gently petted them and seemed to whisper into the animals' floppy ears.

One night, as the two watched over Wolf's sleeping form, Tusk asked Colstone a weighted question. "How long have we known each other?"

The dwarf thought about it for a moment. "Damn near twenty years," he said.

"Promise me something," Tusk spoke, the faintest hint of sorrow upon his voice.

"What is it?" The dwarf asked, looking up at the human with concern.

"When I'm not here," he struggled for the words. "Watch over her."

"Are ye planning on going somewhere?" He asked, concern evident beneath his beard.

Tusk considered himself for several moments, then he pulled down the brim of his shirt to reveal a spreading blue mass beneath his skin. "Rot," he said. "I don't know how long I have."

"Ave you been to see a medicine woman?" Colstone asked though he knew the answer.

"I'm banished from the tribe," he said. "She wouldn't help me."

"You could have come to us," Colstone said, hurt in his voice.

"Would that have helped?" Tusk asked.

"No..." he confessed. "Dwarves don't get sick like humans. We wouldn't know how to treat it."

"Then it doesn't matter," Tusk sighed. "She doesn't understand people. She doesn't deserve to be alone. Please, take care of her."

"I'll try my best, laddie," Colstone placed a hand on his back. "Though I don't think she'll let me."

"No..." Tusk smiled.

***

Wolf held Tusk as he stumbled towards his cot, his hand draped around her neck. She looked at him with frantic eyes, unsure of what to do. Tusk attempted to meet her gaze before erupting into a fit of coughing, a wet and viscous cough that would have dropped him to the ground if his daughter hadn't clutched him so tight. Wolf laid him down onto the mass of animal hides that served as his bed, carefully wrapping him in a fur blanket. He shivered for a moment, but it seemed to be passing.

"What's wrong?" Wolf asked him once he had stopped moving.

Tusk looked over at her, thinking for what felt like hours. At last, he simply said, "I'm dying."

"No," she responded, almost like it was an order.

"Wolf," he began before she cut him off.

"You can't," she insisted.

"I am. Once I go, you need to go to the mountains," Tusk squeezed out. "The Dwarves will take care of you."

"No," she said again.

"Wolf, listen to me," he urged her. "They're our friends. You need them."

"I only need you," she stubbornly stated.

He looked at her with such a look of pity that it cut into Wolf's very heart. Then he said, "Fetch some firewood. I'm so cold."

Wolf rose to her feet and stepped away, her movements slow and sluggish. As she reached the tent flap, she grabbed hold of her two-handed axe and then pushed her way outside. The bitter cold wind instantly began to burrow into her skin and bones, but she ignored it. Wolf made her way to the edge of the camp, where a few trees had already been marked for kindling with charcoal. She raised her axe in both hands and swung it into the trunk, hearing the sound of the blade tearing open wood, but unable to feel the impact. She ripped it out and struck again, causing the tree to tilt to the side. She swung one final time and it came toppling down, sending a white mist up around the area.

As she was dissecting the fallen tree, Wolf grew aware of a strange bird watching her. It was a hawk, of that she was sure, but its feathers were nearly all white with a silver trim along the wings and breast. She acted as though she hadn't noticed the bird, but could tell it was watching her intently for whatever reason. After she was satisfied she had enough wood, Wolf suddenly spun, letting loose the knife she had concealed in her grip. A moment later the bird fell from its perch, leaving a red stain on the snow below.

She gathered up what wood she could carry in one arm, leaving her axe embedded in the fallen tree, then claimed the bird's corpse in her free hand. Wolf quickly returned to the tent. She dropped the bird's body by the entrance and then dumped the wood into a hole at the center of the room. She carefully arranged it, before she took two stones and began to strike them together. Eventually, a fire blossomed, and she returned to her father's side.

"Fire is strong," she said.

Tusk was silent for some time before he said, "This chill runs so deep."

"How did this happen?" She asked, placing her hand on his shoulder.

"Bad wood," he uncomfortably chuckled, before coughing violently. "The Blue Rot. Mushrooms."

She racked her brain, before eventually remembering her once being scolded for foraging a blue mushroom from a dead tree. "But how?"

"I took wood I didn't need," he said. "Nature punishes those who are greedy. The Rot got into my body as I breathed. It eats me from the inside out."

"You don't deserve it," Wolf said as she laid her head across his chest. "Please don't."

"I'm sorry, my daughter," he coughed once. "I love you. In the plains beyond I will wait for you."

"I don't want to be alone," Wolf said and felt tears leaking, yet could not find a way to sob.

"You will never be alone..." he wheezed in sharply. "I will always look after... you."

"I love you," she softly said.

"I love you too," he smiled despite the pain.

It would be many hours until Tusk passed away, his coughing fits growing progressively worse until suddenly they vanished. Relief had flooded Wolf in that moment, for it seemed as though her father wouldn't die. Instead, he was dead within the hour. She noticed immediately when his breathing stopped, and moments later, his heartbeat. No matter how hard she shook him, he would not wake. Refusing to let despair overcome her, Wolf knew there was still one option left to her.

Chapter 2

As the Dread Lord Vhodan spread his might across the land, one by one the realms of man, elf, and dwarf fell. No matter what resistance they put up, the Dread Lord's forces of monsters, undead, and loyal soldiers conquered them. Thousands had been slain, thousands more enslaved, and after the tyrant's one hundred and thirty-two-year reign, Vhodan's conquest showed no signs of slowing as it reached the edges of the lands of Valael. It seemed inevitable that the world was to be swallowed by his evil might, and all hope for salvation would soon be smothered out.

Then the Council of Fate brought forth all the great heroes it could muster from lands far and close, all noble leaders and brilliant masterminds, any who believed they could put a stop to the greatest evil their lands had ever seen. They would meet at The Citadel of Remembrance, secluded deep within the untouched forests of Mulvek. Once fully gathered, there stood no more than a hundred people of all the Valael races, be they prominent or dwindling. A thousand brave souls gathered to save their home. Of them, there were few that could be comparable to the traditional heroes, and even fewer seemed willing to embark upon a quest alone.

The hundred people stood upon a stone floor, looking to a stone altar that hid half the bodies of three sages. Each was dressed in a set of grey robes, which could of course simply be grey robes, but in this case marked them as wizards who have since forsaken magic. Each one possessed a long beard of varying lengths that poked out from their hoods, concealing most of their features. All anyone could tell was that they were human, and had once wielded great power. There were still some legends of their youthful adventures, Apos The Swift, Brindus The Decisive, and Valedict The Trickster.

Amongst these legends were also the rumors that they had once been Vhodan's advisors. In the early years of his campaign, they had supposedly instructed him in archaic and terrible magic, while also aiding in his conquest of Syronul. Then Vhodan had taken to the vampire and gorgon queens and soon began to devise horrible methods of war that disturbed the sages so greatly that they abandoned their emperor and went into hiding. Perhaps because of these tales there were so few that had obeyed the sages' summons.

It was Apos who spoke first, to the hundred or so that had gathered shoulder to shoulder in the stone bastion. "I see all of you that stand before me, and I smile for I know that so long as you stand here, hope still exists. No matter what horrors occur in this abysmal war, I know that we shall prevail, for hope lies upon our side."

Second to speak was Valedict who said, "We have studied the scrolls left to us by those of the First Age. They prophesize the coming battle, events that have unfolded and will unfold. The Emperor's time draws to an end! The scroll tells us of what will make us victorious in this coming age!"

From the crowd spoke Zeydas, a high elf hero who had lost his right arm in an epic battle against a rock troll. He was broad for an elf, and carried about him a peculiar look of disdain wherever he went. His hair was a deep dark blue, and his skin of violet hue. He asked, "What do we do, sages?" He asked, and there was desperation in his voice.

The third sage, Brindus, smiled. He said, "We must send forth a party of heroes into the mouth of the beast. Only a small group will succeed. They will find Vhodan in his castle, guarded by monsters unimaginable, and slay him. Only these few heroes will be able to succeed. Who amongst you will go into the mouth of the beast?"

There were many shocked murmurs amidst the crowd. A thousand brave souls had gathered, yet they had gathered to live, not to embark on a suicide mission. Invading the castle of Vhodan was certain death, for many had tried, and none had ever returned. Facing the Dread Lord alone was an impossible task even in battle, for many there had seen him tear men in two with his bare hands, and never had he been injured. Of course, all also knew that he bred terrifying monsters beneath his castle, which would make even reaching his throne room an impossible task.

"I will go," suddenly said the wizard Jubilatious, a small hint of reluctance in his soft voice.

He was a young man of no real renown, though some mages whispered of his magical potential. Jubilatious was tall and thin, with pale skin and features that were somewhat elf-like. He was dressed in a purple robe and pretentious pointed hat that fell in upon itself, half hiding his piercing crystal blue eyes. These clothes marked him as a wizard of mixed talents - while the pinewood staff with a green jewel pressed into it ensured they all knew he held power. His hair was long and black, badly kept, though his face knew well the blade of a razor.

"As will I," said the regal voice of Zetine, the lost Pharoah of Exia.

Zetine was perhaps the most beautiful woman in the world, which was no easy feat in a world of elves. Her skin was dark brown but heavily concealed by layers of black bandages and a long flowing skirt hemmed with gold. Her hair was obscured by a radiant black and gold headscarf, while several tattoos were presented on the sides of her forehead and her chin. Zetine possessed deep brown eyes that lured in all those who looked at her, drawing attention away from the daggers strapped to her thighs that occasionally were revealed beneath her skirt.

"If we're saving the world, don' count me out," grumbled the dwarf crusader Ironja.

Ironja was somewhat tall for a dwarf, which was still much smaller than the two humans. He had thick black hair and an even thicker beard with flecks of grey in it. His skin was tan and his eyes a modest brown with a slight yellow tint. He dressed in a tunic with heavy dwarven armor over it, while a curved helmet rested under his left arm. In his right hand, he held a hammer, while a short battle axe was strapped to his back.

Last to speak was Mizt-Ied, who stuttered out, "I-i'm not t-too good in a- in a fight, b-but I'm good at sneaking! And I wa-want to help!"

She was a goblin, no more than three feet tall, and with skin as green as grass. Her dark green hair was wrapped up into a bun atop her head. Her eyes were a lovely bright yellow. She dressed in an appropriately sized dark blue cloak with the hood pulled back, and wore a loincloth beneath it. She also carried with her several very small knives and one normal-sized curved dagger that looked a bit too large for her.

"Are there any more here that will join them?" Apos asked, but the room had suddenly fallen deathly quiet.

Brindus said, "Know that we do not consider your silence cowardice. But the four of you are perhaps the four bravest to live for millennia."

Valedict said, "No matter what happens, you are fated to free this land from oppression. It is written. You will face many hardships, many losses, but you will slay the evil once and for all!"

Jubilatious asked, "Great sages, you said our actions were prophesied. Could you tell us of this prophecy so that we may act in accordance?"

The three sages looked between one another, but it was Brindus who spoke first. "Very well, but we ask that no one here tries to affect the prophecy. Be it through assistance or opposition, interference with a prophecy only has disastrous results. Hear these words, and know them to be true.

"As hope is drained from the land, and the army of darkness prospers, there shall be a gathering of scholars and soldiers. From royalty and from squalor, an alliance will be formed.

"A blade will choose a great hero. The vanquished will rise. The children of destiny will stand together against the inevitable. The evil of times past will be defeated, and the land will be united. Until the end, the chosen will fight."

The four heroes listened intently, as did the many others that surrounded them. They all knew never to read into the words of a prophecy, but how could they not? It seemed obvious what the first half meant, though the second half was a complete mystery. Time would have to be the one to shed light upon these mysteries.

It was the human general Carver, a toweringly tall and lanky man in chaimail who asked, "And what of the rest of us? Are we to sit by and wait for the outcome that these four will bring?"

Valedict said, "It will be the duties of the rest of you to hinder the Dread Lord. Whatever battles you can fight, resources you can steal, leaders you can assassinate."

Apos grimly continued, "As the time of his death draws near, he will seek to draw his armies close to his castle. You must not let him. You must send all of your forces at that crucial moment, every man and woman, every elf and dwarf. All must join in the fight to defeat the Dread Lord's army no matter what."

Zeydas said, "My sword will know the blood of our enemies once more, and any dark elves I can gather from the Far Mountains. But how will we know when the time is right?"

Brindus answered, "When the Dread Lord's armies begin to retreat. They will all go to the castle to defend their master, though they likely won't know the reason why. You must follow them and prevent them from being of assistance. This recall, as we have gathered, will coincide with an eclipse that will block out the sun. The eclipse is only three months away."

From the crowd spoke Rain-Upon-The-Rocks, a wood elf with tear-blue skin that had fought in a thousand battles. He said, "This I cannot do. The true elves have fought for the human race time and time again. We have lost more than anyone. I cannot send more of my people to die for you, no matter how noble the cause is. We will not fight in this war any longer, though we will also not stop you."

Under his breath, Zeydas cursed, "Coward."

Apos implored, "I know our fight against the Dark Lord has tried you, Rain-Upon-The-Rocks. It has tried all of us. Every being here has known great loss. Every race has suffered indescribably at the hands of this evil empire. Please, we must stand together if we hope to succeed."

Rain-Upon-The-Rocks shook his head and said, "We shall see what the future holds."

One by one the gathered began to leave, returning to whatever homes and bases they still had. Even the three sages left, retiring to their chambers somewhere in the back of the fort. Soon after the four heroes were left alone aside from each other. Four strangers, two known by reputation, and two utterly alien.

Ironja softly said, "So. Just the four of us, eh?"

"It would seem so," sighed Zetine.

"We can do this!" Mizt-Ied squeaked. "The heroes of the First Age defeated the giants, and there were only three of them!"

"The rules were not as well defined," Jubilatious lamented. "I would love to believe we're more than enough, but magic and body are much weaker than they used to be."

"Don't you believe in the prophecy?" Mizt-Ied asked.

"If you believe in a prophecy," he explained, "It will never come true. Besides, they're infuriatingly vague."

"What do you think, lass?" Ironja asked as he looked at Zetine.

"I think we can do it, but I worry about the cost," she said. "I imagine at least one of us will fall in battle. Perhaps even all of us."

Jubilatious raised an eyebrow and asked, "Aren't you offended by his lack of respect, great pharaoh?"

"We're at the end of the world," she smiled wistfully. "Titles and heritage have little meaning anymore."

Jubilatious stuck his hand out and said, "Then let the four of us, unbound from who we were before, set out to end the suffering that has swallowed our world. My name is Jubilatious, a wizard of modest renowned and savior of farmer's crops."

"What are ye doin?" Ironja asked with a raised brow.

"Oh," he awkwardly mumbled. "I thought we'd do a thing, you know..."

"Like the heroes in the Second Age?" Zetine asked, a coy smile on her face.

"Yes," Jubilatious groaned.

"Why not," she mused. "Maybe it will bring us luck."

The others placed their hands atop his and said their names.

"Ironja, son of Ironskul, slayer of the great rock troll Kanaton."

"Mizt-Ied, humble spy and pretty rogue and raider of bandit camps. Oh! Also, I like to cook! And I saved a guy from a mad dire-llama once!"

"Zetine, daughter of Zelestia and great pharaoh of Exia. Keeper of the restless dead and breaker of the golden chain."

"Until the end of the world," Jubilatious wistfully added.

Together they all declared, "Till the end of the world!"

***

The first real challenge came only a few days later. They rode atop two horses, one black and one white. Jubilatious and Ironja road the black horse, while Zetine and Mizt-Ied rode the white horse.

They had traveled beyond uprooted trees and through burned villages, encountering only the occasional monster or band of corrupted soldiers. It was as they approached the edges of the land of Mulvek that the horses began to act up, neighing and attempting to shake their riders free.

"What's wrong with them!?" Mizt-Ied asked as she frantically held tight to Zetine's waist.

"There's something in the woods!" She replied, holding onto the reigns for dear life. "They can smell it!"

Ironja cursed out, "These damn beasts better be smelling a blasted dragon if they're actin' like this!"

"Don't jinx us!" Jubilatious responded, but it was too late.

What moved out from the forest was not a dragon, though the common man likely would not have known that. It walked upon four scaled legs that ended in the talons of a bird. Its body was long like that of a snake's, and it was covered almost entirely in green and black scales, save for the thick feathers that collected over its breast. Its face was most certainly that of a serpent, only it seemed to be wearing the beak of a rooster, and it possessed both the plume of one and the hood of a cobra.

Typically, a basilisk can only be born when a female serpent and a rooster mate. In all of history, there had only been a dozen or so proven accounts of this actually occurring. But Emperor Vhodan's Beast Lord was a master of alchemy and the shaping of flesh. Each of his abominations could be born by the dozens in a single year and were sent out into the world to cause chaos wherever they went.

Ironja noticed it first, only able to let out a soft, "Oh gods be damned..."

A fraction of a second later Zetine had seen the beast and reacted, drawing her daggers and leaping off the horse. Her reflexes proved lifesaving, for a moment later a glob of thick green acid flew past where her head had just been. Zetine landed in a roll on the ground, quickly rising to her feet to face off against the beast. Though she had never seen anything quite like it, she knew better than to hold still. The others were following in her lead, disembarking from the horses while she strafed around the basilisk.

It hissed, a horrible and guttural sound as it attempted to follow her. Like both of its genetic ancestors, the basilisk possessed forward-facing eyes, but these proved a hindrance as Zetine moved, her bandages forming an almost hypnotic pattern with each twist and turn of her body. This allowed Ironja to swing his axe down upon its backside, which unfortunately was a profoundly useless thing to do.

The dwarf's axe reverberated in his hands, and the basilisk swung about to face him. As it did so, its tail swung into Jubilatious, knocking him to the ground and preventing him from casting any spell. In his haste to avoid the monster's talons, Ironja inadvertently looked into the eyes of the basilisk and found himself utterly paralyzed. Zetine had moved to help Jubilatious and did not notice her companion's predicament. As the monster barred down upon the dwarf, intent on gobbling him whole, it was none other than Mizt-Ied who came to the rescue.

The goblin leaped upon the beast's tail and scampered up its back. As it opened its jaws she reached its head and pulled two of her small knives from their hiding places. Mizt-Ied plunged the blades into the basilisk's eyes, forcing them as far in as they could go without risking her hands touching the green blood that seeped out. The monster screamed a great and horrible screech that made Mizt-Ied flinch and fall from its back, lashing out with its barbed tongue. Ironja took that moment to swing out with his axe, slicing half of its tongue off.

The basilisk turned and clumsily scampered away blind and half-mute. It sent stones flying beneath its talons and crashed through trees. Every now and then a small amount of its blood would fall to the ground, burning through whatever lay beneath. The four heroes gathered themselves and made sure they were uninjured, which luckily they all seemed to be. Even Ironja's axe was undamaged, though he had to hold it out to prevent the acidic blood from dripping onto his hands.

"How is the blade not melted?" Zetine curiously asked.

"Dwarven steel," he replied with a puff of his chest. "Unbreakable and unmeltable by anything other than the very fires that forged it!"

"We need to finish off that monster," Jubilatious said as he looked to the path it had carved itself. "We cannot let it hurt someone else, or alert our enemies to where we are."

"He's right, let's go," Zetine said as she strode forward.

Jubilatious was quick to follow, but Ironja instead walked to Mizt-Ied and gave her a firm pat on the back. He said, "Good work, lass. Ye saved me life."

Then he followed after the two humans, and with a big smile on her face, Mizt-Ied followed after him. The basilisk left an easy trail to follow, which was a great boon since none of the heroes were particularly adept at tracking or navigating forests. It was a bit of an effort to avoid the smoldering puddles of acid, but they made it through unharmed. Eventually, they managed to track the beast to its lair, which was nothing more than a modestly sized burrow with the corpses of some deer and elves strewn around it. There the beast laid, panting heavily with its tongue hanging freely from its jaws, blood dripping into the dirt where it smoldered away.

"How should we finish it off?" Zetine asked as she studied the beast.

"I could hurl a bolt of fire at it," Jubilatious offered. "See what that does?"

"We don't want it to spit acid at us if you fail," Zetine shook her head. "Do you not know of the monster's weaknesses?"

"I never had reason to study monsters," he shrugged. "I just wanted to be able to change the weather. Never expected I'd be saving the world."

She narrowed her eyes as she focused upon the basilisk's breast then said, "The crest of feathers. That may be a weak point."

"I could try hitting it with me axe again," Ironja suggested.

"Do you think you can drive it deep enough to kill the monster with a single strike?" she sarcastically asked.

Ironja looked between his axe and the basilisk for a few moments. Then he said, "Probably not."

Jubilatious said, "I should be able to do this, trust me. But It may take everything out of me."

Zetine nodded and said, "Very well. Do it."

"We'll take care of you, big guy," Mizt-Ied encouraged.

"I'm not that big," he mumbled as he rose to his feet. Jubilatious extended his staff and focused on the monster's chest as he began to chant. "I call upon you, solar flames that burn the cosmos. Let your sparks ignite my enemy and reduce it to ash."

Fire is a natural force of unmeasured destruction, yet it also provides the heat needed for life. The same cannot be said for magical fire, which consumes all it touches and detests the very concept of life. The heroes watched as orange flames began to gather around Jubilatious' staff, centered upon its gem. Then the flames slowly changed to blue, and the air around them all felt intensely hot. Even Ironja had to wipe a bead of sweat from his brow. Without warning the flames shot forward like an arrow, striking through the basilisk's chest. It did not have time to scream, it barely even had time to shake. The flames tore through its insides, expanding to swallow up the monster in its entirety.

The heroes watched as its scales cracked and blue fire sprung out from its maw, quickly spreading over the entire beast. It was quick, yet horrifying, to watch as its body was devoured. Soon all that was left were charred bones and black ash, settled upon the dirt floor amidst the now partially cooked elven bodies. It was an uncomfortable sight, but a relieving one to know the monster would no longer be a threat.

"Good job!" Mizt-Ied squeaked.

"Ye did good, lad," Ironja nodded.

"Thanks," Jubilatious gasped, and they all quickly realized just how sweat-covered he was in comparison to them.

The wizard stumbled back, then fell onto his bottom. He took several slow and deep breaths as he attempted to recompose himself. The other three looked at him with concern, but he merely waved his hand at them. After a few moments, he slowly climbed to his feet and used his staff to keep himself steady.

"Powerful magic," he slowly explained. "It takes a lot of energy. I just need a few moments... then I should be able to make it to the horses."

Zetine took the moment to look around then said, "Speaking of which... where are they?"

"What do ye mean?" Ironja asked.

"We left them to chase the monster," Mizt-Ied reminded her.

"Did none of you take them with us, or tie them up?" she asked.

"When would we have done that?" Jubilatious asked.

"You should have done that before chasing the basilisk!" she cried.

Mizt-Ied looked at her in disbelief and said, "You left first! If you wanted them tied up, you should have said so!"

"And ye didn't even notice the lack of hoof beats?" Ironja asked with a chuckle.

"Well I- no, but," Zetine stammered.

Ironja let out a deep chuckle and said, "Her Majesty doesn't understand she came out here without servants."

"Well now that's not true," she stated.

Jubilatious smiled and said, "We're a team now. We must take equal responsibility, and all work together. Even if some of us *did* stay with the horses longer than others," he looked to his two shorter companions.

Mizt-Ied said, "Well, if you want something done, you actually need to say it!"

Zetine took a deep breath and thought to herself for several moments. Then she said, "Very well. I apologize. I have undoubtedly led a very different life than the three of you, and am used to things being done without having to express it. I will try not to let this create problems going forward."

"And if it does, we'll be sure to tell ya," Mizt-Ied cheekily said, while Jubilatious looked to the goblin in disbelief.

Zetine cracked a small smile and replied, "I'm sure you will, Mizt-Ied."

"I hope they didn't wander too far," Jubilatious abruptly interjected. "I am not up for walking the rest of the day."

"Yer lucky yer in front," Ironja stated. "My ass has never known such a beating."

Zetine blushed at this while Mizt-Ied said, "Mine's known much worse, and on a regular basis too," which caused Zetine to blush even harder and begin walking away.

Jubilatious said, "Thank you for that image. It will haunt me for the rest of my life."

Mizt-Ied shrugged and said, "I don't get what the big deal is. You fall a lot when you scale walls. It tends to hurt."

He replied, "That's not what you meant, and you know it."

She snickered and said, "Yeah, I know..."

**

While the newly named heroes embarked on their quest, there was another who did not have the luxury of a council, of anyone to guide him towards an end goal. Grey, long-fingered hands were clasped in chains as he toiled away, harvesting the turnips that would feed an entire town and the emperor's army. The ceaseless shouting of overseers had grown into white noise in the high elf's ear, drowned out by the beating of his own heart. Rage slowly began to fill the elf as he worked. It wasn't the first time, and many more slaves had been filled with that rage for far longer. It was just the way it was until Kira finally had enough.

It was late evening, and the sun had already set. There were less overseers than usual, most of them having gone back to town to get drunk. The pain that day was no greater than any other, the abuse lessened than usual even. Kira simply could not bare another moment of this existence, and froze up in his spot.

One of the overseers had noticed Kira had stalled in his work and gone to beat him for it. As the orc raised his cudgel overhead, expecting the slender elf to cower in fear, Kira caught the weapon in his fist. The orc looked down at him in shock for just a moment, before Kira drove his thumb through the overseer's eye. He shouted in pain and released his grip on the cudgel, allowing Kira to flip it around in his hand before striking the overseer hard in the head. The orc fell, and then Kira was atop him, beating his head into a thick red paste with the cudgel. By the time he had finished, six other overseers had approached, discarding their blunt weapons in favor of broadswords.

"There's six of us and one of you, elf," one of them called out to him. "Lay down and this doesn't have to hurt too badly."

Kira cast his purple gaze over them before asking, "Have you any idea what I did before you stole me?"

His words fell on deaf ears as they charged him at once. The chains on Kira's legs prevented him from moving too quickly, while the chains on his arms limited him from acting on the offensive. He swung the cudgel into the wrist of the first overseer to reach him, breaking it, before raising up his arms and leaping backward as the next one attacked. There was a flash of sparks as the overseer's broadsword cleft through Kira's chains, and then the elf was rolling across the field as he attempted to get back to his feet. They were upon him in no time, clumsily driving their swords into the ground where Kira deftly contorted to avoid the blades.

They quickly caught on and began to limit the elf's movement range, only for him to wrap his legs around one of the overseer's necks and break it. Kira pulled the orc's sword from his grip and used it to block a strike at his heart just in time. While still on the ground, Kira swung the sword and severed an orc's leg. He used this moment to clamber to his feet, and then quickly parried an incoming swing just in time to avoid a lethal blow. The next orc swung his blade at Kira, only for the elf to parry it as well then follow up with a thrust into his gut. As the orc fell over, Kira severed the chains between his own legs.

Two overseers swung their broadswords at once, but the elf ducked down and their blades connected with one another. Kira then took out the one on the right's leg, before punching into the groin of the one on his left. As that orc fell to his knees in pain and Kira rose back up, the elf brought the tip of his blade through the back of the orc's neck. The last of the overseers looked to the elf, and for whatever reason decided he would still attack even with a broken hand. He charged forward, there was a flash of steel, and he fell to the ground behind Kira.

The elf dropped the broadsword and began to massage his wrists, before speaking to the surviving orcs. He said, "I was master of arms for the entire Northern Coalition. Yet you idiots stuck me out here with the farmers. You could have at least kept me as a gladiator, but no, pulling roots from the ground was such a use for my talents!"

One of the fallen orcs crawled forward, blood still spraying out from his severed leg as he cried out, "Why now!? No one waits years for this!"

Kira carefully stepped towards the orc, then crouched down and took hold of his head in both hands. He answered, "Because you finally broke me. I just didn't break in the way you wanted."

Then Kira proceeded to thrust the orc's head against the ground, before violently pulling it back up. He continued to bash the overseer's skull in again and again until there was nothing left worth bashing. He dropped the corpse and rose back up to his feet, panting as the blood rage wore off. Then he looked around to see the various other slaves, mostly dwarves or humans, all staring at him in a cocktail of anticipation and shock. Kira looked away, instead focusing on the task of stripping the orc he had stabbed through the neck.

The overseer's uniform was twice Kira's size, but it at least did the job of covering up the rags he had worn as a slave. The chains were another matter that needed to be remedied, though he was sure he could find a solution at some point. Kira pulled a scabbard from another orc and looped both between his belt, pulling it as tight as possible which proved to be just a little too loose for comfort with the holes laid in it. Kira sighed and ignored it, before swapping the burlap he had used as shoes for a pair of oversized boots that he stuffed the burlap into so they would fit better. Finally, he claimed two broadswords and slid them gently into the scabbards on either hip.

As Kira began to walk away one of the slaves called back to him, "What about us!?"

The high elf looked back to the woman who had called out, and for a brief moment, more anger filled him. He had been the one to fight back, to risk his life, to kill for his own freedom. Now the cowards that had surrounded him for the past decade wanted to ride his coattails. To use him to secure their own freedom. For just a moment Kira considered laughing in her face and walking away, but pushed those thoughts deep down. There was no point in acting like the same sort of monster that Vhodan employed.

Kira had each of the other slaves line up, and one by one he severed the chains that had marked their imprisonment. He had to replace one of his broadswords after finishing, not wanting to risk it breaking in combat afterward but ensured that each one of them was free to do as they pleased. Once finished, he sheathed his new blade and began to walk away. Once again, one of the slaves called out to him.

This time a dwarf asked, "Shall we follow ye?"

Without slowing Kira answered, "No. Find your own paths."

"But... what if they send catchers after us?" another one asked.

"Then kill them," Kira coldly stated.

He left them without another word, heading east. He wasn't entirely sure of where to go, his mind racing for solutions. Eventually, he recalled a close friend he had for many years, another high elf named Vrias. A few decades before, Vrias had gone to Arkvine in Syronul to study magic. Kira had implored Vrias not to go, but there was no other magic academy for thousands of miles, let alone a magic academy that accepted all races. So Vrias had left to further his education under the thumb of the Empire. Ironically that decision had spared the elf when the Empire came to his homeland, slaughtering thousands and taking hundreds as slaves. Kira could only hope that Vrias was not too attached to the Empire.

The best outcome, Kira decided, was that together he and Vrias would kill Emperor Vhodan The Eternal. That was an impossible task, so instead Kira would strive for the second-best outcome. He and Vrias would reunite, and then together they would flee the country, the entire continent if they needed to. It was unlikely Vhodan had cut off sea travel, port income was too valuable of a resource to be rid of. Even if it meant stowing away aboard a ship, Kira was confident that he could get away from the horrors that had plagued the past decade of his life.

Alone, he set out for the city of Arkvine, for its wretched academy of wizards and sorcerers. It would not be the longest of journeys, but it would be alone and miserable. Despite this, Kira persevered in the hope that his friend would be just as elated to see him as he would be to see Vrias.

Chapter 3

Wolf carried Tusk's body in her arms, her axe upon her back. The corpse weighed her down into the snow, but she marched with all her might, refusing to stop no matter how much her body ached. She had taken a fur coat to help insulate her body, hiding most of her features beneath the grey wolf pelt. She had been unsure of whether Tusk would need more clothing, so she instead wrapped him in a blanket.

Frozen corpses began to appear around her, tied to stakes or held within bone cages. They moaned out a variety of names, of lovers and family, best friends and bitter rivals. One of them even looked familiar, one of the boys that had once beaten her in her youth. His lips were blue and his eyes grey as he called out for a name that could not breach his swollen tongue. Sat atop many of these poor souls were blackbirds, some living, and some clearly dead, often feasting from the corpses.

She continued forward, and instead of skin there became bone. Humanoid skeletons milled about, digging up snow and laying down small pieces of broken animal bones. She saw a pair journey out from the forest, slowly dragging a deer that they had apparently killed by impaling it with a sharpened leg bone they had used like a spear. Then she came across a house that would be impressive, were it not for the skeletal remains that had been used to hold the wood and stone together. Here the birds seemed most plentiful, cawing and chuckling, or wheezing just like Tusk had been doing. These ones she guessed were mocking her, for they were all the live ones.

"DEAD WOMAN!" Wolf called out at the top of her lungs. "I know you're here! Come out!"

There came a creaking as the house's door opened, and there she stood in repugnant beauty. Wolf had no frame of reference, though the dead woman's body had hardly aged a day. Her black cloak was now larger, much more refined and elegant, and completely covered in feathers. Her skin was as pale as ever, and her body as badly concealed as when Tusk first saw it. Her hood had fallen back, revealing black hair, thin sickly lips, noble-like features, and ethereal green eyes. Her only truly inhuman appearance were the skeletal hands that grew from her elbows, held together by thin strands of sinew that seemed about to snap.

"So, you are the one to come here," the dead woman mused. "Fate truly is ironic."

"Bring him back," Wolf ordered, not daring to approach the dead woman.

Instead, the dead woman strode towards her, coming to a stop closer than Wolf would have liked. She said, "I will tell you the same thing I told your father, decades ago. I cannot bring your parents' souls back. The bonds of destiny are too great for me to sever."

"What does that mean?" Wolf asked in confusion.

The dead woman pressed her hand to Wolf's cheeks, her eyes widening as she saw what potential the future held. She said, "You are far too important to interfere with..." though it seemed as though she was talking to herself more than Wolf. "But times of strife make for interesting journeys."

"What are you-" Wolf began before a sharp pain shot up the side of her skull.

She recoiled away from the dead woman, dropping Tusk's body to the ground as she pulled her axe free. The dead woman merely turned back to her home and said, "You may leave now, barbarian. There is nothing I can do for you."

Wolf watched the dead woman retreat, then placed her hand over the spot where she felt the most pain. There was nothing noticeable there, though her finger picked up the faintest dot of blood. She considered storming after the dead woman, breaking her door down, and planting her axe in the thing's chest. But she couldn't see any point in it. Dead is dead, no matter what form it takes. She fell to her knees and cried over the corpse of her father. It would be the first and last cry for what would feel like a thousand years.

As the dead woman peered over her trinkets, she could feel the talons of a bird dig into the undead flesh of one of her pets. Time was drawing to a close faster than she had thought, and the barbarian girl's arrival now seemed as though the strands of destiny extended to envelop her alongside the girl. She had to shift through a mound of dirt and bone to find what she was looking for but pulled it triumphantly from the spot it had rested since she first came to this place. A weapon that she never had reason to use, until now, when her certainty finally began to waver.

It was a blade of twisted black metal, roughly forged with iron and ash, and had been cooled in human blood some fifty years earlier. It was three feet long and perfectly straight, with a somewhat thin blade that once held a sharp edge on both sides and a pointed tip. Unfortunately, it had grown dull, though she wouldn't need to use it for long, and didn't quite understand what a dull blade actually was. Something with boredom, she expected. Lastly, there was the hilt, an elegant white bone that had been perfectly sculpted for the original wielder's hand. Her own skeletal hands awkwardly fitted around it, barely able to properly clasp the weapon.

Satisfied she could make a show of the sword; the dead woman raised her left hand and snapped her fingers. It was an awful sound, more akin to crunching bone than an actual snap. Across her domain, bone cages unlocked and their inhabitants spilled out. The dead yanked spears free from still-moving corpses, gathering whatever weapons they could muster. Their mistress made her appearance only after all available armaments had been taken. She surveyed her several dozen skeletons and zombies, satisfied that they would be enough for the coming attack. Then, she gave her command.

***

In a large artificial clearing several kilometers away, a blind man stood surrounded by a dozen others. The blind man dressed in a brown cloth cloak and a set of rugged cotton and leather clothing. Strapped to his back was a bow and quiver, while a set of small knives was adorned across his chest. On his shoulder was a white crest with a silver throne placed in front of a golden sun with six sharp streamers. This symbol was adorned on each of the surrounding men, who were dressed in leather armor with iron spurs on their boots and iron breastplates on their chests. Spread out across the clearing were also a hundred-odd men in a mix of plate and chain armor, twenty horses, four wagons, and several dozen white falcons.

A falcon dropped a dead crow at the blind man's feet, and then he was no longer blind. He spoke to them in a Mulvek accent, "The necromancer seems allied with the barbarians. It will need to be dealt with. Several of my birds have been slain, either by predators or the barbarians. But they expect nothing. They sleep two hours after sunset and are often drunk enough that they'll be easy pickings. Most of the men are old enough that we wouldn't need to worry about that anyway. There is one spot that seemed to have a small camp, likely a hunting party of only one or two. Otherwise, the nearest major threats are the orc encampments, but they're too far to be of any use."

One of the men in leather asked, "What about the predators?"

"Only wolves," the blind man reassured him. "I have seen no bears in these lands, and if there are any monsters, they're likely slumbering."

"Who should take the necromancer?" Another one of them asked.

"I hate wizards," another nodded.

The blind man said, "Soran, Muller, you two lead your men against the necromancer. Altis, you will send a squad after the camp. The rest of you may lead the charge against the barbarians. I'll watch from overhead and ensure no reinforcements arrive."

One of the men who hadn't spoken, Soran, said, "We'll take care of it, Colonel Huntsman."

They quickly began organizing their forces, climbing atop horses and shouting orders. Two of them went South-East, another South West, the each of them leading eight men with the lone rider leading seven. The others rode alongside their huge mass of soldiers, marching through the woods to the north. Only two of the soldiers remained with Huntsman, each adorned in plate mail and clutching a halberd and shield. The ranger looked over the two with his now green eyes, a small frown creasing across his lips.

"Does the captain not trust me?" He asked them, striding forward with unnatural grace.

"Not at all, sir," the one on the left said.

"We're here in case the camp is attacked," the one on the right said.

"Sure you are," Huntsman sighed. "You may as well make yourselves useful and start packing.

The two exchanged a look with one another then shrugged. "Right away, sir."

***

It was difficult burying Tusk. They had owned no shovel, and so she awkwardly made do with her axe. It was a relief that it wasn't snowing at the moment, for it had taken her half an hour just to clear away the layers of snow that were already built up. The dirt was even harder to remove, for it was frozen and compact. But she steadily made way, until there was a hole two and a half feet deep. She dragged her father's body inside, and then began to use her hands to cover it with a mix of dirt and snow. Once she was done, she laid across the mound of dirt in silence. It seemed as though she was now utterly alone, and had no idea what she was supposed to do anymore.

The crunching of broken twigs caught her attention, and Wolf shot to her feet. Her bow was within the tent, while her axe was held firmly in her hands. She didn't know what approached but was ready to kill whatever it was, man or beast. It was a man. He ran at her from the edge of the woods, greatsword held firmly in his hands as he let loose a battle cry. With a single sweep of her axe, she stole that cry from him, along with his left leg.

The soldier fell to the ground, blood gushing from his stump as he cried out in agony. In but a moment's time she wished she had gone for the bow instead, as a chestnut horse came crashing through the trees. Wolf barely had time to roll out of the way as a lance was driven into the ground where she had stood a heartbeat ago. By the time she had recovered, the remaining seven soldiers were already entering the area, swords and polearms at the ready. Her eyes darted between them, frantically analyzing the situation. As the captain readied his lance for another attack, Wolf moved.

Her knife was embedded in the throat of a soldier before they had even realized what had happened, while she ran towards the captain. A swipe of her axe sent the horse toppling down, letting loose a sound that split the ears of all there as it cried over its missing limb. The captain was crushed beneath his mount, while his men leaped into action. Two men and a woman with swords encircled her, while the three welding polearms filled in their gaps from a short distance. Wolf quickly realized how dire the situation was, and acted upon impulse.

She planted her axe into the arm of one of the swordsmen, leaving it buried as a spear tip pierced her wrist. She grabbed hold of the woman by the shoulders and used her as a shield as she moved forward, two of her allies stabbing at her in an attempt to kill Wolf. The woman's chainmail stopped most of their attacks, but a few struck true. Once the distance was closed, Wolf tossed the woman to the side and grabbed hold of a polearm. She kicked the weapon's owner to the ground and stabbed the tip through the eye of his ally, before turning and driving it through the charging swordsman's gut. He looked down in surprise as his momentum was stolen from him, then back up at Wolf.

"You bitch..." he gasped before his body went limp and his sword fell into the snow.

Wolf yanked the polearm out of his belly then turned, stepping towards the recovering soldier that she had robbed. He looked up at her for just a moment before she brought the polearm over his head, splattering his brains over his shoulders. She released the weapon and he slumped over at an awkward angle, like a stiff doll. Wolf then took the moment to make note of who was still alive. Seeing just the woman, attempting to crawl away, and the man with her axe in his arm, she was satisfied. She strolled towards the soldier whose throat held her knife and ripped it out, before returning to the woman.

She stabbed her knife through the back of the woman's knee and then asked, "Why?"

"Please," the woman begged. "Just let me go, just forget all about this!"

Wolf ripped the blade out and then moved to the felled man. She slid her blade through his fingertip and asked again, "Why?"

"Fuck you, savage," he spat.

Wolf calmly sheathed her knife, stood up, and tore her axe free of his arm. Giving him a moment to cry out in pain, she then began to drive her axe down repeatedly into his legs. Again and again, he cried out as she cut small bit after small bit off of him, his screams graduating into one continuous wail of agony. By the time she reached his knees, she felt as though she was finished. She planted her axe into his skull, and then drew her knife once again. She moved back to the woman and crouched down.

"Why?" She continued to ask.

"I don't want to die..." the woman sobbed.

Wolf tilted the woman's head up with the tip of her knife and ordered, "Tell me why."

"You were just in the way," the woman said. When Wolf didn't seem to understand she explained, "We need these lands. You people would never leave, so we did what we had to."

Wolf slit the woman's throat a moment later, then rose to her feet. She sheathed her knife and moved back to the tent, claiming her bow and a quiver of arrows. After returning outside, she took hold of her axe once again and only then remembered the horse and captain. She moved to silence the beast, with two quick chops to the side of its thick neck. She then looked down to the captain, whose torso was sticking out from beneath his mount. He gasped for breath that would not come, his face purple and bloated. Wolf left him there, as she set out into the night.

***

The village was pure chaos. Tents burned, and with them, so did their occupants. Smoke drowned the air, while the pained and fearful cries of the tribespeople rang out sporadically. The few remaining warriors fought as best as they could, but their ways of fighting lost them any advantage. Each battle cry would only draw more soldiers to them. Some of the women crept about in silence, slitting throats where they could, while most took their daughters and fled. Most of those who fled would survive the night, but come morning, several children and a dozen mothers would be amongst the burned corpses.

Chieftain Shank, though he had yet to realize he was a chieftain, strode through the flames. In one hand he held an axe of bone, and in the other the head of one of his enemies. He chucked the head at one of his attackers, knocking the man to the ground. Another ran around him, sword held high. Shank separated the man's arms from his body and then continued undeterred. He stomped on the head of the man he knocked down, heard a crunch, and then moved on. Another soldier came at him, this one holding a spear and shield. Shank had little experience dodging and was barely able to keep out of the way of the blade. He was saved when a knife was driven through the back of the soldier's neck, before falling to his knees. Behind him stood Spring, panting.

"Chieftain?" She asked, looking between Shank's one remaining eye and the burn across his empty socket.

"Chieftain?" He asked back in surprise. "Papa is..."

"I'm sorry," Spring said as she moved forward, glancing over her shoulder. "Many of the others are already gone too. What should we do?"

Shank spoke quickly, though he wasn't confident in his words. "Run. I'll try and hold them off. Anyone you see- even the warriors, make sure they run too. We can't end like this. Not like this..."

Spring nodded. "You would have been a great chieftain."

He smiled at her for just a moment. "No, I just don't want to die for nothing. Now go."

As Spring ran off, Shank claimed one of the fallen soldier's swords in his offhand. He called out at the top of his lungs, "INVADERS! COME AND MEET YOUR DEATHS AT THE HANDS OF CHIEFTAIN SHANK!"

He hated how that sounded, but it seemed to do the deed. They emerged from the smoke like the devils they were, polearms and spears at the ready. Shank was barely conscious of his actions, but he knew he was at least killing some of his enemies. Blood splattered across his face more times than he could count, and every now and then a limb would fly through the air. He couldn't be sure when he lost his own arm; all he knew was that he was suddenly left with only an axe to use. By this point, the shield soldiers had moved in, and there was no point in fighting anymore. Shank fell to his knees and accepted his fate.

Spring had deftly avoided detection by the invaders, though others weren't as lucky. She had attempted to take Doe and her daughter with her, but fate had other plans. She didn't notice her friend fall, only that she wasn't with her when she made it to the edge of the village. She had gone back for them, but it was too late. One soldier had planted his spear through Doe's back, and another was grabbing Ruby-Gem by her waist. Spring took hold of her knife and hoped her aim was true, and then threw it. It only cut the soldier across his cheek but still caused him to release his grip in surprise.

Ruby-Gem took the opportunity to bolt, and Spring did the same. She heard the soldier's calling from behind her but didn't dare look back. She breached the smoke and kept running until the unmistakable sounds of meat tearing filled her ears. She stopped and looked down, expecting to find herself fatally wounded. Upon finding no wounds, she turned back to see a strange figure standing over the bodies of the two soldiers chasing her. Nearby was Ruby-Gem, fallen to the ground, and looking up at the stranger in disbelief.

He was tall and thin, far too thin for any man to be. He was dressed in black clothing with dirty grey boots and a grey scarf wrapped across his face. He clutched in one hand a curved knife that wrapped over his knuckles and in the other a ritual dagger. The stranger sheathed the knife at his back and practically floated forward, for his movements were so graceful and efficient. He offered a hand to Ruby-Gem, and then together they came to Spring. She could see behind his scarf were silver eyes and pale blue skin.

He spoke in a strange accent, "Forgive my intrusion. I am not one to meddle in wars, but I could not help but take note of this particular event. I hope I have not offended you by stepping in."

Spring was taken aback by this being and his strange way of talking. "N-no," she answered. "Thank you."

He cast his gaze over the two of them and then asked, "Do you have somewhere to go?"

"No," Ruby-Gem automatically answered as she pushed herself to her feet.

"Do you seek sanctuary?" He asked.

"What does that word mean?" Ruby-Gem asked.

"Safety. Shelter," Spring quickly said. Then she asked, "Are you an elf?"

"I am," the stranger answered. "Though my sanctuary is not one of woods nor towers. Should you be willing, I will escort you to the caverns I call home. Your enemies will not follow, though rare is it for human or orc to journey into the darkness."

The two women exchanged looks. Then Spring said, "We would like that. Anything is better than this"

***

Captain Muller fell off his horse as it reared back in terror, two skeletal hands clutching its hindquarters. By the time its front legs were back on the ground, the skeleton exploded, impossibly large spears of bone impaling the horse's underbelly. Muller clambered backward until his back hit a pair of feet, and he looked up into the dead eyes of a zombie. Ir raised its axe into the air, before falling to the ground with a spear sticking out of its eye socket. Muller looked back to see one of his men had covered him and was now using a shield to hold back two more zombies. Muller clambered to his feet and drew his shortsword, frantically looking at where the next enemy attack may come from. Everywhere, it seemed.

Every soldier there was engaged with some form of undead, barely able to keep them at bay. Captain Sorran sat perched upon his horse, two bone spears jutting out from the beast's back and through his torso. One of the men with a polearm had fallen, and the zombies had crowded over him, tearing flesh from his face with their broken teeth. It was nearly impossible for Muller to remember his training, but he managed it, and an air of calm soon came over him.

He strode forward, slicing through two skeletons beneath their ribcages. He never understood why the undead had these strange weaknesses, but he was grateful for it. The zombies were harder to take down, but so long as his blade pierced brains or severed their heads they would fall. Muller grabbed one zombie from behind and threw it to the side, giving his hand to a bloody soldier to hoist her to her feet. It was a miserable and grueling experience to cut down the undead, but they prevailed, and in the end nine of them still stood amidst the corpses.

"Keep moving," Muller ordered as he dragged his wounded leg. "We don't leave until the necromancer is dead!"

There were still more undead that came to face them, but the element of surprise was gone. The soldiers cut through them with relative ease, losing only a single person to yet another bone explosion. At last, they came across their target, standing some twenty yards ahead of her house. She swayed back and forth as though in a trance, a hypnotic dance-like movement that would have aroused several of her enemies, had it not been for the horror of her hands. Then suddenly she stopped and reached into the snow by her side. Muller yelled something, though none of them could quite understand what it was. She drew her sword, and then it seemed obvious, so they charged.

"Die, witch!" Muller growled as he lunged at her.

The dead woman barely managed to parry his strike, stepping backwards, before slicing the blade across the abdomen of another soldier. "You really should know better than to face a mage in martial combat," she chided them.

"Get around her!" Muller ordered, frustrated by the near line-like formation they had taken.

Two of the soldiers suddenly found themselves impaled upon a wall of bone that had seemingly come out of nowhere. It was like the door of a prison cell, and the dead woman looked at them with her otherworldly green eyes. One of the impaled soldiers, caught by his leg, wailed in pain and begged for help. The other was silent other than the gurgle of blood spilling out of his mouth. He had been stabbed through the groin and deep into his body, and there could be no saving him. After getting their senses, the soldiers began to move either way around the wall to cut her off. She could only smile beneath her hood.

As Muller stared daggers into her, the dead woman asked, "Have you ever heard of The First Spell?"

"You wouldn't," he gasped in terror, and though the others had no frame of reference for the spell, the woman's tone made them tremble.

She began to chant, and Muller knew she spoke the truth. "Beneath the skin that binds me, encased in the bone that holds me. Buried in my heart of hearts, of all that is one and all that is others. From first love to last hated, flowing through the blood of life and the blood of death. Of all that is myself I call upon you, held within your prison that is my body. May you finally be free. I release you, Magika Nekras, Magika Eternika, Magika Hema. May my soul find its anchor."

Muller had ran the moment she said the first words and hoped he was at a sufficient distance when she finished. With his back to a tree, he waited for the spell to be complete. The first spear tip would enter the necromancer's thigh as she began the final line, and the last would pierce her arm just as she finished. To call it an explosion would be a fallacy, for there was no tangible force. Every spell she had ever worked save for one came undone, bone crumbling to ash, her constructs falling into their final rest, and her home caving in upon itself. Every other soldier there spent an eternity feeling as though their very being was plucked apart, atom by atom. Flesh slid from their bones, their skeletons warped and melted, while their organs shriveled into mummified husks. The bark from surrounding trees was stripped away and pulp was rotted away into nothingness.

The dead woman fell to her knees, in pain, but alive. She looked down to where her hands had been, finding only infected stumps. "Oh that's right," she quietly mused. "I don't get to just die."

Muller stepped out from behind his cover, barely far enough away to survive the magical onslaught. He dragged his leg forward, clutching his sword tight, as birds fell from the sky. He barely paid attention to the hellscape that surrounded him. The bodies of his men were unrecognizable as anything that had ever lived, and if it wasn't for their intact armor and weapons, he wouldn't have thought of them as anything more than strange puddles. He said nothing as he approached the necromancer, and simply thrust his sword through her heart. She slumped forward into the blade, and then he ripped it out, and sliced off her head with a single strike. Now alone in the forest, he fell to his side, and he did not get back up.

***

Wolf's head split with an intense pain worse than any headache she ever had. In the moment it arrived, she had accidentally stepped too harshly upon the snow, letting loose a soft *crunch*. In the clearing ahead, the cloaked man stopped moving boxes. He was too far to have heard it, yet it seemed as though he was standing right next to her with the way he acted. Wolf watched him to see if he would move, and when he didn't, she silently removed her bow and pulled an arrow back. One of the other soldiers came into her view, carrying a box full of food towards a nearby wagon. Another got out of the wagon and began walking in her general direction. She decided that would be who she would kill first.

"I suggest you drop to the ground," the ranger said.

"What?" the soldier closest to him asked.

"Huh?" the other managed, a moment before an arrow made its home in his skull.

"What the hell?" the first soldier shouted in surprise, looking to the clearing.

The ranger moved around him, leaving the soldier to be hit in the jaw with an arrow. He fell into the snow, gagging on the arrowhead poking into his mouth and writhing in pain. The ranger drew his own bow and said, "Come on out, girl.

Begrudgingly, Wolf moved out from the underbrush she had concealed herself in. She locked eyes with the ranger, and after a moment, realized he wasn't even looking at her. He was blind. Feeling confident, she notched an arrow and released. He was impossibly fast, drawing and notching his own arrow before she even realized he had moved. His arrow whistled through the air with perfect grace, meeting her own. While both arrows were knocked harmlessly to the ground, the ranger's arrow had sliced open the sharp stone she had used at an arrowhead. He simply smiled at her from beneath his brown hood.

Cautiously, Wolf placed her bow back on her shoulder and drew her axe. The ranger changed posture but did not release his own bow. She ran at him with a roar, intent on chopping the man in half. He easily dodged the attack, bending back so the blade carried over him. As he returned to full standing, he swiped Wolf's legs out from under her, and struck her over the chest with the top limb of his bow. She rolled out of the way after being struck and got to her feet, but he was upon her in a heartbeat, delivering quick strikes with his bow as though it was a staff. She could barely react, for each time she realized she had been hit, he was already swinging for the next attack.

The ranger knocked Wolf onto her back, and a groan of pain escaped her lips. "Who...?" she asked in disbelief, never having seen someone so agile.

"The Empire calls me Huntsman," he lamented. "The tragedy of not having a last name is they just call you by your occupation."

Wolf struggled onto her feet, saying, "Shut up. Kill you."

"No you won't," he chuckled. "I have killed far greater warriors than you, girl. Go back to the woods, and maybe you'll get to live a long life."

Wolf spat some blood from a cut on her inner cheek into the snow before turning, pure rage on her face. She raised her axe and charged with a roar, intent on cleaving this Huntsman in two no matter what. Then suddenly he was laid across the ground, and his boot was on Wolf's stomach, lifting her into the air. She saw the notched arrow, and then in a blink felt it buried into her chest. Then she was flying, before landing in a rough roll. She clutched her axe tight, and felt the arrow shaft break off. Snow began to amass around her as she rolled, and she realized she was moving downhill. Wolf attempted to break free before she was buried in a snow bank, but it was no use, and the pain was beginning to sink in. She closed her eyes and let the darkness take her.

***

Several hours later, Captain Bardos walked up and down a line of prisoners on the outskirts of the village. His men had rounded up what slaves they could, mostly of the women and children that hadn't made it too far and hadn't been killed in the battle. Now he had to decide what to do with the surviving men. Most of the elderly had thrown their lives away in the conflict, so he didn't have to worry about wasting time cleansing the pack of useless dregs. Most of these men were injured, some more than others. Even to Bardos, it was impressive that one in particular still lived. Then again, he supposed to himself, orcs are remarkably hard to kill.

At last, he spoke, "Which one of you is the leader?"

"I am Chieftan Shank," the orc began with grim pride in his voice. "I have bashed in the skulls of twigs like you since I was a child. I vow to tear your head off and make a cup from it."

"I see," Bardos chuckled, before drawing his sword. He swung it into Shank's neck then ripped it out, before swinging it again, this time beheading the orc. He calmly asked, "Do any of you feel the same?"

There were a few soft murmurs of the men, amounting to a collective, "No."

"Good," Bardos smiled a thin and despicable smile. "From now on, you are property of the Rizzen Empire. You will work for the betterment of our society, a society that you are now part of. Perhaps you will build bridges, uniting the people of our land. Perhaps you will harvest the crops that feed your brothers and sisters in the nearby cities. One day, should you prove yourself you may even be able to serve in the Imperial Army. To show our might to those that refuse us, and liberate new lands."

Bardos turned away, and said to his men, "Take them to camp. Keep them separated from the women."

The soldiers moved forward and began to drag the barbarians to their feet, making sure the rope tightly bound their hands and kept them from being able to run. Afterward, they connected them all by a single long rope that ended in the grip of one of the soldiers. He dragged them forward, forcing them into a continuous movement that was just slightly too fast for them to comfortably move. They were taken away from the burned-out husk of their home, never to see it again. Their spirits were as broken as their lives, and they had no idea of what to expect from the coming days. More misery, they expected. They were right.

Chapter 4

It had been an arduous journey through the forests of Mulvek, but the four heroes pulled through. Many beasts had roamed the forests, some small, and some far larger than Zetine and Jubilatious. The group had relied heavily upon stealth, moving about unseen and unheard as best they could. In the case of Ironja, this proved easier said than done, for his armor clanked almost every time he moved. On more than one occasion this had scared off a deer that was to be the night's dinner, and once even warned a horde of ghouls that they were nearby.

When at last they reached the fields of Moia, they couldn't believe what they saw. It had been years since any of them had stepped foot upon the lands, and none of them were prepared for it. What once had been endless fields of beautiful flowers and vibrant shrubbery had been reduced to barren wastelands. It seemed as though every field for a hundred miles was burned to nothing. Ash hung heavy in the air, blocking out the sun and choking the life out from the four heroes.

"Cover your mouths," Jubilatious said. "If you keep your cowl over your mouth, you won't breathe the ash in.

He pulled the collar of his robe over his mouth and nose, while Mizt-Ied did the same with the cowl of her hood. Zetine pulled at her headscarf to cover her face, revealing some of her short curly hair. This left Ironja to remark, "Guess I'll die."

"Do you not have a hood or mask?" Zetine asked, looking down at the dwarf.

"What for?" he asked, looking back up into her deep brown eyes. "I have no need to hide who I am, and I certainly don' need to keep my hair tied back."

"You're too proud," Mizt-Ied clucked. "Sometimes a hood comes in handy! Like when you don't want to get rain on you!"

"If I don't want the rain to get on me, I'll stay inside," he grumbled. "Besides, I'm a dwarf. We breathe coal like it's nothin'. I'll be fine."

"Are you sure?" Jubilatious wearily asked.

"I'm sure," he replied. "Come on now, ain't no point standing about."

The dwarf took the lead, pushing Jubilatious out of the way to do so. The wizard gave a look to the pharaoh, who simply shrugged, and then they followed after him. Mizt-Ied followed last, uncertain about heading into the wasteland as unprepared as they were. The ash made it so difficult to see that Jubilatious had to conjure a ball of light to serve as a beacon to the others. It would be an hour of walking until they realized that this was a bad idea.

The group was embroiled in a heated conversation. It was Jubilatious who said, "You're insane. Barbaric. Ill-mannered and rude. Were you in my home, I would kick you out and never invite you back."

"If you were in my home I'd break your teeth," Ironja retorted.

"You horrible little dwarf," Jubilatious spat. "You show disrespect unparalleled in this life or any other. For this alone, I believe you are unworthy of a peaceful afterlife."

"Food needs *salt*," the dwarf exclaimed.

"Which is why the cook salts it beforehand!" Jubilatious insisted.

"Ye know yerself better than any cook does," Ironja shook his head.

"If I were to spend HOURS preparing a fine meal for my friends," Jubilatious began with a huff in his voice. "Adding rare spices and carefully ensuring the meal would be perfect, it should be served as is. My beloved friends who I had labored so intensely for would cherish that meal greater than any they had ever eaten before. But should my dear beloved friend dare to salt their food, should the MONSTER salt it before so much as even tasting it!? Then I would know our entire friendship was built upon a lie. That they were no friend of mine and every experience we had in our past would now be tainted by their vile actions."

"Boy, yer a mad man," Ironja spat. "Salt is the greatest joy in this miserable life. It should be added to everything, be it meat or plant! In the mines of Bastadon, we chew upon salt rocks raw! We lace our gums with salt before heading out for a hard day's work, for its joy is so great that it puts mining to shame!"

"I like salt," Mizt-Ied said quietly from behind them.

"As do I," Zetine agreed. "It is quite tasty."

From somewhere beyond the haze of ash, the group could hear a strange scuttling sound. They quickly drew their weapons and staff, moving back to back as they looked for any sign of their approaching enemy. Eyes darted frantically about, unable to see where the sound was coming from. Slowly, they were able to realize this was because it came from all directions. Multiple creatures, whatever they were, were beginning to surround them.

It was Ironja's dwarven eyes that saw them first. He quickly shouted out, "Salamanders!"

A salamander was typically a creature of no more than a few inches in length. They possessed two arms and two legs, a tail, and lizard-like appearances, though they often lived amidst water. Their monstrous brethren, however, tended to be six feet in length and grew up to three feet tall. They also possessed somewhat hard scales and a rather special ability that made them a danger for anyone to encounter.

Wasting no time, Jubilatious raised his staff up and pounded it into the ground as he declared, "Icen shield, protect us!"

A dome of blue ice sprung up from the ground, quickly enveloping the group. The air inside was freezing cold, but this would last for only a few moments. A spout of fire began to drill into the ice in front of Miz-Ied's face, slowly melting it away. Ahead of Jubilatious, another spout of fire did the same, and a third one took Zetine's spot, a fourth Ironja's, and then two others. Jubilatious focused himself in an attempt to regenerate the ice, but the overwhelming heat of the fires was enough to slowly outpace his best efforts.

"What do we do!?" Mizt-Ied frantically asked.

Zetine ordered, "Get on my shoulders, the moment you have an opening, leap behind our enemies."

"On it!" Mizt-Ied said, before scampering up Zetine's leg, arm, and then onto her shoulders. This caused Zetine quite a bit of discomfort, but she didn't say anything.

Then Zetine asked, "Ironja, how good is your armor at handling flames?"

"It won't melt," he said. "Might burn me a bit though."

"I'm sorry," she said, "but I need you to get in front of me."

"Yes ma'am," he huffed and hopped in front of Zetine.

"Jubilatious?" she asked.

"What is it?" he asked back, straining to control the ice dome.

"Can you lower the wall directly in front of me?"

He thought for a moment about what he guessed her plan to be. Then he answered, "Yes. That will help strengthen the rest of the shield as well."

"Then do it," Zetine ordered.

The salamander's breath breached the dome and enveloped Ironja. The dwarf growled in pain but held steady, even as the flames licked his beard. Mizt-Ied jumped off from Zetine's shoulders, successfully landing behind the salamander, causing a cloud of ash to rise into the air around her. The lizard stopped its attack and turned to see what the commotion was, earning it a slash across the snout from the goblin. The beast hissed in surprise and pain, a moment before Ironja swung his axe into the back of its head and ended its life.

Zetine sprung out from behind the shelter, and all three of the heroes flanked their amphibian enemies. Knives cut through scales, the blade of an axe severed heads, and one by one the flames died down. As the last of the fires subsided, Jubilatious returned the ice dome to nothing more than water vapor and walked forward.

He held his staff high into the air and said, "Great and mighty tempest, scour this land with the winds of the sky!"

From the tip of his staff, a great wind blew, sending all the ash in the air away from it. It was as though a great knife cleaved down upon the world, removing all ash for the next mile ahead of Jubilatious. He could clearly see Mizt-Ied slice the throat of a salamander, and Zetine stabbed another through the head, but that didn't interest him. Much more interesting was a small house, far off but within eyesight.

"We will shelter there," he said as he indicated with his staff.

The other three returned to his side, but it was Ironja who said, "Bagh. If we have to."

Together they set off towards the house, hurrying faster than they had been before, while the ash slowly devoured the group once more. Jubilatious dismissed his ball of light and strode next to Zetine while their two shorter companions followed after them. Soon they reached the house and quickly entered. Ironja closed the door behind them before he pushed a barrel in front of it to prevent the door from being opened again, just in case any stray monster or other enemy happened to be in the area.

The interior of the house was abysmal. It had clearly been ransacked some time ago, and whoever had once lived here was unlikely to ever return. The table that had once been used to eat meals had been crushed, its legs splintered across the ground. The fireplace was cold and devoid of any logs, while the bed that rested in the corner had been sliced open and its straw stuffing torn out. There was also an exposed cross-shaped window, though it didn't seem like it had ever held any glass or other covering. Because of this, a fair amount of ash had been blown into the one-room home.

Jubilatious took a seat and said, "It's better than nothing."

"I wonder who tore up the bed," Zetine mused.

"Probably robbers," he said. "Some people hide their valuables in their beds."

"Do you think they'll ever be back?" Mizt-Ied asked.

"Who, the robbers?" he asked.

"No!" she squeaked. "The people that lived here..."

"I doubt it," Zetine answered for him. "This land is so barren, I don't think anyone will live here come a hundred years or more."

"That's horrible," she moped.

"It's the way of the world now," Jubilatious sighed. "So long as Vhodan lives, this is what will happen to every land and every people. I fear that even if we do stop him, his destruction will have been too great. What if there is never going back?"

"There is always a chance at fixing it," Zetine said. "No matter what he does. So long as people live, the world can be saved. This is but one land, and though the devastation is great, people will ensure it lives again one day."

Jubilatious said, "I don't know how, but I swear that if we are successful, I will see Moia returned to life."

"If I had a cup of ale," Ironja cheekily said, "I'd drink to that."

After a few moments of silence, Mizt-Ied said, "I used to live here, you know."

"In this house?" Ironja asked in shock.

"No!" she squeaked as she turned to look at him. "In Moia!"

"It was your home?" Zetine asked.

"Yes. Er- well, no... I don't know..." she sheepishly said.

"Tell us," Zetine encouraged her.

Mizt-Ied took a deep breath and said, "I moved about a lot when I was young. I mean, obviously, I still move about a lot, but it was different back then. My family never had a lot of money, so we would travel and scavenge what we could. Eventually, though, my folks got sick. I couldn't afford any medicine, or even really a place to stay, not while they were sick anyway. No one else wants to get sick, after all. I tried to care for them, but they died, and I was all on my own."

"That's horrible," Zetine whispered.

Ironja nodded but Mizt-Ied continued, "So I was on my own. I was a teenager when I came to Moia. Thirteen or fourteen, I think. It was so different than all the other places I had ever been. It was so beautiful. As far as you could see, there were flowers of every color in all sorts of shapes. Fruit grew everywhere, and it was good fruit too, that anyone could have! There weren't too many people living here, usually only one or two houses every good few miles. But they were all so nice anyway. I never really saw people so nice, especially not so far from the cities.

"I had been here a few weeks, maybe a month when I met an elderly human couple. Henry and Janet, their names were. When they found out I was a wanderer, they invited me to stay with them. They had had a daughter, much older than me, who had left to fight Vhodan a few years before. She never came back, and they were so lonely. I was suspicious of course, but they seemed nice, so I accepted.

"They would make the most delicious salads, and I'm not even a big leaf fan. I slept in their daughter's room, which was very strange. It's funny to think about how no one ever makes beds for goblins. They still had some clothes from when she was young, and I wore those a lot. I started to stop wearing my own clothes. They became my parents, as funny as that is to say. Even now, I don't think I've ever seen any humans adopt a goblin. I was hurting so much and they took me in, and I became happy.

"One day Janet died. She fell and she didn't get back up and that was it. We cried over her, and we buried her and planted roses above her because those were her favorite flowers. And they burned it down! That's not fair! The burned down mom's flowers and I'll never be able to find her again!"

Tears had begun to drop heavily from Mizt-Ied's eyes. Zetine reached forward and wrapped her in a hug. It was a strange thing, for it was obvious that Zetine had rarely ever hugged anybody before. It still brought great comfort to Mizt-Ied, who hugged her back as tight as she could and stuffed her face into Zetine's bandaged shoulder. She cried noisily for a few minutes, before at last she pulled away.

"Are you alright, lass?" Ironja asked.

Mizt-Ied nodded and rubbed her nose, then continued. "Henry died a few months later. We spent a lot more time together until then. It was a lot quieter with just the two of us, and so much sadder, but it was still nice to have somebody else. Then one day he just didn't wake up. It was hard to bury him by myself, but I did. Next to Janet. He liked the posies best, so I planted some above him. I'll never find him again either..."

Ironja put his hand on her shoulder, and Zetine gave her another hug. She said, "It will be okay. We're here for you."

"I'm sorry," she whispered softly and rubbed her nose again.

"It's okay," Jubilatious awkwardly said as he rubbed the back of his head.

"You have nothing to apologize for," Zetine softly comforted.

"We all have our own baggage," Ironja added.

Mizt-Ied placed both her hands over her large eyes and rubbed the tears away before she said, "Thank you, the three of you. I think I'm gonna lie down now. My heart hurts."

Zetine nodded as Mizt-Ied laid down on the ground, curling herself into a little ball. The other three exchanged awkward looks with one another, not really sure how to proceed. Shortly after, Ironja began to undo his armor. His skin had blistered red and his beard had never been in worse shape, though it was nothing that couldn't be healed with time. He found a nice spot in the corner away from the door and facing the window, then dozed off himself. Neither Jubilatious nor Zetine felt particularly tired, so they sat together in silence for some time.

Eventually, Zetine quietly asked, "Your magic. Why does it need so much from you?"

"What do you mean?" he asked in surprise, the question catching him off guard.

"Magic is much different in Exia," she paused to think of how to explain it. "Our magicians carry ingredients with them to create fire or ice. They also only need to speak for complicated spells. When the priests cast their spells, it lasts forever. When I cast The Solemn Spell, I need only do it once, and the effects would last until my soul absconds to the next realm."

Jubilatious listened to her intently, soaking up every brief detail. "Fascinating," he murmured. Then he said, "Different cultures adapted magic differently, and it is the rules we placed upon it in the Second and Third Ages that shaped it. In the First Age, spells were nothing more than extensions of the will of the users. Come the Second Age, there was little need for conflict and so our ancestors established rules on how to use magic. In the Third Age, our ancestors once again needed to use magic for battle, but it had drifted so heavily from what it once was that magic had to be tangled into a more useful form. So we created our chants to form spells and use catalysts so that the magic does not harm us. I would imagine that your more recent ancestors kept a tighter control upon magic and used it in such a way that they would always obey the masters."

"You are quite the learned man," she remarked.

"Thank you," he smiled. "If I'm being honest, I wasn't the best student. Mages are expected to go into a specific school of magic at a young age, but I could never decide. I tried to learn a little bit of everything, be it conjuration, alchemy, or transfiguration. Of course, the academy also tends to be divided into subgroups of those, which certainly didn't help..."

"But how many of your peers took on this quest?" she asked.

Jubilatious chuckled and said, "I don't expect too many of my peers to still be alive by now, not the good ones anyway. The bravest of the wizards were at The Battle of Solace Hill. No one walked away from that. Of those that do live... I would imagine many of them joined Vhodan. Whether through cowardice or curiosity into what new forms of magic they could learn by studying under him, Vhodan has gathered many wizards and hexblades to serve in his accursed army. Arkvine was one of the first places he conquered, after all."

Zetine frowned and said, "Then they are doomed. To join with evil, no matter what the reason, is utter foolishness. No matter how evil tries, it is fate that demands it be destroyed. I cannot understand why so many sapient beings chose to follow the Dark Lord, especially not those that know as much as you or I would."

"Because evil wants to exist," he sighed. "Good and evil came into the world at the same time, the giants and the heroes of the First Age. For one to exist there must be the other. But when the giants were slain, evil ceased to be. But it needs to be. So, no matter how many times good people destroy it, no matter how it is slain or conquered, or expelled, evil will worm its way back into our world.

This is one of the biggest horrors to be knowledgeable of, I think. It is something that haunts my consciousness. That even if I defeat Vhodan, it ultimately won't matter. Be it a day or a thousand years, inevitably evil will come to be once more. It paints the world in such a hopeless light."

"But it's not hopeless," Zetine stated. "We strive to stop him so that others may live, so that others may prosper, no matter the sacrifice we have to make. It does not matter if another evil arrives the following day because for one day there is peace. It does matter if another evil arrives in a thousand years, for there will be a new generation to stop it. No matter how it tries, evil will always be stopped."

"But how do you truly know that?" Jubilatious asked.

"Because you said it yourself," she said.

"I did?" he asked in surprise.

"You did," she smiled. "When the heroes of the First Era slayed the giants, they slayed the first and only evil. So every time a new evil would arise, it would always follow the pattern set forth by its first iteration. No matter what atrocities may occur, there is an inevitable conclusion. One day, there will be heroes that stand before what seems an impossible enemy. Together they will fell the grand evil, and peace will be brought to the land. Be it for a day or a thousand years, peace will reign, and evil will never be able to truly vanquish good."

"You have such an optimistic way of looking at the world," Jubilatious commented.

Zetine said, "From the day I was born, I was told of death and the honor that it brings. There is inevitability in everything, and when your time comes, you must embrace the inevitable like a lover. You are one and the same. No matter how horrible the world may seem, inevitably it will be made better. All you need to do is wait, and when the time comes, act."

Jubilatious listened to her speak, weighing upon her words. At last, he said, "One day, I hope to see Exia. Your culture is fascinating Zetine. As are you."

She simply smiled and said, "I have been told this. I cannot wait for the day I show my home to all of you."

***

The sun was setting as Kira approached Arkvine. The surrounding fields held many crops from conflicting seasons and were tended to primarily by uncomfortable-looking mannequins. Even with the drones doing the labor for them, there were still a few green mages milling about that Kira had to avoid. Staying as far away from the wizards as he could, Kira stole the tattered brown cloak that one of the mannequins wore and pulled it over his own clothes. As he moved forward with the additional disguise, hiding his overseer's clothes and chains, he still made sure to avoid the wizards entirely.

Like most cities, Arkvine was built within the confines of a thick set of stone walls. Unlike other cities, there were many entrances if one knew to look. Kira had no idea where to look, but at least had the idea to wait beyond the city walls for signs of an opening. At first, he hung about near the stables, where the flow of peasants carried into the city's main gate. While the guards at the gate didn't seem to be checking faces all that closely, Kira didn't like his chances of approaching while still wearing manacles, broken as they were.

Eventually, Kira peeled away from the stables, circling the walls to look for any other methods inside. This proved fruitless at first until a young yellow mage descended from the sky. Kira nearly had a heart attack as he placed his back to a tower corner in the hopes that she didn't see him, but like most wizards, she was too self-obsessed to notice the world around her. Kira watched as she landed on the ground, pulling a seemingly normal broomstick out from beneath her as though it was a stool. The wizard approached a mundane part of the wall and then knocked three times against a specific spot. Just like that, the wall opened into a doorway, which the wizard walked through without ever noticing she was being watched.

Kira hurried after her, but by the time he arrived, the wall had sealed up once more. He proceeded to spend the next three minutes rapping his knuckles against various parts of the walls until they were bruised and his frustration had grown into pure anger. Finally, the wall slid open, revealing a short dark alleyway that led into the city center. Kira slowly walked through the alley, expecting an ambush, but one never came. No one had noticed him, because, in a city of wizards, he appeared entirely unremarkable.

The high elf walked out into the bustling city center, where merchants ranted about their goods and peasants went about their lives. Mixed into the dull crowd were young wizards who wore robes of every color Kira had ever seen, each one signifying their particular school of magic. The youngest of the wizards, who Kira guessed to be a decade or two for humans, seemed to exclusively wear purple robes. Only a small minority of the older wizards seemed to wear purple, while the rest had moved on to more varied schools of magic.

As Kira got a lay of the land, he became aware of his lack of money. It seemed idiotic to try and steal when surrounded by wizards, but Kira felt he had little choice if he wanted to avoid more desperate measures. It took him a good hour of walking the city before he found the libation district, which held such a cacophony of sounds and smells that it made the elf want to vomit on the spot. Even still, he carried on, hoping to find some drunkard devoid of enough senses for Kira to make an easy few coins.

As he passed by the brothels and taverns, more than a few humans called out to him. Most of what they said was some variant of, "Get out of here, nasty elf! We don't want your diseases on our women!"

A few of them actually called out, "Care to join us, elf? We have some ladies here that go nuts over pointed ears."

Either way, Kira ignored them, instead finding the seediest tavern he could see. A trip into the alleyway nearby revealed just what he had been looking for, a drunken goblin passed out beside a dumpster. Kira carefully felt up the goblin before taking hold of his coin pouch, then untied it from the back of the goblin's belt and backed away. The goblin did not stir, and Kira felt sure there would have been someone who saw him, but no one did. He safely walked away, counting the money out one piece at a time.

Six silver and two copper was more than Kira had hoped to find on a single drunk, and it was more than enough to pay for what he needed. Heading back towards the city center, Kira instead veered into the paper district. Here it was almost entirely wizards in their radiant robes, with only the occasional peasant sticking out in their brown and grey attire. Kira strode forward, eyes scanning over bookstores and poetry clubs. It wasn't long until he found a parchment store, about half the size of the rest of the businesses around it.

Kira pushed open the door and stepped foot into the dingy little establishment, taking in the sight of boxes full of scrolls. There was a yellow and a purple mage standing close to one another, whispering about a grey mage who was idly comparing parchment materials. Kira had no idea what the signifying feature of a grey mage was, but based on the way the two teenagers were talking about him, it was something the magical society looked down upon.

Kira headed for the store owner, an elderly man dressed in a fine dark blue coat, and said, "I only need enough to write a single letter. Then an envelope and a quill with ink."

The old man sighed and said, "Follow me. You're not the first to come in here with this request you know, and it's quite rude each and every time. My supplies are meant to be sold as a whole, not small fragments."

"Sorry to hear that," Kira said with a strained tone. "But I just need to send one letter."

The old man found a damaged scroll on a box atop a shelf, which he then tore a small sheet off of with careful precision. He then gathered up an envelope, and a quill, and headed back to the front desk. There he said, "Two silver, and you may use my ink and seal if you would like."

"Very well," Kira grimaced, for he knew the store owner had just ripped him off. Still, he put up with it if it meant finding his friend once again.

Once paid, the store owner passed over a bottle of ink and a red stamp as he said, "Go write on the table over there. And please, do not disturb my other customers while you write."

Kira followed his instructions and went to the table near the entrance, finding a spot that didn't have too many boxes near it so he could craft the letter. He wrote out, "Dear Vrias, it has been far too many years, and through them all I have thought about you. I have come to the city of Arkvine, a stranger to you and this land, though I hope you will welcome me as a friend. Would you see me again, I bid you to the parchment store The Hedgehog's Quill in the paper district. I will wait here until the night after tomorrow when I will know whether or not we were fated to meet again. I truly hope to see you, at least once more before I go. Yours first and truly, Kira."

The elf pressed the letter into the envelope, closed it, and stamped it with the seal. A small hedgehog print stared up at him as Kira approached the pair of wizards asking, "Do either of you know an elf named Vrias?"

"No," the yellow mage quickly replied.

"I do," said the purple mage. She elaborated, "He's one of the older students, right? Purple mage like me?"

"Yes, that sounds right," Kira said. "I need you to deliver a letter to him. Can you do that?"

"What's in it for me?" she asked, crossing her arms with her stave held tight so she could look more confident.

Kira flatly said, "I'll give you four silver."

"Hm," the wizard pursed her lips for a moment. "Very well, I suppose that's fair."

Kira hated how money-hungry every person seemed in this city, but he exchanged the coins and letter anyway. Then he said, "Deliver it fast. I'm expecting an urgent reply."

"He'll get it soon, I promise," the wizard replied with a roll of her eyes. "Come on Miranda, let's get out of here."

Kira watched the pair buy their parchment and ink before heading out of the store, before heading out himself. As he passed through the doorway, he couldn't help but notice the store owner was glaring at him. Still, Kira hung around outside the shop as he waited. The air would soon grow colder as the nighttime progressed, and eventually, the lights in the store behind him were put out. One by one, all of the interior lights in the district were extinguished as the travelers became fewer and fewer. At last only the street lights were left burning, a holdover from the ancient days when light must always burn to keep the monsters at bay.

In the dim light, Kira slumped down against the shop wall. He hoped that Vrias had already read his letter, and was rushing to meet him. Even if he had never received it, Kira hoped his friend was at least happy. He would wait as long as he could in that spot, waiting for when he could finally see Vrias again. Then maybe he too could be happy.

Chapter 5

Wolf awoke, frozen and aching, but alive. Upon remembering what had happened, she spat and felt the glob of saliva land on her chin. Satisfied that she knew which way was up, Wolf began to paw at the snow encasing her, eventually breaking free into the early morning light. She burst out with a pained pant and climbed onto her feet, gazing around at the woods. Evidently, no one had come looking for her, as there were no signs of anyone other than herself there. As she attempted to climb back up the hill she had fallen from, a sharp pain shot across her chest, and she remembered the arrow.

She now knew she needed medicine, that the village might have some, and so she set out for a rude homecoming. It was a slow and horrible walk. She knew exactly where to go, but it seemed that even with her now towering height, it took Wolf three times as long as it should have to make it to her first home. It was nearly nightfall when she came across the charred ruins, still smoking in some places. Blackbirds pecked at the cooked flesh of dead tribespeople, likely the flock left over after the dead woman was slain. How Wolf was so sure the dead woman had been attacked as well, she was unsure of, though it seemed likely with her own attack.

She carefully stepped through the ashes, looking for signs of the granny's tent. She eventually found it, somehow in better shape than every other tent. A stray, alien thought floated through Wolf's mind then. *Apparently, the old hag had a little magic in her after all*. Wolf peered inside and found the granny's body lying across her bunk, stabbed as she slept. She paid no mind to the corpse and began to inspect the various ingredients, taking what seemed right. A jar of pickled boar hearts, a vile of blue flower petals, a vile of salt, a jar of amber fruit, and a roll of some strange herb that Wolf didn't recognize. Then she spent a few moments looking for the granny's gourd bottles and mortar.

Wolf couldn't find the pestle but made do with the hilt of her knife. She began with the flowers and herbs, grinding them into shreds. Then came the heart, and then the fruit, which made a sort of paste. She added the salt, and then frantically looked for any water. Not finding any in the tent, she would have to use her own canteen. Wolf pushed most of the paste into the bottle she had taken, and then grabbed hold of the broken arrow shaft. She screamed as she tore it out, the arrowhead pulling some of her insides out with it. Wolf smeared the paste around the wound, and then stuck her fingers inside it to ensure it got deep. She screamed again, cursing her own rough nails. Finished for now, she poured half of her canteen into the bottle, sealed it, and began to shake it.

Once the paste had sufficiently mixed with the water, it became a slightly thick liquid. Satisfied that this was enough, Wolf opened the bottle and took a swig. It tasted like pure vile in her throat, but she managed to suppress her stomach and drank nearly half of it. Slowly, her wound was closing, and her bruises were fading. Satisfied, Wolf took the bottle and left. She headed back to the clearing she had fought Huntsman in, not knowing if he was still there or not. She didn't care. She would find him, no matter how long it took, and kill him.

By the time she arrived, the army was long gone, but they left obvious tracks. Metal booted footprints, horse hooves, and the marks of wheels, along with a couple of dozen soft footprints similar to her own. She began to follow them, not knowing how far this might take her. Whatever it would take, she would find her enemies and punish them. She barely even thought about the tribespeople.

For several days she followed the tracks, occasionally hunting rabbits or foxes for her meals, though soon she began to subsist off foraged berries. She would carry them with her, eating only at night before resting in hastily constructed snow burrows. She had plenty of water, adding snow to her canteen and waiting for it to melt whenever she needed to, but her appetite was growing and fatigue was setting in. No matter how tightly Wolf bound herself, the cold was seeping into her skin. Like so many before her, it seemed as though Wolf would become a victim of the frost.

Eventually, she fell, close to a row of trees unlike those of her own forest. They were beautiful, she thought. *Beautiful and dangerous*, though she couldn't say why she thought that. With one hand, Wolf began to crawl towards the trees. There were people now, she thought. But that couldn't be right. They were too thin, and they didn't move like people. She could not feel them grab her, but she knew they had, for she was now carried by arms that didn't seem like they could even hold an axe, let alone a fully grown woman.

When Wolf awoke, there was no snow. She lay upon leaves as soft as any blanket, and the air was more comfortable than it had any right to be. She sat up and looked around, finding half a dozen people standing under the twilight with bows all aimed at her. They were all far too thin, and their skin was the color of flowers, not of flesh. She barely even noticed the pointed shape of their ears or the prismatic colors of their eyes, for everything else about them was just too wrong.

"We nursed you back, humans," one of them said in a thick accent, pronouncing the h as a y. Wolf could not tell if it was a man or a woman. "Leave," it ordered.

Wolf rose to her feet, expecting to be sore or delirious, but she seemed so oddly fine and in control of herself. She asked the elf, "Where? I was following..."

The elf looked at her for a moment, then lowered its bow. It said something in elvish, and then the others slowly lowered their bows. It now asked, "Natureman?"

Wolf nodded, "Yes," for she wasn't quite sure of what she was being asked.

"Why did you leave the frost woods?" it asked.

"I was attacked," she growled, memories flashing back to her. "Empire attacked me. Need to find them."

The elf nodded, though it somehow seemed disappointed by this answer. "I will take you to the road. Many travel it, humans and elves alike. It leads longer than I could imagine."

Wolf looked at the strange being as it strode towards her, graceful beyond what she could imagine. Then it was beyond her, moving towards the tree line. She asked, "What are you?"

"An elf," it said matter-of-factly.

"You're an elf?" she asked, vaguely recalling some of the half-elves she had known as a child.

"Yes," the elf smiled. "My name is Mythra. I am a wood elf, as your kind call us. You are most likely familiar with the yai'elves, or maybe cross elves."

"Uh huh," Wolf nodded. "Where are we?"

"The Wooded Land, where all elves originally come from," Mythra explained. "It is not meant for your kind, which is why you cannot stay. But when we saw you, we couldn't just leave you to die. So we took you into our home and made sure you were restored. Do not eat the red berries with blue flowers."

Wolf asked, "Who is the Empire?"

Mythra thought about this for several moments then answered, "I do not entirely know, though they have fought the boundaries of the Wooded Land many times. They originate from a human kingdom but have assimilated many lands and people. They have spread across your lands, but do not intrude upon our world, so I have had no reason to learn of them."

"Where are they?" she asked.

The elf shrugged. "Simply look and you will find them." They then came to a stop and the elf said, "Beyond those trees is your realm. Follow your road as you see fit, and may you find what you are looking for. May it bring you peace."

Mythra turned and walked away, leaving Wolf to look after her. Then she turned to the exit, which looked to be no more than any other row of trees. She stepped forward, and almost instantly the cold air assaulted her once again. It was warmer than when last she had stood in the realm of man, and it seemed as though she had traveled a greater distance than she expected. There was barely any snow or even trees around her, and the sun shone brightly over the land. Sure enough though, there was the road, with the same tracks she had been following. The same tracks, along with several more, though she was unable to discern that.

It would be several more hours of following the road before at last she came to an intersection, the first she had ever seen in her life. Wolf looked at the new road before her, and attempted to tell where her tracks went. She could see wheels and footprints going right, and footprints going straight, but the snow had begun to melt under the sun's harsh glare. She resigned herself to go right, and if need be, come back and follow the other path. This road, it seemed, led to another dense forest that wrapped around a small mountain. It seemed an excellent place for a stronghold. The dwarves had made their fortified home in a mountain, after all. So Wolf followed the path.

The sun was setting when she arrived, and smoke was rising from chimneys blocked by a large wooden door. Two guards stood outside, each holding a spear, and they were dressed in a mix of leather and chainmail. It took Wolf a moment to realize there was a third guard perched atop the wall, occasionally walking around with a bow in his arms. She watched from the shadows of the trees, unable to find a way around. Resolving to do the only thing available to her, Wolf notched an arrow and took aim.

The archer fell to the ground in front of the door guards, an arrow sticking out through his chest. They looked at the body in shock for a moment, before one of them was hit by an arrow as well. He was knocked against the door, leaving his ally to yelp in fear. He clutched his spear tightly and looked around in terror before an arrow hit him in the back. Wolf walked forward, swapping her bow for her axe. She made sure to retrieve her arrows, finding the guard she hit in the chest was still alive. Worse, her arrow broke as she pulled it out from his leather chest-plate. So she kicked his teeth in and attempted to open the doors.

They were firmly barred from the other side, so she resorted to scaling the wall. It was a difficult climb, but she was able to make it to the top, before leaping down. The guards were upon her in a moment, but they were slow and clumsy. She killed one with a chop to the throat, and another by grabbing his face and forcing his skull roughly to the ground. A third came at her with a spear, who she simply threw her axe at. She quickly reclaimed the weapon, and then after a moment's consideration, moved to the doors and removed the large iron bar that had locked them.

From behind her, Wolf heard a sick laughter that sounded metallic and inhuman. She turned and saw the largest man she had ever seen if he even was a human. His clothing was made of several different pieces of cloth that had been sewn together into crude patchwork. Each of his legs was like a tree trunk, leading up into plated armor that must have been forged for a giant, for it was loose even upon his impossible frame. The arms jutting out of the armor were wrapped in metal plates that Wolf eventually realized were entire shields, and the flesh upon them was bulging and purple. He wore a metal helmet with deer antlers affixed to it, and his face was entirely concealed by darkness. Not his eyes though. Those glowed with a familiar green light that filled her with terror.

Every fiber of her being told Wolf to run, but she stood her ground and called out, "Dead man! Where is the Empire!?"

Once again he laughed, then spoke in a voice that was not of this world. "There is no empire here. There is no god and no emperor. There is only me."

"I followed their tracks," she stated.

"The wrong ones, apparently," he said. Then at the top of his lungs, he called out, "PAGE! MY SWORD!"

Wolf watched as a frail-looking teenage boy ran out of a house, holding the biggest scabbard she had ever seen. The dead man took hold of the hilt and then placed a boot upon the boy's chest, pushing him into the dirt so he could draw the blade without lifting his arm. The way he moved was unnatural, as though it should hurt him, but he made no indication of this. He held his greatsword in one hand, though it would have taken Wolf both of her arms just to weild it. They looked at one another, each waiting for the other to make the first move.

The boy scampered back to safety, and then Wolf charged with a roar. She swung her axe and the dead man didn't even bother to dodge. She hit him in the side of the helmet and felt the metal dent, and the blade of her axe crack. Then he grabbed her by the throat with his left hand and simply began to strangle her, suspending Wolf in the air. She kicked uselessly at his chest, before taking an arrow from her quiver and stabbing it into where she expected his eye to be. The dead man grunted and dropped her, allowing Wolf to recover, while she watched in disbelief.

He pulled the arrow out, and there was his eyeball on the end of it, yet the green glow beneath his helmet never faded. With only one eyeball, he looked at her with both eyes. Then the dead man dropped the arrow to the ground and retaliated. He was too quick for his size, for someone who wasn't even really alive. She raised her axe up to defend herself but the brute simply chopped through it, and she felt her chest slice open. Wolf turned, knowing she had no chance against this beast, and tried to run. He sliced her again across the back but she kept running, not daring to look back.

True primordial fear had filled Wolf, overwhelming her almost instantly. It drowned out all the rage, even most of the pain that she felt. There was only the vague stinging sensation that marked her wounds, and the totality of the feeling that she needed to escape. Fear like this was entirely alien to Wolf, and she had no way to combat it. As she ran her breaths turned ragged and a part of her wished she would just scream.

As Wolf made her way down the road, she came across a man dressed in a black robe. He was maybe a few inches shorter than her and didn't seem particularly muscular. The only skin she could see was upon his black hand, holding tight to a staff made of redwood. He seemed almost harmless, a pilgrim of some sort even. Wolf may have been able to ignore the man and just carry on running, were it not for his eyes. They were golden with two black dots at their centers and seemed to glow not unlike the dead people's eyes had glowed. Wolf did not know what this stranger was, but she did not want to know. After the briefest moment of staring at each other, she simply ran past him, clutching tight to her broken axe in case he decided to attack her.

The Black Mage watched her go, taking minor note of her. Then he carried on, calmly making his way up the road and towards the stronghold. A new set of guards were closing the doors, and a moment later they were pulling the lock bar down in place. The Black Mage simply held his hand out, and there came a gust of wind so strong that the doors fell down entirely, taking a guard with them. He looked at the crushed man in pity, but it did not sway him. There were three other guards about, and they all seemed terrified. Of him or his opponent, he wasn't entirely sure.

The dead man looked at him and said, "Ah. I knew I sensed a wizard out there, and I didn't think it was that girl or the thing stuck to her. Have you come to seek an audience?"

The Black Mage ignored his words and spoke in a calm yet grim voice, "Release the body you hold. Allow these people peace. Go forth into your afterlife, whatever it holds for you."

"I don't know what you're talking about," the dead man retorted. "I am the rightful ruler of these people!"

"Do you think I cannot see the color of necromancy radiating out of your eyes?" he asked. "Or the way in which his body has distorted in an attempt to hold the both of your souls?"

If it were possible for the dead man's eyes to narrow, they did so. "This man was a barbaric warlord before I arrived," it growled. "These people raped and pillaged before I came along. I am showing them what it means to serve a proper lord, to find true purpose!"

"The evil of man is a misery, but who are you to interfere?" he asked. "It should be man who puts a stop to the evil of man."

"Who am I!?" the undead lord cackled. "I am Vonasos, Slaughterer of Beghan and Defendor of Bridgeworth!"

"You are all so gullible," the Black Mage nearly smiled.

"What?" Vonasos asked in surprise.

"Vonasos," he said the name with an otherworldly thunder. "I give you your final chance. Abandon this body and cross the rivers to the lands beyond. If you do not, I will destroy you."

The dead thing laughed a horrible, maniacal laugh. Then it charged at him, swinging its massive sword down at the human. He simply held his staff up and the blade stopped before ever making contact. Then the dead thing was thrown back across the stronghold, grinding into the dirt. Vonasos climbed to its feet, while the Black Mage simply moved calmly forward, extending his hand as though to grasp the dead thing. It found itself frozen in place, its chest plate denting inwards and crushing its ribcage. There was a sickening *splat* as its chest imploded, and the undead lord wailed in pain that it should not have been able to feel.

"What in the hell are you!?" it asked in utter desperation.

The Black Mage did not answer it. Instead, he said, "I do not have the right to destroy a soul, even one as corrupted as yours. But I can still ensure you never harm anyone ever again. I pray that your jailers will show you mercy, though I know that they will not. Vonasos, Slaughterer of Beghan and Defendor of Bridgeworth, I banish you. I banish you away from the realm of man and the realm of elf and the realm of dwarf and the realm of the gods and the realm of the devils. I banish you from peace and reality, of body and mind. I banish you to The World That Is Not, from which there is no return. I banish you, Vonasos."

To the crowd of citizens and guards, it looked as though the lights in their overlord's eyes simply blew out. That he keeled over, and that was it. But The Black Mage watched as the otherworldly tendrils wrapped around the errant soul, filling it and mutilating it. A soul has no mouth, but it can truly scream. In pain and primordial terror, it screamed, but there was only one there who could hear it, and he did nothing. The tendrils did not drag Vonasos, for there was nowhere to go. They simply took him, and then they were gone. The Black Mage sighed, for it was a terrible fate to bestow, but inevitably Vonasos would have returned. He hoped he had done the right thing.

One of the women kicked at the corpse's head, knocking the helmet off. She shouted in pain, then nearly doubled over as she looked at the bloated and bruised face of a man she had once known. All of them gathered around, unsure whether to beat the corpse or to burn it. It was a horrid thing, and all they wanted was to be rid of it.

The Black Mage spoke, "I heard truth in the words of Vonasos. Make peace with your neighbors. Make your living off the land, not of the people. I will return in a year's time, and if I find that a single one of the neighboring villages has been pillaged, that a single woman has been defiled because of you, I will treat you to the same fate as your dark lord."

He didn't like to lie, but fear was a terrific motivator. He expected that when he returned, the people would be leading much better lives. If they weren't, he would do what he could, but he was only one man. His path was not to change the world, only to stop others from doing the same.

***

Wolf only had about a quarter of her healing potion left, but her wounds were closed and that was all that mattered. She had discovered that while the potion kept her from dying, it didn't seem to care for leaving her unblemished. She now had two long scars from where she had been cut, and a small white dot where she was shot. The potion also dehydrated her, and the further she went the less and less snow there was to collect. She had not prepared for her journey at all, and it seemed as though this point was being drilled into her at every opportunity. But still, she carried on, for she had no way of knowing if she was almost at her destination or not. She didn't even entirely know where her destination was, for that matter.

It was a relief when she spotted the building in the distance. As she got closer, Wolf could see that it was a large multistory wooden building similar to those in the stronghold. It was seated at a crossroads and had a small building next to it where several horses were. At the crossroads was also a sign, though she couldn't read it. On one side of the building was a set of stairs leading up to the second and then third floors. Hanging over the front door was a painted sign, though she couldn't read that either.

It read, "Tye DeVul's Inn"

There were about a dozen people scattered across the tavern's tables, all with their own drink or food. Half of them were humans, and all of those humans were women who seemed to be flirting with the other patrons. Two were a pair of orcs, and three were elves, while there was also a curious little green fellow seated in the corner. His head barely went over the table he sat at, though this seemed to humor him, encouraging more elaborate ways of getting a bite of his eggs each time he felt like it. It was the sort of place that catered to people from all walks of life, and this made Wolf deeply uncomfortable.

She had no frame of reference for how to interact with a place like this and did not feel comfortable being surrounded by so many people. Yet something compelled her to stay, and so Wolf found the seat furthest from any of the others that still allowed her to look around the room. She placed her elbows on the table and covered her mouth with her hands as she looked around, analyzing the minute behavior of the other patrons. She had always noted how different Tusk behaved than the dwarves, but seeing these wildly different people was mind blowing.

The orcs boasted with one another, roughly moving their mugs for emphasis on whatever stories they took turns telling. Every now and then some foam or liquid would spill out, and if it landed on their wrists, they would lick it up. One of the elves moved about silently, occasionally startling the other patrons as they noticed her, before taking a sip from her mug and moving on. Another elf was seated at a table, playing cards with two of the humans, his movements fast and enchanting as he shuffled the deck. One human sat alone, curling his fingers back and forth with an unnatural determination.

Then there was him. He was seated at the bar with a woman toting on him, but had at some point turned and fixated on Wolf. The man was dressed in tall boots with brown cloth pants tucked into them and some strange white cloth tunic. His arms and face were wrapped in bandages, though they didn't seem related to any wound he may have suffered. Despite the odd regality of his attire, numerous dirt stains had crept onto his clothing during his travels. Strapped to his side was an oddly curved sword, while a strangely serrated dagger was tucked into his belt. It seemed as though each of the serrations was a hook, though Wolf couldn't understand why.

The two looked at one another from across the tavern for an uncomfortable amount of time, before the man rose to his feet. He pulled himself away from the woman and said something to her with a sly smile, before flipping a golden coin into her hand. He made his way across the tavern floor with his back straight and stride efficient. It almost reminded Wolf of the elves she had met, though she had no doubt that he was human.

Upon reaching her the man said, "Rare is it to see someone such as you in a place such as this."

Wolf glared daggers into him and said, "Back off."

"I didn't mean offense," he raised his arms but didn't lose his smile. "I could just see that you're much like myself, and just like me, far from home."

"How?" She asked him bluntly.

He gave her a curious look and then said, "I am from Exia. Surely you've heard of it?"

After a moment's thought Wolf settled on saying, "I'm from the woods."

He then asked, "Where are you heading then, woods girl?"

"To The Empire," she quickly answered, though this felt wrong to say.

"Interesting," he nodded. "I had thought you would want to go to Cairn."

"Cairn?" Wolf asked, and a strange part of her was filled with anxiety that made her heart beat fast.

"A land far to the west, mountainous and dangerous," he explained. "You would have to cross imperial lands to reach it though."

"Where are you going?" She asked him.

He shrugged and said, "I usually go where I am paid. Though my last job was a burn, and I am running low on coin."

"Coin?" She asked earnestly.

"You really are a woods girl," he chuckled. "Money. Within the Empire, it's thrones. The Western Kingdoms usually use crowns, and a few of the Eastern Nations use paper instead of coins. You need it to do just about anything in the real world."

"How do you get coin?" Wolf asked, worrying this stupid-sounding concept might interfere with her plans.

"Doing jobs," he shrugged. "The boring ones pay scraps but it's consistent. Mercenaries can make a fortune, but only if they're skilled and lucky."

"Mercenary?" She asked a feeling she did not recognize as embarrassment growing in her.

He said, "Someone that fights for money. Like myself, though that's mostly only to pay for room and board on my journey."

"Journey where?" She asked him.

He chuckled and said, "Well, I think Cairn is where I'm fated to end up. It is the sister to my homeland, after all. Until that day though, I plan on roaming the land. Taking in the sights. Felling monsters. The usual."

"Where is your home?" She asked.

"Exia," he smiled. "Across the sea. It is a land of sand and sun."

"How different," Wolf mused.

"Quite," he agreed.

She thought to herself for several moments. Though a part of her hated the idea, she asked, "Will you show me The Empire?"

"You want me to take you there?" He asked in surprise.

Wolf nodded and said, "Yes. I need guiding."

"I suppose I could," he said. "What's your name? Or should I keep calling you woods girl?"

The idea of telling him her name was detestable, but she managed to mumble, "Wolf."

"Ah, interesting name," he chuckled. "I am Kazaa."

"When do we leave?" She asked.

"You're so eager to leave?" He responded. "Haven't you just come on from the long road?"

"I   am   ready,"   she
++

"I see," he said to himself. Then he said, "Give me an hour or two. I have business to attend to."

Wolf watched as he walked back across the tavern floor to the woman he had abandoned. He said something to her and she laughed, before rising to her feet. The pair of them left the tavern, and Wolf had the uncanny feeling that they would be making use of the outside stairs. She sat awkwardly in her chair, unsure of what to do next. Something told her it would be best to just leave, but she ignored it. The world was now a terrifying place, and Wolf was grateful for the company, no matter how strange it was.

Chapter 6

It had been a tough several weeks for the heroes. There was nothing to eat save for salamander meat, which was greatly unappetizing for multiple reasons. Slimy, chewy, tough, and laughingly hard to cook. It took Jubilatious' magical fire to prepare it for food, and even then it often took around an hour just to heat it enough so that it was edible. Amongst the four of them, the only one who actually seemed able to gulp it down was Mizt-Ied. The goblin was far less squeamish than the others and was the only one to go back for seconds after she had eaten whatever was initially provided.

"Damn I wish I had some salt," Ironja lamented. "At least then this blasted lizard would taste like something other than death."

"For once," Jubilatious sighed. "We are in agreement. I cannot wait for the day where in which I finally forget this horrendous taste."

"The ash tasted better than this," Zetine agreed.

"It's arright," Mizt-Ied said through a mouth full of slimy white meat.

They had made it to the Barlok Mountains, full of treacherous terrain that would ideally take them around Vhodan's army. The area had long been charted out, with the safe paths marked by green flags. So long as they followed the flags, they would be able to make it through the mountain range without incident.

As they came to the first pass though, the four of them looked on in dismay as the sight of a hundred green flags lay in a smoldering pile. It was Zetine who said, "Those bastards won't discourage us. We have made it this far, and we will continue onwards!"

"Reminds me of home," Ironja chuckled. "Come on, no point standing about."

The dwarf began to walk forward and the other three followed after him, the mountains opening up around them. There was a great scene before them, with massive mountains stretching out beneath a brilliant blue sky. The sun shone down before them, yet the air was pleasantly cool. They could even see some thin woods far below.

It was a slow and precarious trek, but it seemed to be going well for several hours. It was not until nightfall that everything went wrong. There came a tumbling of small rocks from somewhere above, but none of the heroes could make out any sign of what had caused them to fall. From above, an eagle called out, but the animal only served to play into their anxiety. Then suddenly, reverberating all around, was a horrible sound like two inexplicably wet boulders being ground together.

"I know that sound..." Ironja quietly said to himself, gripping his axe tightly. Then the realization hit him like a pound of bricks as he yelled out in horror, "ROCK TROLL!"

Approximately three hundred pounds of brick hit him then, sending the dwarf flying over the edge of the mountain. He went tumbling down past where the others could see him, leaving the three to scatter about as they tried to face down their enemy. Zetine had drawn her daggers, Jubilatious carefully retreated as he conjured a spell, and Mizt-Ied attempted to get behind the massive monster.

A rock troll is much like a normal troll if a normal troll was upwards of three times the size and was made out of solid stone. This particular monster was made from the same brown rock as the mountains, with grey pebbles strewn about its back. Its two black eyes stared out from beneath a hardened brow, while a set of massive teeth poked out of its maw. Its fingers, if you could even call them that, were like miniature stone spears. It stood at fifteen feet tall, and it was clear upon sight that killing it was no easy question.

Zetine slashed across the monster's chest, resulting in little more than sparks. It retaliated by swiping her to the side, sending her hard into the ground. Mizt-Ied hopped onto its back and raced up to its shoulders, intent on gouging the troll's eyes out. Instead, it grabbed her by the scruff of her cloak like a kitten, then hurled her into Jubilatious. The pair were knocked to the ground and left defenseless as the troll approached them.

Each lumberous step seemed to shake the mountain. The guttural growl of the rock troll filled their ears, a promise of their doom. It stood before Jubilatious and Mizt-Ied, no remorse in its black eyes, no reasoning. There was nothing more than the inevitable. It raised its fist overhead, a strike that would squash the both of them. Then something fell onto its head, and the troll fell away from them, letting loose a roar that could be heard from a hundred miles away.

The unmistakable sound of a rattlesnake tail filled the air, and Jubilatious watched in disbelief as the rock troll grabbed at its body, attempting to loose the snake from itself. Never had he seen a snake move with such dexterity, narrowly escaping from each grasp. But then the rock troll flung itself onto its back, and there was the subtle but unmistakable sound of wet meat being splattered. The rock troll rose back to its feet and set its eyes back upon the wizard and the goblin.

Then Zetine was there, delivering a strike across the back of its knees. Somehow her blades found soft flesh and the troll buckled, its growl intensifying. But then it spun around and grabbed her by the head. It stood, and despite the blood that still stained the monster's thighs, it was unharmed. Zetine cried out in pain as it slowly began to squeeze her head, enjoying the pain it caused her. There was little Jubilatious could do to save her in time, but his brain worked in overdrive to come up with a spell.

He pointed his staff and said, "Air of life, meet air of poisonous death."

A cloud of green appeared around the troll's head, and Jubilatious rejoiced for a small moment as he could see it breathe in the toxic fumes. Then he despaired as it took a continuous long breath, clearly enjoying the poison he had tried to kill it with. He looked to Mizt-Ied who lay unconscious by his side, and in that moment understood how truly hopeless their mission had been. How there had never been any chance of them succeeding.

Fortunately, Jubilatious never understands anything correctly.

A single arrow appeared as if from nowhere, engulfed in flames, and struck the rock troll in its eye. The monster roared in pain and dropped Zetine to the ground before it stumbled backward. Then it seemed to realize that the arrow was on fire, and screamed. Words could not do justice to the terror that emanated from the rock troll's throat. An immortal unkillable monster that delights upon death and destruction, finally meeting the one and only thing it is capable of fearing. Jubilatious would never forget it. It was true primal fear, beyond anything a man could ever hope to envision, a fear so powerful it transcends this mortal coil.

The rock trail flailed wildly, too frightened to remove the arrow and yet too terrified to attack. Zetine was barely able to roll out of the way of its stomps, each one risking her life. At last, it resorted to bashing its own head upon the mountain, driving the arrow deeper into its skull but smothering the flames. It fell back, satisfied that the threat was vanquished, but now horribly scarred. It turned and looked to Jubilatious with its left eye, its right nothing more than a burn with a charred arrow jutting out of it.

It stormed towards him, raised its arms into the air, and then once again screamed. A voice that Jubilatious did not recognize shouted, "Back! Leave them alone! I said BACK!"

The troll turned and fled, crawling up the mountain in desperation. Jubilatious turned to see a cloaked figure approaching him, gripping a lit torch in its left hand and a yew longbow in its right. The figure was tall and broad, dressed in a dark blue hooded cloak. As it grew closer, Jubilatious could see the dark green skin and protruding tusks of the figure's face and knew instantly that this stranger was an orc.

"Are you alright?" The orc asked in his gruff voice, sliding his bow over his shoulder.

"I- yes," he awkwardly replied. "I think so."

"What about your friend?" He asked, indicating to Mizt-Ied.

"I think she hit her head," Jubilatious replied. "But she's breathing."

The orc looked up and asked, "What of you?"

"I'll live," Zetine replied, struggling to stand. "The damned beast nearly tore my head off."

"Count yourself lucky I was here," the orc said. "Snarlgor has a habit of killing whatever he finds."

"Its name was Snarlgor?" Jubilatious asked, finding that fact darkly hilarious.

"It had a name?" Zetine asked, equally humored.

"Every being has a name," the orc said. "No matter how great or how small."

"Why didn't you kill it?" Jubilatious asked as he rose to his feet, carrying Mizt-Ied in his arms.

"Because every living creature deserves life," he explained. "It is not my place to end the life of a creature that does not understand what is right or what is wrong."

"It almost killed us!" Zetine hissed.

"It was you who came into Snarlgor's domain," he said. "Speaking of, why have you come here?"

Jubilatious motioned to remain silent but Zetine said, "We are on a quest to defeat the Dread Lord Vhodan. We had hoped the mountains would prove a safer route than the plains."

"You hoped wrong," the orc sighed. "Though you have a noble task, you did not think through your actions. Many rock trolls now roam these mountains, though most cower at the sight of Snarlgor. The only thing they truly fear is fire, for it is the one thing that can kill them. And you didn't so much as bring a torch."

"We didn't know," Jubilatious said.

The orc turned to look at him, his eyes washing over Jubilatious' clothes and appearance. He said, "You are dressed as a wizard. In all of your studies, did they not teach you of trolls?"

"Well," Jubilatious nervously replied, "Our studies tend to be more practical."

"More practical than life-saving information?" He asked.

Jubilatious spent a moment remembering how he spent several weeks learning a spell that would let him make realistic shadow puppets. After that, he said simply, "Yes."

"We had another with us," Zetine spoke. "A dwarf. He was knocked somewhere below by the troll, and fear whether he lives or died."

"He lives," the orc reassured her. "I have sent a friend to rescue him."

"Thank you," Zetine said.

Deep down below, Ironja had rolled to a painful stop against a tree. Though his armor protected him from any real harm, it didn't stop the impact from sending a wave of pain across his small body. After some time of lying down, waiting for the pain to subside, he eventually hopped to his feet and looked around. Ironja cursed at the thought of having to climb back up the mountain, but it seemed like the only way to rejoin his companions.

Then there came the snapping of twigs and tree branches as something large approached. Ironja frantically looked about for his axe, which he had dropped in the fall. He found it near the tree line and dashed for it, hoping to defend himself against whatever beast came for him. The rock troll to finish him off, most likely. He grabbed the axe from the ground but then the beast was upon him, face to face.

"Well screw me then," he huffed as he stared into the deep brown eyes of a grizzly bear.

The bear looked at him, then slowly reached its head forward and gently bit Ironja's armored arm. It pulled his arm to its shoulder then let go, and gave him the strangest look. In confusion, the dwarf asked, "Do ye want me to get on you?"

The bear said nothing because it was a bear.

Ironja slowly climbed up onto the bear's back, which was an awkward thing both due to his height and due to bears being notoriously ferocious. He tried to hold onto the bear's neck without being too tight, and the bear didn't seem to mind as it moved forward. Ironja shook as the bear began to climb the mountain far quicker than he could have hoped. It was a terrifying experience for the dwarf, but he would be lying if later he said it wasn't an experience he delighted in.

When at last they breached the mountain ridge, Ironja was quick to ask, "Who the hell are ye?"

"Is that a bear!?" Zetine asked in disbelief.

"That's a bloody bear," Jubilatious gasped.

"Ay, we've all seen a bear before," Ironja smugly said. Then he threw in, "Well, probably. I don't know yer lives."

"This is Jermaind," the orc said, striding forward to gently rub the bear's ears. "And he would like it if you got off."

"Right," Ironja awkwardly said and clambered down. "Ye didn't answer my question though. Who the hell are ye?"

"My name is Garr," he softly answered.

"Is that it?" Jubilatious asked.

"Yes," Garr replied.

"What are *you* doing out here, Garr?" Zetine asked.

"I watch over the animals," he explained. "I stop people, rare are they may be, from causing unnecessary harm or getting killed. When needed, I step in to ensure an animal causes no long-lasting damage."

"Yet you let the rock trolls stumble about," Jubilatious said.

Garr looked to Jubilatious as though he was the biggest moron in the world and said, "Animals know to stay far away from trolls. They only kill what gets close to them. It was you who angered Snarlgor, and you who cost a brave snake its life."

"The snake attacked on purpose?" Jubilatious asked.

"Yes, Ratatatat chose to try and help you," he said. "He was always kind-hearted."

Jubilatious looked down to the unconscious goblin in his arms and then asked, "Do you have any healing potions with you?"

Garr looked at him suspiciously then said, "No. But I know of a wise elven lady that lives in these mountains. She is likely to have some. Come."

Garr turned and began to walk away, side by side with Jermaind the bear. As the others followed him, Zetine asked, "Does she live out here all by her lonesome?"

"Yes," Garr said. "She is unwell. She moved out here to stay away from other people, save for those that truly need her help."

"If she's all the way out here," Jubilatious asked, "how does she help anyone?"

"Because they come to her," he said as though that was an adequate answer.

Garr led them across the mountain, a task which was far easier said than done. They were all exhausted and injured, though little fuss was made about it. Zetine lagged behind the most, with Ironja and Jubilatious about equally paced. Jubilatious' arms screamed for rest as he held onto Mizt-Ied, though he dared not let her go. Eventually, though they were led up a winding path to a cave with a narrow entrance, not unlike a door.

Jermaind the bear took a seat outside while Garr led them into the cave, dismissing the torch he had been using to keep any suspicious trolls at bay. It was far darker than the two humans would have liked, though Ironja greatly enjoyed the dark cavern. About fifteen feet into the narrow tunnel it opened into a modestly sized chamber that could fit all of those there five times over and still have some amount of room.

There were a few dozen candles spread out across the cavern, most of which were lit with blue fire. Several tables and racks lined the walls, along with a great many trinkets. There was everything from weapons to whole suits of armor, children's toys, a crown, vials of poisons and medicine, even an anatomically correct human heart that beat ominously whenever someone looked away from it. But there were also spaces where something clearly had once been, some leaving behind dust prints, others leaving nothing more than the empty spaces that showed they had belonged there.

Seated upon a cushioned chair was an elf, her frame slender even for her people. She had pale hair and skin a subtle pink. Her eyes were closed as she slumbered peacefully. She was naked save for a blanket that was wrapped tightly around her, a withered and tragic-looking thing that urgently needed to be replaced. Like all elves, she looked to be in her twenties, yet somehow this frail little slumbering elf carried with her the weight of a hundred thousand years. She was like nothing they had ever seen.

"Lady Pricilla," Garr softly said, causing the elf to stir.

She opened her violet eyes and instantly met a single person's gaze. She exclaimed, "Ah, Jubilatious! I didn't expect you to visit again so soon! Tell me, did it work?"

"You know her?" Zetine asked in surprise.

"No," he replied in confusion. "I have never seen this elf before in my life."

Pricilla pursed her lips then looked around at the others, "Zetine, shouldn't you be in Exia? And Ironja, your arm looks... Oh! Mizt-Ied! I see... I must have fallen asleep."

"What's happening?" Zetine asked.

Garr looked to her and solemnly said, "Lady Pricilla can see the future."

"It's not the future if it's already happened," Pricilla smiled.

The elf rose to her feet, dropping the blanket, and Jubilatious quickly averted his eyes. Ironja elbowed him in the thigh and said "It's the more perverted thing to look away, lad."

Each step Pricilla took was slow and uneven, as though she didn't quite remember how to walk. Garr moved to assist her but she pushed him away, a pathetic use of her arm which barely even nudged him. She hobbled to a basket and slowly bent over, which caused Jubilatious to cover his eyes in shame.

Zetine sarcastically hissed, "She's clearly elderly, you degenerate!"

"She looks my age!" he whined in response.

Pricilla pulled a small vile full of red liquid from the basket and slowly moved towards Jubilatious. She pulled the cork from the bottle and placed it against Mizt-Ied's lips, pouring the contents down her throat. The goblin's face reacted to what was undoubtedly a foul taste, and then her tongue clicked. She slowly opened her bright green eyes to look up into Jubilatious' brilliant crystal blue eyes. Then she tilted her head left.

"Those are some tits," she said in surprise, causing Jubilatious to drop her on the floor and walk away.

"They are," Pricilla said with a small laugh as Mizt-Ied picked herself back up.

"What happened?" she asked, rubbing her head.

"We were attacked by a rock troll," Zetine explained. "This orc, Garr, saved us and brought us to an oracle."

"Thanks," she said as she looked up to Garr.

"You're welcome," he replied, offering up a small smirk to the goblin.

Mizt-Ied looked to Pricilla who was returning to her chair and said, "Thank you too, ma'am."

"Anything for you, my dear," she smiled. "Have I made you your list yet?"

"My list?" she asked in confusion.

"Ah," Pricilla sighed. "Not yet. Sorry about that. All of you have come here for a reason, not just to help sweet Mizt-Ied here."

"How do you know that?" Jubilatious asked.

"Because that's why you always come, silly," she said. "You've come to kill someone. Now... was it Vhodan, or Mountain-Eater? Oh, please don't tell me it was that sweet girl. If you just talked to her, you would understand that you wanted the same thing deep down."

Jubilatious and Zetine exchanged a curious look before he said, "It was Vhodan. We need to stop the Dread Lord."

"Ah yes, of course," she said as Garr pulled her blanket back over her. "Take your items; I've been keeping them safe for you."

Mizt-Ied asked, "What's ours? All of it?"

Pricilla chuckled and said, "Sweet Mizt-Ied. One item each belongs to you at this point. Though if it's wrapped with something else, it belongs to you as well."

Zetine asked, "How will we know what's ours?"

"You'll know," she smiled. When the others moved to look around at her collection, Pricilla then said, "Garr. This is your last time to choose an item. Go find what's yours."

He looked to her with concern for a moment but then nodded. Sure enough, each of the heroes found something that seemed to call to them. Zetine found a golden scepter that radiated a strange familiarity. Mizt-Ied found a group of six strange black balls bound together in a red bow. Ironja found a necklace made of a silver cord and a brass pendant. Garr found himself a scimitar with a strange red glow about it. Then lastly there was Jubilatious, who stared intently at a golden dagger resting upon a pedestal. He took it, and for the first time realized he had been incomplete his entire life. Now he was finally whole.

Pricilla looked upon Zetine and said, "Ah, Ama's scepter. First pharaoh of your homeland."

"That's not possible," Zetine said. "Ama's sarcophagus was stolen a thousand years ago, it's been lost to time."

"And yet," Pricilla grinned. "A piece of history has been found by its rightful owner." She then looked to Mizt-Ied and said, "Those are smoke bombs. Simply throw them to your feet and you'll disappear from view. Move fast though, for the smoke lasts only a few seconds."

"Will do," Mizt-Ied clucked her tongue.

To Ironja she said, "You hold the amulet of Turk-Na, slayer of gorgons. It will protect you from petrifaction."

"Ah, handy that," he grinned at her.

She continued, "Noble Garr. The weapon you have chosen has no grand history, but it is a great one. A blade imbued with magic, capable of setting aflame any enemy it touches. A useful tool for one who lives amongst rock trolls."

"It will do," he nodded.

"Then there is Jubilatious. Your true weapon, though you will often act as though it's not. The dagger of Ahk-Zul, hero of the First Age. It will stay by your side for as long as you live."

"It's beautiful," he said as he gazed upon the blade.

"It is a part of you," she said softly. "Keep it well, for one day it will be part of someone else."

"I will," he nodded.

"You are all ready to leave," she said. "I ask only that Mizt-Ied remain behind for a moment.

Mizt-Ied looked back to the others, who all gave her nods of approval. Ironja said, "We'll wait for ya, lass."

One by one they all took their leave, until at last Mizt-Ied stood alone with Pricilla. The elf beckoned her forth, "Come here dear. I don't want them to overhear."

Mizt-Ied said, "Alright," and nervously approached her, leaning forward so that her ears poked up just below Pricilla's mouth.

She said, "Do come back to me. I would love to see your beautiful face once more."

Mizt-Ied looked up at her, blushing intensely. She gave a nod then turned and ran, heading out after the others. She found them all waiting outside, Garr petting Jermaind's ears. It was a pleasant enough scene, and in that moment she realized just how haggard everyone looked. Zetine's bandages hung from her body and a number of small scrapes covered her exposed skin. Ironja's face had a red tint and his beard would take years to regrow properly. Jubilatious' clothes were caked in dirt, and his patchy beard was beginning to grow out.

"What did she say?" Zetine asked curiously.

"She said I had great tits too," Mizt-Ied shrugged, causing Jubilatious to awkwardly look away, lest he accidentally gaze upon them. "I mean, she's not wrong, but I guess she was embarrassed about saying it in front of everyone else."

Zetine smacked Jubilatious on the back of the head and said, "Stop acting like a eunuch."

"Yes ma'am," he softly muttered.

"We all set to move then?" Ironja asked.

"If I may," Garr spoke.

"You may," Zetine nodded.

"I would like to come with you," he said. "Vhodan threatens all of Valael, and I would like to help put a stop to him. Already his soldiers have moved across the mountain, and though their actions were minor, the signs of their evil here are already obvious. I would not be able to live with myself if I did nothing about it.

The others looked to one another to make sure they were all in approval. Then Zetine said, "You may come with us, Garr. We would be glad to have your help."

***

It had been a rough night, but far from the harshest Kira had endured. No matter how tight he had wrapped the tattered robes around his arms and legs, the cold air continuously dug in. His backside hurt as he leaned against the shop wall, before eventually settling for laying atop the pavement. At multiple points during the night someone passed by, making rude remarks and thinly veiled threats towards what they perceived as a vagrant. At least they hadn't seen his swords, or Kira was sure the city watch would have come for him.

After the night had passed and traffic began to flow back into the district, Kira rose up to his feet and began waiting once again. There first came the shop owners who didn't live in their stores, unlocking their doors and getting ready for the day. Then an hour after sunrise came the wizards, intent on buying supplies and books once again. Kira had no idea how someone could possibly spend as much money as they seemed to on mere paper and ink, but it seemed quite fruitful in Arkvine.

Not long after the door behind Kira opened and the store owner said, "Oh, you're still here. Did you sleep on the street or something?"

"I'm waiting for someone," Kira replied.

"Of course you are," the man shook his head. "Just... try not to talk to any of my customers. I don't want you scaring away any of my business."

"You'll be fine," Kira grunted.

After the store owner headed back inside, Kira continued to stand motionless in his spot, stomach growling. He didn't dare leave, and instead waited patiently as wizards drifted past him. Every set of purple robes on an adult filled him with hope, but each time that hope was dashed as they walked away without even turning their heads, or Kira saw them to be a human or orc instead of an elf. Each and every time this happened, Kira's heart broke just a little bit more.

It wasn't until midday when a soft voice rang out, "Excuse me? Are you Kira?"

Kira spun around, eyes taking in Vrias' every feature. He wore loose-fitting purple robes and a pointed black hat that looked so out of place on his head it was almost adorable. His skin was a pale green color in stark contrast to Kira's own pale grey skin, to say nothing of his eyes which were a bright gold while Kira's were a deep violet. Vrias had a look of amusement on his face, but also of excitement. He carried with him a pinewood staff with a sapphire embedded in the end.

Kira resisted the urge to embrace Vrias in a hug and instead said, "It's so good to see you again... I didn't think you would come."

"I might not of if I hadn't gotten your letter in time," Vrias replied. "That youngling had barely remembered to give it to me. How come you didn't find me in the academy?"

"How could I have?" Kira asked. "I'm not a wizard."

"Those are a wizard's robes you're wearing," he chuckled. "Please tell me you didn't buy those off some con artist."

"Took them from a mannequin," he replied.

"Ah, that would explain it," Vrias nodded. "Only two types of wizards wear brown, Kira. Beast Shifters and Lowbornes, who are basically just regular people with a few fancy tricks. What are you doing here anyway? Shouldn't you be home?"

Kira's eyes widened in surprise at that and he asked, "Haven't you heard?"

"Heard what?" Vrias asked back, equally surprised by Kira's demeanor.

"They killed our people, Vrias," Kira lamented. "Thousands of us, slaughtered like feral dogs."

"Who did that!?" Vrias nearly yelled, horror dawning on him as he thought back to all those that he had left behind decades ago.

"Your Empire did," Kira somberly informed him.

"That can't be right," Vrias shook his head. "A few years back there was some issue in the North, but that was just some terrorists. The Empire resolved that peacefully."

"The Empire invaded our homeland, Vrias," Kira told him. "They killed indiscriminately. So few of us made it out, and those of us that survived-"

Vrias cut him off saying, "I don't believe you! I don't know why you've come here now with your lies, but the Empire has been nothing but good to me! Go home, Kira... just go home and forget about me."

As Vrias turned away, Kira grabbed his wrist and pulled him back. He then rolled back his sleeves to reveal the chains he had wrapped around his arms from making noise. He said, "They made me a *slave*, Vrias. They killed nearly everyone we have ever known and made the rest of us slaves. For years I toiled away for them, enduring the beatings and starvation, the endless fieldwork. They invaded our homeland so they could butcher and enslave our people, and you've joined them! It doesn't have to be this way, just come with me!"

The wizard stared at him for several agonizing moments. The wizard took in the sight of the chains, saw the fear and anquish in Kira's eyes, before at last he asked, "But where would we even go? All I have is the Empire, the academy. It's my home."

"It doesn't matter," Kira replied. "Together we could set off, find a home somewhere outside of Valael entirely. Travel the seas or take residency in some far-off land. Far away from the tendrils of this Empire, or anything else that would seek to hurt us."

"I just don't know if I can do it that easily," Vrias lamented. "I have... grown comfortable here. The rest of the world has never been as accepting of mages as Valael. For all I know, the moment I cast a spell in some distant land, I'll bring their entire army down upon us."

"The Empire's entire army is already trying to kill me," Kira stated. "Claiming my freedom came at a price, and there will be a target upon my back for as long as I live. No matter where we go, no matter what happens... as long as I will be with you, everything will be well."

Vrias smiled and tucked a strand of his hair behind his ear as he considered Kira's words. Then he said, "Very well... I'll go with you. I have to admit, a part of me has always wanted to see the outside world, no matter how dangerous it may be..."

From behind Vrias a voice mockingly asked, "Consorting with brown mages now, Vrias? What, are you scared that soon that pretty little purple robe will be ripped away from you?"

They both turned to see a red mage standing about fifteen paces back, with a signature red hat shading his face, while also making him look like a particularly dangerous mushroom. The wizard held a long metal rod in his hand in place of a staff, with a large sparkling diamond rising out of the rod's head. While most of his face was hidden, Kira could see the subtle glow of his eyes. The orange swirl that marked him as a pyromancer who had embraced the eternal flame perhaps a little too much for a person to safely do.

Vrias was quick to say, "It's nothing of your business who I can consort with, Marten."

Kira attempted to hide his chains, but the pyromancer's eyes widened as he saw them a moment before Kira pulled his sleeves back down. The red mage asked in shock, "Why do you have- are you a- YOU ARE!"

Vrias cried out, "It's not what it looks like!"

The red mage chuckled and said, "Consorting with an escaped slave? Whatever will Headmaster Hrafasaf say?"

"I'll handle this," Kira coldly stated.

All Vrias managed to say was a quiet little, "We don't have to do this," directed at the both of them.

Marten abruptly shouted a spell and pointed his staff, causing a spout of flame to lash out at the two elves. Kira quickly pushed Vrias out of the way and rolled to the side, drawing one of his swords as he rose back to his feet. Never before had he wished he had a whip than at the moment, for he could have severed the wizard's tongue without closing any distance. Instead, he was left wide open as he ran at the red mage.

Another spell sent three flaming swords at Kira, which he deftly ducked down to dodge. Instead, the flaming missiles shattered the window of the parchment store, setting it ablaze behind the elf. Vrias looked on in shock and horror, while Kira pressed forward. Before Marten could cast another spell, a chain-wrapped fist struck him square in the face, breaking his nose and knocking him to the ground, and sending his hat drifting away. Kira was atop him in a heartbeat, unwrapping the chain from his left hand so that he could strangle the human.

Vrias called out, "Don't kill him!" as the various other wizards in the district came by to watch.

Kira let out a subtle groan, tightened the chain so that Marten gasped for air, then slid his sword forward. The tip of the blade split open the wizard's tongue, then pierced the roof of his mouth in a quiet gesture of cruelty. Kira could see that tears had formed in Marten's eyes, yet they evaporated before ever making it to his cheeks. The elf twisted the blade, severing the end of Marten's tongue and slicing open his mouth, before releasing him onto the ground.

Marten lay choking on his own blood, before spitting the tip of his tongue out onto the pavement. He crawled away for a moment before he got up and stumbled away with the unmistakable sound of sobbing. The red mage's departure did not lessen the weight upon either of the elves' shoulders, for now, they faced the entire collected gaggle of wizards. Kira slowly stepped back, until he felt Vrias' hand upon his wrist.

"Do you have an escape plan?" Kira asked quietly.

Vrias replied, "If we can make it two streets east, there's a door we can go through. Otherwise... no."

"On my mark, we run," Kira told him.

The wizards all looked at them expectantly, eagerly. They were all young, some even children, but mostly about twenty years old or so. There were just over a dozen collected, and while Kira would fancy those odds against warriors, these were unpredictable spellcasters who had never seen a proper fight before. That worked in Kira's favor somewhat, for none of them knew who should make the first move, or even that they should all work as a single unit.

He watched them with the same eager eyes that they all held, then suddenly ran.

With his hand still latched on Kira's wrist, Vrias ran after him. Spells of all sorts were cast wildly through the air, lightning bolts and fireballs, gusts of wind, and molten metal. A few vines even grew out of the ground, pushing cobblestones aside to grab at the two elves. Kira easily sliced them apart as he ran, not slowing down for the feeble obstacle. A few spells nearly hit them, but Vrias was able to quickly counterspell them and send the attacks back towards their owners.

Three of the wizards happened to be in possession of enchanted rods, namely two broomsticks and one's own stave. They flew out over Kira and Vrias on their rods, intent on cutting them off at the end of the road. Two of them were yellow mages, one was blue. Kira laid his chances squarely upon his guess that the blue mage was more dangerous, and threw his broadsword at the wizard. It soared through the air as the wizard recited a spell, cleaving straight through the wood of his staff. The blue mage fell to the ground several feet below with a surprised cry of pain but was left relatively unharmed.

The two yellow mages each reached into their robes, where they produced a handful of different items. One held small clay blocks, the other a fistful of hair. The one with the clay threw it at the elves, where they exploded like grenades around the pair. Still, they pressed forward, clothes ripped and small cuts littering their faces and hands. The second yellow mage threw the hair to the ground, where it grew horrifically larger and took on the shape of a spider. The hair construct snarled at them, despite its lack of vocal cords, and moved to intercept them. Kira leaped up onto the top of the spider, then with all of his strength, threw Vrias forward.

The elf screamed in surprise before he collided with the hair construct's master, knocking the wizard to the ground below. Now seated upon the broom, Vrias quickly cast a gust of wind at the other wizard, blowing him harshly against a wall where he too fell to the ground. Kira hurriedly leaped onto the broom behind Vrias as the spider nipped at his heels but was left unharmed by it. Vrias then willed the broom forward, and the both of them flew through the air at a frighteningly fast speed. In that moment, Kira vowed he would never fly again, because it was truly one of the worst experiences he had ever been a part of.

With spells still being flung after them, Vrias pushed the broom to steadily rise higher into the air. They were going up and beyond the walls now, then were suddenly over and beyond. For just a moment it seemed as though their backs were to the entire world, and they could go anywhere their hearts pleased. But then the broom began to slow and tilted down towards the ground on the other side of the wall. As beautiful as the greenery was, Kira did not want to stop with their enemies so close.

"Why are we landing?" he asked.

Vrias chuckled then asked, "So you know how enchantments can be repealed by the wizard who placed them?"

"...no," came Kira's uncertain reply.

"Well they can," Vrias stated. "I can feel the magic being peeled away, absorbed back into the enchanter we stole it from. If we stay up high, we will end up crashing into the ground and turning into elf-colored paste."

"You can't fly on your own?" Kira skeptically asked.

"Are you kidding?" the wizard generously laughed. "I was never any good at flying on my own. The best I could manage is a slowed descent, and with you here we would still get flattened!"

"You're a terrible wizard, aren't you?" Kira lamented.

"I'm passable," he shrugged. "Get ready to hit the ground..."

Had Vrias not slowed their momentum, the lack of magic inside the broom would have sent the both of them flying violently forward. Instead, the pair made it close to the ground before they fell off. Kira landed in a steady roll across the field, while Viras landed on his side and went tumbling forward. Kira was quickly back on his feet, while Viras continued to lay on the ground. The warrior strode forward, placed his hand on the wizard's shoulder, and then hoisted him up onto his feet.

"Ow," Vrias groaned. "You could have given me a moment."

"We need to keep moving," Kira replied. "Not the nearest village, but I need directions to a settlement close by."

"Why not the nearest?" Vrias curiously asked.

"It's the first place they'll look," he informed.

Vrias thought about it for a moment then said, "Yes, I know a place. It will take a bit to get there, but I'll show you the way."

Chapter 7

It was strange to walk side by side with another person again. No matter how she tried to distance herself from the thoughts of her father, Wolf found herself thinking of him. For years he was the only real company she had, and living without him now was strange and desolate. Traveling with Kazaa made this worse, for his presence was now a reminder of what had been taken from her. He couldn't know this, of course, but Wolf still felt like somehow the man did. Every so often she would catch Kazaa giving her a strange look, as though he knew something she didn't. As innocent as it appeared, it made her deeply uneasy.

Despite all this, Kazaa proved himself to be a reliable companion. He caught on quickly that Wolf could not read, and would read aloud each sign they passed for her. He was also quite knowledgeable of The Empire and gave her detailed accounts of their customs. Each piece of information she learned about them fueled her quest for revenge, and there seemed no end to the information. He also knew of many other peoples and cultures, though Wolf hardly cared about them.

Kazaa himself seemed quite entertained by Wolf's hunting prowess and confessed it was a skill he was never able to improve upon. Once a day for six days she would leave him at a small camp they constructed together, and return an hour or two later later with a pair of rabbits or a fox to roast. He found it humorous how she knew next to nothing of farming, though it hardly mattered here. Still, she managed to find more berries and mushrooms than he would have expected on her hunts as well after he complained about the lack of vegetables.

On their seventh day together, the road they traveled passed through a densely wooded area. Kazaa froze in place, telling Wolf, "Stop."

"Why?" She asked, turning back to face him.

"Eyes forward," he said, and Wolf once again faced the woods. "It's likely to be an ambush up ahead. Plenty of cover and hiding spots, easy to cut off escape. Keep your weapon ready, move slowly, and keep an eye out for anything unusual."

"Are ambushes common?" Wolf asked as she drew her bow.

"In some places, yes," he answered. "In the lands that The Empire has annexed, many are left without home or food. They turn to banditry to survive, and in turn, often take the lives of others."

"Let them try," she grunted.

Kazaa drew his own sword, and for the first time, Wolf got a good look at it. It was made of bronze and had a hilt slightly curved, wrapped in a white bandage like Kazaa himself. The blade was similar to a normal sword for the first several inches, before curving drastically. The tip of the blade was actually slightly behind the hilt, though it ended two feet higher. Wolf would have considered it closer to an axe than a sword, though the grace with which Kazaa held it made her think otherwise.

He strode forward with the khopesh drawn, taking the point for Wolf to cover him. Kazaa held the weapon in his right hand, yet did not draw his dagger. Instead, he steadily walked forward, eyeing the surrounding trees with suspicion. Wolf kept an arrow half-notched as she followed after him, her own gaze steadfast on the overarching tree branches. It was a silent and slow walk forward, but caution proved monumental.

The bandits came at them from the sides, clearly intending to take the travelers by surprise. Judging by the overturned cart by the side of the road, Wolf could guess they weren't the first to have fallen into the trap. Three came at them from either side, while a seventh stood to the left with a crossbow and an eighth to the right with a short bow. Wolf quickly dispatched the eighth bandit with an arrow to the throat but was immediately thrown onto the defensive.

Three of them attacked her, one with a bastard sword and the other two with cudgels. She managed to leap out of the way as the bastard sword swung down at her and drew her axe head as the other two charged at her. She forced the broken weapon into one of their jaws, sending him to the ground but taking her axe with him. The next she delivered a punch to the gut, and as he gasped for air, took hold of his cudgel and bashed him over the head.

White hot pain shot through Wolf's body as the bastard sword was driven through her hip, causing her to let out a cry of pain. She looked into the blue eyes of her attacker and snarled in his face, before grabbing hold of the blade that jutted from her body. He watched in surprise as she gripped it so tight she bled from her fingers, and then began to pull it from her body. The bandit attempted to rip the blade free but Wolf held tight, before jerking the blade closer to herself. She head butted him as hard as she could, resulting in a satisfying crunch of the bandit's nose, and smiled as he let go of the blade.

"You psycho bit!" He cried in pain and shock.

Wolf said nothing. She merely twisted the sword around and took hold of the hilt, before raising the weapon into the air. The bandit looked up, and a heartbeat after the realization set in, Wolf split his skull in half. His body fell to the ground, and she took a moment to catch her breath.

Kazaa moved gracefully around his own opponents, refusing to let them encircle him. His biggest threat was the bandit with the crossbow, who made sure to keep Kazaa in his sights. Without a moment to spare, Kazaa managed to strike the bolt before it could land but nearly received a sickle to the throat for it. He leaped back and parried an oncoming sword strike before kicking the bandit in his chest, knocking him into two others. Seeing his opportunity, Kazaa ran forward and cut the archer's head off before he managed to load another bolt.

Three more bandits were on top of him in that moment. He dodged from a sword jab, caught an axeman in the arm with the curve of his blade, and then severed it just in time to parry a sword strike. The injured bandit fell to his knees shouting in pain, but Kazaa paid it no attention. He quickly moved forward, punching one swordsman in the throat while slicing open the other one's side. Before the two men could recover, he slit the bleeding man's throat and then lopped off the other one's head in the same motion.

Already the last three were attacking him, sword jab, sickle slash, axe strike. Sword jab, sickle slash, axe strike. They were so predictable. Within only a few repetitions of their attack pattern, Kazaa had them beat. He dodged the sword, hooked the sickle, and ripped it free from its owner's hand in order to parry the axe strike. With the momentary opening, Kazaa let the sickle fall into his left hand and attacked with both weapons. He slit the two men's throats, and then moved towards the lone swordsman.

The bandit raised his sword into a crude defensive stance, but he couldn't possibly compete with a master swordsman. Kazaa easily hooked both weapons beneath the man's arms and split them open, before kicking him down into the mud. He silently sheathed his sword and tucked the sickle into his belt as he watched the man attempt to stand, unable to use his paralyzed arms.

"Get out of here, and don't forget the mercy you have been granted," he said.

For a moment the bandit stood dumbfounded, panting as blood slowly seeped out from his arms. Then he turned and ran off into the woods, screaming like a madman. Kazaa turned himself to see how Wolf had faired and smiled to see she was mostly intact. Far more injured than he would have liked, but she had fared better than the average warrior would have.

"You should rid yourself of the sword," he said as he approached her.

Wolf quickly spun her head to look at him and asked, "Why?"

"It's a bastard sword," he said. After a brief moment, he thought to add context. "Within the lands of The Empire, bastard swords are reserved for their namesake. They are the lowliest of grunts, near second-class citizens that find service only as arrow fodder."

"It will do for now," she simply said, ignoring his advice.

"Very well," Kazaa sighed. "Come, let's loot their bodies and see if they have anything of use."

"Grave robbing?" She asked as she joined his side.

"Is that a problem?" He asked.

"No," Wolf said. "But I know the dead are supposed to be left as they are."

Kazaa chuckled and said, "It depends on where you are, and who the dead are. Shall we?"

"Very well."

***

Late into the night on the following day, Kazaa patiently stoked the fire the pair had built. It was his turn to keep watch as Wolf slept, curled up around her newfound sword on the opposite side of the fire. He looked out into the surrounding area, dark and ominous, listening to the hooting of owls and calls of small predators and the chirping of insects. It was peaceful, all things considered, and he found himself as relaxed as one could be while still on guard.

Then Wolf sat up. It was not in a natural way, more like her body was pulled upwards by strings. She nearly cut herself on the sword but pulled away from it without a scratch. Her arms jerked downwards and gripped the hilt of the blade, but did not raise it. Her eyelids opened one at a time, revealing glowing green eyes. Kazaa looked into the gaze of the dead woman without flinching and instead smiled.

"So," he quietly said. "You finally show yourself."

"What do you want with the girl?" Said Wolf's mouth, though it was not her own voice.

"With her?" He asked. "Nothing."

"Then with me?" She asked, slowly dragging the blade upwards.

"Also nothing," he said.

"Then why?" She pressed him for n explanation.

Kazaa dropped a handful of leaves into the fire and said, "In Exia, we know death. It is part of our culture. Of our religion. Necromancy is one of the highest honors performed by our priests. When I saw the girl, I knew that something possessed her."

"And you risk to rid me of her?" The dead woman asked, Wolf's eyes unblinking.

"No," Kazaa answered. "That would not be my place. Though I am surprised she has not yet noticed. She must have seen you in her dreams at the very least, yet she has said nothing."

"The girl is naive," the dead woman said. "She knows nothing of magic nor spirits. Answer me what it is you want."

"I journey to Cairn," he explained. "I assumed that was where you wished to go as well."

"It is," she hissed at him.

"Then let us travel together," he smiled. "Me and the girl work well together, and the last thing you want is her rushing off to fight an Imperial battalion."

The dead woman considered his words in silence for some time. The fire flickered between them, thirsting for more fuel. Kazaa patiently fed it more sticks he and Wolf had gathered, waiting for the dead woman to answer. All that time she looked at him with unblinking eyes, hand clasped upon the hilt of Wolf's bastard sword.

Then she said, "Very well. Ensure we arrive in Cairn, and you will be rewarded."

"Do you have a name?" Kazaa asked, but no answer was given.

Then Wolf collapsed upon the ground, her eyes snapping shut while her body went entirely limp. She slowly put her hands onto the ground below her and pushed herself up. She rolled her shoulders and looked around, looking down at Kazaa and then her sword. She knew she had fallen asleep with it, and yet there it stood planted in the dirt.

She asked him, "What happened?"

"You were sleepwalking," he lied. "They say it's bad luck to wake a sleepwalker, so I just made sure you didn't grow close to the fire."

Wolf looked at him silently, trying to judge his words. At last, she said, "I see," then sat down. "I will take over."

"Very well," Kazaa said, then stretched and laid down where he sat.

Wolf continued to watch him as he drifted off into sleep. She didn't quite believe him, though she couldn't understand why he would lie. Once she was satisfied he wouldn't wake, she spread out her belongings and took careful inventory. There was the sword, of course, along with her bow and eight arrows. She had her hunting knife, along with a pocket knife she had taken from one of the bandits' bodies. Then there were several pouches filled with red metal that Kazaa called coins. She still couldn't quite get her head around how they were valuable but was sure to hold onto them anyway.

Once satisfied that everything was as it should be, she put her belongings away. Her hunting knife went into the back of her belt, while the pocket knife was slid into her right boot. She strung the pouches along her belt, save for one that she tucked into her left boot. Once all was ready, she sat cross-legged with her sword across her lap and bow by her side. Should anything come for them in the night, she would be ready.

***

Colstone stepped out from the mountain for the first time in sixty years. The cold wind bit into his skin and he was quickly reminded of why he hated the outside world. But still, he had a duty to perform, and he would be damned if he didn't see it through to completion. He gave a gesture back to the entrance and along came three other dwarves, one of which mushed a sled pulled by two goats. Together they began to set down the mountain path, journeying to the bottom where an old friend resided.

When they arrived at Tusk's hut one of the other dwarves, Brock, remarked, "Doesn't look like anyone's home."

"Ay," Colstone nodded. "But these are humans. A weird folk. Maybe they have no lights inside."

He approached the door and pulled it open, finding no signs of his two friends. It was noticeable that Wolf's bow and axe were gone, but much more noticeable that Tusk's were still there. He said, "The girl's stuff is gone but the man's are still here."

"Strange," said Limecrack as he rubbed his beard.

Marblekeeper, who tended to the goats, then noticed one of them was licking at something buried in the snow. He cried out, "There's something here!"

Together the dwarves moved in and began to clear out the snow. Quickly they realized it was a gauntlet, which was alarming for all of them. They continued to dig it up though, until at last the entire body was exposed. There laid an Imperial soldier, though they had no idea what The Rizzen Empire even was. The body had been stabbed through several times by some type of spear and had been almost perfectly preserved aside from the places where birds had picked at its cold flesh before the snow buried it.

"Any idea who she is?" Brock asked.

"None at all," Colstone shook his head. "Keep digging though, there's gotta be somethin' here we're missing."

The dwarves worked for several hours to clear up the snow, finding each of the bodies that Wolf had left behind. Each one was a horrible sight and just seemed to raise more questions. Eventually, though, Marblekeeper uncovered a large patch of dirt that didn't seem to be shaped right, and together they pulled out several large frozen clumps. Resting below them was a face that brought tears to Colstone's face.

"He dinnit make it," the dwarf choked back sobs.

"What do you think happened to the girl?" Limecrack asked.

"Probably left after," Colstone quietly said. "Couldn't bear to stay where her da died. But these blokes," he kicked a soldier's pauldron. "These I don't know about. We'll head to their village next, and see if she went there."

"The barbarians don't like us," Marblekeeper reminded him.

"Ay, but they don't like anyone," he said. "They don' just go around killin' either. So long as we respect them, we're fine."

When they came to the village, all hope of finding Wolf vanished. It was a horrible scene, even weeks later. Nearly everything had been burned to the ground, and numerous bodies littered the ruined landscape. Some of them had been stabbed through or dismembered, but far too many had been burned to a crisp. It made all of the dwarves sick, but still, Colstone marched through the camp. He had to find her. He had to know what happened to his best friend's daughter.

Then he found the bodies. They were far away from the village, which is likely why the soldiers missed them. Their throats had been slit and they lay in a heap, half buried in the snow. They wore the same armor and crests as the bodies at Tusk's home. It was clear that whoever these people were, they were responsible for the massacre.

"There wasn't enough bodies for the whole of 'em," Brock said.

"Either they left..." Limecrack proposed.

"Or somebody took them," Colstone finished. He then ordered, "Look for any signs of where they went! We're finding that girl no matter what!"

***

Huntsman dunked his head into a pail of water, the ice-cold liquid quickly enveloping his long black hair. He held his head down for a few minutes before quickly surfacing, biting his lip as the cold stabbed down into his skin. He then took a wool rag and soaked it in the water, before dabbing at his armpits, then his groin. Once finished he found a fishbone comb and began to straighten out his matted hair. It would clearly take some time.

A beam of light fell upon Huntsman as the flap to his tent was pushed open. He turned to see some low-grade soldier standing there, taking a look around at the abysmal decorum. Huntsman's clothes sat in a neat pile, while his weapons were a foot away. Otherwise, there was a bedroom on the opposite side of the tent, and the washing basin at the center. While none of the soldiers was allowed to carry any large items, they were still permitted any personal items they could carry and often decorated their own tents with small trinkets.

"What do you want?" Huntsman asked, practically hissing at the young man.

"The general's arrived, sir, colonel," he quickly said. "He um, wants to speak to you. Now."

He replied, "Tell him I'll be right with him."

"Yes sir," the soldier replied.

Huntsman groaned and said, "You're dismissed, private."

"Yes sir," the soldier said again before turning and leaving.

Alone in the dark once again, Huntsman was left to dress himself in peace. He first pulled on his shirt and made sure to lace the chest closed, then his leggings. After this were his trousers, then he stuck his feet into his boots and laced them tight. Before he donned his cloak, Huntsman fastened both his belt and his bandolier. Then he equipped himself with his bow and quiver. All set, he left the safety of his tent.

Outside the sun glared down upon the Huntsman, along with many of the others. He pulled his hood on to shield his eyes from the light and walked across the camp. Many soldiers sat around chatting or eating, while the occasional patrol strolled past. Many tents had been erected, many of which were occupied. Huntsman winced at the sounds coming from within, be they moans or screams, for they were one and the same in the camp.

Huntsman found General Raeon near the edge of the camp, along with several of his personal guards and another ranger. Raeon was adorned in silver plate armor and a white cape, the Sigil of Rizzen painted across his breastplate. He held a fox-like helmet under his arm, while his thumb was tucked into the sword belt that carried a saber. He was an older man, but fairly attractive, with neck-length grey hair and golden brown eyes.

The ranger next to him was a woman, with flowing blond hair and crystal blue eyes. She dressed in a leaf-green cloak over leather armor and carried a soldier's bow upon her back. Unlike Huntsman, she also carried a shortsword against her hip. She was followed by a large sleek black cat with large claws and protruding tusks. Huntsman recognized it as a Northern battle cat, a beast that nearly went extinct after the Empire annexed the Northern Reach.

Raeon smiled his usual pretentious and fake smile as he said, "It's good to see you again, Whistler."

"General Raeon," Huntsman said as he offered a small bow. "I hope your journey wasn't too difficult."

"Not at all," the general responded. "There's not much of a rebellion left to be a threat. I expect we'll be able to send a few dozen brigades into the Southern Reach by next year. We're doing good work, Whistler."

"Yes sir," he automatically responded. "Am I clear for leave?"

The general tipped his head, his smile wavering. He said, "Yes, you can leave by morning. I've brought your replacement."

The woman bowed and said, "Charmed. My name is Savia."

"Whistler," Woodsman repeated the bow. "What rank are you, Savia?"

She grinned at this and said, "Brigadier, colonel."

Whistler looked to Raeon and asked, "What are you planning? I thought the troops would be returning to Imperial Heart."

The general said, "Calm down, Whistler. They will. Savia is to escort them to the sanctuary, then Imperial Heart. There I'm gathering my own men to hold Oshack, while your own will have time to recover."

"Oshack?" Whistler asked. "We finally took it?"

"Oh yes," the general nodded. "A handful of the higher-ups have already gone to oversee it and lay claim to its lands. The Emperor himself was present for the final battle."

"I see," he said more to himself than Raeon. "What of my birds? Are they to remain with you, or may I take them with me?"

"You can have a dozen of them," he said. "Savia will maintain most of the flock. When you return to Imperial Heart, you may regain control of them."

"Very well," he sighed. "Is there anything else I should know about?"

"No," he stated. "But I'm getting the idea that you don't appreciate how lucky you are."

"I know," Whistler said, though was quickly cut off.

Raeon continued, "If Bardan hadn't spoken for you, you would be dead. Not just the fact that you're alive, but the fact that you're commanding men speaks legions to the amount of faith that man has in you."

"I know," Whistler said with more frustration in his tone.

The general finished, "Appreciate the gift that lays before you. If I had been present when you withdrew, I would have killed you for treason. Be grateful, Whistler."

Whistler only said, "I am more grateful than you could ever imagine."

***

It had been over a decade since Wolf stood amongst a thriving village. Her malformed memories of what they were like were filled with the imagery of annoying children and abusive older boys. Her last fight with the boys was barely even remembered, just a haze of anger and blood. Now that she approached a new village, her nerves were filled with anxiety.

She lagged behind Kazaa as the bustling little village grew in size, already visibly larger than her first home. The smell of roasting meats filled her nose and it made her hungry, yet the distant laughter of children made her want to scream. A few people stood along the village outskirts, talking amidst one another or performing chores. As the pair passed by though, most turned to stare at her. It made her nauseous.

"I don't like it here," she whispered to Kazaa as she matched his pace.

"It is fine, woodsgirl," he said. "These are a peaceful people, you have nothing to worry about."

"They're staring at me," she hissed.

"No," he corrected. "They're looking at your sword. I warned you it would draw attention."

"I don't like it," she said.

"It will be fine," he replied.

They reached the entrance of the town, where log walls protected it from the outside world. No longer were the fields of crops tended to by stray farmers or lone homesteads. This was not a village, but a new daunting type of settlement. Now there were dozens of houses in a row, of which there must have been several dozen. Mixed in were the stores and storage buildings that drove the town's economy.

At either side of the entrance was a guard, dressed in chainmail and wearing helmets that resembled iron hats. They each held a poleaxe in their hands and looked fairly bored. Kazaa knew they likely dealt with little real action and should be fairly docile, though would always be on the lookout for trouble where it didn't exist. To Wolf though, each of these guards was a threat waiting to spring out at her. Following Kazaa's lead, she was barely able to keep herself from drawing her sword.

"What's your business in Fragrant Meadows?" One of the guards asked.

"That's the name of the town?" Kazaa asked as he sniffed the air, but failed to spot anything other than moss and meat. Then he said, "We're simply passing through. We figured we would try the local cuisine, maybe buy some supplies and stay the night, then be on the way."

The other guard said, "Keep your swords sheathed. We ain't got no patience for troublemakers."

"Will do," Kazaa smiled politely at them.

The first guard said, "Get in there then, we don' have all day."

The duo entered, and all at once the strangeness hit Wolf. She could see a group of children playing with a hoop and stick, two drunkards arguing over something trivial while sitting on their porch, and a dozen cooks preparing their foods. Bread was placed upon tables for anyone to purchase, the ringing of metal upon metal occasionally split the air, a dog ran down the street with a sausage in its mouth, and there was so much talking that it made Wolf want to vomit.

She could hear them saying, "Look at that bastard."

"You would think that thing knows it's not wanted."

"What kind of woman looks like that?"

"I wish she'd use that sword on me."

"Bitch doesn't look like she's bathed in a year."

"Could you imagine laying next to something like that?"

"I'd never live with myself if I was a bastard like that thing."

"This is too much," Wolf said from beside Kazaa.

"They're gossips," he replied. "Their words mean nothing, they talk of us only because we're new."

"I don't WANT them to talk about me," she hissed.

"This is how the real world is," he replied. "You must face it, one way or another."

Wolf's lips distorted as she tried to form a response but failed. She remained silent with pursed lips, following after the man as he wove around townsfolk and looked over small market stalls. Wolf had to admit that some of the stalls looked interesting, serving strange foods or selling odd trinkets, unlike anything she had seen.

Eventually, she stopped at one stall, looking down at a large canine tooth with a thread through it. "Do you like it?" The vendor asked, smiling gently at her.

"I do," she said without pulling her eyes away.

"It belonged to a dire wolf," the vendor explained. "It makes a great trophy necklace, only five silver."

"Five silver?" Kazaa asked from behind her. "What a load of hogwash. The thing's probably not even real, and definitely not worth more than eight copper."

"Eight copper!?" The vendor gasped. "Sir, this is fine craftsmanship right here! I risked my life to slay that beast, and slaved away carefully carving that hole! The least I can go for is a silver and a half!"

"A silver and two is the highest we'll go," Kazaa replied.

The vendor grimaced but nodded and said, "Fine. Only because the girl wants it."

Kazaa fished around in one of his coin pouches and then produced a silver coin and two copper pieces. He tossed them at the merchant and walked away, leaving Wolf to grab the tooth and follow after him. She admired it for a moment longer, feeling the bone between her fingers before she strung it around her neck. The feeling of a necklace was foreign to her, yet it was almost natural. Soon she would learn to forget it was even there.

Eventually, Kazaa led her to a building, not unlike the inn they had first met at, several weeks before. This one was far wider, and not nearly as tall. The door frame had been painted purple, a color Wolf had previously only seen in the rarest of flowers. A few townsfolk hung about outside, drinks in hand as they bickered. When Wolf and Kazaa passed by though, they fell silent and quickly moved out of the way. Wolf could feel their eyes burrowing into her back though, and knew their conversation would quickly become about her.

Inside the tavern, there were six long tables, where a dozen and a half people sat spread around them with plenty of seats to spare. A woman in a white shirt and long green skirt carried trays with three bowls of soup to a group of young boys, while an angry-looking older man chopped something just out of eyesight while standing behind a bar counter on the opposite end of the hall. As the woman headed back towards the bar, Kazaa followed after her, and Wolf went with him.

Kazaa placed his hand upon the counter and said, "Hello, sweet flower, whatever are you serving on the menu today?"

The woman softly smiled at him and said, "We have cabbage soup, eggs, and a few roaches left."

"I never much cared for fish," he said. "I'll take a bowl of your soup."

"And what about you, miss?" the girl asked, leaving Wolf to feel awkward that she didn't quite know what any of those things were besides eggs.

"I'll have soup too," she muttered.

"It's great this time of year," she said. "You folks came at the perfect time," then she yelled out, "Horace! Two bowls of soup!"

"Gah!" replied the older man.

"That's gonna be four copper each," the girl said.

Wolf watched as Kazaa reached for his money pouch and mimicked him. She carefully selected the four coins he had chosen and did the same, offering them to the girl. After this Kazaa asked, "Any trouble around town?"

"No," the girl replied. "Aside from the war, everything's been fine around here. You two can take a seat, and I'll bring your food to you when it's done."

"Very well," Kazaa said, before flipping her a silver coin. "Take that as a tip."

"Thanks," the girl nonchalantly replied and pocketed the coin.

As he and Wolf headed for a mostly empty table he remarked, "I miss the working girls. They're much easier to charm."

"Working girls?" Wolf asked.

Kazaa frowned at that and said, "I forgot you're from the woods. Some girls offer... services for money. Not unlike how I may offer my sword. Only their services are more intimate."

Wolf nodded, thinking of how it made sense for a woman to make money from slitting throats. She took a seat and asked, "How long have you been fighting?"

He thought for a few moments then said, "I killed my first person when I was twelve. That was... twenty or so years ago. Yourself?"

"I've fought since I was young," she replied. "Killed someone when young. Killed many people now."

"You say that like it means nothing," he said.

"Why would it?" she asked in response. "Death is death. If you kill an animal, you live another day. If you kill a person, you live another day. People aren't special. Everything dies."

"True, I suppose," he said. "My people have a much more revered sense of death than yours do, apparently."

"You worship death?" she asked.

"No," he chuckled. "But there is nothing greater than dying, for it means you've lived. Death is your final true act upon this world, and it is a holy right. As such, when you kill someone, you are giving them their final honor. However, there is often a sense of guilt that lingers when you kill someone before their time. I must admit, that traveling the world has instilled a minor sense of agnosticism upon me. Every now and then there's a life I take that leaves me awake at night."

"Why would you do that?" she asked him, genuinely baffled by the idea of guilt.

Kazaa looked at her with a look of pity, something Wolf could recognize far too well. He said, "Because some people kill to survive, and by killing them, I am ending their survival."

Two bowls of hot soup were then slid in front of the pair, and the barmaid joyfully said, "Eat up!"

"Impeccable timing my dear," Kazaa smiled up at her, but the girl was already walking away. "Damn Oshack women. I can never read them."

"What's an Oshack?" Wolf asked as she played with her spoon, spinning the soup around.

"The region we are now in," he replied. "Do you really not know any geography?"

Wolf stared at Kazaa. Kazaa stared at Wolf. She placed a spoonful of hot broth between her lips. He still stared at her. She swallowed and then said, "No."

He let out a dramatic sigh and said, "I suppose it does not really matter. But it is good to learn your places and your peoples."

"Okay," she said, abandoning her spoon to carefully slurp the soup out of the bowl.

Kazaa raised his own spoon, blew on it, and then consumed his soup. Wolf prodded a piece of cabbage with her finger. Kazaa took another spoonful of soup. Wolf slowly plucked the vegetable from her bowl and plucked it into her mouth. Kazaa savored the rich taste. Wolf cringed as she chewed on the horrid thing. Kazaa went back for another spoonful. Wolf copied him. Kazaa took yet another spoonful. Wolf grew bored and picked her bowl up. Kazaa looked at her. Wolf chugged the bowl of soup until only the cabbage remained.

"What are these things?" she asked as she carefully examined the vegetables as though they were explosive.

"Chunks of cabbage," he informed her between mouthfuls of soup.

"I don't trust them," she sternly said.

The cabbage looked particularly sad at that.

"Why not?" Kazaa asked, a sly grin spreading across his lips.

"Look at them," she said. "They look so sad and strange. And they taste bad."

"They're vegetables," he replied. "They're good for you. Eat up."

She begrudgingly picked one up, put it in her mouth, and nearly died from chewing it. She said, "I don't believe you. Nothing good could be this bad."

"No, they very much can," he said before chewing some cabbage. "Though cabbage is delicious. You're just too used to meat."

She looked at him with what Kazaa could only describe as puppy dog eyes and popped a piece of cabbage into her mouth. Then she said, "I would rather eat a raw pheasant than this."

"That's disgusting," he replied.

"Just like this," she said in retaliation. "I'm not eating any more of it."

"Then I'll eat it," he said as he reached for her bowl.

Wolf smacked his hand rather hard and said, "It's mine. You said money is important and I gave money for this."

Kazaa rubbed his hand and replied, "I did, and I see how quickly that betrayed me. So you're not going to eat it, but you're not going to give it to me?"

Wolf looked at him with fierce eyes as she ate another piece of cabbage. "I'll eat it," she said with a mouthful of the disgusting food.

"Then chow down," he said.

They continued eating for several more minutes before Wolf finally finished her meal. The barmaid watched Wolf rise to her feet and follow Oshack towards the exit, a sigh escaping her lips. The pair left the building, passing by the few people outside who had failed to move since they entered.

"Where to?" Wolf asked.

"The inn," Kazaa shrugged. "May as well get a good night's rest before we continue onwards."

"It's still daylight," she obviously pointed out.

"But it will be weeks before we have another bed," Kazaa retorted. "Enjoy it while you can."

It would cost them another silver each for separate rooms, which Kazaa had personally insisted upon despite Wolf's ambivalence. Each room consisted of a bed, a small trunk, and a small end table with a flimsy chair. Each bed had two straw pillows and both a small and large blanket. All in all, they were fine rooms, though Wolf found herself uncomfortable sitting alone.

After a few hours had passed, she got up and left. She made sure to slowly close the door to not disturb Kazaa, and then made her way outside. The sun had set a short time before, and there were still streams of pink and violet in the sky. Wolf silently walked through the town, which was now much more silent than it was upon their arrival.

Virtually alone, Wolf passed through the town undisturbed. As she reached the Gaye, there were two new guards waiting for her. They gave her strange looks, but seeing she came from within, let Wolf go without a word. She found the river that the town fished from and made her way upstream, traveling until the town was nothing more than a small hut in the distance.

She kneeled by the riverside and submerged her hands in the flowing water, before bringing them to her lips for a sip. The water was ice cold and didn't taste the best, but it was good enough for her. She drank as much as she felt she needed, and then refilled her waterskins. Once finished she looked around for signs of anyone else.

Satisfied that she was alone, Wolf placed her weapons on the ground and stripped down completely. She entered the river, wincing as the water cut through her skin. She continued deeper into the water until only her head was above the surface and began to relax. It required a small amount of effort to keep from flowing downstream, but otherwise, it was peaceful.

Wolf stared up at the stars in the sky, taking in their beauty. It was a waning moon, and there was even a comet passing by. She watched the comet streak past the moon, curving around the planet on its way somewhere far away. Then she fixed her eyes on the constellations. She could make out The Hunter, The Bear, The Wolf, The Mountain, and The Pup. She could not see The Boar and The Tree, and for some reason, this made her sad.

She would not have long to wallow in the sadness though. Emerging from the underbrush was a grey wolf, wearing its spring pelt. The girl focused on the animal, which returned her stare. It moved towards the riverside slowly, as though it would pounce upon her. Then it lowered its head to drink from the river, and Wolf relaxed. Once satisfied, the animal ran away as the girl watched it go.

She swam back to the shore and emerged from the water, shaking her hair dry. She wiped as much of the water as she could from her body, then quickly dressed and rearmed herself. Once ready, Wolf headed back towards the town.

***

An ornate cart traveled down a dirt road late at night, pulled along by two fine white horses. The horses were beckoned forth by the snapping of reigns held by a sore guard dressed in chainmail. Both he and the cart were adorned with the Empire's crest. The cart also held a great many intricate carvings that served to make it all the more beautiful. Amongst them was a wizard standing above an army, a knight plunging a sword into the heart of a dragon, and a diplomat making peace with an elaborately dressed pharoah.

Inside the cart, there were just two men and their charcuterie board. One of them was dressed in a white shirt and light blue cloak. He was a small and somewhat pudgy man with a long thick mustache and glasses that bounced on his nose as the cart rocked.

He held with him a ledger book that he continuously inspected, and occasionally reached for a piece of cheese.

The other man was tall and of questionable build. He dressed in an overly large pristine white road that hid most of his features. His skin was somewhat pale, and his well-kept hair was the exact shade as his robe. His brilliant crystal blue eyes pierced out from behind his crows' feet like beacons in the dark. He looked to be in his fifties and was exceptionally well-groomed and handsome. He would leisurely take a sip of wine without spilling it, or reach forward and take a small sausage or cheese slice.

"You must try the sausages," the man in white said. "They're to die for."

"I could imagine," the man in blue responded. "I'm not much of a meat eater. Especially not pigs. Filthy creatures."

"Are you implying I'm filthy?" He asked grimly. The two stared at each other in silence for several moments before bursting into laughter. "I had you going there!" He chuckled.

The other man laughed and said, "Did not! You can't keep a straight face to save your life!"

"Sure I could," he said. "I would just have to glue it straight first."

The man in blue reached for his goblet, only to spill it on himself as the cart violently shook. "Blast it!" He hissed. "I hate these lousy dirt trails. Why don't you ever take the highways?"

"Because that's just begging for attention," he stated.

"We've spent a fortune on constructing them," he grumbled. "We should get some use out of them."

"Highways are for the peasants and the soldiers," he explained.

"Speaking of which," he sighed. "I also wish you would take some guards with you. These back roads make me so nervous."

"The more guards you have," he explained. "The more attention you draw to yourself. We wouldn't want to get ambushed by some Oshak legionnaires."

"True, I suppose," the man nodded as the cart slowly came to a stop.

The two looked to one another, but it was the man in white who took the initiative. He said, "Stay here. I'll see what's wrong."

"Good luck, Val," the man in blue said.

Val swung the door open and stepped out, closing it behind him. He looked around, his eyes passing over each of the armed men before him. There must have been at least two dozen, dressed in a hodgepodge of leather and studded armor. They all held some sort of weapon, mostly axes and sickles, while a few had bows or swords. Each of them was clearly malnourished, and many were scarred or disfigured in various ways.

"We'll don't you look lovely," the one Val guessed to be the leader spoke in an Oshack accent.

He was dressed in a steel breastplate over leather armor, while the left pant leg had been removed. Val could see a crude prosthetic foot had been installed, made from lead by the look of it. The man also had an eyepatch over his right eye and a small burn scar to go with it. He held a shortsword in his hand that he pointed towards Val's throat with a smug smile.

"Here's what's gonna happen," he said. "You're gonna come with us. We're gonna send a nice little letter to your empire and send a finger with it. They're going to give us some money, and you'll get to live. Sound good?"

Unphased, Val simply asked, "How many of you are there?"

"What?" The bandit asked in surprise. "About thirty. Why?"

"Hm, not a lot," Val mused. "Where is my driver?"

"Dead,," the bandit stated. "Which I'm sure you don't want to be."

"Tell you what," Val sighed. "I am in a generous mood. If all thirty of you leave, you can live."

"Are you daft?" The bandit growled. "You're outnumbered thirty to one!"

"No," he smiled. "You're outnumbered one to thirty."

The bandit watched in confusion, and then horror, as an array of golden daggers appeared around Val's head. It was cold and bitter recognition that filled the man's veins. Before he could speak, a dagger had already taken out his other eye. Val grabbed hold of the shortsword's blade as the bandit fell, easily twisting it around in his hand. He walked forward, golden daggers flying through the air faster than the arrows that targeted the mage. Each arrow was destroyed before it could make contact, and soon each archer would be slain.

The bandits ran at Val as one, but it was a useless gesture. He weaved out of their attacks with an otherworldly ease, parrying blows only out of sheer boredom. Each time he riposted, it resulted in a limb being severed. His opponents fell to the ground one by one, blood gushing from cleanly cut stumps. Still outnumbered ten to one, the bandits reached a mutual agreement with one another.

One of them cried out, "Fuck this!" Then turned and ran.

Val dropped his sword to the ground as the vagabonds ran, but he was not done with them. He sent forth his daggers, harpooning two of them through their wrists and elevating them high into the air before turning them to face away from their allies. He bent his right hand as though he intended to scoop something, and with his left extended his fingers as far as they would move. In Val's right hand, he conjured a ball of fire, and between his left fingers, a powerful string of lightning began to grow.

He threw the fiery ball, no larger than a head, into the crowd of fleeing bandits. Then he shot his left arm forward and unleashed a bolt of lightning, striking the ball just before it could make contact with the back of a bandit. The resulting explosion was deafening, and then suddenly devoid of all sound as the last remnants of air were swallowed. Skin melted and blood boiled in the blink of an eye as skeletons were reduced to ash. The light could be seen for a hundred miles, and yet Val looked upon it with unwavering eyes.

Val pulled the two survivors down from the air, still crucified upon his golden blades. With his left hand full of lightning he approached them, gasping for the air that was just now returning to the area. To the one on his left, he placed his hand on the man's face and remained unflinching as he screamed in pain. Electricity coursed through his brain and into his skull before the spell was abruptly abandoned. He was left sputtering and with smoking hair as the daggers removed themselves from his wrists. For the other man, the daggers instead chose to remove his wrists altogether.

"You may go," Val said to them as his daggers returned to his head like a halo. "Tell all you know of what happened. Warn them of what happens when they cross the Rizzen Empire."

The two men looked at him in pain and terror, frozen in place. But then the one whose hands had been severed rose to his feet and began to stumble away. The electrocuted man followed after him, his footsteps far less certain. With a satisfied smile, Val returned to the carriage and opened the door.

"Brelos you old dog," Val smirked. "It would appear as though our driver didn't make it. Be a pal and take the reigns?"

The man in blue looked at him in shock. Then after several moments, he let out a defeated sigh. "Right away, my lord."

Val then looked down to his dirt and blood stained robes, holding in a curse. "I *liked* this outfit," he muttered to himself.

Chapter 8

It had been a strange few days getting used to Garr, but the heroes had welcomed him with open arms. Now five, it seemed as though they stood an even greater chance against the forces of evil. His bowmanship was also greatly admired, and a skill that none of the others possessed. Really his only drawback was his reluctance to hunt, which made the others rely more steadily upon the plants he foraged.

"I'm sick of roots," Ironja huffed.

"I need meat," Mizt-Ied agreed.

"You do not need meat," Garr explained. "You simply enjoy meat more than others foods. You can learn not to eat it."

"I thought orcs ate almost exclusively meat," Jubilatious said.

"Most of us do," he replied. "But I only eat the meat of an animal that either gave itself to me, or that had to die. It is not right to kill something solely because I was hungry."

"But why roots," Ironja wailed. "At least pick some mushrooms!"

"Or some nice tasty berries," Mizt-Ied added.

"I would fancy some berries," Zetine quietly said.

"There are none in this area," Garr straitforwardly explained.

"What about the bear!" Ironja said as he gestured to Jermaind. "You let HIM eat meat!"

"Jermaind is a bear," Garr said. Jermaind said nothing, because he was a bear. "If he catches a foal, that is his business."

"Yer a hypocrite," Ironja grumbled.

"Quiet," Garr said.

"But I'm-" he began, before being cut off.

Garr hissed out, "Quiet! I hear something!"

They all stopped to listen and sure enough, there was a noticeable sound. The flapping of a great many wings. Occasionally a strange cry would echo, not quite bird like but entirley inhuman. It was dreadful waiting for Garr to listen, each one of them entirley motionless.

Then he simply said, "Harpies."

"What's a harpy?" Zetine asked.

"A landlady," Mizt-Ied badly explained.

Garr properly explained, "A harpy is a creature similar to an elf but with the limbs of a bird. They are usually scavengers, but The Emperor has introduced a new breed that has infiltrated many flocks. These new harpies are highly aggressive, killing anything that isn't one of their own, even if they do not hunger."

"Gotta love these new monsters," Ironja groaned.

"Are they dangerous?" Zetine asked.

"In groups," Garr nodded. "But they are also weak. If you can keep your distance, they are no real threat."

"Any elemental weaknesses or resistances?" Jubilatious asked.

"They are bird people," he pointed out the obvious. "Throw a rock at them or light them on fire, it kills them just the same."

"And you're fine killing the harpies?" Mizt-Ied curiously asked.

"Yes," Garr stated. "I have no tolerance for invasive species."

Together they moved forward until they reached a ridge where they could overlook the gossip of harpies. There were a dozen and a half of the creatures, as beautiful as they were disturbing. Each one was its own special blend of colors, and it seemed as though they could be every color of the rainbow, much like elves and birds alike. Sometimes their skin matched their feathers, sometimes it did not. Wings jutted out from where elbows would be and talons jutted from bird-like feet. They did not have beaks, luckily, and were almost beautiful. It was strange to see a starved elf though, for these creatures were certainly starved. Their ribcages were clearly visible and they had a mad look in their eyes as they fought with one another for scraps of warm flesh.

The creature they eviscerated had once been a human, or at least looked human. His brown cloak had been torn away and was stretched across a boulder, the wind unable to lodge it free. Talons pulled free his intestines, lifting his body into the air for a moment before the organs tore and the corpse fell back to the ground. A harpy would swoop down and bite a piece of his face off before quickly flying away. They fought over his arms and legs, tearing the limbs off as they played a gruesome tug of war with one another. Every second there would be a fraction less of the man there once was.

"That's horrible," Zetine gagged.

"Lucky birds," Mizt-Ied grumbled.

"Who was he?" Jubilatious asked.

Garr's eyes turned white for a few moments, before returning to their usual yellow. He said, "I believe he was an Imperial ranger."

"All the way out here?" he asked in surprise. "Though I suppose that explains the path markers."

"A what?" Ironja asked.

Garr said, "Many of the monsters require rangers to lead them, so they do not turn on their own forces or eat one another. Despite our vows to protect the natural order, some rangers have been seduced by the Dread Lord. Evidentially, this one was not a good enough ranger to stop his pets from growing too hungry."

"Can we sneak past them?" Mizt-Ied asked him.

The orc spent a few more moments watching the harpies then said, "Possibly. If we remain quiet and skirt around the area, it is unlikely for them to notice us. At least, until they run out of food."

The group then spent the next few agonizingly slow minutes creeping about the minute. Never had it been so apparent just how loud Ironja's armor was. It went *clank. Clank. Clank.* Every time he moved. Never did Zetine realize how her daggers occasionally scrape against something nearby, resulting in a subtle skrieeek. Never had Jubilatious noticed just how much his cloak fluttered when the wind blew, resulting in a steady *fwlfwlfwl* sound. Mizt-Ied did not notice any noises coming from herself, as she was entirely silent. Garr also did not notice any noises, as he worked particularly hard to ensure he remained silent.

They had gotten nearly halfway around the harpies when a cacophony of screeches filled their ears. Fearing the harpies would be swooping upon them in seconds, the group looked over the ridge in fear. Instead they saw a lone rock troll, smaller than Snarlgor, walking towards the gossip. It held a thin tree trunk in its hand and looked particularly angry, even for a rock troll. The first harpy swooped in at it, and the troll simply swatted it from the air. Then they all descended down upon the monsters, trying to avenge their fallen sister and find a new meal. One by one, they would all be felled by the superior beast.

"Thank the gods for that," Mizt-Ied said.

"Truly a minor miracle," Garr agreed.

They continued onwards, slow and steady, offering only the occasional glance towards the carnage. Though they were grateful for the rock troll's interference, it reminded them of wounds that were all too recent. Mizt-Ied couldn't help but feel bad for the harpies, for every few moments they would cry out in agony, and then were swiftly silenced. No matter how hard the monsters fought, there was no use fighting a rock troll. Soon there would be no more sounds from the creatures, save for the steady growl of the troll before it began to feast upon the spoils of victory.

It would be another two hours of careful journey before they reached the decline, overlooking the brilliant Oshack landscape below. To get down they would have to move slow and carefully, which the group had grown used to by this point. Each step sent fall stones tumbling down, and their feet would regularly slide. Despite this, there was no incident for the first twenty minutes.

A soft pleasant whistling was pulled along by the wind, an innocuous and almost joyful tune. As soon as he heard it, Garr turned towards the direction the noise had come from with wide and frightened eyes. Then Zetine, who had been standing ahead of him, slipped. Distracted, he was unable to catch the woman as she fell to the ground and began rolling downhill. She passed by Mizt-Ied, nearly knocking the goblin over herself, and then passed Jubilatious. As the hard and sharp stones dug into her skin, it was Ironja that managed to catch her, swinging his axe into the ground with a subtle *chip* on order to block Zetine.

Zetine grabbed hold of the shaft as her life depended on it, and let loose a series of adrenaline filled pants. After rising to her feet, she asked Garr, "Where were you?"

The orc barely paid attention to her, instead focusing on the source of the noise. He said simply, "I heard a song I have not heard for a long time."

"Is that it?" Zetine asked, aggravation abundant in her voice.

Garr then looked to the sky and a deep frown appeared on his lips. He said, "The sun will set in an hour. We will make camp then. No fire tonight."

"No fire!?" Ironja asked in disbelief. "It's bloody freezing at night! We'll be dead by morning!"

"You will be fine," Garr stated. "Though if needed, simply lay with another."

Ironja pursed his lips for a moment then said, "Only if there's no funny business. Jubilatious."

"Why ME!?" The wizard asked in distress.

"I seen the way you looked at that elf," he huffed. "The mind of a pervert, that one 'as."

"Yes," nodded Mizt-Ied. "He is the pervert. Which is why Zetine and I should lay next to one another."

Zetine looked across at her, and had a moment of weirdness as the elevation made Mizt-Ied almost eye level with her. She asked, "You just want to put your head on my chest, don't you?"

"Busted," the goblin snickered.

Garr continued forward at that, causing the others to get back to moving. They continued their slow climb downwards, eventually reaching their final ledge before they would need to scale the wall to the bottom. It was easily a fifty foot drop, and after several minutes of inspection, no one really wanted to make that journey at night. So they began to set up camp, laying down what small rolls of fabric they had to serve as blankets and bedrolls.

Garr and Mizt-Ied set out to forage for dinner, much to the goblin's dismay. Eventually they each came back with several pouches filled with mountain roots. Unbeknownst to Garr, Mizt-Ied had found a birds nest and taken three blue spotted eggs from it and hidden them beneath her cloak. As she walked back to camp, she was doubly careful not to crush them.

"I hate roots," Ironja grumbled as he tore one in half with his teeth.

"They somehow taste better raw," Jubilatious gasped in confusion as he bit off a small piece.

"It's the rock dust," Zetine gagged.

"Crunch," said Mizt-Ied.

"What?" Jubilatious asked.

"I dinni' say anything," she replied while barely opening her mouth.

Jermaind laid his head across Mizt-Ied's own head and began sniffling while Ironja said, "I cannot wait for the day we reach a town or somethin. I'm ordering the biggest platter they have."

"With what money?" Jubilatious asked.

"I have money," the Dwarf replied with an upturned chin.

"What, dwarven runes?" He asked with a playful smile.

"Coins," Ironja said matter of factly.

"Right," his grin grew. "And what if they don't have the same currency?"

Ironja's face froze and he asked, "What do ye mean?"

"Well, most countries have different forms of currency, and sometimes no currency at all," he said. "Why when I was studying in Arkvine, they would often send us to lands where you had to work for everything instead of being paid. A breakfast would usually be about an hour of washing dishes or a hundred pieces of chopped wood."

"Madness," the Dwarf shook his head. "First you humans invent money, and then you don't even commit to it."

"Crunch," said Mizt-Ied.

"Did you say somethin, lass?" He asked.

"No," she replied as Jermaind softly poked her cheek with his nose.

Zetine spoke up, "Garr. What was that music you spoke of?"

The orc looked at her carefully then said, "If I tell you, you may all have difficulty sleeping, and it may have been nothing."

"Well now I'm intrigued," the human purred.

"Yes, do tell us," Jubilatious encouraged.

"Preferably loudly," Mizt-Ied said while leaning away from Jermaind, who looked as sad as a bear possibly could be.

Garr sighed and said, "Very well. These mountains were not always my home. Once I lived close to Cairn, where the shadow of Black Mountain homes the vilest of monsters. In a realm of rock trolls, wyverns, wargs, and the dead there is one monster we feared above all.

"Though a wyvern was more dangerous, they had well defined territory and many preferred to feast upon rock trolls. Though they were intelligent, orcs are hunters, and wargs were only ever a threat to someone on their lonesome. But the manticore is a beast that kills for pleasure, and it has no true territory, going only where it can cause suffering.

"I was still a child when I first heard that song. The stories of lantern spirits had been pressed upon me since birth, and when I heard that whistle all alone in the woods, I knew my time had come. But as the seconds kept into minutes, no apparition appeared. No ghastly screams or horrifying faces plagued me. I was simply alone.

"When I returned home, I found out why I was alone. It had torn my mother in two with its claws. My father had been pierced through the chest with its tail. As they had tried to run, my older sister and younger brother were shot by the beast's spines. There were a dozen other bodies of my friends and neighbors, all hardly recognizable.

"As it fed upon my parents, I covered myself in the blood of the dead and hid beneath the bodies. I do not know how long I hid there but it felt like an eternity. Then I watched as my sister's hand began to twitch. Slowly she regained control of her paralyzed body, and began to crawl forward. All I could do was watch at what happened next.

"Slowly and quietly it moved after her, before grabbing hold of her leg and dragging her back. It placed one paw upon her back and tore her leg from her body. Her cries still haunt me to this day. Then it tore off each of her arms and left her there, bleeding and screaming, until she eventually felt silent.

"Come the next day, a group of hunters would find me. I was too terrified to speak and tell them of what happened, but the spines in the corpses told them all they needed to know. They took me in and trained me to be a hunter, then eventually, a ranger."

"That's horrible," Zetine said with her hand over her mouth.

"Makes me wonder how many of us were spared the horror of this world as children," Jubilatious quietly said in a wistful tone.

"My childhood was great," Ironja grunted.

"Fantastic, no one asked," Jubilatious replied.

"You think this creature is nearby?" Zetine asked.

"Perhaps," Garr said. "I thought Iheard its song, though it could be just coincidence."

"Let us hope we have no more monsters to worry about for now," Jubilatious said.

"What do you think, Mizt-Ied?" Zetine asked. "You've been awfully quiet."

They all then looked to the goblin, who had one hand wrapped around one of Jermaind's teeth while she stuck her entire arm down the bear's throat in an attempt to recover her final egg. She turned to see everyone staring at her, and then looked back to the bear. She looked back at them, then back to the bear.

She then looked to the group one last time and said, "Oh no! Jermaind is trying to eat my arm!"

"Jermaind," Garr softly spoke. "Is this true?"

"Grrr," said Jermaind, which was about all he could say with an arm in his mouth. Also, he only had the vocal range of a bear.

"I see," Garr sighed. "Please refrain from eating our companions."

Mizt-Ied pulled her arm from the animal's mouth and whispered into its ear, "Thanks for covering for me."

***

The morning had been spent carefully climbing down the mountainside. For Jubilatious, this was not an issue, as he could simply cast a spell that would slow his fall to a comfortable pace. Jermaind proved surprisingly capable, but then again, bears are much better at climbing than most people. On par with the bear was Garr, who had spent many years learning the intricacies of the mountain range. Mizt-Ied was not talented in scaling mountains, but her experience climbing up and down various other surfaces helped keep her steady. Trailing behind was Zetine, who had to move slowly and carefully to avoid falling to her death. Lastly there was Ironja, who moved much like a turtle that someone had glued to a wall.

On the ground, Jubilatious looked up at the others. He had grown quite bored waiting for them, and the glaring sun made it hard for him to focus upon their shapes up above. Then he heard a sound so beautiful it nearly made him weep. It was a song, not unlike one he had heard many years before, when he had been just a child.

***

Lydia had lived a hard life, with every day proving a new struggle. But she persevered. Women were barred from practicing magic in Syronul, yet she did not let that stop her. As a child she had watched whenever she saw a wizard, memorizing their motions and the movements of their lips. When alone she would practice what she had seen, often to disastrous results. But day by day her skills improved and she began to adapt the half formed spells into useful tricks. Her favorite amongst them was the Candle Spell.

Learning to create fire was the hardest, and her one and only successful attempt had nearly burned her arm off. But Lydia refused to be stopped from putting her knowledge to the test. She was twelve years old when she mastered the Candle Spell, something that many wizards would laugh at as nothing more than a child's idea of magic. Whatever fire existed around her, she could bend to her will.

It would be another four years until she met Tyruden. Lydia had posed herself as a mystic from lands far beyond and set up shop in an abandoned little building in the city of Arkvine. When a customer would enter, the candles she had posed around the room would cast ominous shadows to help sell her act. They most often came to speak with deceased loved ones or for insight into the future. Lydia could do neither of these, but no one needed to know this.

Then Tyruden came, dressed in his flowing blue robes. The fires burned bright and the shadows took the shape of terrifying demons, but he did not care. The half-elf strolled forward, the candles snuffing out one by one as he passed them by. Lydia couldn't help but notice the air had grown thick with moisture as he approached her, peering down through the illusion she had cast over herself and into her true face.

"You have quite the talent," he said to her. "Who taught you?"

"No one," she answered as she stared up into his lightning-storm eyes. "I taught myself."

"Fascinating," he said in the way that wizards often say the word. "What is the name of the fascinating creature standing before me?"

"Valeen," she lied without breaking eye contact.

"Of course," he grinned at her answer. "I have come a long way, Valeen. Will you offer me a cup of wine, a loaf of bread, and a bed for the night?"

She resisted flinching at his request but nodded and said, "Of course. Anything for a guest. May I have your name?"

"A wizard does not give his name," he said. "But I have always had a weakness for beautiful women. So you may call me Tyruden."

Lydia led him into a back room where she ate and slept. There was nothing there more than a bedroll, a few bags of food, and a trunk. She said, "The bread is probably stale, but the wine is unopened. I hope you don't mind drinking from the bottle. Or sharing."

"I don't," he said, sitting down on the ground.

Lydia moved around him and sat on the bedroll before producing the bread and wine. She broke off a piece and watched as he muttered a quiet word before the cork popped from the bottle. She passed both to him and asked, "Why have you come here?"

"In truth?" he asked, and then said, "I am lonely. I have traveled the world for many years now, and will spend many more years away from my homeland. It is rare to find a woman capable of magic that I may hold myself with."

"And what of elves?" she asked quizzically.

He laughed at that and answered, "I've always much preferred humans."

They talked for many hours that night, but eventually their conversation grew into something much more. Lips locked together, legs were entangled, and a single night of passion was shared between the two mages. Afterwards they laid together, a strange peace overcoming Lydia as she slowly drifted off to sleep.

In the morning she woke to find Tyruden dressed and standing by the door. She asked him, "Where are you going?"

"Where my duty takes me," he simply said.

"You're just leaving?" She asked, a spear piercing her heart. "What about last night?"

"It was fun," he grinned. "But I have responsibilities that do not permit a relationship."

She stared at him in a mix of shock and disgust, before she only said, "You made me feel special. Important."

"And maybe one day the child will be," he said, and the words cut straight through her. "If it is a boy, I will come for it once it reaches the right age. If it is a girl, I'm sure you can raise it just fine."

As he turned she cursed at him, "You bastard!"

"Perhaps," he said with a dry smile still on his lips.

"Flames engulf the world, burn and devour," she growled.

Tyruden spun around, extending his hand outwards as a massive tornado of fire spewed out from Lydia's hand. He blocked the flames with his own hand, yet found himself amazed that she cast a spell of that magnitude without a catalyst. Then the flames began to spiral throughout the room, setting fire to the walls and table. All the while Lydia channeled all of her energy into the magical attack, trying with all her might to kill the wizard.

Then she collapsed upon the floor, and her tornado vanished in Tyruden's grip. Before he left he said only, "Hope that it is a boy."

Her desires did not matter. Eight months later she gave birth to a boy, frail and unlikely to live for more than a few days. Lydia named the infant Jubilatious, her first joy, and ensured his survival. She nursed him into a healthy babe and took great care on protecting him. She made sure to leave not just the city but the region entirely, heading to a rural village in Oshack. There she found a home by the riverside, nothing more than a small hut, but it would do just fine.

As Jubilatious aged into an adventurous young lad, Lydia wove her magic into every piece of clothing she crafted for her one and only child. She made sure he stayed healthy and happy, that he could live a life nothing like the one she had lived before his birth. For all her efforts, it worked wonderfully. Even the news of Vhodan's growing armies did little to disturb their peaceful way of life.

Then one day, late into the evening, Lydia realized her son had not come home for supper. She left to look for him, storm clouds hanging high in the sky. Then a mournful melody reached her ears, and she knew something horrible was about to happen. Nothing human could sing so beautifully. Lydia raced for the river as fast as she could, hoping that she could make it in time.

The woman stood suspended over the water, a cloud of fog surrounding her. She was adorned in a purple dress that hung from her pale shoulders and fell past her ankles. The woman's wet black hair fell over her face, obscuring it entirely. She seemed to sway ever so slightly, her arms remaining motionless as her body moved to the rhythm of her song. By the riverbank there stood Jubilatious, transfixed on the melody.

Lydia screamed as loud as she could, hoping it would be enough to snap Jubilatious from his trance, forming an impromptu spell from her cries. The air turned to ice around the thing that was not a woman, a dozen icicles taking shape before impaling it. The thing cocked its head to the side and its hair fell just enough to reveal a lifeless grey eye staring out at Lydia.

Jubilatious cried out in terror and fell to the ground. Lydia was almost to him when the thing raised its arm, sending a torrent of water into Lydia. It knocked her onto her back but did not subside; engulfing her entire body as it continuously buffeted her. Jubilatious looked on as the water flowed into his mother's mouth, drowning her. He looked back to the thing that was not a woman, and opened his mouth to speak.

Lydia never heard the words he spoke, but with a blast of lightning the river spirit was vanquished. Lydia was left spitting up water as Jubilatious looked on in disbelief at his own power, before running to his mother's side. He cried into her shoulder as she recovered, more relieved than anything else.

Then a half forgotten voice said, "It is time."

Lydia turned and looked up in horror as Tyruden stood there, a copper staff in his hand. She could say only, "No."

"What is your name, boy?" He asked.

Jubilatious looked up at him in confusion, then to his mother's pleading eyes. He then said, "I'm not to tell my name to strangers."

"A smart child," Tyruden said. "Would you like to learn magic, boy?"

"My mother already teaches me magic," he replied.

"This is nothing like her parlor tricks," he grinned just as he had so many years before. "I offer you power beyond what you can imagine. True magic that goes beyond anything your mother could ever dream of teaching you."

"I-" he began.

"You're not taking my son," Lydia growled as she slowly rose to her feet.

Tyruden barely glanced at her as he said, "This was always going to happen. Come, boy. I will take you to the academy of mages, where you will be at home with those like you. Where you can become a true wizard."

Jubilatious looked back to Lydia, and then spoke.

***

The following hours had been spent carefully treading the forests. Throughout their trip, the song of the manticore was always just around the corner. Occasionally it would disappear and they would not even notice until suddenly it began again. Undoubtedly the beast preyed upon other beings, though it would be many hours until they came upon signs of its conquest.

The first body they found had been a dire wolf, filleted and impaled to a tree by a thin black spine. Soon there came the remains of its pack, though what was left behind was far from recognizable. Then they discovered human bodies, some torn to shreds, others crushed or bitten open. Many of them were also filled with the signature black spines of the manticore.

"Who are they?" Zetine asked as they made their way through the dozen or so bodies.

"Perhaps hunters," Garr said as he took note of a bow clutched in a severed hand.

"So far into Imperial territory?" Mizt-Ied asked.

Jubilatious informed her, "Many people live normal lives in the Empire. Vhodan desires obedience, not death."

"How can they live in a place run by such a monster?" Zetine spat. "They're all monsters themselves."

"No," Jubilatious sighed. "They just don't know any better, or are too afraid to fight back. Besides, if we get into a city, it will be easier to pass as civilians than out in the wild."

"We haven't even seen any soldiers yet," Ironja grumbled. "I've been lied to."

"We'll find you some soldiers to fight," Jubilatious snickered.

Suddenly Garr said, "Stop."

The others froze in place and drew their weapons. The ranger notched an arrow and looked into the trees, beyond anything that the others could see. In the silence they could make out the unmistakable sound of twigs snapping, coming from all around them. The realization that they now stood in a circular clearing hit them at once, and the obviousness of the trap made them feel like fools. The others carefully positioned themselves in a circle around Garr, waiting for the attack to come.

In a thickly accented voice came the words, "Whatever has me here?"

Ahead of Ironja, a face appeared shrouded in darkness. It was pale skinned and dark bearded. The face seemed to float forward, before its thick yellow main came into view. A lion's body stalked forward, with large black claws digging into the ground. Nestled to its side were bat-like wings, and almost hidden on its back were the thousands of sharpened spines. It's scorpion-like tail waved back and forth as the manticore began to circle them, a wide smile on its face.

"You following me?" It asked in its strange cadence, sharp teeth beaming out from its thin lips.

"Let us pass," Garr said firmly. "We do not need to fight each other."

"No?" The monster asked, its grin spreading horrifically upwards. "Too bad. I want to."

It pressed its paws down and raised its rear quarters, shooting a volley of spines towards Garr. Jubilatious barely managed to aim his staff in time to send a strong torrent of wind into the path. The spines were blown harmlessly away, but the manticore took the opportunity to leap. Garr rolled out of the way while the others attempted to circle the beast. Ironja was too slow however, and found himself pinned beneath the beast's paws.

The manticore's tail rose into the air and prepared to stab through the dwarf's face, when two small knives embedded in its side. It turned to see Mizt-Ied glaring at it, before Zetine slashed its back legs with her dagger. The manticore spun around, attempting to hit any of its opponents in the progress. Both Mizt-Ied and Zetine dodged out of the way, while Garr and Jubilatious were too far away to be hit. This left Ironja to be trampled, though luckily he avoided any serious injury.

Garr dashed forward, bow strung over his shoulder as he drew his new scimitar. The weapons blade sliced through the manticore's shoulder, searing it like a steak in a pan. The beast roared in pain and swatted at him, knocking the orc against a tree. Garr looked up as the manticore pounced at him, before a mound of dirt collided with its ribs and knocked it back to the ground.

Garr looked over to Jubilatious who shrugged and said, "Telekinesis. Who knew?"

"Wizards," the ranger groaned and pulled himself up.

Before the manticore could recover, Ironja hurried forward and slammed his hammer into the beast's back right knee. It howled in pain as its kneecap was obliterated, partially imobilizing it. As it raised its tail up, Zetine leapt upon the monster's back and quickly severed the limb. The beast's blood squirted out into the air, leaving both Zetine and the dwarf covered in the disgustingly thick fluid.

Garr asked, "Do you remember me, demon?"

The manticore looked to him, a look of intense pain spread across its face. The beast's lips distorted as it tried to place him, before relenting and answering, "No."

"I recognized you," he said. "You took everything from me, but I would have let you live. All you had to do was let us pass."

It smiled up at him as Garr now stood over the monster and meekly said, "You can still let me go... just walk away, leave me to my woods."

"We both know I won't do that," Garr replied.

He raised his scimitar into the air and brought it down in one quick, fluid motion. The manticore's face split upon and burned, the wound practically cauterized. Then a moment later it fell to the side, nothing more than another corpse in the clearing. Garr sheathed his scimitar, and looked to make sure the others were okay.

They all seemed to be in good order; with no more than a few scrapes and bruises on ironja. Zetine strode towards him and asked, "Are you okay?"

"I'm fine," he grunted.

Then she asked, "How did it feel?"

Garr considered this for several moments. Then he answered, "Like nothing. I have killed many monsters, and this was no different. It was simply an animal that had to be dealt with to protect the natural world."

A look of concern flashed across Zetine's face but she nodded and said, "I understand. Let's go, we don't want to stay around here too long."

Chapter 9

In the morning, Wolf and Kazaa ate breakfast in the tavern from the previous day. This time they had the fortune of eating eggs and more cabbage. Kazaa was more than grateful for the meal, while Wolf once again picked at her food. She found that the taste of the cabbage was much more bearable if coated in the slimy yellow yolks, but it still tasted like a snake spat in her mouth. The taste of the eggs also wasn't too good, though she was at least used to eating them.

Kazaa swirled a mug of milk with his finger, tasted it, and then said, "I should have stuck with water."

Wolf gagged as she swallowed a whole piece of egg coated cabbage and said, "We should have just left instead."

"We still need food," he replied.

"Blegh," she gagged.

Across the room, the tavern's front door was roughly thrown open, causing it to hit the wall with a loud bang. A few heads turned at the noise, but most didn't seem to care. Wolf looked to see a boy standing there, no more than fourteen, dressed in a torn green shirt and muddy pants. He was covered in small cuts and scrapes, and was panting desperately for breath.

At last he cried out for the whole tavern to hear, "The legionnaires are dead!"

An older man with long silver hair and a massive bald spot rose to his feet. He demanded, "What do ye mean, boy!?"

The boy gulped and said, "I was at Heroes' Bluff. I saw the Emperor! He wasn't human, I tell you! He ordered his men to stand down, and he killed them all without breaking even a single a sweat!"

"And ye ran, you coward!?" The man barked at the boy, stalking forward to lift him into the air by his shirt.

"They sent me back to spread word!" The boy cried in a mix of fear and misery. "Even if I was there, even if we had a whole 'nother army, there's nothing we could have done!"

Kazaa silently rose to his feet, and Wolf mimicked his motions. She was barely able to suppress the rage building up in her chest, begging to be released. As she slowly walked away from the table, she could feel it seeping out from her ribcage and into her throat. Her head began to throb with pain, and something told Wolf not to listen to the boy, but she did her best to ignore that voice.

The old man dropped the boy to the ground, where he let out a whimper and scurried out of the way. Then the man turned towards Wolf and Kazaa and asked, "Are ye two sellswords?"

"Not against the Rizzen Empire," Kazaa replied without making eye contact.

"Fuckin cowards," he spat. "They'll come for yer land one day too!"

"My land lies across the ocean," he retorted. "Tell your new emperor good luck with that."

The man then turned his gaze to Wolf and asked, "What about ye, lass? As scared as yer lover?"

Wolf's face turned crimson but before she could respond, Kazaa cut in with simply, "We're leaving."

Outside, Wolf asked him, "Why did you say no? I could have killed The Empire at its heart!"

"First of all," he sighed. "That kid has no idea what he saw. The battlefield plays tricks on the mind to even seasoned soldiers, much less a child. Second, there is no way we can fell an entire army. I'd wager not even a single battalion, though I hold out hope for that one. Third, if the kid was right, then The Emperor is not a being that you could possibly hope to face one on one."

Wolf's fists clenched and she growled, "It's my right to kill him."

"Maybe one day you will," Kazaa calmly replied. "But this is not the opportunity you think it is. Focus on the small ones for now. Claim the lives of those directly responsible for whatever tragedy befell you, and prepare for the day you have a chance at revolution."

From behind him, Kazaa heard the unmistakable sound of a blade sliding against leather. He sighed once more and said, "Don't do this, pup. I don't want to break that quaint little face of yours."

Wolf charged at him, needing only to close five feet before she could bring her bastard sword down upon the man. Instead her eyes widened in surprise as she realized Kazaa had turned and caught her blade with his dagger, finally understanding the strange hooks in the weapon. Her eyes flickered to the side as Kazaa pulled his fist back, and punched her square in the nose.

She stumbled back, blood gushing out of her broken nose, then quickly regained her composure. Once again Wolf charged at Kazaa, but he simply side stepped her and delivered a kick across the back. She yelled out in anger and turned, swiping at him with her sword. The man easily avoided the clumsy attack. She attempted a thrust which actually caught Kazaa off guard, but he still managed to dodge out of the way at the last second. Wolf took a step after him, raised her sword into the air, and swung down with all her might.

Kazaa raised the dagger in both hands, catching the falling blade. Wolf spat in his face but he ignored the insult, and then kicked her hard in the left knee. Wolf's leg buckled and she let out a yelp of pain as she fell to the ground. Kazaa punched her across the side of the face, pushing her further to the ground, mud coating her face. Wolf attempted to stand up, but instead Kazaa kicked her in the head. Barely conscious, she attempted to push herself up one last time.

"You are far too stubborn," he muttered, and then kicked her one last time in the head, ending Wolf's consciousness.

***

It was rare to ever see dwarves embarking upon a long journey. Even the hill dwarves, who long ago settled in Oshack and Mulvek hardly ever left their homes. So for those few that got the chance to see Colstone and his company, they felt as they were being treated to a marvelous show. This particularly annoyed the dwarves, who not only were in the midst of an important mission, but also hated to be gawked at. Especially by humans, who seemed to always be the ones doing the gawking.

The group had mushed their goat sled for quite some time, and dangled a salt covered mushroom for even longer. At last they had arrived at an inn, tall and sleazy. The tracks that had been left had vanished, and it seemed as though their leads were drying up. Still, Colstone was determined to find Wolf no matter what. He would pursue her to the ends of the world until he found definitive proof of what happened to her.

A pair of drunken men stumbled outside, their gaze falling upon the dwarves and their sled. One of them let out a laugh, pointed, and said, "Look! A gaggle of stump fuckers!"

It took everything in Colstone, Brock, and Marblekeeper to stop from verbally assaulting the men. The same could not be said for Limecrack who huffed and declared, "If ye inbred dickwankin drunken layabouts say another word, I'm gonna bust yer bloody kneecaps!"

"Easy, Limecrack," Colstone softly said, though his words were coated with anger towards the men.

"Shut your fuckin trap, dwarf," the second man quite literally spat.

Limecrack took his hammer, walked forward, and broke that man's kneecap. As he fell to the ground, writhing in pain, the dwarf said, "I told ye so."

The first man cried out, "Mad dwarf!" And ran off towards the inn's stable.

Limecrack chuckled, "Some friend ye got there," then swung his hammer down into the man's other knee.

"Limecrack!" Colstone sternly said.

"What? I told him both knees," he replied. "I'm a dwarf of me word."

Colstone groaned and said, "Marblekeeper. Get the dullroot."

"On it," Marblekeeper said before rummaging around in a chest. He produced a small shriveled black root and passed it to his friend.

Colstone took the root, broke off a small piece, and crumbled it in his hand. He walked over to the man and forced it into his mouth as he said, "Swallow."

The man resisted, but the horrid taste practically forced him to swallow. His cries soon began to die down, and the tears streaming from his face ceased to flow. Colstone took a step back and flicked his head to the side, indicating to Limecrack to walk away. The dwarf quickly complied.

The man sat up and whimpered, "It doesn' hurt anymore..."

"I'm looking fer a girl," Colstone said, straight to business. "Tall even by your standards. Looks like she could lift a boulder. Dark hair, brown skin. Ye seen her?"

The man shook his head and said, "N-no."

"Waste of time," Colstone grumbled and walked towards the door.

"I-I still can't walk!" The man called after him.

Limecrack chuckled and said, "That's what ye get for insulting a dwarf."

Colstone pushed open the door to the inn's tavern and looked around. There were ten humans, three men and seven women, three elves, and a goblin. Colstone almost didn't notice that there was also a half-orc, since she was bundled up so tight against one of the women he mistook them for a single overly large person. Then of course there was the human tavern keeper, who looked like he was about to drink himself to death but unfortunately couldn't stomach the taste of ale.

Colstone sauntered up to the bar, where the woman and half-orc sat along with an elf who had watched the dwarf enter. The elf continued to follow the dwarf's path with his eyes, making Colstone uncomfortable. It was usually the wood elves who were the most distrustful of dwarves, and this particular elf certainly didn't seem to be a wood elf, but the idea of the elf harboring animosity dug at Colstone's nerves.

He asked the tavernkeeper, "Have you seen a girl?"

"I've seen lots'a girls," he replied as he placed a mug down and began to pour some sickly yellow ale into it. "If you want to talk, you drink."

Colstone grumbled out, "Fine," and awkwardly climbed onto the bar seat. He reached into his pocket and pulled out a small copper bar before placing it on the table. He asked, "Is this enough?"

The tavern keeper did his best to remain calm as he picked up the bar and looked it over. If the thing was solid copper, which it absolutely was, it would be worth most of the furniture in the tavern combined. So of course the tavern keeper said, "It will have to do."

"Right," Colstone nodded. "This girl. She's big an' tall. Coal black hair. Brown skin. Brown eyes. Weird around people, sticks out like a sore thumb."

The tavernkeeper shook his head and said, "Sorry, not ringing any bells."

"She goes by the name Wolf," Colstone said, earning a subtle gasp from the woman next to him. "She may have been with other people. Soldiers?"

The man's eyes widened and he said, "If your friend was with the war party, she's as good as dead."

"War party?" Colstone asked in surprise.

"Empire sends them out every now and then," he explained. "They're supposed to cull small populations of undesirables. Usually goblins or kobold. Every now and then, humans and elves. It's so when the Empire eventually expands into the region, there's no local resistance."

"That's horrible," he coughed.

The man pursed his lips for a few moments then asked, "Your friend. She's a soldier?"

"Ney," Colstone shook his head. "Just a girl."

"Then she's dead," he said. "The only time they let someone live is if they need slaves. And if she's a slave, there's no way you're gonna be able to find her."

"And why's that?" He grimly asked.

"Because they take them halfway across the land. Then either sell them off to regional lords, or ship them to Imperial Heart to make new buildings."

"And where's this Imperial Heart supposed to be?" He pressed.

"You're not a hill dwarf, are you?" The tavernkeeper quizzically asked.

"Does it matter?" The mountain dwarf responded.

"I suppose not," he grunted. "All the roads lead to it. The Emperors have always insisted on the roads being laid, long as even the elves can remember. It's between Syronul and the Northern

Reach. Though both of those places are some of the Empire's oldest states."

"And where's the place they go before that?" He asked, eager to resume the hunt.

He said with a shrug, "Just some place in Moia. I don' know it."

"As good a lead as any," Colstone grunted, then began to climb off the stool.

The woman next to him moved after him, and the elf hissed out, "Don't!"

But Spring ignored the order. She asked Colstone, "How do you know Wolf?"

The dwarf look her up and down before asking, "Are you a ba-"

Spring slapped him across the face before he could finish and said, "Don't you dare finish. How do you know her?"

Colstone scowled at the half-elf woman and rubbed his reddening cheek before he said, "I was friends wit her da'. He asked me to look after her 'fore he passed."

"Tusk is dead?" She asked in disbelief, another part of her heart breaking. "Those monsters took everything from us..."

"Wasn' no monster that killed 'im," Colstone replied. "Not a man, either."

She blinked in surprise and then asked, "Then what happened?"

"He got sick," the Dwarf explained. "Real sick. The girl though, she was fine last I saw her. Same can't be said for some of the soldiers that found her."

"So... his daughter is alive," she said more to herself than him. "And you think she was captures by the soldiers?"

"Has to 'ave been," he said. "We found a few bodies, but Wolf was gone. Some of her stuff too. She wouldn't just leave her home."

Spring shook her head and said, "No. They killed all of the warriors in our tribe. Those that didn't fall in combat, they executed like feral dogs. They wouldn't take her prisoner if she fought back. They only wanted the pretty girls and the meek men."

Colstone rubbed his beard then asked, "Do you think she was chasing them?"

A memory flashed through Spring's mind and she said, "That girl was a monster herself. If she wanted to... she would chase her prey to the ends of the world. So I think if you follow the trail of those that attacked us, you'll find her in the end."

"If ye know her, why don't you come wit' us? We could use more help, especially from a..." he trailed off for a moment. "A woodswoman."

Spring looked over her shoulder, and for the first time Colstone noticed the elf was standing directly behind her. She said, "No... I can't... I have a responsibility now."

Colstone frowned as he looked between the two but nodded and said, "Ay. I understand."

"I hope you find her," Spring smiled sadly down at him.

"I will," Colstone promised.

When the dwarf had left, the elf took hold of Spring's wrist and guided her back to Ruby-Gem. Now that they were together he said, "If you wish to join our order, truly join us, then your past lives are dead. The women you were died that night, and you are nothing like they once were. Should you ever see those you once knew, or have shared history with, you do not address them. You do not speak of the past, or make their acquaintance, or anything that would tell them who you once were!"

"I don't see the harm in it, Dancing-Lights," Ruby-Gem said. "I mean, if we see a friend from our past, why wouldn't we greet them?"

Dancing-Lights shook his head and said, "Our order embraces the death of the past, and the murder of the future. What if someone links who you were to your actions? Would they not seek vengeance upon you, even if it meant killing those who believe you truly dead? Or give them reason to hunt you down, now knowing you were still alive? You must use your heads, and abscond from all illusions of the past."

"This is so much easier for you," Spring said as she crossed her arms. "You were born into this life, we were brought into it. Of course we'll make mistakes you never would, because we lived lives outside of your order."

"And this is why few ever join," Dancing-Lights replied. "It is far too dangerous for outsiders to join us."

"Then why even bother?" Ruby-Gem asked.

The elf sighed and said, "Because I have a soft spot for defenseless girls, what else? I didn't want to see you dead, and I didn't want you to die as soon as you left my protection."

"Some noble savior you are," Spring scoffed at him.

"Would you rather I left you to die?" Dancing-Lights asked.

"I would rather you treat us with more respect," Spring retorted. "We had enough of a time living under the "protection" of the men in our tribe. If we have to, the both of us will willingly face the wilds than live with any sort of debt to you. Right, Ruby-Gem?"

"That's right," Ruby-Gem chimed in. "We want to learn from you, but that doesn't mean we'll put up with you being as callous as everyone else about it."

Dancing-Lights grabbed a cup from the table and quickly downed its contents. He placed it down upon the table, cleared his throat, and spoke once more. He said, "I hear you. For a complete lack of weapon's training, I have seen how well you adapted to your daggers. We will work on your decorum, and hopefully... we can make some progress."

**

Kazaa had barely managed to carry Wolf back to the inn, expecting someone to attack him at any moment. In the time it took him to reach the door, it seemed as though the town had erupted into chaos. People were running in every direction, and it seemed certain that his duel with Wolf was the reason for it. So it was only obvious that he would be targeted as the aggressor.

But then Kazaa watched as an elderly couple rolled out a wagon to the town square and hitched a donkey to it. A handful of parents had brought far too many children that the group of them could have fostered, and together loaded the children into the cart. Some of them cried, others were deathly silent, and others said words too quiet for Kazaa to hear.

He gently laid Wolf onto the ground beside the doorway and hurried towards the group, desperate to know what was happening. He asked, "What are you doing?"

One of the parents, a middling aged woman looked at him with tears in her eyes and said, "It's over. We lost."

"Lost what?" Kazaa asked, though he already knew the answer.

She shook her head and said, "The rebellion. The legionnaires are all dead. Soon the Empire will come for us."

"You don't know that," he said, trying to reassure the woman as she loaded another child onto the cart.

"I do," she said. "My great grandparents freed us. They lived in a world without trees, without hope. The empire killed everyone that ever tried to resist them and burned our land to the ground. There's nothing we can do now."

"But your kids!" He practically cried out.

The woman looked at him as though he was the stupidest man in the world and said, "We're giving them a chance. Maybe they can get away, if we stay here..."

The horror of what the woman meant quickly washed over Kazaa, but he more than understood. As he turned away he said, "You're braver than the greatest of warriors. Fight well."

Then he cried out, "Get away from her!" As a pair of teens cut the pouches from Wolf's belts

Kazaa drew his khopesh which was enough to scare the youths away, but not enough for them to drop the money. He sheathed his sword and hurried back to Wolf's side, scooping her up in his arms. It was difficult to get her back up, and once firmly held they were almost knocked over when the inn's door swung open. There stood the daytime innkeeper, a grizzly looking dwarf with a thick brown beard, a scar across his left eye, and a large bald spot. Held tight in his hand was a doublesided handaxe, which due to his small size, was just a regular doublesided axe.

"What do ye think yer doin with that girl?" the dwarf growled, his gaze flickering between Wolf's unconscious body and Kazaa.

"She's my friend," he quickly replied. "I don't think you want to stay here, The Emp-"

The dwarf cut him off by saying, "Don' tell me what ye think, lad. Put the girl down and I'll let ye keep both legs."

Kazaa considered his words carefully. Then he said, "Fuck you," and kicked the dwarf in the face.

The dwarf grunted with pain as he was knocked onto his backside. Kazaa wasted no time in spinning around before bursting into a short sprint. He quickly lowered his speed into a much more manageable jog, but Wolf's weight in his arms would soon begin to slow him even further. The dwarf climbed back to his feet, axe still held tight, and brushed the blood away from his now broken nose with his sleeve.

The dwarf looked around and asked himself, "What in the name of Bastadon is happenin'?"

Kazaa made his way towards the village's back gates, hoping that they would be open. Fortunately, they were. Unfortunately, it seemed as though the guards had gotten wind of the evacuation and were using it as an excuse to line their own pockets before they ran off. There was a row of a dozen or so people and five carts slowly moving towards the exit, each and every one being stopped to give out some of their belongings. Kazaa watched as one man began to yell at a guard rummaging through his cart, only to receive a pike through the gut for his efforts.

With a sigh, Kazaa forced his way through the crowd then awkwardly dumped Wolf's body in the back of the recently abandoned cart. The guard that had killed the man demanded, "What in the hell do you think you're doing!?"

Kazaa tightened the bandages on his hands and stated, "I am taking this cart. You can either let me, or I can kill you and all of your friends. Which sounds better?"

"The hell do you think you a-" the guard never got to finish his statement, as he found himself now devoid of a head.

The crowd gasped and made space as Kazaa stood with his khopesh drawn, the guard's headless body falling to the ground before him. He said only, "Everywhere you go, pigs are always the same."

"You killed Franberr!" another guard cried out at him as he and three others approached.

"Obviously," Kazaa said. "Are you going to make some dramatic speech or are you just going to yell and charge?"

The guard responded with, "I'll fucking kill you!" as he ran at Kazaa with a longsword.

Kazaa said only, "The exact same."

He easily dodged the attack, delivered a kick to the man's jaw to knock him off balance, and then pierced his jaw with the hook of his sword. Kazaa tore the blade out, taking the guard's lower jaw with it, then swept his feet out from under him. The guard was basically as good as dead, but Kazaa was more than trained enough to never take chances. He took a step forward then stabbed the blade down through the guard's upper face, ending his life.

The other three guards looked at him in disgust and horror, then to their two fallen comrades. One of them said, "Remember your training! All at once, disable him first!"

Then they attacked. Two pikes and a longsword. Kazaa quickly drew his dagger and let his own training take over. He danced away from the sword, caught a pike with his dagger, and then parried the third attack with his sword. They repeated, though the first pikeman's blow was delayed as he rescued his weapon from Kazaa. Pirouette, parry, parry, repeat. They were slowly pushing him back, and with each step Kazaa grew more and more unsure of his surroundings. He really hated guards.

"Spearmen are cowards," he grunted before catching the longsword with his dagger. With a grin he said, "Gotcha."

"What!?" the guard said in disbelief, though it would be his final word.

Kazaa slit his throat with the curve of his sword then sent the guard's body into the second spearman, momentarily knocking him down. With his attention firmly planted on the first spearman, Kazaa was able to easily catch the pike with his dagger. He retched the weapon from the guard, delivered a kick to the groin, and then quickly severed his head.

Pirouette, feint, thrust.

The final guard had stood, and managed to take a single step towards Kazaa. He now stared at the man with wide unblinking eyes. He looked down to see the tip of the khopesh piercing through his shirt. Slowly red began to spread out into the fabric, marking the wound he had suffered. The guard looked back up into Kazaa's eyes, a look of utter disbelief held in his own gaze.

"That's not fair," the guard muttered.

"Honestly," Kazaa agreed. "I messed up. Your armorer must just be horrible."

He pulled the blade out and the guard stumbled towards him, but Kazaa simply stepped out of the way. The man fell to the ground and curled up in a ball, holding his hands tight against his chest as he began to sob. Kazaa looked back to the cart to make sure that Wolf was still there, and that no one had touched her, and then marched back towards it. The villagers gave him a wide birth, which made things much easier.

Kazaa sheathed his dagger then wiped the blood from his khopesh with his forearm, before sheathing that as well. He climbed into the driver's seat of the cart and took note of the two cows that were tied to the reigns. Viewing them as better than nothing, he whipped them into motion, and guided the cows around the carts ahead of them. Slowly the cattle made their way out of the village, heading deeper into Oshack.

In the distance, a large smoke cloud rose up, nearly blocking the site of a far off mountain. Kazaa hoped that he would be fortunate enough to avoid the empire. Of course, he never had been particularly fortunate before.

Kazaa had spent several hours alone on that desolate road. It had seemed as though the villagers had circled about and gone in the opposite direction, likely hoping to resettle in the Southern Reach or find sanctuary with the orcs or barbarians of the region. He doubted they would find much. Wolf had laid motionless in the back of the cart, and more than once had he looked back to make sure she was still breathing. He knew of how dangerous a concussion was to a normal person, though believed that she couldn't be hindered by such a lowly injured. His belief in this was beginning to waver.

After doing his best to make sure the cattle would continue straight towards the mountain, Kazaa turned around and climbed into the back of the cart. He kneeled down beside Wolf's head, watching as she rhythmically breathed for a few seconds. Then he reached down to touch her forhead, only for Wolf's hand to grab his wrist and squeeze down hard enough to make him squirm. Her eyes opened, one slightly after the other, and she looked up at him with otherworldly green eyes.

"You injured the girl," the dead woman said to him with Wolf's lungs.

"I had to," Kazaa said as he attempted to pull away from her iron grip. "The girl wanted to go fight the whole Empire at once. A suicide mission, in case you couldn't tell!"

Wolf's body began to sit up, and Kazaa was sure the process would dislocate her shoulder. It nearly came close, but then the puppeteered body turned around, sparing the shoulder and allowing Kazaa just a few extra inches of freedom. In that time she did not release him, and he wondered if he would soon find himself with only one working hand.

The dead woman said, "You did well in that regard. More than I would have expected from a sellsword. Then again, I suppose you must be used to... precious cargo."

"I am not a fool," he said. "I will not endanger either of you, or let the girl endanger you."

She smiled, or at least Kazaa thought she was smiling as she said, "You are an excellently obedient dog. I would almost think you were dead, if it weren't for that beautiful skin draped over those bones."

She squeezed his wrist, sending sparks of pain and a clear message into Kazaa. He replied, "I am doing just as you ask. She strives to fight the Empire, but I'll be there to stop her. We will reach Cairn, just as you want. You have my word."

"Yes, I do," her mouth hung open at this. "Do be careful of the head, sellsword. You wouldn't want to damage anything important."

Then Wolf's body fell limp, releasing Kazaa. He backed away to the end of the cart, and then watched as Wolf bolted awake. He knew it was her, the fluidity of her movements and the obviousness tension in her muscles could only come from a living creature. She took a few moments to take in her surroundings, looked to Kazaa with her brown eyes, and then drew her knife.

She was upon Kazaa in a heartbeat, which was barely had enough time for him to draw his own dagger to fend off the attack. He caught her blade in the hooks of his own, but then her free hand was upon him, clamping around his throat. She choked him mercilessly, driving out all the air from his lungs as she stared unblinking into his eyes. Kazaa grasped at her wrist, attempting to break free, before dropping his dagger. As his face began to turn blue he held up his arms in a clear sign of surrender, hoping she would take it.

Wolf raised him up by his neck then forced him back onto the cart, cracking the wood below Kazaa, and then released him. She moved back, like a predator waiting to pounce, and sheathed her knife. Kazaa looked at Wolf with a fresh set of eyes. Gone was the image of the socially awkward and naive girl he had cultivated. Wolf was entirely a predator, one that he was now chained to. Almost as quickly as that image appeared in his head, Kazaa pushed it deep out of his mind. He knew she was still just a girl, no matter how intimidating she was.

After he had breathed enough, Kazaa said, "You could have killed me..."

"I would have," she bluntly replied.

He shook his head and said, "I saved your life, you know."

"I don't," she said. "I could have won."

"There were hundreds of them!" He said in dismay.

"And I am ready," was her only response.

Kazaa took her in as best he could, the enigma of this strange girl from the woods. He tried to explain, "I have fought in dozens of conflicts. Killed hundreds of men. In my homeland, I am a legendary warrior. But even I cannot fight off an entire army. No matter how good you are, no matter what resources you have, eventually you will fall. If your enemies far outnumber you, there are two inevitable endings. Either they overwhelm you and die a pointless death, or you grow tired and they kill you in your moment of weakness. Either way, it was all for nothing, and you are dead. Do not die, Wolf, for you are young and have so much to live for. No matter what has happened to you, it is not worth dying for."

She looked to him with suspicion for a few moments before asking, "Where are we going?"

Kazaa breathed a sigh of relief then answered, "Through the mountains, hopefully. The empire is powerful throughout Syronul, so crossing over would be a death sentence for you."

"I want to make them suffer," she said firmly.

"You will," he nodded. "But first, we need to reach Cairn."

"Why?" She asked. "What's so important about that place?"

For just a moment, panic overtook Kazaa, but he kept a cool face. He said, "Allies. People who can help you fight the Empire."

"Who are these people?" She asked, filling him with more fear.

He told the half truth, "Necromancers. They can raise the dead, and are the most feared faction in the world. Untouched by conflict for thousands of years. But now they may wish to finally fight."

"Why?" She asked, her eyes glaring down into Kazaa's soul. "Why is now so special? I'm not going anywhere with you unless you tell me."

He said, "I cannot be certain... but I believe the Empire plots to destroy them. That it may have already killed a number of their kind."

Wolf took this in then said, "I see. So we go to them, so together we may fight the Empire?"

"Yes," he said in relief. "That's exactly it."

She then said, "Very well. I'll go with you. But don't try and hurt me again. If you do, I'll cut your head off and leave your body by the road."

"Very well," he said. "Just please try not to act so recklessly."

Kazaa climbed back into the driver's seat to steer once more, while Wolf began to check over her possessions. Soon she said, "I had more pouches. Where are the other ones?"

"Some kids stole them while you were unconscious," he answered.

"Oh," she said. Then she sat down, and waited.

Kazaa was silent for some time, but eventually he spoke. His words were innocent, but to Wolf, they felt anything but. He asked, "What is wrong with you, woods girl?"

"What?" she asked in surprise, hands tightening into fists once again.

He said, "I have known many warriors, good and bad, and none of them were as foolish or determined as you. Some of them, even just as you, were motivated by revenge. But they all knew better than to fight an army. They knew better than to draw a sword on their friends. So i ask simply, what is wrong with you?"

Wolf resisted the urge to punch him in the back of the head, and instead thought to herself. Her skin *hurt*, it was hot and she could feel blades poking her in the upper back. It was an uncomfortable long amount of time that she sat silent like this, neither of them sure what to say. But eventually, she managed to muster up some words.

"There's nothing wrong with me," she said. "Just because you don't understand me, just because you know more than me, doesn't mean there's *anything* wrong with me. I am just different than you. Like it or don't. But don't talk to me like that."

"Like what?" he asked in surprise.

"Like I'm..." she struggled to find the words. "A child? Dumb? That I can't be as much of a person as you are."

"I never meant to insinuate anything like that," he replied.

She bit her tongue at that word but continued, "Then don't. I can't stand it."

Kazaa thought to himself then said, "Would you like to hear a story?"

"Why?" she suspiciously asked him.

He said, "Because I think it will help you understand me."

She thought to herself for just a moment then answered, "Fine."

He smiled and said, "When I was young, very young, I was an apprentice to a stonemaker. It is a common profession in Exia, stones are what every home and temple are made from. My master was a crotchety old man, stern and foul, always with a scowl upon his face. I had come from a poor family, and though we had no possessions, we had each other. But to apprentice under someone, you must leave your home. So I had come with no more than the clothes upon my back to study beneath him.

"The first thing he had said to me was, "Boy. Are you the new apprentice?" I told him, "Yes master, I am. My name is," and he scoffed at that. Why should he know my name? I was just yet another child come to learn the trade. Another mouth to feed, to bed, to care for. He then insulted me for not coming with my own tools and said it would be added to my debt. Every meal, every piece of misshapen rock, it was all written down so that I might pay it back once my apprenticeship was over.

"I hated that old man more than I had ever hated anyone. I dreamed of killing him, of destroying his home with a pickaxe. But I kept myself quiet and did my job. Day after day, week after week, month after month, for an entire year. Then one day, I was sent into a crypt to make note of any structural damage. It was centuries old, and the owners were worried it may collapse at some point. So my master inspected the outside, while I was sent inside with a torch, a quill, and a roll of parchment. It was the blackest black I had ever seen in there, the light from the entrance disappearing within only a few steps. The light from my torch provided just enough for me to see my hand if I outstretched it to its limit, but not my fingertips.

"I went over every inch of that mausoleum, making note of every crack and fracture I could see. Every particularly moist spot or strange shift in the air. My quill dried up, so I stuck my fingers until I drew blood and used that to write. I continued deep into the crypt, far underground, beyond rows of cracked and dusty sarcophaguses. In that deepest of recesses, I learned what true fear was.

"A corpse stood there, moldy bandages hanging from dead black skin. It was so painfully thin and I could see the scars from where some of its organs were removed. It turned to look at me, with empty eye sockets yet glowing green eyes. As it turned, I could hear every vertebra in its neck pop and crack. Then it took a step towards me. It was slow, and moved in such a horrible way, as though its body could not properly follow the instructions on how to move. For five whole minutes, our interaction lasted. It walked up to me, nearly tripping over its own bandages, bones cracking beneath its dead skin.

"Then it gave me a pat on the head. It turned around, walked back to its sarcophagus, climbed inside, and pulled the top close. I ran away as fast as I could, retracing the steps I had taken in my mind. I found the exit and practically leapt out, and then I was wrapped in my master's arms. I don't know how long I had been crying, or how long I continued to cry, but he held me tight and said it would be okay.

"He took me home after that, and once I was ready, asked what had happened. I told him, and he didn't laugh, though I know he must have wanted to. He explained that it was simply a guardian. That when great people die, we keep their bodies occupied so that nothing else can get inside. It had probably heard me moving and came out to make sure I wasn't a graverobber or ghoul. When it saw I was just a child, it did what it was told to do in this situation, and returned to its rest.

"After that, we talked a lot more beyond what was required of the apprenticeship. He taught me to read, not just the measurements, but language. Books. He told me of lands far and close alike, and of how when he was young, older than me but still young, he had been a sailor. He told me of how truly terrifying the sea was, but of how it called to him, even in his old age. Of how he hoped it would be where he was laid to rest, even though that is not the way of our people. He told me, "But it's the way of *mine*. Of sailors. The sea is our tomb." He told me of how one should truly experience life..."

"How?" Wolf asked, finally interrupting.

Though she could not see it, for his back was to her, Kazaa gave her a sad smile. He said, "By living it. One cannot do what is expected of them, one cannot live the same life for their entire life. They must experience all of what the world has to offer. I grew to love that old man, and when my apprenticeship ended, I would still visit him regularly. On the first night I had ever spent in his home, I lay awake shivering in the cold. He had entered my quarters and without a word, gave me his own blanket."

Wolf asked him, "What was the point of that story?"

He shrugged and said, "I thought it was a nice story, that's all. So you can see who I was, and how it led to who I am now, at least in some small way. Though there's another part I withheld from you. Maybe I'll tell you one day, though not if you keep being so rude."

She stared at his back then said, "I have a story too."

"Oh?" he grinned. "Let's hear it, woodsgirl. I am curious to how well of a storyteller you are."

Wolf fidgeted in her seat at this before saying, "Well... okay. I only ever had my papa. There was a village, once. I remember tents, and a never ending fire, and that it always smelled like blood and cooking meats. There were more girls than men, I think. I hated that place. Too many people, always looking at me and judging me. One day I beat some of the boys half to death, and the elders were furious. They said that only a boy should be allowed to hurt someone like that. So they kicked me and papa out. Papa said it was the first time in many years that anyone had been kicked out, but it used to happen a lot when there were more men.

"It's supposed to be dangerous for someone to be kicked out of the village, but papa wasn't scared, so I wasn't either. No one else knew it, but papa was friends with dwarves, and they could help. He found us a nice place at the bottom of the mountain to live and cut down trees to make a house. He went to the dwarves to ask them to help, and they complained, but they helped. Then we had a house, and it was better than anything the village ever made. It was just ours.

"We would visit the dwarves a lot. Papa was the best of friends with one of them. Sometimes he would go alone, but mostly we went together. The dwarves taught us to take care of animals instead of just hunting them, and we worked together a lot. One winter, there was a bad snow storm, and so we couldn't go to the dwarves or out to hunt. But one day, there was a knock on the door, and a man stood there.

"Papa took him in and gave him some of our stew to warm up. The man told us stories of how he was traveling the world, meeting all sorts of people, eating their food, and learning about them. Late at night, the man stabbed papa and said he was going to eat him. So I killed him. I stabbed him through the back of the knee so he couldn't stand, and then stabbed his neck so he bled out. Papa was okay, even though he bled a lot, but he seemed so scared of me.

"I love papa more than anything, but he would ask questions like you did. He didn't like how I acted a lot, especially after that. Of how I looked at the dwarves or made noises that weren't words. But he still loved me, and we were happy together. Until he died. Then the Empire ruined everything. So I am going to ruin everything for them, I am going to kill all of them, so that papa can rest."

"What about the dwarves?" Kazaa asked.

"What?" she asked in surprise.

"The dwarves," he said. "Did they know he died?"

This froze Wolf in place as she contemplated Kazaa's question. Eventually she said, "No. This is more important."

"They didn't deserve to know?" He asked her. "They were his friends, I'm sure they were yours too. They could have helped."

Wold shook her head and said, "No! This was my duty. I had to do this. Alone!"

"Why?" He asked her. "No one should have to fight no. You're hurting, Wolf. You shouldn't have hid from the people that were there for you."

"You don't know anything about me," she growled.

"No," he agreed. "But I know people. You're hurting. This quest of yours, as much as I understand it... it won't bring you happiness."

"I'm not going home," she stated.

"No, I didn't think so," he replied. "Just know what path you're going down... no, not even that, just understand that at the end of all of this, you'll have even less than when you started."

"What are you talking about?" She asked, confused by his words.

Kazaa turned to look at her, making eye contact. He said, "No one becomes a mercenary because they lived a good life. Revenge kills nearly all of you that there is. Once you're finished, you're left with nothing. Nothing to live for, nothing to die for. If you truly want your revenge, understand that it will kill you, but you won't get to die."

She stared back at him, lips twitching in frustration. She then growled and said simply, "I know what I want."

***

The dark elf Dancing-Lights watched as a white bird with a silver breast soared through the air. It had been longer than he would have liked, and he was beginning to worry if it would ever come. Seeing the bird now flooded the elf with relief, though he was still prepared for it to bear bad news. The bird swooped down, heading straight towards him.

Dancing-Lights extended his arm so that the bird could land, which it quickly did. As it perched on his wrist, Dancing-Lights unfurled a small letter it had tied to its leg. He quickly devoured the letter's content with his eyes, and then shook his arm so the bird would release its grip and fly off. He headed back inside the tavern, crumpling the letter in his hand. Dancing-Lights strode past Spring and Ruby-Gem, towards the tavern's hearth. He tossed the letter into the flames and watched as it burned away into black ash entirely. Only then did he turn around.

Ruby-Gem asked, "What did it say?"

He answered, "We have a location. We move now, and keep walking through nightfall."

Spring asked, "We can't rest?"

"No," he simply said. "We don't have enough time to rest the first night."

Ruby asked, "Can't you just take us there? I mean, you're an elf after all."

He chuckled softly and said, "Wood elves do not like those of the cavernous path. We also do not know if they have elves in their number, who would be upon us the moment we arrived. Now come, we're going."

Dancing-Lights led Spring and Ruby-Gem out of the tavern, once again embracing the cool night air. He wasted no time in heading back onto the road, both women walking by his side. After a few minutes Ruby-Gem broke the silence by asking, "Where is it we're going?"

"To the north," he responded.

"More specifically?" she asked.

He groaned and elaborated, "There is a place in Moia. They call it Sanctuary, for whatever ironic purposes I have no idea. It is a prison where they house slaves, before moving them either to Imperial Heart or to work the fields. It is likely that is where your fellow surviving tribesmen ended up."

Spring quitely said, "I see."

He continued, "I have worked for a few people that needed work done in the area before. This one in particular likes to see quick strikes performed without collateral. He wants us to kill Sanctuary's warden, as well as any Imperial generals that may be in the area. Curious, that one."

Ruby-Gem then asked, "So we just go there and kill those people? Nothing else?"

"That's right," he replied. "Think of this as an excellent test for you. Should you bare any mark of an assassin, you will resist the voice that tells you to reunite with those you once knew. If you still return to them... then there was never any point in me saving you. You were just the same wives and mothers your tribe always viewed you as."

Spring pursed her lips as she struggled to think of an appropriate insult that wouldn't draw her too much ire from the elf, but Ruby-Gem surprised them both with her bluntness. She said, "You haven't done nothing to show you're not the same prick as the rest of them."

"Ruby!" Spring chided, though she was secretly quite proud of the young half-orc.

Ruby-Gem said, "No, I'm getting sick of his words! Dancing-Lights, all you ever talk about is how we're damsels you had to save! How our tribe hated us for being women! You think you're better, but you're just the same as them, only you think you're better than them for some reason! You're not, you're just another male bossing us around and bragging about how great you are compared to us!"

Dancing-Lights listened to her vent her frustrations, and then he laughed. He asked, "Is that really how you feel, Ruby-Gem?"

She then punched the dark elf square in the jaw, the force of her punch nearly knocking him off of his feet entirely. Dancing-Lights held his sore mouth in shock as Ruby-Gem said, "Don't talk to me like that. I'm not a child."

The elf recomposed himself, and still holding his jaw said, "Okay. Very good. Ow. Who taught you to throw a punch like that?"

"Myself," she retorted, rubbing her freshly bruised knuckles.

Dancing-Lights took a step away and said, "You hit well... could use some work, but very good none the less. What about you, Spring? Care to take a shot at me?"

Spring looked to him dubiously for a moment, before delivering a punch to the opposite side of the elf's face. Almost instantly she asked, "Are you okay?"

Dancing-Lights nodded and said, "I am fine... nothing that won't heal anyway. Tomorrow night, we'll work on your technique. Ruby-Gem my dear, that right hook of yours is a gift. But for now, we really can't waste any more time."

Chapter 10

Though they were travelling through Oshack in an attempt to avoid Vhodan's armies, the group had decided against staying within the dense forests. They would follow the Ozshaka River, which flowed down from the mountain and across the entire western border. This way they avoided being caught by any more unexpected monsters, though more than once the heroes had to wait several hours for a company of soldiers to pass by.

Garr was always the first to notice them, often several minutes before there would be any evidence that the soldiers were even there. He would simply stop, lay his ear against the ground, and then declare, "There are a hundred of them. Northeast."

Whenever he did this, the group would quickly find any hiding place nearby and wait with bated breath. Eventually the soldiers would appear, crashing through the woods with reckless abandon. Their blades were frequently dull from slicing through tree branches, but this still didn't make anyone want to fight them. Luckily, the soldiers didn't seem to be activley pursuing them, and so once they had gone the group could continue by unscathed.

Then Garr stopped, put his ear to the ground and said, "Maybe ninety of them. Southwest. They have prisoners."

"How can you tell?" Zetine asked in surprise at this.

"They're being dragged," Garr responded as he stood up.

"We have to help them!" Mizt-Ied urgently said.

Jubilatious shook his head and said, "We can't. If we make any commotion here, it will alert every soldier for a dozen miles at least."

"But we can't just leave them," she said in what was almost a whimper. "We have to do something."

"I agree with Mizt-Ied," Zetine said.

Jubilatious ran his hands across his face, flinching at the hair that was beginning to form a small beard. He said, "How do you two propose we do that?"

"How is your illusion magic?" Zetine asked.

"Passable," he groaned. "I would have to maintain mental clarity and a line of sight. Once they're out of view it would dissipate."

Ironja said, "Use the rock like ye did earlier. Drop a giant one on them and crush 'em flat!"

Jubilatious shook his head and said, "That wouldn't work. There's a reason wizards almost never use telekinesis."

The others all stared at him in silence for several seconds. It was broken by Mizt-Ied who asked, "Are you going to explain it to the non-wizards orrrrrr?"

He looked at each of them, let out a dramatic sigh, and then explained. "Okay so, pyromancy. It burns everything, but you can point it in the right direction. Cryomancy freezes water in the air around you, and is much easier to control. Even necromancy is basic in a certain way; you just need dead things... more or less. Telekinesis isn't bound by a natural element though. So how do you control something with no basis in the natural world?"

"By... focusing?" Zetine asked.

""You don't," he corrected. "With telekinesis, you can try to grab a small rock. Okay, that might work, it's just a rock. But let's say you try and grab a fistful of sand. That's a million rocks, all bundled up close together. You try and lift a handful of that and your magic will try to lift the entire bloody beach, draining you before you even manage to get more than a few grains up. Try and focus on a tool and you'll find that your magic can't distinguish between the individual parts. Where does it hold a sword? Maybe you get lucky and it will be the hilt, or you end up having it held by the pointy bit, or worse it just completely separates the blade from the hilt. It's essentially worthless magic, unless you're in a panic."

"That's why ye learn practical skills," Ironja muttered under his breath.

Zetine said, "We are not leaving those people to their fates. We're supposed to be heroes! A true hero does not permit suffering, even in the name of the greater good!"

"This is for the *ultimate* good!" Jubilatious shot back. "If we die here, then Vhodan lives! He'll kill and enslave the entire world! We can't let that happen, for crying out loud! We're so close!"

"It would take us a month of restless travel, minimal," Garr replied. "While I agree that our quest holds greater weight, I cannot say with confidence that this would hinder our progress."

With a frown Jubilatious said, "Then one of you has to come up with the plan. I cannot conceive of a way that we can rescue those held prisoner without being captured ourselves. And no, that is not an indication to fake a capture. Mizt-Ied."

"Why me?" she asked in surprise.

"I know how much you love picking locks and escaping from places," he replied.

"Eh, you got me there," she shrugged.

Zetine spoke up, "What if we light a fire as a diversion? While they're distracted, we swoop in and free the prisoners."

Garr said, "That would not be enough, and there's no guarantee that would divert all of their attentions."

"Well, we DO have a bear," Mizt-Ied suggested.

"And if worst comes to worse..." Zetine mused.

After another several minutes of deliberating, the group had formed a plan. They encircled the soldiers' camp, a large artificial clearing near the river bed where their backs were to the Syronul forest. Garr used his scimitar to ignite five arrows which he strategically fired into the woods behind them. Soon the fires had spread out, forming a half circle that drew the attention of many of the soldiers. They began to run back and forth, using whatever buckets and waterskins they had to try and put out the flames, refilling them in the river.

Then, a roar from beyond the flames struck fear down into even the laziest of them. The soldiers quickly formed up, making several tight rows as they prepared to face whatever terrible beast lay beyond. From behind them, their prisoners were left with their hands tied to roughly chopped wooden logs placed over the back of their necks. It was here that Mizt-Ied and Zetine quickly began to untie the ropes once it was evident their blades were ineffective. Once the prisoners were freed, they guided them away and headed back across the river.

It was here that a soldier turned, saw the fleeing prisoners, and shouted. They all began to turn, realizing how they had been fooled. That's when a red dragon flew from overhead, landing by the river bank. The soldiers froze mid-run, some even turning and sprinting off entirely. Those that maintained their composure watched as their prisoners, along with the two heroes, were quickly devoured by the massive winged beast. It turned to face the soldiers, and at last they all ran off into the wilderness to fend for themselves.

Across the river, Jubilatious collapsed to his knees. He maintained consciousness long enough for Zetine to appear above the water then said only, "I hate illusion magic."

He then proceeded to pass out, falling into the mud.

"You forgot the sound," she said to his sleeping body. "Did everyone make it over okay?"

The five people they had rescued were elves, and though their bodies were beaten, they seemed in good spirits. Their leader, a pink skinned elf with lilac hair said with a thick accent, pronouncing hard Hs as Ys, "We did. Thank you, brave humans, dwarve, and brownie."

"We go by goblins now," Mizt-Ied politely corrected.

"Where will you go now?" Zetine asked.

"The trees are our home," she said. "So long as they stand, we will always have a home."

"Why didn't ye just run off into a tree earlier then?" Ironja grumbled.

The elf persed her lips, then bent down to show him their wrists. "There was iron woven into their rope. It prevented us from returning home."

"That's horrible," Zetine said.

The elf nodded and said, "Iron does not belong in The Land of Wind and Trees. It is an evil thing."

"Maybe for you," Ironja said beneath his breath.

"We will return home now," the elf said. "But I thank each and every one of you brave heroes. Even the sleeping one."

"He made the dragon!" Mizt-Ied chimed with a smile. "He didn't think he could, but I knew Jubilatious could do anything he set his mind to!"

"Indeed," Zetine nodded. "He lacks confidence, but is a powerful wizard."

"I see," the elf murmered. "But there is still one thing that I don't understand..."

"And what's that?" Mizt-Ied asked.

"How ever did you make that sound?" she asked with quite a perplexed expression.

"I sent my bear friend," Garr spoke up. "His name is Jermaind."

"And where is Jermaind now?" she asked with a tilt of her head.

"He is moving away from Vhodan's forces before we regroup, so that they do not attack him."

"I see once again," the elf said. "Farewell then, noble heroes. May we never have reason to meet again, but meet again we do."

One by one, the elves left the river side. Each one of them chose their tree and simply walked into it, bodies disappearing behind bark. It was a strange sight to behold, especially for Zetine who hailed from a land without elves. But once they knew their new friends had successfully escaped, all that was left was to pick Jubilatious up and set off at once. This was a task no one wanted to do however.

Mizt-Ied squeaked out, "Not it!"

"Not it?" Zetine asked in surprise.

"Not it," Garr simply but quickly stated.

This left Ironja to be the last one to say "Not it! I... oh you cheeky bit! I'm only four feet tall!"

Garr said, "As the humans say. You slumber, you do the number."

"That's not an expression," Zetine gently informed him.

***

When Jubilatious awoke, he found that he was laid atop a very soft material. It was perhaps the finest blanket he had ever touched, though that wasn't saying much as most would agree the best blanket he had ever slept with was mid-tier at best. It was made from thick brown fur that felt incredible beneath his fingers. Much more interesting though was the moving early morning sky above him. Also, something kept awkwardly jostling his back.

Jubilatious attempted to roll over, only to find himself face down on the ground. He mustered up only a pitiful, "Ow."

Jermaind did not call him a moron, though it was clear to everyone that the bear thought it.

Zetine helped Jubilatious to his feet and said, "It's good to see you awake. You slept through most of the night."

"I told you illusion magic was draining," he grumbled as he wiped the mud from his face.

"Up and at 'em, lad," Ironja chuckled. "About time ye get some exercise after yer snoring."

"I was snoring?" he asked in surprise.

"Just a bit," Zetine politely said.

"It made me want to spit in your mouth," Mizt-Ied said.

"Please tell me you didn't," he gagged.

"Only if you pay," she giggled.

"I hate you," he groaned before quickening his pace to reach Garr's side. "How much longer do you think until we cross over?"

Garr said, "We have not seen any soldiers since you fell asleep."

"That is SO not what happened!" he cried out in disbelief.

"So I would say another day without spotting them would be good," he concluded.

Jubilatious stretched out his arms and took a look around at their surroundings. A look of confusion flashed across his face, catching Garr's attention, though the orc remained silent. Jubilatious began to look around more frantically as he recognized more and more of the area, though he couldn't be sure quite where from. At the mage academy he had been taught of liminal spaces, the strange locations your dreams conjured up, but this seemed different. It was far more real.

"What is it?" Garr asked at last, unable to ignore Jubilatious' frantic eyes.

"I... I think I'm home," he said at last.

"What?" Garr asked in surprise, not expecting the statement.

"That's right, you are from here," Zetine mused.

"No, I'm..." he gasped at his own realization.

Then Jubilatious ran off, further along the muddy beach, leaving the others to chase after him. Jubilatious was never the most athletic of the group, in fact he was the least athletic of them all.

But something motivated him to outpace even Garr as he sprinted beyond a tree line. When Garr broke through the trees he found Jubilatious bent over and panting several dozen yards away. Ahead of him stood a quaint riverside cottage, though it could use a bit of upkeep, and there was quite a bit of wild grass in the garden.

Garr slowly approached him, but by the time he and Jermaind got close, and the others also made it into the area, Jubilatious began to move again. He called out, "Mother! Mother it's me! I'm home!"

Gar followed after the man, and though he knew nothing of who Jubilatious was, he now knew of the sorrow that had lurked behind his heart for countless years. He couldn't gather up the strength to say anything to Jubilatious, knowing it would break the fragile human heart even more than it already was. So he simply followed in silence as Jubilatious called for his mother again and again to no avail.

Jubilatious pushed open the cottage door, a line of dust falling onto his hat as he said, "Mother I'm finally home!"

But the interior was empty. Dust rested across nearly every surface, and the growth of two separate types of mold showed that no one had been there for years. The cottage had been completely abandoned, left to rot by the river. Jubilatious stepped inside, looking around with the look of a saddened puppy. His eyes were wet but he still bore a smile as though some part of him still thought it was all just a prank.

He stooped down to pull a roll of parchment out from beneath his mother's bed. He unfurled it to find carefully illustrated designs for a hat. There were even notes on small enchantments to give it. How the fabric would never decay, the wire would never bend, and it couldn't be burned. He had worn the hat for a decade, and in all that time never known who gave it to him.

"I don't understand," Jubilatious whimpered.

"She's gone, Jubilatious," Zetine softly said from behind him.

"She would never leave me!" he cried, anger in his voice at the misconceived disrespect.

"I don't know what happened to her," she gently said as she calmly approached him, and then wrapped her arms around him from behind. "But she's not here, Jubilatious. She hasn't been for a long, long time. No matter how it hurts, we need to keep moving."

"I can't," he sobbed, and realized tears were flowing from his eyes. "I was supposed to come back a great wizard... to see her after all these years as a hero. This isn't FAIR!"

"I know," Zetine whispered into his ear. "But there's nothing you can do now. Come, we need to go."

"Well, isn't this a heartwarming scene," a strange voice cut the tension.

Jubilatious and Zetine looked behind them, passed their friends who also looked behind themselves, to see a dark elf standing in the doorway. His skin was a light purple and his hair, long and braided, the color of moonlight. The elf's green eyes pierced into them all, as though he was seeing into their very souls. He was dressed in what had to be a mockery of leather armor, for it protected barely anything save for his heart and abdomen. He had strapped to each of his thighs a dagger, the left shaped like waves, while the right was of a traditional design. On his back was also a falcata.

"Who the hell are ye?" Ironja asked, brandishing his axe and shield.

The elf smiled politely and said, "We-Will-Reach-Sanctuary."

"No..." a gasp escaped from Zetine's lips.

"Get down!" Jubilatious shouted, fully turning to raise his staff.

Time moved in slow motion. Mizt-Ied drew one of her knives and threw it before diving to the side. Ironja charged at the elf. Zetine crouched low and drew her daggers. Garr fell to his back and quickly notched an arrow. Fire erupted from Jubilatious' staff. It was overkill for a single person, and all the attacks were centered upon his heart. Not a single one had a hope of landing a hit on the dark elf.

He fell to his knees, bending backwards to dodge Jubilatious' flames, then grabbed Mizt-Ied's dagger from midair before it could enter the fire. Garr readjusted his shot and let loose, only for the elf to twist himself onto his side to avoid the arrow, then swept Ironja's feet out from beneath him. As Garr notched another arrow, We-Will-Reach-Sanctuary leapt back to his feet to avoid the quick slashes of both Zetine and Mizt-Ied. The elf deftly avoided the attacks from the both of them, before kicking Mizt-Ied in the gut to knock the wind out of her. He disappeared behind the doorway before Garr could fire another arrow, leaving Zetine to chase him.

"No! Don't!" Jubilatious called out after her.

They all moved towards the exit, but in a heartbeat We-Will-Reach-Sanctuary had returned. He held Mizt-Ied's knife to Zetine's throat, who now lacked both her weapons, and spoke with a smile. Vhodan's top assassin said, "I would like to parley."

***

When the original four heroes set out on their journey, there was one who watched them go not with hope, but with fear. No matter how noble one is, no matter what cause they might fight for, war inevitably corrupts everyone it touches. In his heart, Rain-Upon-The-Rocks knew that Vhodan would win. There was just no hope fighting against a being so powerful, especially not one with such a vast array of armies and monsters. So there was only one option left that may preserve the wood elves.

A century before, Vhodan had erected a castle of black rock and salt above a spirit so ancient and primordial that it has never been named. Though rumors persist about every inch of the castle, there is hardly an ounce of truth known. Save for but one detail. In the throne room, which is believed to be at the center of the castle behind wall after wall, defense after defense, there are two trees. A cherry tree and an ashwood tree, their branches intermingling with one another. A gateway for all of elven kind.

When Rain-Upon-The-Rocks stepped foot in that horrible throne room, he found himself struggling to see and immensely cold. The braziers did little to illuminate the vastness of the hall, let alone the people inside. He guessed about two dozen soldiers, the two hands of The Emperor, and Vhodan The Eternal himself. Seated upon a throne of ashen bone and black salt was The Emperor, nothing more than a shadow, flanked by his two hands.

The right hand was We-Will-Reach-Sanctuary, the master assassin who had no need to conceal his face. The left hand was The Storm Caller, dressed in blue robes and a wide-brimmed hat. The Storm Caller's piercing blue eyes stared out from beneath his hat, swirling with lightning filled clouds. He raised his stave to Rain-Upon-The-Rocks, a clear act of annihilation.

"Why do you stand before me?" The Emperor's words were simple but powerful, thunderous across the hall, his voice deep yet elegant.

Rain-Upon-The-Rocks mustered up all of his courage and said, "The Three Mystic Sages of Syronul have uncovered The Citadel of Remembrance! They called a meeting of all peoples to plot out your demise!"

"You say this as though I did not know the moment they stepped foot outside the academy," The Emperor said and Rain-Upon-The-Rocks knew his life hung upon a thread.

He said, "In the end, only four heroes were joined together! They were prophesied to slay you, great Vhodan, or so the Sages said! I come to warn you of their mission!" after an afterthought, he took a great bow.

Vhodan said, "Tell me of these heroes," and it was as much a request as a slit throat was a scratch upon the skin.

Rain-Upon-The-Rocks said, "The pharaoh of Exia, though she is aided by none of her own peoples. She is of great talent with twin daggers, and a superior duelist. Little is known of her magic prowess, though likely she possesses some air of necromancy. Next is a brownie named Mizt-Ied. Fully grown, yet with the aptitude of a child. Still, she is an expert escape artist and is known to be quite skilled with throwing knives. The dwarve Ironja, former Keeper of Stone. Like most, the dwarve is a brute that uses its hammer to resolve all conflict. Lastly is their wizard, a schoolless welp though quite proficient at many of the schools despite this. The wizard goes by the name of Jubilatious."

At this, the Storm Caller inhaled sharply, but did not speak. Vhodan said only, "When will they arrive?"

"They will likely evade your armies instead of fighting. It is planned for you to realize they are close, moving to assassinate you. When that happens, the Sages predict that you will draw your armies close to defend you. When this happens, your enemies will all attack at once to provide distraction. Then the heroes are said to slay you."

Vhodan said, "Enough. I tire of the elf."

In that moment, Rain-Upon-The-Rocks realized he had lost sight of We-Will-Reach-Sanctuary at some point. There was a sharp pain in the wood elf's back and out through his belly. He looked down to see a knife protruding from his gut. As he looked back up, a purple hand gripped his face, and his head was forcibly spun around backwards to stare at his killer. We-Will-Reach-Sanctuary ripped his dagger free and watched as Rain-Upon-The-Rock's lifeless body fell to the ground, blood pooling around it.

The dark elf took a knee over the body and asked his master, "What is your bidding, my Eternal Emperor?"

Vhodan thought for a moment then said, "Find the heroes. Kill them before they ever reach Syronul. Bring me their heads so I may place them with the others."

"It will be done," said We-Will-Reach-Sanctuary, his gaze fixed upon the intricate stonework beside his boot.

***

"Let her go," Jubilatious growled as he focused his staff at the dark elf's head, though he didn't dare cast a spell.

"Promise you won't hurt me," he replied.

"What games are ye playing at?" Ironja spat at him.

"No games," said We-Will-Reach-Sanctuary. "All I want is your word that none of you will harm me."

There was silence for several agonizingly long moments before Mizt-Ied said, "Done. We won't hurt you."

"Mizt-Ied," Jubilatious hissed.

"What?" she asked. "Not like we can do anything without him killing Zetine!"

"Fine," he said. "You have my word."

Garr said, "Mine as well," though he did not loosen his arrow.

Several more moments passed before Mizt-Ied encouraged, "Ironja, come on."

"Fine," the dwarf groaned. "Ye have me word, murderer."

"Now yours as well, pharoah," the elf said into Zetine's ear.

"You have it," she hissed. "So long as no harm comes to any of us."

He released her, causing Zetine to stumble forward, and for a moment every single one of them expected someone to attack. Then We-Will-Reach-Sanctuary sheathed his dagger and brushed himself free of the dust and ash that had collected on his person during the scuffle. They all looked to him anxiously, causing him to give them a curious look back.

"Aren't you going to ask what I'm doing here?" he asked.

"What are you doing here, assassin?" Zetine aggressively asked.

He smiled and said, "I have come to defect. Go Team Heroes."

"That's a stupid name," Jubilatious muttered.

"No way The Emperor's top stab-guy wants to switch sides," Mizt-Ied said.

"That's a stupid title," We-Will-Reach-Sanctuary retorted.

"She makes an excellent point though," Zetine said.

"Thank you!" Mizt-Ied beamed.

Zetine continued, "What makes you think we would fall for this obvious trap?"

"It is not a trap," he said, the smallest twang of hurt in his voice. "I have stood by Vhodan's side for years, watched the atrocities he has committed, claimed a thousand lives for him. But that does not mean I believe in his cause. Vhodan seeks the annihilation of anyone who opposes him, the oppression of the entire world, no matter how long it may take. Inevitably my hand would have been forced, though my confidence in killing him is weak."

"If you're such a master assassin," Jubilatious said, "then why don't you think you can kill him?"

"Because I have seen him die on three separate occasions," We-Will-Reach-Sanctuary said. "Vhodan does not truly die. Were I to slay him in his sleep, poison his wine, or even behead him, he would rise again."

"What, is he a vampire?" Jubilatious asked with a sarcastic tilt of his head.

The elf replied, "No. It is some form of magic that I do not understand. He has kept it as his greatest secret, that even after a century of serving at his side I know nothing of it. Save for its existence, though that was from my own deductions."

"What exactly are you proposing, assassin?" Zetine asked him.

We-Will-Reach-Sanctuary smiled at this and said, "I wish to be of use to you, the last of the heroes who will strike at Vhodan's heart. My blades are yours to stab with, my bones yours to break, my mind yours to plot with. No matter what it takes, from this life into the next, I will stand with you against Vhodan. I, We-Will-Reach-Sanctuary, pledge myself unto thee."

As he took a formal bow, Ironja commented, "Ye act like a prick."

"Pardon?" We-Will-Reach-Sanctuary asked as he rose back up.

"We need to take a team meeting," Jubilatious said.

"Okay," he replied.

"Alone," Jubilatious added.

"Ah, I see," We-Will-Reach-Sanctuary nodded, before awkwardly leaving the building.

The group all huddled together and Jubilatious said, "I don't trust him."

"Obviously," Zetine responded. "That elf has probably killed more people than we've all ever met combined."

"His deeds are notorious, even in the most remote of reaches," Garr agreed. "However, even the most vile of people should be given the chance of redemption. If this is what he wants, who are we to stand in his way?"

"It is not a matter of redemption," Zetine said. "But if we can trust him."

"Never trust an elf that stabs people in the back for a livin'," Ironja said.

Mizt-Ied said, "I think it's only fair to give him the benefit of the doubt. I mean, everyone's done bad things. If he wants to help us, we should let him."

Jubilatious responded with, "Okay. Let's say we trust him. Then he betrays us and kills us all, or offers us up to Vhodan. What then? I would rather not be a slave to the Empire."

Zetine said, "I believe that ultimately, it is whether or not the danger outweighs the potential benefit of our alliance. He is the Right Hand of The Emperor. His knowledge is invaluable. It could be what secures our victory."

"An excellent point," Garr nodded.

"What would he even know?" Mizt-Ied asked.

"The layout of Vhodan's castle, the number of his troops, their placements, even what monsters there may be surrounding the castle," Zetine explained.

"You've got to be fucking kidding me," Jubilatious groaned. "Okay fine, you make an excellent point. He's useful. Maybe even worth keeping around. But how do we protect ourselves from him?"

"We never let him stand watch," Zetine offered. "Always have someone watching him. Bind his hands. If he ever seems to be a threat... we could kill him."

"Do we really want to do that?" Mizt-Ied asked. "It's so cruel..."

"If it's what must be done," Garr said.

"Alright..." Jubilatious said. "I have a spell that should keep his hands together."

The group left the house one by one, expecting to find We-Will-Reach-Sanctuary eavesdropping on them. Instead he was some thirty paces away, petting Jermaind's ears. He even had a few fish at his feet that he seemed to be occasionally feeding to the bear. That certainly explained how We-Will-Reach-Sanctuary was able to sneak up on them, though it didn't fill anyone with confidence that their watch-bear could be swayed so easily. That said, Mizt-Ied thought it was a particularly cute scene.

We-Will-Reach-Sanctuary looked to them and asked, "What decision have you reached?"

Jubilatious took a deep breath and said, "We will allow you to travel with us, and be of assistance against the Emperor Vhodan.

On the condition that you are never granted the right to stand watch, freedom away from the group, or to carry weapons. Furthermore, your hands will be bound by magic so that your threat is diminished. However, should it ever become apparent that you are a danger to our group as individuals or as a whole; we will not hesitate in killing you. Do you consent to these terms?"

"I do," the elf said. "On the condition that should the time come when you need me, you grant me the right to kill your enemies.

Jubilatious nodded and raised his staff as he said, "Very well. We-Will-Reach-Sanctuary, I bind your hands until the time that you are of use to me. Your hands will never raise a weapon again so long that I, Jubilatious, will it. In the event of my death, your hands will be removed from your body."

A sharp coldness spread up We-Will-Reach-Sanctuary's wrists. Then a weight seemed to drag them down, before both of his arms were forced together. The elf looked down in curious surprise as two silver bracers appeared on his arms, before they were suddenly forced together. While his hands were seemingly free to move, and elbows were more than capable of bending, We-Will-Reach-Sanctuary found himself devoid of the arm movements he had been so used to. He had no doubt the magical cuffs were far stronger than any physical manacles, and to attempt to break them would be entirely useless.

He looked to Jubilatious and asked, "What will I do if I have an itch?"

"Hope it subsides," the man responded with a sly grin.

Zetine stepped past Jubilatious and began to remove We-Will-Reach-Sanctuary's weapons. She stripped him of both daggers, the falcata, and even managed to find a knife hidden in each boot, as well as a sharp pin hidden in the braids of his hair. She took several more minutes trying to find anything, before growing satisfied the elf had no more weapons. She then brought each one of them to the others. Mizt-Ied received the knives to replace her lost ones, Ironja received the falcata, Garr his conventional dagger, and Zetine kept the wavy one. She then stepped away to retrieve her own abandoned daggers.

"Ye look good like that," Ironja chuckled.

"I've heard manacles bring out my eyes," We-Will-Reach sanctuary laughed back, though his own laugh was slightly strained.

Jubilatious asked, "Where is the best place to cross into Syronul?"

We-Will-Reach-Sanctuary answered, "Honestly? Probably no more than three miles downstream. That part of the region is hardly populated, and patrols are rare. However, there are tribes of ogres scattered throughout the region, and in this area griffins were released to hunt the local centaurs.

"That's horrible!" Mizt-Ied gasped.

"It is war," We-Will-Reach-Sanctuary said. "To prevent an uprising in the region when we expanded into it, we had to ensure there would be no one left to stand against us."

"You killed all of them?" Zetine asked.

"I didn't, no," he said. "But it was eighteen years ago when we sent forth three hundred griffins into the wilds. We haven't so much as seen a centaur in all that time. They are all dead."

Jubilatious said, "We only have a single archer, and myself for magic. How are we supposed to get past a cavalcade of griffins?"

He explained, "Most likely, two thirds of the griffins are dead. Maybe more. The centaurs would have killed many of them, and after their prey died out, they would have turned upon each other. Griffins are highly territorial and aggressive even with their own kind. Cannibalism is common when they don't have a steady supply of food."

"That's still a hundred winged hell beasts roaming the region," Jubilatious stated coldly.

We-Will-Reach-Sanctuary continued with, "But not alongside one another. If we do encounter one, it is important that we lay flat upon the ground and don't move. Though griffins have excellent eyesight, they have difficulty differentiating between motionless objects from far off. Potentially, our bodies may seem as little more than rocks."

"Some plan ye got there," Ironja grumbled.

He shrugged and said, "It's the best we can do. Though if you prefer, we can just run and hope the griffins forget how to dive."

"Point made," Ironja frowned. "Ass."

Jubilatious asked, "What more can you tell us of Syronul's current state?"

We-Will-Reach-Sanctuary thought for a few moments then said, "There are a few villages scattered across Witchway River. Some coastal towns by the ocean as well. It would be best to go through one of the villages. There we can all acquire disguises."

"Why would we need disguises?" Zetine asked.

"Because Vhodan knows exactly who you are," he said.

"How?" Zetine asked in surprise.

He smiled sadly and said, "You were betrayed the very moment you embarked on your journey. It is why I was able to wait for you at Jubilatious' childhood home. I knew you would eventually reach it if you traveled along the route The Unknowing King laid out for you. All i had to do was wait."

"Who would do that?" Mizt-Ied asked in shock.

"Someone that won't ever betray you again," he said. "Now, the villages and towns will be heavily guarded. It would be best if only one person enters initially to procure the disguises. Once that is done, we should leave that village and head to another. There we can rest and prepare for the following journey."

"We are not staying in a village," Garr firmly said.

"Pardon?" We-Will-Reach-Sanctuary asked in his own surprise.

"It's too dangerous," he replied. "We stick to the wilds."

"Very well," We-Will-Reach-Sanctuary thought to himself. "Well, from there, we are likely to find many soldiers and loyalists. The mage school is completely under the Emperor's control-"

"Obviously," Jubilatious cut in. "You said The Unknowing King chose our path?"

"Indeed he did," the elf nodded. "He has the ability to control people's minor actions even from a great distance. Ensuring you would face select challenges instead whatever the wilds may have in store for you."

Jubilatious stroked his chin and mumbled, "Facinating."

He continued, "There are likely to be many mages blending in as commoners. The Storm Caller named them his Secret Guard, to ensure Vhodan's followers remain docile."

"How powerful are they?" Jubilatious asked.

He said, "Not very. The most powerful wizards are generals. If anything, these mages are the ones who could barely graduate. Still, they pose a substantial threat to non-mages."

Jubilatious thought to himself for several moments then asked, "Is it worth trying to infiltrate Arkvine? Could we take it off the map before attacking Vhodan? Or get rid of The Storm Caller?"

We-Will-Reach-Sanctuary shook his head and said, "It would be entirely pointless. Far too many wizards for just six people, and a bear, to take. The Storm Caller also resides within Imperial Heart. He rarely visits Arkvine anymore. Instead the mage school is overseen by a puppet. A spineless wizard named Hrafasaf."

"Damn," he cursed under his breath. "Once we get close enough to Imperial Heart, to Vhodan's keep, how are we supposed to get inside?"

"There are several ways," We-Will-Reach-Sanctuary said. "There is a sewer system that can be accessed from a distance. Aside from the expected hardships of that, it is also filled with basilisks and scale beasts. I doubt you will want to risk that."

Ironja shrugged and said, "Could be worse."

He continued, "The forest gate is the only direct entrance, though it is of course heavily guarded. There are two trees in the throne room that can be used for direct entrance, though if you seem to be a threat, you will be filled with arrows the moment you step foot inside. This method of course requires myself, or another elf. Short of scaling the outside walls, which obviously wouldn't work, there's one other method of entrance. The Unknowing King resides within the tallest tower in the castle. If, as I have been told, there is to be an intense battle... he will provide a way inside."

"Why would he do that?" Zetine asked suspiciously.

"What do you know of the Unknowing King?" he countered.

"Little," she meekishly said.

"Nothin'," said Ironja.

"An unknowable amount," Mizt-Ied whimsically said.

"Only that he is a powerful wizard of some kind," Jubilatious said.

"He is not a wizard at all," We-Will-Reach-Sanctuary said. "The Unknowing King made a deal with a being of immense power at the cost of his soul. He only leaves his tower when directly summoned by Vhodan, but is perhaps his most essential asset for the battle. He drives madness into the minds of all those around him by changing what is real and what is not. He will inflict a mass hysteria upon the battlefield, and will likely claim half of all the lives there at once. It is vital that when that happens, you enter his eye as one. It is the only way for you to be teleported into the castle, bypassing any guards or monsters."

Jubilatious asked "What do you mean by enter his eye?"

He only smiled and said, "You will know it when you see it. But don't worry, I'll help you through it."

Zetine asked, "What of Vhodan's other commanders? The Monster Queens, King of Bones, and the Lord of The Beasts?"

We-Will-Reach-Sanctuary answered, "Each of them are powerful in their own right, but rarely fight alongside with one another. Torrn seldom leaves his workshop beneath the castle. There he experiments with the various monsters and animals Vhodan has gifted to him, creating new and more dangerous monsters. He has even taken to grafting new body parts onto his own anatomy, and claims some otherworldly being speaks to him when no one else is there to hear it. If this were true, I expect Vhodan or The Unknowing King would have intervened in some way by now.

"Kerotin is an errant necromancer from Cairn, though I know little about him. He serves as a general to Vhodan's infantry, and has branded each and every one of his own personal soldiers with some necromantic mark. It bids them to obey every one of his commands, in life or death. Artessa sticks to the dungeons below the castle, collecting her statues. Vhodan has little use for her anymore, but keeps her around in case he needs to collect new gorgons in The Northern Reach.

"Then there is Barragu, an enigma I have attempted to crack for many years. She is ancient, and if you take her at her word, she is older than even the entire history of the elves. The only way to kill her is to drive a blade through her heart then sever her head before she can retaliate. Of all the other commanders, it is her I fear the most."

"Sounds like we got our work cut out for us," Mizt-Ied quipped. "I mean, it doesn't matter how strong these guys are! We're the good guys, so we're going to kick their asses and save the day!"

We-Will-Reach-Sanctuary smiled softly and said, "I admire your attitude."

Zetine said, "This information will have to do. Thank you, Sanctuary."

"Of course, great pharaoh," the elf bowed.

Soon after, the group had begun to move once more. They carefully reorganized their supplies and made sure to have the humans and Garr carried their belongings, along with Jermaind. Then one by one they entered the river, cold water washing over them and sending icy daggers across their bodies. While at first it seemed as though it would be easy enough to get to the other side, no one had taken into account the depths of the water, and the height of everyone in the group.

As they travelled across the deeper part of the river, Ironja and Mizt-Ied had to sit on Jermaind's back in order to keep their heads above the water. This was humiliating for everyone involved. Zetine proved to be a surprisingly graceful swimmer, while Garr struggled to keep up, and We-Will-Reach-Sanctuary walked on the tips of his toes in order to keep his nose above the water line. Jubilatious calmly walked ahead of them, occasionally circling back to look down at them and ask if they needed help.

"Yer such an ass," Ironja grumbled.

"I never learned how to swim," he shrugged. "Not my fault that I'm magic."

"You could cast a spell on us!" Mizt-Ied shouted at him.

"But alas," Jubilatious dreadfully said. "The spell is only for oneself. It cannot affect others."

It absolutely could affect others.

Zetine pushed her head up above the water and called back, "There's people under the water!"

"What?" Said almost all of them in unison.

"Oh, right," murmered We-Will-Reach-Sanctuary.

"You know what this is?" Zetine asked sharply.

The elf spit out some water and said, "Yes. I'll tell you later. Out of the water."

They traveled for several more minutes before at last they all made it to shore. As he passed Jubilatious, Ironja walked the wizard in the back of the knee, causing him to stumble backwards then fall into the shallows. As Jubilatious flailed his arms and shouted for help, the dwarf and goblin laughed to one another.

We-Will-Reach-Sanctuary came up last; gagging on the water he had swallowed. Zetine asked him, "Well? What were they?"

The elf looked back over the river sadly and said, "Humans, once. From before The Empire completely took over. Their feet and arms were bound with chains, and they were tossed into the river as punishment for rebelling."

"By all that is godly," Zetine gasped. "That's such a horrible way to go."

"You have no idea," the elf agreed. It was such a beautiful day for something so terrible."

"You were there?" Mizt-Ied asked with a tilt of her head.

He sighed and said, "I was there for all of The Empire's greatest achievements, and most horrendous atrocities. I pushed more than a few of them off the boat myself."

"Why would you ever take part in something as vile as that?" Zetine asked.

"What choice did I have?" Was his response. "All I knew was to serve The Empire. So I did as I was told."

"And..." she thought back to what she had seen. "They were moving."

"I would think a child of The Dead Sanda would know the reason for that," he said. "Commit a big enough atrocity, and the dead come back. I'm sure they'll be down there until their bones are eroded entirely. Until there's nothing else to hang onto. Maybe they'll find peace after that."

"You're a monster," Zetine shook her head and stepped away from him.

"I know," he quietly replied.

Jubilatious struck his staff into the ground and created a small flame above its tip, which he then used to dry his clothes. Once satisfied, he cast it over the clothes of Zetine, then Ironja, then Mizt-Ied, and then Garr. He did not offer the flame to either We-Will-Reach-Sanctuary or Jermaind, and instead extinguished it. The wizard then strolled forward, looked around, and nodded confidently.

"I have no idea where to go," he said.

"North-east," We-Will-Reach-Sanctuary replied. "We'll want to reach the woods as soon as possible. Or the griffins will get us. Probably."

"Right," Jubilatious nodded. "North-East. I knew that."

He began to walk forward, leaving the others to catch up with him. Though they had been somewhat dried, the wind still blew daggers through them, and the shelter of trees couldn't come soon enough. Every now and then an inhuman cry would fill the air, but the skies remained clear.

It had been an hour of walking, but a forest now stood proudly in the distance, with tows of thick trees and dense foliage. Ironja hated the fact that they were about to enter even more woods, but he supposed it was better than the water. Every step he took still caused the horrid liquid to squish between his toes, and it slowly seeped from his armor insistently.

Once more a cry filled the air, but this time there was a beast to accompany it. Its wings stretched far and wide, growing out from the back of a four legged creature. The monster's body was built sleek yet muscular, and it was covered in tan feathers. Each of its legs ended in razor sharp talons that wouldn't look out of place on a torturer's wall. Its head was indistinguishable that of an eagle, with ever staring yellow eyes and a beak like the blade of a sword.

"GET TO THE TREES!" Garr roared, quickly loosening an arrow at the beast before sprinting for the tree line.

The arrow embedded in the griffin's breast, but it didn't so much as slow its pursuit. One by one the heroes reached the forest, first Zetine, then Garr, then Jubilatious, followed by Jermaind and We-Will-Reach-Sanctuary. They turned back to watch as the dwarf and goblin's little legs proved to be a hindrance to their survival. Doom seemed so certain as the griffin swooped down, talents outstretched...

But then We-Will-Reach-Sanctuary stood there, pushing Mizt-Ied to the ground with his body. She looked up to him, eyes widening in shock and awe as he looked back to her with a face of utter determination. Then he was gone, whisked away by the winged beast. They all watched as it steadily rose into the air, the elf held tight in its back right talons.

We-Will-Reach-Sanctuary grinned in the griffin's grip, straining his hands. He flung his head back and declared, "You're so beautiful! I'm going to feel so bad about this!"

Blood ran down the elf's wrists, telling him that he was doing well. He maneuvered his legs up and wrapped them around the griffin's leg, then continued to put more pressure on his arms. With a masochistic laugh, We-Will-Reach-Sanctuary ripped his arms free from the beast's talons, spilling his own blood onto his face. Now that he was free, the master assassin set about proving his title to be true.

He climbed up the griffin's flank, which caught it by surprise. The monster looked over its shoulder and squeaked in shock. Then it twisted, and We-Will-Reach-Sanctuary was falling through the air. He rotated his body in free fall, keeping his eyes upon the griffin's as it swooped back in. Its beak opened to take a bite out of him, and the elf took his chance. He flung his bound hands out, letting the griffin bite down upon them.

With a loud clang, he was caught, and no longer had to worry about falling. We-Will-Reach-Sanctuary wrapped his legs around the monster's neck this time and pried his arms free, then slammed them back into the beast's beak. It howled in pain and attempted to peck him, but a quick shift caused it to slice open its own neck. He laughed maniacally as he beat the griffin with his manacles, cracking its beak and causing it to injure itself with well timed movements.

Then they were both falling.

The world raced up to consume We-Will-Reach-Sanctuary, who had only a few precious moments to act. He climbed up the griffin's body, barely able to grab ahold of its feathery hide with his bound hands, until he reached its upper thigh. With a single second left to act, the dark elf pushed himself off of the beast, which proceeded to crash through the treetops and landed with a sickening splat on the forest floor. We-Will-Reach-Sanctuary himself hit the tree branches hard, which snapped beneath his weight and velocity, but slowed his fall. He landed in a roll upon the ground, coming to a stop a dozen meters away on his feet.

The group of heroes came bursting through the shrubbery not long after, looking to We-Will-Reach-Sanctuary in shock. He grinned up at them and said, "I killed it. Dinner, anyone?"

Zetine's stomach rumbled, so she said, "It sounds as though Ironja is hungry."

"That wasn-" Ironja began, before a gentle kick at his side silenced him.

She continued, "I think it may be best if we gather some of its meat, carry on a bit, then we can cook it and take a rest."

"I agree," Jubilatious quickly said.

We-Will-Reach-Sanctuary rose to his full height, then rolled his shoulders and began to awkwardly stretch as he said, "Very well. The best meat is from its chest, though the thighs can certainly be appetizing."

"You've... eaten a griffin?" Jubilatious asked in shock.

The elf shrugged and said, "There's not much produce around the castle. Half of our diet are the monsters that are unfit for battle."

"And I thought it was terrible eating salamander," he shuddered. "I can't imagine what else you must have eaten."

"Oh trust me," the elf smirked. "You don't want to know the half of it."

Garr spoke up, "We need to hurry. The scent of the dead beast will soon draw scavengers."

"On it," Mizt-Ied said as she sauntered up to the griffin's carcass. She drew one of her pitiful little knives and began to slowly slice off thin pieces of meat. Seeing this, Ironja brandised his axe and began to hack up a leg. Zetine herself stepped in to fillet the beast as well. Working together, the three of them were able to make decent progress. They began to fill their carrying sacks, which dripped red with blood, and knew they wouldn't need to worry about food for a few days at least.

Behind them, Garr said, "Good work. It takes impressive skill to take down such a formidable beast as a griffin."

"Thank you," We-Will-Reach-Sanctuary smiled over at him.

"This doesn't mean that we trust you though," Jubilatious added on with a side-eye.

"Of course not," the elf nodded.

"Because," the human continued. "If I was in your position, nothing would prove my loyalty more than an act like that. Killing a dangerous monster, but also one that's no longer useful to Vhodan? Why, I'm sure anyone would trust me after that. But we will never trust you, not after everything you've done."

"I'm trying to be better," he said, and there was true sorrow in his voice.

"And we're letting you," he replied, bitterness in his tongue. "But atonement does not bring forgiveness. Especially not for someone with your past."

Jubilatious began to walk away to assist the others in chilling the meat, leaving Garr and We-Will-Reach-Sanctuary alone together. Garr looked to him and asked, "What is it that makes them so resentful of you?"

"Do you really not know?" he asked in surprise.

Garr said, "Only rumors that you are the deadliest person alive. I am from the wilds, and rarely concerned myself with the rumors of hunters and travelers. In all of the names of evil I have heard, yours was perhaps spoken least."

We-Will-Reach-Sanctuary smiled sadly and he said, "Well, I killed a lot of people."

"Many have," Garr stated bluntly. "That alone does not mark you as a pariah."

The elf sighed then said, "I will tell you of one of my many monstrous acts. It will tell you of all of them, an interweaving pattern that only recently has ended."

"Very well," the orc nodded.

We-Will-Reach Sanctuary said, "It was a few decades ago, in the Northern Reach. I led my own forces, the Shadow Stalkers, into the lands due to rumors of a rebel cell. My spies pinpointed the town where they operated, a few thousand people in total, a mix of high elves and hill dwarves. We suspected the cell to be ten, maybe twenty people in total. They had stolen various supplies from the army and drowned a basilisk before it could be deployed. Nothing too big, though with the obvious knowledge that their efforts would eventually escalate. Not that it matters. All traitors are treated the same way.

"I do not know exactly where my failing lies. If I was too vague when I gave orders, if I had misspoken, or even just not expected the Shadow Stalkers to go so far. When I arrived after my advance team, they had set the entire town ablaze, encircled it with fire so that there was only one visibly safe exit. They had made what we call a "kill hole." It is a single exit that leads directly into the line of sight of archers, leaving the victims with no cover.

"They were running low on arrows by the time I had arrived. I told them to fall back while I took over. Alone, I waded through the bodies in the kill hole. There weren't many survivors, but those that had lived, huddled together in the town square, drawing water from a well to cover themselves and the surrounding area with. They looked to me, and I saw recognition in their eyes. They knew who I was, and why I was there.

"So I did the only thing I could do. I cut down each and every one of them. I made it quick, clean cuts to the throats, direct stabs through the heart. They barely felt anything. I had killed the entire town just to prevent an uprising for my dark master. As I left though, I found a child standing just before the kill hole. She clutched a scorched doll and was more terrified than any child ever should be. She knew perfectly well what waited for her beyond, and what waited for her behind.

"Maybe I would have done differently if I could have... but The Shadow Stalkers returned, come to pick over the scraps I left behind. There was only one thing I could have done..."

"You killed her?" Garr quietly asked.

We-Will-Reach-Sanctuary nodded and said, "Yes. Before I did, she turned from them and saw me standing there, daggers drawn and coated with blood. I made it quick, so that The Shadow Stalkers couldn't hurt her. A dagger straight through the heart, drawn out in the same instant so that she wouldn't suffer. She fell into my arms and I held her as she went limp, as I laid her upon the ground and watched the light fade from her emerald eyes."

"I see," Garr simply stated.

"I am a monster, Garr," We-Will-Reach-Sanctuary said, and though he smiled, there were tears in his eyes. "That is one tale of a thousand, all exactly the same. I have killed more people than you have ever met, given the orders to kill far more. I just want to prevent that from ever happening again... not just to stop myself, but to stop anyone else from ever becoming me. Please, I do not need your favor, your appreciation, even your care. All I ask is that you believe I am trying to do better."

Garr looked to him and said-

"We're ready to move," Ironja grunted as he hoisted his sack over his back. "This stuff's heavy for a bird!"

"You were'nt supposed to pack it full!" Mizt-Ied cried. "Look at it! It's too big!"

"Nonsense," the dwarf retorted. "This 'ill hold me over fir a week or so, your little bag will barely last you two days."

"This is as much as I can carry!" she hissed, horribly lifting the bag to show that she was telling the truth.

Zetine said, "Children, stop bickering."

"I'm twice yer age," Ironja grumbled but complied.

"Yes mommy," Mizt-Ied eagerly said.

"Never call me that again," Zetine said as she walked away with her own sack over her shoulder.

Jubilatious called back, "Garr! Can we use Jermaind to carry the meat?"

"Jermaind," Garr called to the bear, who had been picking at the opposite side of the griffin. The bear poked its head up over the carcass and Garr asked, "Can we place heavy bags of meat upon your back?" the bear popped out of view and Garr said, "He said yes."

"You have such an ear for language," Mizt-Ied beamed up at him.

"No, I just pay attention," he replied. He then looked back to We-Will-Reach-Sanctuary and said, "You have a long road ahead of you. No one can say what lies at the end, though I hope for your sake it is a peaceful conclusion."

"As do I," We-Will-Reach-Sanctuary smiled back at him.

***

The woods proved to be not nearly as dense as they would have liked, especially the more north they traveled. While no griffins appeared to attack them, they were plagued by lesser beasts. Wolves, mainly, who were too starved not to risk attacking such a dangerous group. There were also smaller creatures, like foxes and rats, which followed after them with the hope of stealing some griffin meat. This proved bothersome to everyone, but most of all Zetine, who was disgusted by rats.

"They're just little babies!" Mizt-Ied told her.

"They are far more disgusting than babies," she retorted.

Mizt-Ied pressed, "They're furry and cuddly! Plus, they like to play with you!"

"I am NOT playing with a rat!" she angrily said.

"Garr," Mizt-Ied called, "Tell Zetine that rats are adorable little angels!"

"They are," he agreed. "They make excellent friends, as well."

"Jubilatious," Zetine pleaded. "Please tell me you at least stand by my side."

"Actually," he said, causing Zetine to groan with frustration. "I used to have a pet rat when I was first studying at Arkvine. He was adorable and liked buttered bread."

"I am surrounded by lunatics," she wailed to herself.

Garr abruptly stated, "We are being followed."

"By a monster?" Jubilatious asked.

"There shouldn't be any monsters," We-Will-Reach-Sanctary stated. "The griffins were the only control measures, and they would have eaten anything else that made its way here."

Garr elaborated, "It's not a monster. Keep walking. There are several of them, three to our right, one behind us. They walk on hooves. Four legged."

"Centaurs?" Zetine asked with surprise. "I thought you said they were dead!"

"They ARE dead," We-Will-Reach-Sanctuary said. "We haven't seen signs of them for years. If there's one thing The Empire is good at, it's wiping out populations."

"Well they certainly don't *sound* dead," she shot back at him.

"One of them is notching a bow," Garr said. "Get ready to fully stop. Three. Two. One."

The entire group stopped in their tracks and watched as a wooden arrow landed on the ground in front of them. Then suddenly they were back to back, drawing their weapons. We-Will-Sanctuary pushed himself into the center of the group, hiding behind Garr and Jubilatious who stood ready to face their attackers. Ahead of Ironja, a centaur emerged from behind a bush, with chestnut fur and olive skin. He held a shortbow in his left hand, and notched an arrow made from a stick with his right.

Ahead of Garr emerged four more centaurs, of black, brown, and tan fur who began to circle the group. The chestnut centaur said, "Hail, ootziders!"

"Hail?" Jubilatious dubiously asked.

The centaur shook his head and pointed to the ground, repeating, "Hail!"

"I think he means "heel,"" Zetine pointed out.

"Lower your weapons," Garr said, placing his own bow upon the ground. Begrudgingly, the others complied.

The centaur said, "Why do ootziders come hair?"

"You have a wonderful grasp of common tongue," Jubilatious sarcastically stated, earning him an elbow from Zetine.

Garr said, "We mean you no harm. We are passing through, seeking to end the scourge of Vhodan."

The centaurs exchanged looks from one another. Their leader asked, "Art you zeeking truth?"

"He is!" Mizt-Ied squeaked. "We're going to kill him!"

The centaur cautiously lowered his bow and said, "Revenge uz, if you do."

"But you live, do you not?" Garr asked.

The centaur smiled at him, and it was the same smile We-Will-Reach-Sanctuary often wore. "No," he said. "We are dead, only zmall left. We are dead."

"We will," Gar promised. "He will never kill another people again."

The centaur nodded to the others, who trotted back off deeper into the woods. Then he said, "Travel zave, good luck," and left.

"Well that was stressful," Jubilatious said as he stretched out his back. "At least some centaurs survived, even if they're stuck in these woods."

"They didn't survive," Garr said with a slow shake of his head.

"You mean they were ghosts!?" Mizt-Ied asked in disbelief.

"What? No!" Garr exclaimed. "There's only a few of them left, not enough to repopulate. They have maybe a generation left, if none of them are killed, until they die out no matter what we do."

"That's truly awful," Zetine sighed.

"It is," We-Will-Reach-Sanctuary said, and all of them turned to look at him after that. The dark elf was too ashamed to meet any of their eyes.

After several moments of silence, Mizt-Ied said, "I wonder if we'll see a unicorn too! I've always wanted to see a unicorn!"

"Yer never gonna see a unicorn, lass," Ironja gently said from beside her.

"What? Why not?" she asked frightfully.

"They've been extinct for a century," he somberly said.

"Nooo," she whispered sadly.

"Also," Jubilatious interupted. "They only appeared to virgins."

Mizt-Ied thought about this for a moment then meekly said, "I mean, how would they KNOW..."

"They would," he stated. "That's why so few people ever actually saw them."

"And how would YOU know, HUH!?" she stubbornly asked.

"Because I'm a wizard," he retorted. "We have a whole chapter in our textbooks about unicorns and how snorting their ground horns can get you high."

"Noooo," she once again wailed quietly.

Zetine said, "Enough. We need to continue on, we're losing too much time."

"She's right," We-Will-Reach-Sanctuary said. "Come on, we shouldn't have more than a couple hours left in the woods."

Chapter 11

Kazaa bit his tongue and held tight onto the reigns, hoping that Wolf knew well enough to keep quiet. The soldier rounded the cart, looking over the various bags, then up at Wolf who sat with barely concealed anger. The soldier reached into one of the bags and produced an apple, before casually taking a bite as she watched him. Then he walked back towards the front of the cart, taking another bite.

He said, "Alright, you're clear to pass. Be careful on the road though, we have reports of Oshack guerillas killing people on the highway. Barbaric bastards."

"We'll be careful, but my sister and I can hold our own if worst comes to worst," Kazaa replied with an awkward grin.

The soldier stared at him for a few seconds then said, "Okay. You can go now."

"Right, sorry," Kazaa said, before flicking the reigns to drive the cattle onwards.

Slowly the cart began to pass by the two rows of soldiers, all standing with their weapons at the ready. There couldn't have been more than a few dozen, but Kazaa had no desire to fight even half of that many. He had to commend Wolf though; she was doing remarkably well compared to how he expected her to act. When he turned around, Kazaa could see that she was glaring at each and every soldier they passed by, sizing them up as though she could fight the entire platoon at once.

"Eyes down, sister," he said to her. "The good soldiers are just doing their job."

Wolf resisted the urge to growl at him and instead bit her tongue as the cart slowly passed by the procession. Once they were far enough away that Wolf knew there was no way for them to hear her, she asked, "Why did they let us go so easily?"

Kazaa sighed at that question and thought how to best explain it. Eventually he said, "Because we are not Oshackian."

She then asked, "How do they know that?"

It was a question that made Kazaa deeply uncomfortable but he explained, "Because of our race, and because of our skin. If we were elf or dwarf, they would have stopped us for sure. If we were pale skinned or red haired, they also likely would have stopped us. Those features are common for Oshackians."

"And our features are not?" she pressed curiously."

"Yours are less common, but still present," he said. "My own heritage leaves me looking quite different. As do my clothes. Side by side though, I doubt the Imperials would give you a second look as anything other than Exian."

Wolf was silent for just a minute before she asked, "What are they going to do to them? The Oshackians. Are they going to kill them?"

"Many of them, yes," Kazaa said quietly. Then more clearly he said, "Officially, The Empire believes in liberating people. Those who fight back will be killed, be it in battle or through execution. Some of the peaceful men may be taken as slaves, though likely they'll just be given labor jobs for the Empire. Building their ever growing sprawl of a land."

"And the women?" she pressed more.

"We can talk about something else," he said, poorly attempting to change the subject.

"I want to know," she insisted.

After several seconds of silence Kazaa answered, "They will be given husbands from The Empire, whether they want them or not. They will bare children to those husbands, so that their offspring are true children of Rizzen."

Wolf's answer came slowly, more thoughtfully than she was prone to being. She said only, "That's horrible."

"It's not the first time it has happened to Oshack either," he said. "The Empire claimed them once before, but after a few generations they fought back. They won their freedom, their independence. And now the Empire has returned to crush them back into submission."

"They'll fight again, won't they?" she asked, feeling some shred of empathy for the people of Oshack.

"Perhaps," he mused. "But then eventually The Empire will just crush them again. I want you to understand that it's not just an army of men who are the threat. The Empire of Rizzen is a powerful force, one who can afford to take massive losses as though it was just spare grains. One that can wait for as long as it takes to reclaim what it views as its own property."

"Which is why I must cut off its head," she grinned at the thought. "Once its head dies, the beast will fall upon itself."

"Perhaps," he said again. "Though there have been plenty of Emperors before who were cut down early. Countless noblemen, too. But so long as the line of succession continues, there will be someone else to continue what someone else started."

"What's a line of succession?" Wolf asked outright.

"Oh, right," he said. "You weren't educated."

This made Wolf wince but she said, "Yes. What is it?"

He explained, "A father's son, and his son, and his son, and so on. Each time a ruler dies, with rare exception; their eldest child takes control of their domain. Almost always, whatever the previous ruler had done is continued. Sometimes deeds are undone, but this is rare, and usually only done if the new ruler hated the old one."

"So even if we kill The Emperor..." she said to herself more than Kazaa. "There will be another emperor waiting to take his place?"

"That's right," Kazaa nodded.

She then asked, "So then how does one kill an empire?"

"If only I knew," he replied.

Wolf thought on all she had been told for the next several minutes before she asked, "Kazaa?"

"Yes, Wolf?" he responded, though he had grown tired of her questions.

"Where are we going now?" she asked, which caught him somewhat off guard.

"To the Barlock Mountains," he said. It's more dangerous, but it will be a much quicker way of getting to Moia than travelling around them."

"Why is it more dangerous?" she asked. "Are there more soldiers guarding them?"

He laughed at that and said, "No. None at all, in fact."

"Then how can they be more dangerous?" she asked in confusion.

Kazaa explained, "They are infested with monsters. Harpies, rock trolls, basilisks. The Empire steers clear of it though, and if we can handle a few monsters, we can make it straight on through to Moia within a day or two."

"Then that sounds good," she said. "This journey is making me feel sick, and it would be good to test my blade against a monster's hide."

He winced at that but said, "How about instead we hope we don't encounter any monsters? I don't know about you, but I rather like having all of my limbs attached to my body."

"Then don't let them hit you," she replied nonchalantly.

**

The sun was now setting as the cart approached the mountains, the forest well behind them. The cattle had grown extremely sluggish, and it seemed time to cut them free. Before Kazaa could say anything though, he noticed a figure in the distance. It was too far, and hidden in the mountain's shadow, for him to make out any specific detail. Whatever the figure was, it was not a welcome sight.

"Be on guard," Kazaa said to Wolf.

"What is it?" she asked as she gripped the hilt of her sword tightly.

"Someone's blocking our way," he replied. "I'm going to check it out."

Wolf pulled her bow free and said, "I'll keep watch."

"Good pup," he smirked and hopped off the cart.

As Kazaa approached the figure, he drew his khopesh and scanned the surrounding area for any sign of an ambush. Finding none, he drew closer. Now he could see it was a knight of some sort, dressed in bulky black platemail. It had a grip upon a massive greatsword embedded in the earth, while a shield rested by its side. Without warning the knight rose to its feet, faster than Kazaa could have expected, but with a strange sort of jankiness that could not accompany any normal living being. It pulled its shield up, and ripped its blade from the ground, then turned to bare Kazaa witness. Behind the slits of its helm there was only ethereal green.

"Have you come to end me at last, Lady Selena?" it asked, words echoing out without emphasize or weight.

"I don't know who that is," Kazaa replied. "I'm just a traveler, and ask your permission to pass, whatever you are."

The knight seemed to tilt its helmet, and the sound of grinding metal filled the air. "You are a warrior," it said. "Will you be the one to end me?"

"I don't want to fight," Kazaa responded.

"And yet you're here," it said as it took a lumbering step forward. "I am Sir Donovan, Lost Soul of Cairn, Prized Thrall of her Lady Selena the Third. Stand and face me, or be struck down."

Kazaa drew his dagger and entered a defensive stance as he said, "Just stand aside, Donovan. We don't need to do this."

"Yes we do," Donovan replied, stalking forward.

Kazaa sidestepped, then did so again to position himself behind the knight. He scanned its back for any sign of a weakness, but found it to be a seemingly impenetrable defense. Silently, Kazaa cursed himself for not carrying a cudgel or mace, then leapt back as Donovan spun around, slashing blindly at his backside.

The sword's tip landed in the ground at the knight's side, spraying coarse dirt into the air. It took a step forward, and didn't so much as flinch as an arrow shattered upon its back. It slashed forward again, and Kazaa leapt back while taking note of the knight's movements. Not quite slow, but seemingly mundane. Donovan raised the sword into the air and brought it down over Kazaa, who side stepped to his right. In that moment Kazaa was knocked onto his back by the knight's shield, having successfully feinted an attack.

"I needed more from this," it stated.

"You're going to regret that," Kazaa replied as he spit into the ground.

Donovan raised its sword into the air, and then suddenly turned as it heard the roar of a feral beast. In its moment of shock and confusion, Wolf drove her blade through Donovan's visor as deep as she could. The knight stumbled back, nearly crushing Kazaa who rolled out of the way just in time. Green light flowed from its helm like fire, head held back in place. She pulled the blade free, nearly falling onto her own back, and panted as she locked eyes upon the recovering knight.

If Donovan still possessed lungs, he would have gasped, "It can't be... *you*?"

As Kazaa returned to his feet he shouted, "Mordhau it!"

"What!?" Wolf shouted back in confusion, before leaping back just in time to avoid a swipe from Donovan's sword.

"Take the blade in your hands!" he quickly explained to her. "Keep your right hand close to the hilt, and use the pommel to strike him!"

"Lady Velena..." the knight uttered in shock, enraptured by the sight of Wolf.

Wolf quickly complied, spinning her bastard sword around in her hands before taking hold of it as Kazaa had instructed. The blade dug into her palms and fingers, but she held as tight as she could. Wolf dodged out of the way as Donovan stabbed forward, then received a strike from his shield, followed by a thrust. Wolf barely managed to avoid the brunt of that attack, but was still stabbed through the shoulder as she leapt backwards.

"For gods' sake girl!" Kazaa yelled at her. "You're using a two-handed sword, so block his strikes with it!"

Wolf did her best to take his words in stride, and raised the sword to block Donovan's next downwards slash. As the knight recoiled, she took the opportunity to strike at his ankle. The armor was dented inwards, and the blow seemed to carry enough momentum to force the knight to drop to his knee. Donovan looked up at Wolf as she raised the bastard sword overhead then brought it down atop him. The knight's helmet was knocked from the rest of the suit of armor, which collapsed into a pile of pieces mere seconds later.

"What was he?" Wolf asked in disbelief as she stared at the ruined suit of armor.

"Yes, what was he?" Kazaa asked as Wolf's eyes began to glow green.

"A soul bound to an enchanted suit of armor," The Dead Woman nonchalantly replied. "Amateur work, really. Most curiously is *who* he was."

"Well then," he groaned. "Who was he?"

"Donovan of The Ash Tree," she said. "He and Lady Selena left Cairn many years ago, when I was no more than a child. Neither of them were ever seen again."

"So what was he doing out here?" Kazaa asked.

"I would imagine Selana left him here to guard something," she mused. "It's not uncommon for necromancers to leave their thralls behind. Though much more interesting is that this happened after he died, and that she never came back for him. Perhaps something killed her not long after... but then you're left to wonder what it was."

"You seem awfully talkative," Kazaa replied. "Why?"

"I am growing quite used to the girl's body," she said. "I must say, it's taking a lot of work not to swallow her soul at this point. The girl has virtually no subconscious to defend herself with."

"And why don't you just do it?" he asked. "You could be alive again, and wouldn't be relying upon either of us."

"Because her body isn't *my* body," she said. "I could never live in someone else's body, not truly. Besides, there would be no chance of me recovering my magical prowess in a body like this. It's as devoid of magic as a, well, as a you."

"Charming," Kazaa grimaced. "We're close to Cairn now, maybe a month longer at most."

"Yes, I know," she smiled with Wolf's face, which was a truly horrible gash between the girl's cheeks. "I cannot wait to be home, to be alive again. To be in a body that does not smell of meat and sweat."

Kazaa sheathed his blades and said, "I hope you remember who made that possible."

"Of course," the Dead Woman replied. "You will be well rewarded upon arrival, I'll see to that."

"And what of Wolf?" he asked.

"Who? Oh right, the girl," she said, and Kazaa could not tell if she was joking or not. "Yes, she'll be granted everything her little heart desires."

"She deserves it," he said. "You have no idea what she's been through."

The Dead Woman looked at him, and through the swirls of necromantic energy Kazaa could see pure amusement in Wolf's eyes. She said, "Sweet boy, I know quite literally everything the girl has ever been consciously witness to. She's a barbarian, as true as one that's ever lived. That deserves no pity. Now hurry, before he puts himself back together again."

"That thing's still alive!?" Kazaa asked in disbelief as he stared down at the pile of armor pieces.

"Of course he is," she chuckled, a dry and horrid laugh. "It would take magic to remove his soul from that armor, magic that I am in short supply of."

Kazaa hurried away from Donovan's remains and said, "I just have to cut the cows free."

From behind him, Wolf asked, "Right, but what was he?"

As Kazaa drew his dagger to sever the ropes he answered, "A necromancer's thrall, whose soul was bound to a suit of armor. A tragic fate for anyone, especially a warrior like he must have been."

Wolf looked to the armor, and then to the sword still held in her bloody hands. She asked, "Do you think that might happen to us, when we arrive in Cairn?"

"No," he lied. I don't think that will ever happen to us."

***

Though Kazaa and Wolf had no way of knowing it, they climbed up the same wall of the same mountain that Garr, Ironja, Jubilatious, Mizt-Ied, and Zetine once climbed down. There was no longer any trace that the heroes had been there, nor was there any trace of anyone else who had ever climbed that part of the mountain. The few places where blades had been inserted to assist in climbing simply looked like naturally formed crevices, and now aided Wolf and Kazaa in their own climb.

By the time they had made it to the top, the sun had long since set and storm clouds were gathering. The cold wind cut through Kazaa like daggers, but Wolf didn't even notice it. To her, it was the closest to home she had felt in ages. Kazaa had to readjust his bandages to better protect himself from the cold, while Wolf strode forward. She found what seemed an obvious path not too far away, and looked down the twisting and winding passage.

"It seems so familiar, yet I've never been here before," she remarked.

Kazaa walked up behind her and said, "Most mountains are like that, I think. If you've been to one, the next one will feel just the same, at least until you grow to know it."

"How far do you think we should travel?" she asked.

"Until we find shelter," he replied. "I'm sure a mountain like this has plenty of caves and caverns. I have a few torches I found in the cart, too."

He proceeded to hold up a backpack he had found for Wolf to see, then produced an oil-soaked torch from inside. Kazaa then spent a good thirty seconds trying to light it as Wolf watched in silence. She then took it from him, reached into the bag, and rummaged around. After a few moments Wolf pulled out a strange piece of metal. She held the torch close to a boulder and struck the rock with the metal, producing a few sparks that caught the torch aflame. Satisfied, Wolf handed both back to Kazaa.

"Show off," he mumbled.

"How did you not know to do that?" she asked, walking forward.

As Kazaa followed he said, "I haven't lit many torches. I'm not one of those sellswords that goes around plundering tombs or venturing into ominous dark abodes. I travel by day, usually sleep at night, and make my campfires naturally."

"It is natural," she said. "Metal and rock make fire. Our ancestors figured it out ages ago, and I'm sure even some animals could figure that out."

"Well now you're just being rude," Kazaa suppressed a laugh. "Stop walking ahead of me, I have the light."

"I can see fine," she replied just before the ground gave way beneath one of her feet, nearly sending her stumbling over a ledge. She then said, "Okay, you first."

Kazaa strode forward and swept his torch around them, illuminating the ground and the path they were meant to walk. The ground seemed heavily eroded and combined with the mass of clouds overhead and limited light, travelling down the path seemed to be the last thing anyone would want to do. Even still, Kazaa carried on with Wolf in tow.

He said to her, "Keep an eye out for a cave or wide crevice. We need to seek shelter as soon as possible."

Wolf didn't reply, but kept as best a look out as she possibly could while still traveling safely. The pair slowly made their way down the path, pebbles and small rocks occasionally falling beneath the impact of their feet. Eventually they reached a spot where it seemed as though the path continued straight forward, with only dips and rises standing in their way, instead of a fall to the death. By the time they had reached this point however, the first cracks of thunder were beginning to play their serenade.

They almost weren't able to distinguish the sounds, but quickly Kazaa and Wolf become aware of a steadily approaching torrent of aggression. ***Boom. Boom. Boom. Boom.*** It was like the drums of an approaching army, practically shaking the mountain beneath their feet. Kazaa drew his khopesh and Wolf raised her bastard sword, the pair moving back to back to scan the mountain ridge for signs of their approaching foe.

Wolf was the first to see it. Massive, towering over twice her height, and with muscles that made her own look like nothing more than flabby skin. Its flesh was made from brown rock and was spotted with grey stones, each the size of Wolf's fist. Its hands if they could even be called that were massive claws, while its rows of sharp teeth seemed capable of chewing the toughest of boulders with ease. The beast stared out at them with a single black eye, practically glowing red in the reflection of Kazaa's torch.

There stood Snarlgor, the great rock troll of the Bartok mountains, ripper of flesh and breaker of bones. He who had been branded by the orc ranger Garr, and now lived with an eternal reminder of the pain and humiliation the fleshling had bestowed upon him. Suffice to say, Snarlgor was furious.

The rock troll let out a roar that could shake the heavens, but found that the measly little human girl before him returned his roar with one of her own. The troll found this amusing, like a pet owner seeing their dog try to make human sounds. Snarlgor decided to kill the human girl after he killed the human boy, who did nothing to entertain him.

Both Wolf and Kazaa now watched as the troll approached them, each footstep taking it over rock that the pair would have needed to climb. It was so hopelessly massive that its mere movements seemed to be a threat, which was entirely correct. There was little the two humans could do against a great rock troll, even with fire on their side.

With panic in her voice, Wolf asked, "What IS that!?"

"A rock troll," Kazaa choked out.

"I've slain trolls," she replied. "That's not a troll!"

"Rock trolls are much worse," he shook his head. "Focus on its joints, you might get lucky. I'll try and scare it with the torch."

"We're fucked, aren't we?" She asked.

Kazaa took in a deep breath and replied, "Yup."

They dared not rush the troll, fearing the instability of the mountain, so they let it come to them. The sky cracked with lightning and thunder, and then the downpour was upon them. Wolf roared and charged while Kazaa leapt forward, dancing around the monster. Wolf swung at the back of its knee, only for her body to shake as her blade was harmlessly deflected. Kazaa thrusted the torch at the beast's face, but it didn't so much as flinch.

Snarlgor delivered a punch to Kazaa's face which sent him flying backwards, where he hit his back upon a boulder. The air quickly fled from Kazaa's lungs, leaving him to gasp in pain upon the mountain floor. The rock troll stalked forward, ignoring successive strikes from Wolf which did little more than scrape against its stone skin. It reached forward for Kazaa, who took as deep a breath as he could and grabbed for the torch. The troll grabbed him by the head and hoisted him into the air, only his right eye visible between its thick and hard fingers.

"Kazaa!" Wolf cried out, genuinely distraught over his fate.

The troll began to squeeze Kazaa's head, sending waves of pain throughout it, as Snarlgor opened its mouth to laugh. Before it could tighten its grip to a concerning level though, Kazaa thrust the torch forward, forcing it between the troll's parted lips. Flames licked at Snarlgor's tongue and mouth, burning it from the inside out. The rock troll cried out in pain which quickly turned to panic, before tossing Kazaa away like an unwanted doll.

Wolf watched as his body went sailing overhead, landing somewhere on the slope behind her. She turned back to Snarlgor, who had bitten down upon the torch, reducing it to splinters. It spat out the oil-soaked cloth, now barely even ignited, and stared her down. Wolf returned its gaze, locking eyes with the beast. The two predators reached an unspoken understanding, and each waited for the other to make the first move. Wolf roared. Snarlgor roared back, shaking the mountain beneath them. She roared once again.

Lightning flashed and at the same moment, thunder cracked.

She charged the troll, roaring all the while as she held her sword high. The troll struck forward but Wolf slid upon her knees, tearing the flesh from her legs upon the rocks as she did so. As she rose to her feet the troll spun around to face her. Wolf's knees stung like hell but she stood confidently against the troll's might.

One and the same, there was lightning and thunder.

The troll raised its arms into the air and brought them down upon Wolf, who barely managed to leap out of the way in time. Stone of all shapes and sizes flew into the air, before raining back down. One large stone hit Wolf on the back as she recovered, nearly knocking her back onto her stomach. But still she stood tall, while the troll moved to attack her once again.

Together the thunder and lightning came, as bright and magnificent as the heavens.

Wolf charged at the rock troll with her fiercest of roars, only for it to grab her by the waist as though she were nothing more than a small pup. She growled at Snarlgor as he lifted her up to its twisted stone face, then let out its own roar. The smell nearly made Wolf pass out, and the impressive amount of saliva that hit her face left her feeling like she needed to set herself on fire. But she was in the best position she could possibly be in.

Taking the bastard sword into both hands, Wolf thrust the blade as deep as she could into Snarlgor's remaining eye. The rock troll screamed in agony, one it had not felt in quite some time, and threw Wolf to the ground. She landed hard but pushed herself up to watch as the troll stumbled around, tearing at its face. It took hold of the sword's hilt and for a moment Wolf thought her plan ruined. But then Snarlgor broke the hilt free from the sword in his own stubborn attempts to rid himself of the blade. The troll flung his head back and roared for the entire world to hear him.

Thunder cracked and lightning flashed, and struck the blade of the broken bastard sword.

Snarlgor's entire body spasmed violently as electricity coursed throughout his veins. Every muscle attempted to rip itself from their bones. His heart, which had been beating at a consistent rate only barely elevated by the thrill of the hunt, was rendered motionless. Stone skin was rendered black from the heat. All that was left of the troll's one eye was vaporized almost instantly. The monster's brain was torn asunder and burned away into ash and sludge. The troll took a single step forward, and then fell over dead.

Wolf stood still for a few moments, watching the creature's still and lifeless body. Even with the smoke rising off its carcass, she didn't feel safe enough to turn her back to it. As the adrenaline washed away though, her senses returned to her. Wolf quickly ran over to where the rock troll had thrown Kazaa, scanning the ground below for any sign of him. With only the flashes of lightning serving as a light source, it seemed impossible for her to find him if the worst had happened.

"Kazaa!" she called out, her voice wavering from the intense pain she was beginning to feel.

There came a groan and then, "I'm here!"

Wolf carefully walked in the direction he had spoken from and looked down below, waiting for the lightning. In a flash she saw him upon his back, clutching his blood soaked right side, but otherwise seemed okay. He was even still clutching his khopesh. Wolf hopped down, her boots sliding atop the loose rocks, before she came to a stop near Kazaa. She took another step towards him, then crouched down and looked over him.

"Can you walk?" she asked.

Kazaa attempted to lean up, before falling back down. He said, "No. I think I broke my rib...s. It's not too hard to breath though. Did you kill it?"

Wolf nodded, then waivered for a few moments. After recovering, she began to rummage around in her carry bag. She produced the healing potion she had brewed in what now seemed like a lifetime ago. She said, "Swallow this. It will help."

She uncorked the bottle and pressed its rim to Kazaa's lips. He slowly began to swallow the contents, gagging at first on the taste. Wolf watched as his superficial wounds began to close, though it seemed at a slower rate than she remembered. A part of her told her it was due to the potion expiring. She couldn't see if the wound on Kazaa's torso closed or not, but his whole body shuddered, and then he began to relax. After the whole bottle was gone, Wolf tossed it away and waited.

Kazaa leaned up, and then twisted his torso to pop some of the vertebrae in his back. He grinned and said, "Oh that worked like a charm! What was that?"

"Potion," she shrugged. "I dunno."

"I haven't had a potion in years, much less a healing potion," he shook his head. "But I couldn't imagine them tasting that bad..."

"Potion's a potion," she replied. "It tastes what it tastes like."

"Come on," he said as he rose to his feet with some amount of effort. "I think I saw a cave somewhere around here..."

Wolf followed after him and said, "The troll ate the torch."

"Of course it did," Kazaa groaned. "How did you kill it, anyway?"

"I stabbed it in the face and it got hit by the sky fire," she replied matter of factly.

"Sky fire," he mused. "I like that name. In Exia we call it krakovos, which means fire of the gods. More or less. I've heard it most commonly called lightning by Imperials and their neighbors though."

"That's a bad name," she said. "Do they call the sun the light as well? Or the moon the night light?"

"No," he chuckled. "You share those names in common."

They came across the entrance to a small cave, only just barely big enough to fit the two of them inside. Kazaa and Wolf exchanged a look, and then prepared for slumber in the hovel. Kazaa slept with his dagger clutched under his pack which he used as a pillow. Wolf slept with her back to the cave wall, looking out through the entrance. Both of them were only awake for a few more minutes.

Eventually the rain dissipated, and in the early morning the sun began to shine through the remnant clouds. Wolf awoke to the sounds of birds calling outside, and the warm sunlight quickly filled her eyes. She looked to Kazaa who twitched in his sleep beside her, then back out towards the exit. Without a word she rose into a crouching position and stilently stepped outside, letting the warm light bask over her.

Her entire body *hurt*, it was unlike anything she had experienced before. From the tips of Wolf's toes to the top of her head, everything was in pain, and each part of her body seemed to possess its own unique type of pain. She tried to sit down, but it seemed as though that suddenly was too much effort, and Wolf instead collapsed upon the ground. Consciousness soon began to fade...

Then with a scream, she was jolted back to reality. Her legs burned with a pain even greater than what she had previously felt, leaving Wolf to thrash around in agony. Her foot connected with something soft and she heard Kazaa cry out, "Ow!"

She steadied herself and saw him kneeled over her, a canteen in his hand. He said, "Hold still. I need to clean your wounds."

Wolf didn't quite understand, but she nodded and held still. He poured the liquid over her and once again the pain was amplified beyond reason. She scremed, but quickly the feeling began to recede. She then watched as Kazaa pulled a roll of bandages from his pack and began wrapping them around her left leg. Once satisfied, he cut the bandage free with his knife, and used the rest of it on her right leg.

"These aren't meant for wounds, but they'll do," he said once done.

"What did you do?" she asked.

"I disinfected your legs," he explained. "You would have gotten sick if I hadn't, and likely died. The bandages will keep anything from getting in, and your blood from getting out. I wish you had showed me last night, we could have taken care of this before it worsened."

Wolf gently touched one of the bandages, and flinched almost instantly. She said, "It didn't feel like much last night."

"It was your war lust," he said. "We need to take you to an actual healer, unless you have any more potions I don't know about."

"I don't," she replied. "Just had the one."

Kazaa frowned and said, "Then let's pray we find someone who can heal you soon. We don't have any time to waste."

"Then let's go," she simply replied.

Chapter 12

It was another day's journey across the plains of Syronul, various hills and burrows rising up every now and then to put everyone on guard. We-Will-Reach-Sanctuary had assured them that there shouldn't be any more monsters, and that the worst of the dangers were behind them. Of course, he also pointed out that within a few days they would also need to sneak past Vhodan's endless armies. Still, everyone was rather relieved to not be attacked by any more winged beasts.

"I don' like these mountains," Ironja complained. "They ain't shaped right."

"They're hills, not mountains," Zetine corrected. "Are you not a hill dwarf?"

"You best watch yer tongue, lass," he growled up at her. "I was born in the stone-lands, and I will die in the stone-lands."

"Well, ideally," Jubilatious said from ahead of them.

"Really, Jubilatious?" Mizt-Ied asked from the back of the group.

"What?" He feigned ignorance. "No one really knows when they're going to die. Why, you could be struck by lightning in just a moment and not even know it hit you."

"Is that a threat, boy?" Ironja asked with as much bravado as he could muster.

"Not at all," he replied. "But we are in the domain of the wizards. Our lot tend to be arses. If you meet one, best not to anger him."

"Or you could just be nicer," Mizt-Ied suggested.

"You clearly have never met a wizard," he retorted.

"I... met you?" She said with a hint of confusion.

"And I'm as nice as we get," he replied. "Trust me, once you see another wizard, you'll find it a miracle I have empathy. You'd swear it's a requirement to remove it if you want to graduate."

Garr suddenly stopped, and with him so did Jermaind and We-Will-Reach-Sanctuary. The orc said, "Quiet," and all were quiet.

The others carefully drew their various weapons, and Jubilatious readied his staff, while We-Will-Reach-Sanctuary did his best to look intimidating while still shackled. Slowly, with an arrow notched, Garr turned around in a circular motion. His face was unreadable, completely devoid of any emotion as he took in the surrounding nature.

"What is it?" Zetine asked from his side.

"Trolls," Garr replied.

"Ogres," We-Will-Reach-Sanctuary corrected. "I thought we were too far away from their domain, but I suppose they've moved north..."

"What even is an ogre?" Mizt-Ied asked nervously.

"Bastard children of the giants," We-Will-Reach-Sanctuary explained. "They eat sapients almost exclusively. Humans are their preferred meal."

"At least that gives me a running chance," she awkwardly joked.

Zetine asked, "Can you tell how many there are?"

"Not without listening to them move," Garr said. "But four, at least, from each of the cardinal directions."

"Do they have any weaknesses?" Jubilatious asked.

We-Will-Reach-Sanctuary informed him, "Cutting the head off usually works. Vhodan breeds monsters to kill, not for them to be defeated."

"Of course he does, the twat," Jubilatious grumbled.

"They're coming," Garr suddenly said, the faintest hint of fear in his voice.

The beings that appeared over the hills certainly seemed to be giant. Their skin was a sickly purple that contrasted horribly against We-Will-Reach-Sanctuary's own purple skin, and it was covered in rough patches of hair. Their front teeth were sharp for ripping flesh, and their back teeth flat for breaking bone. Each of the ogres wore their own unique set of badly fitted clothes, for they were far too large for a normal tailor to have anything that would fit. Each of the ogres held what at first seemed to be a club, before it soon dawned on the heroes that they were thin tree trunks.

Jubilatious quickly spat out the words, "Torrent of flame, be my spear!"

From his staff appeared a spiral of fire that shot out towards the ogre in front of him, striking it square in the chest. The ogre was knocked backwards, but didn't fall. Instead it grasped at its seared flesh and roared in pain, before charging. Each of its allies, five in total, charged as well.

Garr fired off his arrows as quickly as he could, hitting one ogre in the face six times before it fell to the ground. That victory was shirt lived, for its mate quickly threw its tree at Garr, knocking the orc unconscious and flattening him against the ground. Jermaind roared in anger and charged at the giant, tackling it with all of the bear's might. It was enough to push the ogre back, but not to drop it.

Jubilatious looked up at the incoming tree trunk and said only, "Shield m- oh shit."

Zetine watched as Jubilatious fell, and then spun around. She called out, "Where in the hells is Sanctuary!?"

She narrowly dodged the grabbing claws of an ogre, before delivering a retaliatory strike that nearly cut the monster's forearm free from the elbow. It then swept her feet out from under her, and Zetine's last conscious sight was the incoming tree trunk that came down upon her skull.

Ironja held his shield tight as he blocked the strike of an ogre, the pure weight of the blow sending him skidding backwards. Another one came at him from the other side, grabbing him by the chest and lifting the dwarf into the air. The ogre began to squeeze Ironja, slowly pressing the air out from his lungs. The dwarf's feet failed wildly, before they slowed, then stopped. Satisfied, the ogre dropped Ironja's unconscious body to the ground.

Mizt-Ied was working hard to avoid the ogres' attacks, leaping out of the way of blows and diving between legs. She even climbed up the back of one ogre to escape from another. One by one, she watched as her friends were taken down by the monsters. She was unable to tell if they were alive or dead, which did her no help.

Then she saw Jermaind the bear, Garr's loyal companion, wrestling with the ogre that had knocked the orc unconscious. The bear had split the ogre open and bitten into it several times, but was nowhere near strong enough to overpower the monster. It knocked the bear to the ground, raised both fists into the air, and brought them down upon Jermaind. Blood leaked from the bear's mouth, but the ogre wasn't done. It lifted Jermaind into the air by the throat, then grabbed hold of his feet, and began to twist both ends.

Mizt-Ied fumbled for the smoke bombs upon her bandolier, just barely managing to grab one as she dodged a grab from an ogre. She threw the bomb to the ground, enveloping her and the surrounding area in smoke, as a sickening crack filled the air. The ogres poked around the smoke as it slowly dissipated, but found no sign of her. So they gathered up the meals they had gathered, including the corpse of their fallen kin, and began to carry them back to their home.

From a hill a short distance away, Mizt-Ied held back tears as she watched the ogres drag her friends away. "I'm so sorry," she pitifully said to no one in particular."

"No need to give up just yet," We-Will-Reach-Sanctuary said from behind her.

Mizt-Ied spun around pointing her knife at the elf. She hissed out, "Where were YOU!?"

"My hands are quite literally tied," he said bluntly. "There's nothing I could have done in that fight, so I hid."

"It's not like I can release you," she shook her head. "Only Jubilatious could."

"And I would never ask that of you, Mizt-Ied," he said with what he hoped to be a reassuring smile. "I cannot fight, but I am still useful when attacking from the shadows. As are you, are you not?"

"You want to sneak attack the ogres?" She asked in surprise, rubbing the tears from her cheek with the back of her left hand.

"Much better than attacking head on," he said. "Ogres prefer live meals, so I wouldn't think the others would be dead... injured most certainly, but not dead."

***

Jubilatious' eyes slowly opened, though he wasn't quite sure of this at first, because there was absolutely no light at all. He could feel that his arms and legs were bound, though he wasn't sure by what. After a few moments he also realized he was being pulled by something, to which he guessed it to be an ogre. His head hurt fiercely, and there was definitely a modest amount of blood leaking out from somewhere.

Soon a light began to glow from a chamber up ahead, and now Jubilatious could see the silhouetted form of his attacker. The ogre pulled him into the chamber then roughly tossed him into a corner, where a sick smell filled Jubilatious' nostrils. He could also make out the sound of a crackling fire, and shuffling from another chamber.

He then heard talking, low and guttural, from two distinct voices. The first said, "I want a stew. Humans make good stew."

"A stew!? Are ye mad!?" The second voice demanded. "Ye should roast 'em for two minutes, then eat 'em toasty!"

"Noooo!" The first voice lamented. "The human should be BARELY cooked! That way you get a nice but of tenderness, but the flavor is still sealed in."

"At that point, why not just eat 'em raw?" The second voice inquired.

"Because of the tenderness!" The first voice insisted.

"What if I don't like tenderness?" The second wanted to know.

"Then you're mad!" The first barked.

Jubilatious held his eyes shut as tight as he could and focused with all of his might. There was discomfort in his back, which grew into a decent amount of pain, before his binding was cut through. From his backside emerged the dagger that had been gifted to him by the oracle. It slowly split open the rest of Jubilatious' bindings, so that he was able to crawl out and rise to his feet.

It was insulting how effective telekinsis had worked out for him lately. Jubilatious' mind wandered, and he began to wonder if perhaps his teachers had intentionally lied about it. After all, the last thing you want is for other wizards to be as powerful as you... or worse, even more powerful.

Upon the ground was a mass of spider silk, which Jubilatious quickly realized was used to tie him up. Looking around he spotted the two ogres nearby, oblivious as they faced a large iron pot bubbling away over a fire. Across the room, he could also make out the unconscious body of Zetine, bound in spider silk just as he had been.

"Zetine," he said in what was nothing more than a whisper.

The ogres turned around at this, causing Jubilatious to curse himself, and he could see one of the ogres was missing a freshly lost arm. It called out, "It's awake! You forgot to tie it up!"

"Did not!" The other grunted, taking a step towards the lowly human.

Jubilatious focused, and the dagger flew upwards, piercing the ogre through its skull. The ogre's eyes trailed upwards to focus on the blade perched between its brow, slowly digging in deeper. Then it fell to its knees, and then it fell completely limp and lifeless. Jubilatious recalled the dagger to his side, and marveled at how useful telekinesis was compared to the way his teachers had described it.

"Listen up, ogre," Jubilatious sternly said. "This is what's going to happen-"

"DIE HUMAN!" The monster roared, leaping forward and grabbing Jubilatious off the ground.

It hoisted him into the air and began to squeeze the life out of him, shaking him like a rattle toy. The dagger began to furiously stab in and out of the ogre's one arm as Jubilatious vainly tried to push its fingers away so he could breathe. Slowly the blade was working its way up the monster's arm towards its head, but it was far too slow. He was beginning to see red, and knew consciousness would soon leave him.

But then Jubilatious saw quite an unbelievable sight. The ogre fell away, dropping Jubilatious to the ground. It thrashed and grasped madly at its back like it was possessed. For just a moment he could see We-Will-Reach-Sanctuary with his cuffs wrapped around the ogre's throat, before the ogre stumbled away towards a cavern wall. Jubilatious took the opportunity to send the dagger straight into the monster's skull just as he had the first. It quickly keeled over, and We-Will-Reach-Sanctuary was free to step away.

Jubilatious said, "You ran away."

"It was a tactical retreat," the elf replied. "We came back for you."

"We?" Jubilatious asked with a raised eyebrow.

"Mizt-Ied and myself. She should be freeing Ironja and Garr just about now. Come, let us remove the webs from Zetine."

Jubilatious watched him wearily for a moment then said, "Let us."

As We-Will-Reach-Sanctuary approached Zetine's unconscious body, Jubilatious instead looked to his hovering dagger. He reached out and gripped the hilt, before pulling the weapon from the air. He approached the pair and moved to assist, though the elf had already pulled her up onto his shoulder.

"Do you know any healing magic?" We-Will-Reach-Sanctuary asked.

"It was never by specialization," Jubilatious replied. "Once we're in the clear though, we should have a look through the riches. There might be some healing potions in there."

***

"Ye'll hate eating me," Ironja spat. "I'll punch and thrash and bite all the way down yer throats! I'll kick your stomachs from the inside! I'll set a fire in yer bellies and chew my way out!"

"I like this one," one of the ogres said. "He reminds me of Jorug."

"Ah I miss Jorug," said another one wistfully with a slow nod of his head.

"Whatever happened to Jorug?" Asked the third.

"He called The Emperor a pansy," the second one solemnly informed. "Split him right in half- and didn't even eat him after."

"Such a waste," the first sighed.

From beside Ironja on the ground, Garr carefully scanned his surroundings. There were a few stalactites growing from the ceiling that could be useful, and the chests and carts lining the walls seemed like they may be hiding weapons or other useful items. The silk that bound Ironja and himself told Garr that there was likely some giant spider or worm somewhere else in the cave, though he hadn't seen any direct sign of it. Most of his personal belongings had been taken while he was unconscious, though one of the ogres seemed to be using his scimitar as a toy.

"Look at me, I'm the little goblin," the ogre who had spoken second said while he waived the sword around. "I'm gonna cut the big bad ogres down with my toothpick!"

The ogre then brought the tip of the sword to his open maw, intending to clear some old meat from the gap in its front teeth. A few seconds later, the ogre was wailing in pain and hopping around, throwing its arms about. The display nearly crushed Garr and Ironja, who had to tactfully roll back and forth to avoid being hit. This was far easier said than done.

"What is it!?" The ogre who had spoken third asked.

"It burns!" The other cried, throwing the sword to the ground. "My teeth burn!"

"Go drink some soup an-" whatever the first ogre was going to say would never be heard.

A stalactite fell from the ceiling, piercing the ogre's skull. It fell to the ground instantaneously, the tip of the rock jutting out of its jaw. Garr wormed his way towards the fallen scimitar as the other two ogres looked around in confusion, finding some apparent threat by the chamber's sole entrance and exit. The orc pressed his body to the blade and winced as the heat washed over him, but did not turn away.

With a triumphant rip, Garr sprung to his freed feet, grabbing the scimitar from the ground. The threads of burned silk fell from his body like a cape, still smoldering as they hit the ground. He hurried to Ironja's side and cut the dwarf free, which unfortunately claimed some of Ironja's belly hair in the process.

"Me dwarven pride," Ironja lamented as he stood up.

"I thought that was your beard?" Garr quizzically asked.

"A dwarf can be proud of many-a things," he smugly replied.

"I can imagine," Garr said as he turned to face the ogres, whose backs were turned to them. "A shame you have no weapon."

"I don' need one," Ironja grinned.

The pair charged the ogres, Garr slicing one's leg off at the knee, while Ironja used his body as a ram in an attempt to knock the other onto the ground. Suffice to say, this didn't work. As Garr's ogre fell with a wail of pain, Ironja's merely turned in confusion. Then it slapped the dwarf against the wall, knocking the wind out of him before setting its ire upon Garr.

The orc leapt back as the ogre swept at him with its malformed hand. He sized the beast up, weighing his options for how best to attack. When the ogre lunged for a grab, Garr jumped back against the wall, and struck forward with the scimitar. The tip of the monster's middle finger went flying off as smoke wafted up from its hand. Unfortunately, this did little more than anger the ogre.

While Garr struggled, Ironja went for the easier victory. He huffed in as much air as he could and hurried towards the fallen ogre, who clutched its severed keg desperately to its seared stump. There was no conceivable way the limb could ever be reattached, but in that moment, the ogre was convinced it would fit back on if only they bound it tight enough.

"Hey, dung fer brains," Ironja called out.

"What?" The ogre asked, wiping tears from its face as it turned to look at the dwarf.

"Eat this!" Ironja cried, before jamming his fist into the ogre's right eye.

The monster's wails were amplified greatly, and were quickly accompanied by a sickening tearing sound. Ironja tore the monster's eyeball free from its stomach, then stuffed it directly into the ogres mouth. The great beast seemed both disgusted and enthralled as it tasted itself, but blood loss was now making quick work of it.

Ironja turned as he heard a high pitched battle cry, then saw Mizt-Ied perched atop the final ogre's shoulders. She stabbed her blades into the monster's neck, causing it to flail its arms up at her. Before the ogre could make contact, Garr cut it down to size, by cutting its leg out from under it. As the monster fell, Mizt-Ied rolled away towards Ironja, leaving Garr to finish the ogre. He raised his scimitar into the air, then brought it down into the cannibal's face.

Garr panted with exhaustion, and then looked to Mizt-Ied. He said, "You did well. Who else is with you?"

"Sanctuary should be saving the humans any second now," she responded as she sheathed her knives.

"Do not let your guard down," he stated.

"There's a spider er somethin' round 'ere," Ironja added.

"A spider?" The goblin quizically asked.

"We were bound by silk," Garr explained. "A giant spider seems the most obvious culprit, though it could also be a silk worm or some other strange animal."

"Right, well, I haven't seen it," she said.

"You said We-Will-Reach-Sanctuary was rescuing the humans?" Garr asked.

"That's right!" She chirped.

"What about Jermaind?" The orc asked, and suddenly all joy from rescuing her friends flooded from Mizt-Ied's body.

She took an uncomfortable moment to reply, "He didn't make it..."

"Are you sure?" Garr asked, and she couldn't read his emotion.

"I'm sure," she stated.

"Then we must move on," he replied, though his words rung hollow. "Let's get to the others."

It wasn't long before they crossed path with the humans and elf, though it seemed as though they were drawn to the same place. From opposite sides of a deep and dark cavern did the two groups look at one another. Zetine was still unconscious in Jubilatious' arms, a thick trail of blood running down her forehead and onto her face. On the edge of the shadows, thick webs marked the walls and ground, practically drawing them inside.

"What's wrong with her?" Mizt-Ied asked.

"She's not waking up," Jubilatious said with tears in his voice.

"She may have a concussion, or..." We-Will-Reach-Sanctuary trailed off.

"Or what?" Ironja grunted.

"A coma," Jubilatious quietly said. "We need healing magic, and I don't know any..."

"There's a town half a day's walk from here," We-Will-Reach-Sanctuary said. "They are likely to have potion sellers or a white mage."

"Who can go?" Mizt-Ied asked.

"Garr and Jubilatious," We-Will-Reach-Sanctuary said. "Orcs and humans are the most common of Vhodan's followers. You may pass as well, though goblins are a rare find in these lands. Dwarves are killed on sight, and as for myself... well, you can guess that wouldn't go well."

"What about the monster?" Ironja gestured into the shadows. "We can't just leave it here."

"It is only an animal," Garr replied with a forlorn voice. "It has done no wrong."

He began to walk away, following another tunnel. Mizt-Ied said, "Well I guess we follow him?"

Follow him they all did, and after several minutes light began to shine through the cave system. They followed it to the exit, though there was little joy to be found in freedom. At the mouth of the cave rested Jermaind's body, bloody and broken, tossed between the stalagmites. Everyone drew deathly silent at the sight, but it was only Garr who approached.

He fell to his knees beside Jermaind and said only, "I will join you later. Go."

"Garr, we're here for you," Mizt-Ied said.

"I told you to go," Garr replied. "Let me mourn alone."

She exchanged a look with Ironja then said, "Okay. Find us when you're ready. We can't do this without you."

Before they took their leave, Garr drew We-Will-Reach-Sanctuary's dagger and tossed it into the dirt beside Zetine. He said, "Take this. I have no need of it anymore..."

Mizt-Ied picked the dagger up and said only, "I will."

They left the ranger at the cave, following We-Will-Reach-Sanctuary as he led them to Imperial civilization. Each of them would turn and look, hoping Garr had begun to follow, but each time they saw nothing. Once Garr was sure they were too far to notice, he pressed his face into Jermaind's fur and began to weep. He held the corpse of his friend tight and cried for longer than he had ever cried.

***

The sun was beginning to set over the village, casting long and dark shadows, as Kira and Vrias scaled one of the log walls that sealed the village off from the outside world. They were careful not to be seen by any of the guards by the entrance, or from the few peasants that had taken leave of the village to return to their homes in the wilds. Kira had scaled the wall quickly and efficiently, while Vrias struggled behind him.

After several moments of landing on his feet, Kira was accompanied by Vrias who fell onto his hands and knees behind the warrior with a quiet thud. Kira offered a hand to Vrias, who gratefully took it and was hoisted back up to his feet. The wizard then hurriedly looked around himself, before pulling a tome out from beneath his purple robes. He let out a sigh of relief at the sight, and held the book tight against his chest.

Kira watched him for a minute then said, "It's just a book."

"Yes but it's *my* book," Vrias retorted. "I've cared for it some fifty odd years, and I'll be damned if I lose it now."

"Whatever," Kira grunted as he turned around, tuning his ears to the faint sound of a hammer clanging against steel. "Come on. The blacksmith's still working. I don't imagine he'll be out much longer."

"You go see him on your own," Vrias replied. "I haven't eaten a proper meal in two whole weeks, there's no way I'm passing up a chance to grab a bite of whatever they serve at the tavern."

"Probably flour soup," Kira stated.

"Still better than foraged roots," Vrias pettily stated as he sauntered off.

Kira let out a sigh then went his own way for the time, zoning in on the sounds of the forge. He passed by a cluster of teenage girls on their way home for the night, and then ducked behind a house as a pair of guards walked down the street. Once they had rounded a corner, Kira moved back onto the street and continued his walk. There was no one else to see him that night, save for an old crone who watched him from her window.

The forge rose into view, a beautiful building of slate and iron. A muscular human with a large belly and thick red beard tended it, putting the finishing touches to a longsword. As Kira approached, the blacksmith slid the sword into a bucket of black oil, which proceeded to hiss as it cooled the molten blade. Only then did the blacksmith indicate he noticed Kira, looking up with a disinterested scowl.

"Whaddu you want," he slurred, and even from where Kira stood some ten feet off he could smell the stench of alcohol on the man's breath.

"We should talk inside," Kira stated. "I have need of your services."

"Shop's closin," he replied as he pulled the sword back out of the oil.

"It's urgent," Kira pressed. "And it won't take more than a few moments."

The blacksmith let out a strained groan then said, "Alrigh... come on in then. Wipe your boot on the mat."

Kira followed him into the store, and while he did look down to wipe his boot, he found there was no mat on either side of the door. Inside, the walls were decorated with all manner of weapons. Some three dozen swords of five different designs, spears, halberds, maces and warhammers. Some of the weapons were of much better quality than others, and Kira took a wild guess that the current blackmith had inherited the forge from someone else.

The man leaned against a counter and asked, "So what do ya want then?"

Kira pulled the sleeves of his brown robes back, revealing the chains wrapped around his arms. He said, "There's another set on my legs. I want you to take them off of me."

The blacksmith looked over him carefully then asked, "Are you a slave, elf?"

"I'll pay in gold," was all Kira said.

Kira watched as the blacksmith moved behind the counter, where he produced a tool similar to a pair of tongs. The tool ended in sharp prongs that resembled some cruel torture device, which Kira nearly winced at. The man moved back towards the elf, before roughly grabbing Kira's arm so he could slide the bit beneath his manacle. He squeezed down, and a small part of the metal was torn open. He repeated this process several times before Kira was able to slide his arm free from the manacle, only to suffer through the next three limbs.

It was an agonizing sludge of anxiety for the next five minutes, until at last Kira was freed from the last reminders of his enslavement. He flexed his fingers and toes in relief, then quickly began to massage his raw wrists. It took him a moment to even remember the blacksmith was there. Only then did he produce a small bag of coins from beneath his robes. He tossed it to the man, before pulling his robes back down over his limbs.

Kira said, "I'll be going now."

"You best," the blacksmith replied. "I'll be reportin' you to the guard after ya leave."

The elf sighed at that and said, "I really wish you hadn't told me that."

The blacksmith leapt for a spear to his left, but the next thing he knew he was sprawled out atop his back. Kira strode forward before placing his hand on the hilt of his broadsword looming ominously over the man's field of vision. He pulled his eyes downward past the elf's hands, down the blade, to the point that rested in his chest. The blacksmith attempted to scream then, but no air filled his lungs. Blood began to sputter from his lips as he gasped uselessly, until Kira pulled his sword free and ended the man's suffering with another quick strike.

Kira then began to move around the shop, taking careful inventory of anything he found useful. There was one particular sword Kira was drawn to, but he found it massive, thick, and far too heavy to wield. So he left it and moved on to look over more practical weapons, before another thought entered his mind. There were a few mannequins wearing armor that looked to be in good shape, and Kira would need protection for any more fights he found himself in.

Kira stripped himself of all his clothes, then redressed quickly in a red outfit that had been kept in a locked display case he smashed open. Moving onwards, he pulled only the most essential pieces of armor from a mannequin so that he wouldn't be slowed down. Then he found two new broadswords that he sheathed at either hip, and a bandolier of throwing knives just in case. Finally, Kira pulled a crimson red cowl and cape over his shoulders, and set off into the night.

He found Vrias reading his book in the tavern, which was mostly cleared out of people, save for a few soldiers eating their evening meal. Kira sat down next to his companion and said, "It's done."

Vrias replied, "That was nice of the blacksmith. Did you tip him?"

Kira informed him, "He was going to rat me out, and moved for a weapon. I killed him."

"Oh, that's less nice," Vrias softly said.

"How was your meal?" Kira asked.

"Impressively passable," the wizard said. "They had small bits of fruit mixed in with porridge and milk. I would have killed for a piece of meat, but unfortunately they just didn't have any."

"How tragic," Kira chuckled. It felt nice to hear such minor problems, yet oddly haunting to him.

Vrias then said, "I also heard some of the local militia talking. They've heard rumors that there's a group of people moving across the country to kill Emperor Vhodan. What's more, an entire army is going to meet them at his castle during the next eclipse."

Kira's face went white and he asked, "When is the eclipse?"

Vrias grinned then falsely said, "Next month. I've studied the stars, and it is exactly one month and thirteen days from today."

Kira shuddered as he thought of the battle it would take to claim the fortress then asked, "What do you want to do about it?"

Vrias was quiet for a moment then answered, "I've thought about it. Kira, I know you want to run away, but I don't want to leave my home. I would like to join these people, whoever they are, and reclaim this land from the evil that has corrupted it. Maybe with our help, they'll stand a better chance. Maybe not, either, but we have to try! Together with them, we could see that Valael knows peace once again."

Kira took in all of his words then said, "Alright. If that's what you want. A month from now, we will meet these Empire killers and join them."

Vrias smiled and placed his hand upon Kira's. He said, "We're going to make history."

Chapter 13

Sanctuary was a miserable place filled with dread. Though it was surrounded by fields of wild flowers, which themselves were surrounded by pleasant farmlands, Sanctuary was anything but. It was an open wall prison, where freshly gathered slaves were kept tied to posts and barely fed. Patrolled by three dozen guards and a warden at any given time, the slaves were frequently beaten or assaulted without warning. Many of the weaker ones would die, and their bodies were flung into a mass grave that was perpetually being expanded upon. The only two buildings in the whole prison were the barracks and the warden's home, a quaint little cottage that mocked the misfortune of the prisoners.

Savia gazed upon the place from a distance, and then closed her eyes. From the sky she peered down at the hundred or so slaves already imprisoned there. She could see a handful of guards playing cards at a table under the shade of the barracks, while various others threw darts or picked on the slaves. She blinked, and her eyesight was restored to normal.

The brigadier-colonel turned back to her troops and said, "Alright men, you are all well aware of the drill. You will assist the guards in tying down the prisoners and making sure they're secure. Once completed, you have half a day to recuperate. Eat, drink, sleep, fuck, I don't care. Just be ready to march by evening."

"Sir yes sir!" Came the chorus of confirmations.

"Good boys and girls" she cooed. "Now get to it."

The soldiers began to flow past her, forming two neat lines as the wagons followed. She watched as the barbarian slaves, and a few other poor souls they had abducted during their travels, barely managed to stay on their blistered and bloody feet. It was a tad unusual to see just how many women were included amidst these slaves, for typically men made up the brunt of the work force. Still, she had no sympathy in her icen heart to give them.

Once all had passed her, Savia strolled forward with her battle cat in tow and eventually met the assembly. Having taken note of them, the warden had gathered up his guards and gotten them as presentable as possible in the short time they had. The guards' armor was barely secured, even missing in some cases, and they stood awkwardly as they waited to be addressed.

The warden himself was nothing impressive. A short human man in his late 40's. He had graying hair and a thick beard, with even thicker sideburns. He held a wicked and malicious look in his eyes, and strode about as though he was far more important than he was. The little man even had the audacity to wear his old commander's uniform, with faded blue fabric and a medal of service pinned over his heart.

"Warden Deitrus, I presume," Savia said as she parted her own troops.

"And whom may I be speaking to?" The warden asked, a certain air of pompousness in his voice.

"I am brigadier colonel Tracker, standing officer of these troops, and as of this moment, your little prison."

"I know how this works," Deitrus grunted. "How many more mouths do I have to feed?"

"Do the farmers not supply you with enough to keep your cattle fed?" She asked with a raised eyebrow, but no judgment in her voice.

"They do," he admitted. "A waste though, if you ask me. These lot aren't fit for anything more than flour soup."

"Perhaps, but you have a duty to see them properly maintained for the Empire," Savia replied.

"You did not answer my question," he growled at her.

Savia looked down at him for a moment then answered, "Seventy-three. They will be exchanged for your current stock, who are all bound for Imperial Heart. How many do you have, warden?"

"Surviving?" He asked with a grin. "Thirty-six, provided the ditch crawlers haven't passed on."

"Ditch crawlers?" She inquired.

"A sanctuary slang term," he explained. "Some of the prisoners fail to have their spirits broken by traditional means. We send these ones to work the ditch, day in and day out. We toss our leftovers in there for them of course. When we remember. And they always have their fellow slaves to eat, if they're really hungry..."

"You're referring to the mass grave?" She asked, finally disturbed by his actions.

"If that's what you want to call it," he nodded. "It's just the ditch to us. A place for garbage."

"Show me to these two prisoners," Savia ordered.

The warden complied, leading her through the sanctuary. They passed by the nearly three dozen slaves who wore chains around their throats that connected them to concrete blocks in the ground, along with the six guards who had stayed to watch over them. Savia looked over the barracks with a look that showed she was unimpressed, though her head tilted at the sight of the warden's home.

"Only thirty-six slaves?" She asked.

"Oh yes," he replied. "We weed out the weak wonderfully. The Emperor needs strong workers, after all."

"And I won't find any more squirreled away in your home?"

The warden stopped at that then said, "I have my own personal slaves that attend to my need. They are mine, not the Empire's."

"You forget that the Empire owns everything, yourself included," she said with a satisfied smile. "But do not fret, warden. I have no need of your concubines, and I doubt our glorious Rizzen Emperor has a care in the world what you stick your arrowhead in."

Deitrus blushed then continued, leading Savia to the ditch. It stretched some fifteen feet down, and much of it was filled with corpses in various states of decay. Some parts of the ditch, mostly those closer to the center of the camp, were filled nearly to the top. Others barely had so much as a skull strewn about. It soon became apparent though that the ditch carried on for longer than Savia first realized, as they spent several minutes walking along its ridge.

Eventually they reached the end, though it wouldn't be the end for much longer. Below were two figures working tirelessly, scraping dirt away with their bare hands. They would then walk to one of two iron tubs connected to a pulley system and dump the dirt into them, before returning to their task. Apple cores and depleted corn cobs littered the ground around the pair, though it was clear they had even eaten some of them in their desperation for food.

One of the two slaves was an orc, who Savia imagined had once been a burly and impressive sight. Now he was thin and wiry, just muscular enough to get the job done, and solely in his arms. One of his tusks had been broken off, which Savia remembered was one of the greatest dishonors in most orcish cultures.

The other was a dwarf, with pale skin and black hair. He was slender, nauseatingly so, and his beard had been shaved down completely. While it had partially grown back, it was nowhere near what it should have been. The dwarf was covered in runic tattoos that littered nearly his entire body, even the sides of his head.

"What do the tattoos mean?" Savia asked Deitrus.

He replied, "I have no idea. He was an Oshack legionary, once upon a time. I imagine that may have something to do with it. Or perhaps it's some foreign hill dwarf custom. You know how the dwarves love their little rituals."

"Of course," Savia nodded. "Get them out of here, they're coming with us."

"They're never going to serve the Empire," Deitrus said.

"Then they can act as target practice for new recruits," she replied. "Just get them out of here."

"I'll send some men to pull them out," he said.

"I don't care, just get it done," Savia stated coldly.

The battle cat by her side suddenly snarled, causing Deitrus to squeak out, "Is that thing safe to have out here without a leash?"

Savia replied, "Daisy here wouldn't hurt a fly, unless I told her to," before walking away.

After she had moved a comfortable distance away, Detritus mumbled, "Whores and their beasts..." then he mockingly called to the slaves down below, "Hear that men? Looks like you get to join the Empire after all!"

Savia suddenly stopped, which caught Deitrus' attention. Though he couldn't see, her eyes had gone entirely white. He jogged up to her and asked, "What's wrong?"

"We're being watched," she simply stated.

"Probably just some farmers," he replied. "The local kids sometimes come and try to sneak food to the slaves."

"It is neither farmers nor children," Savia stated. "There are two warriors with their backs to the mountain approaching the sanctuary."

"Just two people?" The warden chuckled. "What can two people possibly do?"

"Enough," she said before she bolted into a sprint. Deitrus had no idea whether she meant enough damage, or if she tired of his words.

***

Wolf asked, "What is it?"

"A slave camp, from the look of it," Kazaa grimly replied. "It seems as though they've just brought in a new procession."

Wolf looked to where he pointed and strained her eyes as she analyzed everything in sight. Then she said, "We should do something."

"We should," he agreed. "But we are merely two people, and they must have fifty soldiers there at least."

"So we let them suffer?" Wolf asked.

"It's our only choice," he replied. When he looked over to see why she wasn't responding, Kazaa found his companion already heading down to the slave camp.

Wolf easily cleared the distance from their little ridge to a boulder at a lower elevation, still overlooking the camp, but with only about seventy yards from the procession. She drew her bow and notched an arrow, before leaning out from the cover. In the distance, Wolf could hear someone yelling something that was causing the soldiers to abruptly move, but couldn't make out what it was. She took aim and let loose an arrow, hitting one of them in the head.

She quickly notched another arrow and sent it flying, hitting a running soldier in his chest. The arrow didn't kill him, but she was already onto her next target. This arrow hit a soldier in the side, and he wouldn't be getting up again. As she notched her fourth arrow, a retaliatory strike embedded in the boulder close to Wolf's head. She looked to the arrow in shock for a moment, then returned her focus to her enemies.

She sent the fourth arrow into the chest of one of the unarmed guards, but by the time the arrow had landed, Wolf was entangled in vines. They grew rapidly from the arrow shaft in the boulder, wrapping around Wolf's body and binding her tight. She could not step away, and her right arm was being pulled towards the boulder.

Wolf struggled to free her knife with her left arm, but soon that too was captured by the growing plant.

Then Kazaa was there, slicing through the tendrils with his khopesh. Green fluid spilled from the severed vines, but he paid it no mind. Before the plant could resume its attack, Kazaa sliced the arrow in half, and the spell ended. Even the plants that had still been gripping Wolf died instantaneously, turning black and lifeless as they fell away.

"What was that?" Wolf asked, peeling dead plant off of her right arm.

"Elemental arrow," Kazaa replied. "They must have a ranger with them."

"A ranger?" Wolf looked back over at the gathered soldiers and guards, most of whom were hiding behind the carriages and barracks as they waited for a dozen shield carrying soldiers to bridge the distance, while two squads followed them for support.

"In tune with nature, almost universally use bows," he explained. "But more importantly, we have that whole army over there coming after us!"

"We can take them," was all Wolf replied as she readied another arrow.

"You are insane, woodsgirl," he groaned.

"You take these ones, I'll clear a path," she said almost like she had an actual plan.

"You're still not healed!" Kazaa hissed, but she was already gone.

Wolf ran forward and leapt, her momentum carrying her over the head of one of the soldiers who failed to strike her with a spear. She notched arrows as quickly as she could while she ran, letting them loose at whatever soldiers ran at her. She made it halfway before an arrow slices through her left shoulder, delivering a powerful electric shock that forced Wolf to the ground.

She gasped for air, smoke rising from the singed hairs on her arm, as the soldiers began to surround her. Wolf drew her knife and lashed out, stabbing into an ankle. She pulled a woman to the ground and slit her throat before rising to her feet, striking out randomly. This set the six nearby soldiers into defensive postures, but it quickly dawned on them that Wolf would be easy prey. Or so they thought.

As Wolf fought her own battle, Kazaa faced down the dozen shield carrying soldiers who had gone to meet him. He acted quickly, for he knew how dangerous a phalanx could be, and threw his dagger into the face of one of them. He ran forward, sheathing his khopesh, and then claimed the fallen man's spear and shield as his own. The closest soldier stabbed at him but Kazaa blocked the attack, and then retaliated with a sweep of his spear that knocked the soldier to the ground.

He thrust the blade into the man's throat then said, "Well? What are the rest of you waiting for?"

Wolf pushed through the crowd; her blade soaked with blood, and knocked two soldiers onto the ground. Finally her gaze rested upon the ranger, who Wolf was angered to see was a woman and not the man she believed to be her rival. The ranger notched an arrow, to which Wolf retaliated by throwing her knife.

A soldier swung her bastard sword at Wolf, another took aim with a crossbow, and one rushed to tackle her. The blade of Wolf's knife connected with the arrowhead and there was a fiery explosion that ripped through the area, knocking Wolf and her surrounding enemies to the ground, along with the ranger herself.

As Wolf pushed herself up, her bandages growing red, she watched as a flaming guard ran by screaming. She reached for an arrow and grimaced as she felt her last one in the quiver, then notched it. A soldier stumbled for her, raising his bastard sword in the air, but Wolf simply shot him in the throat. She ripped the arrow out, and then continued to march forward.

Behind her, the slaves who had been tied to the carriages saw their moment. Many of them wrapped their ropes around the throats of the soldiers who had taken them from their homes, while a few others beat them with their fists. As those first few soldiers died, the slaves claimed their weapons as their own, and freed their fellow slaves from their bonds. Then together they brought the fight to the soldiers who had hidden amongst their ranks, unleashing bloody vengeance.

Kazaa panted with exertion as he ripped his spear free from the abdomen of a soldier, and then looked over at the last one standing. Kazaa wagered that he was no more than nineteen, and was clearly scared out of his mind. So the mercenary put a foot forward, held his shield straight and his spear aloft as he stared into the boy's eyes. It was enough to make the boy piss his pants, though Kazaa had no way to know that.

"Get out of here, boy," Kazaa ordered. "Leave this place behind or I'll impale you like your friends."

The boy cast his eyes over the nearby corpses, and then threw down his weapons. He turned and booked it, stumbling over himself. Kazaa watched him go, making sure the boy wouldn't have a change of heart mid-flee. Once satisfied, he turned back towards sanctuary, and his breath caught in his throat. The flames that had encompassed the barracks were magnificent and horrifying. Without wasting any more time, Kazaa hurried to rejoin Wolf.

The barbarian was flung back by a gust of wind created by an arrow at her feet, but it didn't stop her. She stalked forward like a thing possessed, not that she knew she was, and refused to be felled. Her foot landed upon the head of a soldier who had been attempting to crawl away, crushing it into the scorched earth.

She raised her bow, but before she could notch her last arrow, the ranger fired upon her.

The enchanted arrow tore through the air, and then sliced through Wolf's bow, her arrow, and even the drawstring, before lodging in her sternum. Wolf grasped at the air, coughing from the force of the blow, before ripping it from her chest with a squirt of blood. She roared in anger and pain, then pushed herself to move as fast as she could forward.

The ranger notched another arrow, aimed low, and then fired. Wolf attempted to leap to the right, but it did little good. The arrow sliced the bandage on her left foot, and then embedded in the ground behind her. In half a second it had exploded into a blizzard, sending thick torrents of snow flowing through the immediate area. Wolf was consumed by the snow almost instantly, though the ranger found herself partially buried as well.

Savia pulled her legs free and stumbled back, before quickly shifting into a bird's eye view. Her eyes snapped back open a second later and she fixated upon the slave carts in the distance, and how they had freed themselves and attacked their guards. Instead of worrying about it herself, Savia willed her battle cat to attack the slaves as nonlethal a way as possible. She notched another arrow and was about to fire when a tan arm sprung up from beneath the snow. Its hand landed flat, and then began to push down until a head of raven black hair appeared from beneath the wintery grave.

"Can't you just DIE!?" Savia asked in frustration, loosening the arrow. "I mean, seriously lady! I shot you! Have the common decency to just keel over already!"

"Kill you," Wolf growled as she freed her other arm, still clutching Savia's arrow.

"What was that, savage?" She asked.

"Kill you," Wolf growled again as she crawled out from the snow bank.

"Adorable," Savia chuckled a dry and hate filled laugh, before notching her arrow again. "Enjoy hell."

A bird caw suddenly caught her attention, leaving Savia to ask "What!?" In surprise.

She closed her eyes to gain the bird's sight; only to open them again as Kazaa grabbed her arms from behind. He forced them up, causing Savia to release her grip on the bowstring, sending the arrow high into the sky. She struggled with Kazaa for a moment before pushing him away, then drew a knife. He reached for his own dagger, before remembering he had failed to retrieve it after the start of the conflict. As he drew his khopesh, Saia sliced his chest open and delivered a punch to his jaw.

Kazaa retaliated with a sweep of his blade, but the ranger easily danced out of the way. As he went in for a thrust she parried his sword away, but then Wolf tackled her to the ground. The pair of them rolled down a snow hill, leaving Kazaa behind as they exchanged punches. They landed with Savia on top, and she delighted in delivering a series of punches to Wolf's face. Wolf then grabbed her by the shoulders and rolled over positioning her on top to strangle the ranger with her left hand.

As Wolf raised her right hand into the air to strike the arrowhead down into Savia's heart, the misfired arrow landed beside their heads. The both of them looked to it in shock, and for the split second before it activated, they both had the same thought. Savia barely managed to kick Wolf off of her as snow erupted from the arrow and scrambled away, but in moments the both of them were completely buried.

A pale hand broke through the snow, accompanied by a second. Then a head full of straw colored hair rose up, and Savia gasped for air. She slowly began to pull herself free from the snow, straining from the effort. Sensing her master was in trouble, Daisy the battle cat released its grip upon the arm of the slave it was attacking and hurried to help Savia. Then Wolf burst up behind the ranger and roared like the barbarian she was. Savia looked over her shoulder in terror, and then attempted to escape her cold prison.

"Why won't you die!?" She cried in vain.

Wolf pulled herself free and tried to stand, but quickly fell back onto the snow. Instead she began to crawl forward, determined to finish Savia off. When the ranger freed her last leg she thought she had escaped, but then Wolf stabbed her through the ankle. She grabbed Savia by the foot and pulled her close as she ripped the arrow out, before driving it into her ribs. Again and again Wolf stabbed her as the ranger screamed in pain, until at last the arrowhead broke off inside of her.

Then there was Daisy, landing harshly upon Wolf's back. The cat dug its claws deep into her, and then bit down onto her shoulder. Wolf struck blindly at the beast, punching it only three times while the rest of her blows missed as it continued to bite at her arm. Then Wolf took hold of the fang around her neck, tore it free, and stabbed into where she expected the cat's face to be. She hit it in the throat, and then dragged the tooth to the side, spilling the animal's blood over both her and Savia.

Wolf rolled Savia onto her back, and the woman looked up at her with tears in her eyes. In a ragged voice she pleaded, "Please... let me go... I don't deserve this," then she saw the corpse of her beloved companion. She croaked out, "Daisy! No! No... please, no..."

The barbarian said nothing. She only growled softly as she clamped her hands tight around Savia's throat and began to squeeze. The ranger struggled as her face turned red, grasping and clawing at Wolf's hands. Then as her face began to turn blue her movements slowed, until she fell motionless. As the woman's eyes rolled to the back of her head, Wolf continued to choke, feeling the pulse leave her body. After several more seconds she finally let go, and then fell over.

***

There was only white. As Wolf opened her eyes, it seemed as the snow had swallowed up absolutely everything. She still lay next to Savia's body, and her blood left a scarlet stain beneath her, but that was all. There were no trees, no distant fields or mountain, no Kazaa. There was only the snow, which strangely seemed to fall from above like the natural snow in The Southern Reach. It was almost nostalgic for Wolf, but accompanied by deep sorrow.

She sat up and took another looked around, this time finding another person several yards away. This person was dressed in a hooded black cloak, but seemed to be a woman from the way it clung to their curves. Even without seeing the person's face, Wolf was strangely attracted to this person. Something about them drew in all of her fascination.

"Who are you?" Wolf croaked, and her voice was not her own.

"You already know who, girl," said a voice from Wolf's side.

She looked to her left and saw a near mirror reflection. However, this reflection of herself possessed glowing green eyes. It also did not move in the same way as her, and took cumbersome breaths through her mouth. It was in that moment that Wolf realized neither her nor her reflection's breath seemed to be creating any fog.

The figure said in a voice so beautiful that Wolf wept, "She does not know, Velena. Not that it matters. Death rarely matters."

"Velena?" Wolf asked, looking to her reflection. "You are not me..."

"No," said the figure. "She merely hides in your body like a parasite. Shall I free her from you?"

"NO! Not yet!" Velena pleaded. "We're so close! Don't take me now!"

"But you are dead," the figure simply stated.

Then it turned, and Wolf wished for nothing more than to be able to scream in terror. Half of its face was truly beautiful, with a radiant blue eye and soft pale skin. But then the other half was bloated and yellow, its left eye missing entirely. The figures chest was exposed, and Wolf could see it was littered with maggots and spiders that feasted upon rotting flesh. But then there was no rot, and its body was divine, save for the stark white skull upon its shoulders.

"All things die," it said in that same beautiful voice. "You just need to let go."

Wolf looked to her reflection then asked, "You want to kill her?"

"Nothing so evil," the figure said. "Man kills. I merely take."

Wolf looked between the two of them them then asked, "Why do you have to take her now? Whatever she is, you didn't do it before."

"Because you are so close to the end, child," the figure whispered from Savia's lips. "You can give it all up now. There is nothing easier than simply giving up."

"I am never abandoning my quest," Wolf growled. "No matter what enemy or monster stands before me, I will have my revenge!" Though she said the words with all her heart, she waivered ever so slightly at the end.

The figure cackled, and turned as its arms became bone. It took a step forward, and then turned its head. It said, "Remember, child. In the end, Death always gets its due. Nothing more. Nothing less. There is no subverting destiny, because there is no destiny. There is only The End."

Then it was gone, leaving Wolf alone to speak with her reflection. She could only ask, "What did she mean?"

"You will find out at the end of your journey," Velena promised.

"Fuck you," Wolf growled. "Tell me what you are."

The reflection flinched then meekly answered, "A friend you thought long gone. I have been there since the start of your journey, and I will be there until it ends, watching over you the entire way."

"Do you mean... you're-" before Wolf could articulate her thoughts, there came a gentle neighing.

She looked in surprise to see a magnificent thin white horse standing hear her. It silently drew its front hoof across the snow a few times as though to tell them it was impatient. The horse's wispy white beard reminded Wolf of a goat, but the most eye catching part of it was the sharp horn upon its forehead. Though she could not truly appreciate the myth standing before her, Wolf was stunned none the less.

"What are you doing here?" She asked.

The unicorn did not respond, because a horse is a horse. But it rolled its eyes and waited. Wolf looked back to Velena, but she had vanished. She looked to her right, and Savia had vanished as well. Wolf struggled to her feet, and then gently stroked her fingers across the unicorn's side. Seeing that it was passive, she cautiously climbed up onto the beast's back.

The unicorn slowly galloped forward, carrying Wolf away from the strange land. Wolf's consciousness quickly began to fade, the galloping strangely lulling her to sleep. No matter how hard she resisted the siren's call, there was no fading it. The endless sea of white was replaced with black, and Wolf fell into a deep slumber.

Chapter 14

Jubilatious walked side by side with Mizt-Ied, though he didn't slow his pace for her. She had to nearly jog just to keep up with him, but took it in stride. Despite how horrible everything was, she couldn't help but admire the beauty of Syronul. Vhodan had ruined the beauty of every other place he touched, whether it was uprooting trees, burning the fields, or poisoning the waters. But it seemed as though he held a soft spot for his homeland, and had spared it from the worst of his fury.

"Do you think we'll find anything cool in town?" Mizt-Ied asked nonchalantly.

"I don't know," Jubilatious replied, finding her questions deeply annoying.

"I hope there's like, an enchanted weapons merchant there!" she happily squeaked, unaware of her companion's frustration. "I mean, I know we don't want Vhodan to have any *more* magic weapons, but it would be cool to get some of our own. Like a boomerang that always returns to your hand!"

"I don't care," he flatly stated.

"Oh come on, tell me there's not something you'd want," she pried.

"Just an apothecary," he said.

She crossed her arms and then asked, "There isn't a single thing in the whole wide world you'd want to find?"

"No," came the simple answer.

"Come on Jubilatious," she pleaded with him. "We're so far from normal lands, there's no telling what kind of crazy treasures we might find here!"

"You forget I was raised here," he shot back quietly.

"Oh, right..." she ruminated on that for a moment. "Still, wouldn't that mean you know what's here better than anyone? And I mean, you *are* a wizard. I bet you've seen, like, a statue that turns you into a dragon, or a staff that makes you have crazy eyebrows."

Jubilatious spun on her and shouted, "Do you EVER shut up!?"

"I- what- wh... what?" she stammered, suddenly terrified of the human that towered over her.

"Zetine could die!" he hissed. "Yet you sit here prattling off about toys! You never just shut the hell up and let anyone think!"

"It's- it's n-not like t-that," Mizt-Ied whimpered.

"Like what?" he asked with a sneer. "You can't take anything seriously! All of our lives are at stake- this whole gods damned country is at stake! Yet from day one you've talked your head off about things that didn't matter! Just... shut up. Let me think, and keep your mouth shut until the moment calls for it.

The goblin looked up at him with big wet eyes and whimpered out, "I'm sor-sorry."

Jubilatious sighed and said, "Forget it. Let's just get this over with, and hopefully, things don't take a turn for the worse.

The rest of their trip was done in silence, awkward and uncomfortable, but silence none the less. Mizt-Ied desperately tried to distract herself by focusing on the scenery, but that was tainted now too. As hurtful as Jubilatious' words had been, they stung true. As beautiful as Syronul was, it was a place of evil and tyranny. A living symbol of what had been ripped away from several other regions. Then on top of that, even this land was plagued by monsters to keep the population passive.

When they eventually arrived at the town, it was no great thing, though nothing to scoff at either. A few hundred buildings had been constructed, while the perimeter was surrounded by log walls. A few other buildings were situated outside of the walls, such as two guard towers, a stable, and what looked like a simple little hut. There was a dozen guards situated by the front entrance, which was about a dozen too many for Jubilatious to like.

"Do you think we should sneak in?" Mizt-Ied suddenly asked him.

He looked down at her and she flinched, but he only said, "I don't think it will be necessary. Though we should change our clothes somewhat."

"I don't have any spares, do you?" she asked.

"None at all, but I have a scarf," he answered.

"What good's that gonna do?" she further questioned.

He elaborated, "I can change clothing pigment, replace my hat with the scarf, and voila I look like a different wizard."

"What about me?" Mizt-Ied demanded, tapping her foot.

Jubilatious suppressed a laugh and said, "If you pretend to be my servant, they won't even look at you."

"That's horrible," she pouted.

"That's the business," he replied. "Wizards are assholes."

When they approached the town gate, Mizt-Ied hefted the both of their bags and had hidden her knives, but otherwise looked the same. She only made sure to look at the ground and did her best to stay quiet. Jubilatious had removed his hat and wrapped a long scarf around his head, concealing everything save for his piercing blue eyes. Both the scarf and his robes were now scarlet red, giving him the appearance of a pyromancer, or more colloquially, a red mage. It also had the added benefit of making him far more intimidating than he would have been otherwise, especially in his normal purple.

One of the guards closer to the gate stopped them and asked, "What's your business in South Daggerspark?"

Jubilatious gave the guard what was his best intimidating glare and answered, "Travel supplies on my return to Arkvine. Now get out of my way, I have shopping to do."

"Yes, my excellence," the guard bowed and stepped away.

After the duo had gone some distance into the bustling little town, Mizt-Ied quietly asked, "What was that about? Your excellence, I mean?"

"Wizards are practically royalty in the empire," he replied just as quietly. "We're Vhodan's most powerful resource, so we tend to enjoy a much finer quality of living than everyone else."

"Wow," Mizt-Ied gulped. "I would have loved to have been born a wizard, huh?"

"Absolutely," Jubilatious agreed. "Now... how are your thievery skills?"

"I'm offended you ask," she replied.

"That good?" he asked.

"That good," she moped.

"Go steal us some money then," he ordered. "We need to be able to buy those potions after all."

"On it," Mizt-Ied chimed before scurrying off.

Long before Mizt-Ied had ever taken on the responsibilities of being a hero, she had been a thief. As any thief would tell you, there are only two types of pickpockets. The good ones and the dead ones. But to say Mizt-Ied was good was an understatement. She had mastered the art in childhood, and since then only grew more talented. The shadows of alleyways were a cloak, the bustle of crowds a smoke screen. There was nothing save for the clothes on your back that Mizt-Ied couldn't get to, and even then she could still pull a cape or a hat off someone before they realized anything was amiss.

Under Jubilatious' instructions, Mizt-Ied peeled away and set to work. She moved into a crowd of human women who seemed to be coming back from the market, for each of them carried a basket full of produce. She took a potato, a bulb of garlic, an onion, and two plums, along with five small pouches of coins without any of them noticing she was even there. Mizt-ied pocketed the treasures and moved on, passing through an alley to reach an orc who had fallen asleep outside of a tavern. She pulled his heavy coin purse from his waist, then considered for a moment. She decided to enter the tavern.

The place was fairly rundown, the ceiling sloping inwards after one too many rainstorms. The candles were in various stages of melting, and the various stains on the walls and floor told her that the place was prone to bar fights. The tavern wasn't particularly large at all, but there were over two dozen humans, orcs, and dark elves spread about talking. Behind the bar were an older human and a younger woman, each with brown hair and brown eyes. Mizt-Ied wagered they were father and daughter, and made sure to stay out of their sight as she crept about.

It was remarkably easy to steal from a drunk, though every now and then one was far more alert than they had any reason to be. As Mizt-Ied crept about, her ears twitched at every slight sound made throughout the entire establishment. From the pouring of drinks to the rambunctious laughter, she heard it all. Unsurprisingly, these drunks didn't have too many coins on them, and she'd wager all of their money that they each owed a hefty debt to the tavern keeper. Still, money was money.

As she passed by, Mizt-Ied overheard a conversation between a human man and a dark elf. The human was saying, "I'm telling you, I heard the report just before I was cycled out of rotation. There's an invading army from the West, set to take on the capital. Supposedly we've got someone else coming from the south, too."

"I can't move again," the elf shook her head. "I've lost too much already... what happens if they get to Daggerspark?"

"I don't know," the man shrugged. "The Emperor wants to pull back most of the army to guard the capital. I don't know if anyone will even be left to protect the town in a couple'a weeks."

Mizt-Ied took her leave after hearing that, and hurriedly crept out the door. As she did so, she thought she spotted the tavern owner's daughter looking at her, but she couldn't be sure. She hurried back to where she left Jubilatious, but found something much more interesting along the way. Plastered against the wall of a general goods store were wanted posters for a number of criminals wanted by the empire.

Amongst the crudely drawn illustrations were an elf named Kira who seemed to be some sort of vigilante, a goblin named Crued-Shake who had stabbed a captain, a weirdly handsome human pirate named Torrent, and her friends. Each of them was horribly rendered, which Mizt-Ied found humorous. Her drawing had massive teeth and pupiless eyes, while Zetine's depicted her like a half-naked harlot. Ironja's was almost entirely beard, which wasn't exactly untrue, and Garr didn't even have a poster. Strangely enough, Jubilatious was the only one who looked exactly like himself.

Mizt-Ied peeled her eyes away from the poster as a human woman stepped up behind her. "Horrible, isn't it?" the woman asked.

"Sure is," Mizt-Ied instinctively responded. "A damn shame."

"A damn shame is right," the woman nodded. "I can't believe what's happening to our beautiful country."

"Really?" Mizt-Ied asked, masking her shock behind mild interest.

"I thought The Empire was supposed to keep us safe," the woman said, which shook Mizt-Ied down to her core. "Yet lately we've had all these brigands rampaging around. I heard that just last week, that psychopath Kira killed a poor blacksmith and his forgehands!"

"That really is horrible," Mizt-Ied nodded along.

"Then there's those lot," she gestured to the posters of Mizt-Ied's friends.

The goblin meekly asked, "What did they do?"

"From what I heard," the woman began with quite the air of confidence. "They're a pack of escaped murderers from The Emperor's dungeons. He showed them mercy by imprisoning them, and they repaid it by going on a killing spree across the countryside. All those poor people they've hurt... this is why we need to just execute all criminals. No more garbage preying on the innocent."

"Yup, you've got the right idea," she awkwardly said. "Hang 'em all, let the gods sort them out. That's what I always say."

"But our noble Emperor Vhodan is just too kind hearted," the woman sighed. "He would never allow anyone to be harmed, no matter how evil they are. I'm sure he'll just imprison these monsters again, I just hope he punishes them properly when he finally captures them."

Mizt-Ied turned around and mouthed the words, "What the fuck," as she walked away.

It took her far too long to find Jubilatious again, which drove nervous daggers deep into the goblin's heart. At first she thought that he had been arrested, or worse, that he had abandoned her. But eventually Mizt-Ied was able to find the wizard, leaning against a wall a few streets down. He was muttering a brief spell incantation under his breath and snapping his fingers, each time creating a spark. A couple of kids cheered at him from their home's window each time he did this, and Mizt-Ied had to admit it was a little cute.

"There you are, er, master," she said as she walked up to him.

"What took you so long?" Jubilatious asked before snapping his fingers to create yet another spark.

"I wanted to make sure we were well stocked," she said. "Also I uh... did some eavesdropping."

"Find out anything useful?" he asked.

Mizt-Ied looked over both her shoulders, saw only the children, so she grabbed Jubilatious by the collar and pulled him down to whisper in his ear. "These people- they don't know they're the bad guys!" she hissed.

"Well, obviously," he simply replied. Then he said, "Wind and flame, rise and spiral," then slapped his hands together to form a small burning tornado that quickly went out. The children were ecstatic at this.

"You don't get it!" she continued. "They think we're a bunch of crazed killers! And that the Army of Hope is some evil invading force! And that Vhodan is too nice to ever kill anybody!"

"Mizt-Ied," Jubilatious said, and there was something otherworldly in his voice. Mizt-Ied looked up at him as he rose to his full height, and for the first time the goblin fully grasped just how powerful the wizard could seem. "We are within the heart of the beast. All these people have ever known is their homeland, their ruler. They could not fathom the idea of being evil, because they have only been told that they are good. In fact, I'm sure they all do good deeds on a regular basis. But each and every one of them would kill for Vhodan, would eradicate entire peoples if it meant preserving their tranquility. It is does not matter for what they think, because they know they are the heroes, and we are just the monsters that want to steal their peace."

This mystified the little goblin for a few moments before she gingerly asked, "Then what can we do?"

"Nothing," he said as though it was obvious. "We cut off the serpent's head, but the body will do as the body does. Now, have you any money?"

She nodded and said, "Yeah. More than enough, I think."

"Good," Jubilatious replied, and that was that.

They then walked in silence for a few minutes until they reached a market square. Mizt-Ied found it to be quite awkward, but Jubilatious enjoyed it. The market square was bustling with activity, and the pair had to stick close by one another in fear of being separated. There were nine stalls in total, three of which sold crops, one sold jewelry, two bottled ale, one sold potions and the remaining two sold a variety of miscellaneous goods that one wouldn't find at a normal store. Of those latter two, Jubilatious could see that one sold enchanted garbage. Though it was garbage, he still found himself enthralled.

"Where are you going?" Mizt-Ied asked him as he got into the small queue for the trinket stall.

"I'll only be a minute," he replied. "I want to see what they have."

"But! Potion!" she squealed after him, but none the less followed.

"Hand me a few coins, will you?" Jubilatious asked.

Begrudgingly, Mizt-Ied pulled one of the smaller coin pouches out from her pocket. As she passed it to him she sternly said, "Here, take it."

"Thank you, servant," he replied. "Now go buy us some potions with the rest of the money."

"As you command, oh great master," Mizt-Ied rolled her eyes then went into the other, considerably longer line.

Once Jubilatious reached the front of the line, he could see the stall's owner was a dark skinned woman in her mid thirties. She dressed in a commoner's garb, with her hair braided tight against her head. Spread out on display were all sorts of knickknacks, mostly simple necklaces or totems, but also a few crystals and small toys. Some of them looked like she made them herself; while others were likely things she had collected. But most interestingly, each and every single item held a minor enchantment.

Jubilatious picked a small wooden figure of a knight off the stall and asked, "What is this?"

"A great toy for your son, your excellence," she beamed at him. "He's sure to love it."

"And the enchantment?" Jubilatious asked casually.

"I beg your pardon?" she said a little too quickly.

"The enchantment," he said. "To me, it looks like a luck spell, but I was never the best at enchanting. Always more of a conjurer than an artificer."

"It's a fortune spell, not a luck spell," she quietly replied.

"What's the difference?" Jubilatious asked curiously.

"Luck gives you what you want," she explained. "Fortune will keep you safe. If a boy keeps that toy on him, he won't grow up to be a soldier or sellsword. He'll find a passion for something much safer."

"I see," Jubilatious murmured, putting the doll down. He then pointed to a hammer and asked, "A blacksmith's aid?"

She shook her head and said, "Keeps the nails from rusting."

"What about this?" he asked as he lifted up a silver pendant.

"If you give it to your true love, she'll see you for who you really are," the woman smiled innocently. "It helps her get to know the real you."

"Interesting," he said. Then Jubilatious asked, "How much do you want for it?"

"Three gold," the woman quickly replied.

"You sell your wares for too little," he replied as he fished around in the pouch. "The average person would think these are just trite trinkets."

"That's the point," she said. "I don't want anyone to know how special they are. I want them to find that out on their own. Or at least experience the magic on their own."

Jubilatious placed down four gold coins, two silver coins, and ten copper pieces, the first four of which came out of his own personal stash. He said, "Keep the change."

"Thank you, your excellence," the woman smiled as she took the coins and poured them into a drawer.

When Mizt-Ied reached the front of her own line, she found a male goblin perched on top of a stool. He was older, and had a long wispy white beard that would have made him stand out from any other goblin. His ears had been clipped, causing them to somewhat resemble a human's more rounded ears, and he possessed a sharp glare that stared into the soul of anyone unfortunate enough to be looked at. Suffice to say, Mizt-Ied thought he would be a blast at parties, and she was certainly right. He was also absolutely surrounded by a plethora of potions that came in all sorts of different colors and consistencies. They hung from the frame of the stalls, were placed on racks, and lined the countertop. He also very obviously had crates more placed behind him.

The old goblin croaked out, "What do *you* want. Oh! Let me guess... stimulant potion so yeh can keep given it t' yer old lady?"

"No, I just want to buy some healing potions," Mizt-Ied casually replied.

"What are yuh? An adventurer?" he asked as he perused the selection of bottles.

"No, just health conscious," she shrugged.

"Then you'll love this!" he shouted as he handed he held a yellow potion over her head.

"What... is it?" she asked, not taking it from him.

The old goblin replied, "Poop potion. Keeps yeh regular."

"Not that kind of health conscious," she awkwardly said.

The merchant pulled the potion away and said, "Fair enough. What else can I get yeh? Strength potion? Fire potion? The kind that protects against fire, not sets yeh on it. The kind that sets yeh on it? I have one that makes everything yeh drink taste like milk."

"No thank you, I-" she paused at that last one and thought it over. Despite the vast potential for a milk potion, Mizt-Ied said, "No thank you. I just need some healing potions and that's all."

"Suit yourself," the crotchety old goblin shrugged. "Just tryin t' spark up your life."

"It's appreciated, really, but I just need the healing ones," Mizt-Ied rushed him along.

"How many do yeh want?" he asked.

"How many do ya got?" she asked right back.

"Bout a few," he replied, before jumping off his stool to approach a crate full of eight red potions. "Thirty gold for the whole thing! Whudda'you say?"

"I'll take it," Mizt-Ied eagerly replied as she began to count out the coins.

The goblin hefted the crate up and walked around the stall, before dropping it at her feet. He then said, "For an extra silver, yeh can keep the crate."

"...I don't need a crate," Mizt-Ied stated.

"Don't need a crate!?" the merchant gasped. "How are yeh gonna get these potions home!? Just bouncing along your belt!? Yer sure to break 'em that way! You need the crate to keep 'em safe!"

"Huh, good point," she murmured. Then Mizt-Ied produced another gold coin and passed thirty one pieces over to the old goblin.

After counting them all out, he placed one coin in his mouth then bit it in half. He handed one half back to Mizt-Ied and said, "Yer change!"

"You can keep it," she politely replied. "Also... one silver is not half of one gold."

"Yeh try biting a coin in half ten times at my age," the goblin crossed his arms and stated. "I damn near broke my tooth!"

"Okay geez," she replied, before hefting the crate up herself and stepping away.

When she rejoined Jubilatious, the wizard asked, "Why do you have the crate?"

"It was only a little more," she replied. "And this way the potions won't break on the way!"

"...Mizt-Ied, potion bottles are meant to withstand being dropped on stone," he informed her. "You got scammed."

She took this all in before replying, "Well you try haggling! It's hard!"

"It's hard to turn down a piece of wood?" he asked. "All you have to do is say no!"

"But he was so OOOOOLD," she protested. "What if I broke his heart so bad he DIED???"

"By saying "no" to a BOX!?" Jubilatious practically cried.

As they left, neither noticed that they were being watched. From the shadows of a nearby alleyway stood an elf, tall even amongst his race. His magnificent violet eyes studied them from beneath a red cowl that covered his face just like Jubilatious' scarf. He was also dressed in lightweight platemail and a red cape that flowed behind him as he walked. Strapped to the both of the elf's hips were scabbards holding twin broadswords, and a number of throwing knives lined the bandolier on his chest.

Once the pair had disappeared into the crowd, the elf turned and departed deeper into the ally. He found his partner around the corner, sat upon an overturned crate and reading from a musty old tome. This high elf was adorned in purple wizard's robes much like Jubilatious' own, along with a large black wizard's cap. From beneath the cap's shadow, golden eyes twinkled, and pale green hands flipped the pages.

"You were wrong about the date," the warrior stated in a husky voice that would sound completely alien on any other elf.

"Whatever do you mean?" The wizard asked without looking up.

"I just saw two of the seers' champions," the warrior said.

"Are you sure?" Came the uninterested reply.

"One of them was in disguise, but it was them," he matter of factly stated. "The wizard and the goblin. They were buying potions and charms."

"I could have sworn we had a whole other month," the wizard said as he looked up to the sky. "I swear, you can never trust the stars anymore. They lie far more than they tell the truth these days."

"Are you ready to move?" The warrior simply asked.

"Yes, yes, yes," the wizard nodded as the warrior took hold of his collar and hoisted him to his feet. "You have no patience, Kira. It's not like the castle is going anywhere."

"You don't know that," came the annoyed reply from who Mizt-Ied would recognize only as a serial killer.

"It's a castle," Vrias cackled. "It would take a hundred mages of my power just to lift it, let alone move it anywhere."

"Let's just go," Kira urged. "I am tired of waiting around this boring little outpost. I need excitement."

"You didn't get enough when you killed the blacksmith?" The wizard asked with a raised eyebrow.

"Course not," Kira retorted. "He barely put up a fight."

***

When Jubilatious and Mizt-Ied returned to camp, they found We-Will-Reach-Sanctuary and Ironja looking after Zetine who they had lain against a tree. She had still not woken, and her skin had paled. We-Will-Reach-Sanctuary strained a wet cloth over the grass before placing it upon Zetine's forehead for what little good that would do. Both he and Ironja were beyond ecstatic to see their companions had returned, baring a supply of potions.

Ironja said, "Took ye long enough! She don' look too good..."

Jubilatious took one of the potions and sat down beside Zetine. He quickly popped the cork out and held it to her lips as he said, "Here, this will make it all better. Please make it better..."

The red liquid seeped down Zetine's jaw as he poured it down her throat, hoping that all would be well. Quickly her complexion began to return, and soon after her eyes fluttered open. Zetine looked up at Jubilatious, then to the bottle between her lips. Instinctively she slapped the bottle from his hands and into the grass, before she began to wretch and heave.

"What was that!?" She asked, rubbing her tongue on the back of her hand.

"It was just a healing potion, not poison or anything," Jubilatious tried to dissuade her fears.

"Poison!?" Zetine spat. "No poison could taste that vile... ugh, I hate medicine."

"Are you really okay?" Mizt-Ied eagerly asked.

"I am..." she said before looking around. Then Zetine asked, "Where are Garr and Jermaind?"

"Jermaind," Ironja awkwardly grunted, looking for the words.

"The bear did not make it," We-Will-Reach-Sanctuary said bluntly.

"Garr said he'd meet us again, but we have no idea when that will be," Jubilatious added on.

"That poor orc..." she murmured. "How long was I out?"

"Only fer a day," Ironja reassured her.

"A whole day!?" She asked, not reassured at all.

"Don't worry, I don't think there's many dangers left," Jubilatious said.

"What do you mean?" Zetine asked.

"Jubilatious and I did some scouting!" Mizt-Ied eagerly informed them.

Jubilatious elaborated, "From what we can gather, Vhodan is withdrawing all of his forces to his castle. His subjects are being left under defended, and they're preparing to do battle with The Army of Hope."

"So we've finally arrived," Zetine dryly laughed.

"In just a few more days," We-Will-Reach-Sanctuary said. "Then we arrive at Vhodan's castle, and face down everything he has."

"Then at last, we reach the end," Jubilatious stated. "No matter what happens. No matter what we lose, or what Vhodan does, we kill the bastard."

Soon after, Jubilatious excused himself from the group and approached Mizt-Ied as she took stock of her inventory. She didn't like the idea of holding onto We-Will-Reach-Sancturary's dagger and had given it to Zetine to hold onto. Now she just had her last two smoke bombs and three knives. The goblin glanced up at Jubilatious nervously, not wanting to break the silence.

Jubilatious raised his arms to show he came in peace and said, "I want to apologize for earlier. I shouldn't have snapped at you like that."

"It's fine," she grumbled.

He sat down beside her and gestured to her knives as he asked, "May I?"

"Knock yourself out," Mizt-Ied shrugged.

Jubilatious arranged the knives in front of himself and began to recite, "Iron ore and wood of tree, grow and split and form to what you once were, may one become two and two become three."

The pair watched as one of her knives seemed to spontaneously blossom into two equally sized weapons, almost as though it had simply slid in from just below the original knife. After a moment, another knife grew out from the first duplicate. Jubilatious meanwhile looked a bit haggard; though it wasn't the worst she had seen him after casting a powerful spell. The wizard was certainly getting better.

Mizt-Ied quickly snatched the new weapons and inspected them before saying, "Thank you, Jubilatious."

He cracked a weary smile and tiredly said, "Any time, Mizt-Ied."

Chapter 15

When she awoke, Wolf opened her eyes to a wooden ceiling dimly lit by candles. She had been laid upon a cot, which proved refreshingly soft, and a thin sheet covered her. As Wolf sat up the sheet fell away, revealing that she had been stripped down in her sleep and had been covered in bandages. This aggravated her greatly, but before a growl could escape from Wolf's throat, her attention was caught by the myriad of people moving around her.

Each cot, of which there were twenty, was occupied by people with various injuries. A few were badly burned and had been covered in bandages, while most had been stabbed or cut. One of the men laid rasping in bed lacked a leg, and the bloody stump leaked thick yellow pus. Around them all were dozens of people, barely more than skin and bones, most of which bore minor wounds themselves. They almost all held a strange and haunted look in their eyes, and some of them had chosen to simply sit alongside the walls in quiet little huddles.

"Oh good, you're awake," said a weasel-like voice with an accent identical to Wolf's.

She looked to her side to see a young man dressed in a guard's trousers and no shirt. He was just as starved as the rest of them, though he had also been tattooed with tribal sigils across his arms. The man's hair was as black as Wolf's, though his skin was remarkably pastier, and his eyes weren't quite the same shade of brown. He was vaguely familiar, but in the same way any stranger can seem familiar.

"I am," Wolf replied before rising to her feet.

"Easy now," the man held his arm up in front of her. "You were shot, and suffocated, and whatever else happened to you. You need bed rest."

"I'm fine," Wolf retorted and pushed his arm away. Her steps were uneven and she nearly fell, but Wolf didn't stop. As she walked she asked, "Where is Kazaa?"

The man caught up with her and said, "Outside preparing supper with a few of the others. Wolf, do you not remember me?"

She stopped, looked him over closely, and then answered simply, "No."

His face soured at this and he said, "It's me. Splitter. You beat up a bunch of the older boys for me when we were kids?"

"I don't remember that," Wolf answered honestly, though she left out that she certainly remembered getting bloody with them.

"I've thought about you constantly since then..." he said, hoping to spark something within Wolf.

She simply said, "Okay," then turned around and left.

As Wolf pushed open the door, the bright early evening sun filled her eyes. It stung and she quickly clenched them shut, but continued to step outside. After her eyes had adjusted she opened them and looked around, taking in the new sights of sanctuary. The place was certainly recognizable, though it seemed far different than when she had last seen it.

The snow had completely melted away, and had assisted in putting the fires out before any serious harm could be done. The bodies had all been cleared away, and at first she had assumed they were simply thrown into the mass grave with the others. But then she noticed a great number of swords sticking out of the ground near where the slaves had been chained, each a few feet apart from the other. Some even had flowers placed upon them, and Wolf assumed those graves belonged to the slaves who had fallen in battle. Lastly, there were a few long tables set up in the middle of the courtyard, along with a large fire and two kettles that boiled away while a dwarf, Kazaa, and a woman tended to them.

Wolf approached the long table and nearly collapsed onto it, but caught herself at the last minute and sat down. She muttered, "I hope that's not cabbage soup."

"Rice and apple, actually," Kazaa replied as he peeled one of the aforementioned fruits with a chef's knife.

"An' mystery meat," the dwarf grunted.

"Ah yes, and the mystery meat," Kazaa added. "Personally, I think it's horse. It would explain the shortage."

"There are many sheep pastures in Moia," the woman piped up. "I'd say it's salted mutton."

"An excellent theory as well," Kazaa nodded.

"How long was I out?" Wolf asked as Kazaa sat down across from her.

"Two days," he replied without looking up from the apple. "Are you okay?"

"I think so," she replied, before suddenly her face was pointed ninety degrees to the right and a loud ringing filled her left ear.

As her cheek began to sting Kazaa pulled his hand back and said, "You could have died, pup. I THOUGHT you had died! I pulled your body from the snow and nearly lost you as you bled out all over me!"

Wolf looked back to him, embarrassment and rage flooding her system, before he slapped her across the other cheek. Kazaa continued, "You left me to fight a dozen men YOU had drawn to us!? You were reckless! Idiotic! Both of us could have died, and these people would have been far worse off."

"Don't touch me," Wolf growled at him.

"Do you understand what I am trying to tell you?" he asked.

"No," she practically barked back at him.

"I didn't want to lose you," Kazaa said, and that cut through Wolf like a dagger. He continued, "I know you have your death wish and that I have failed to sway you from it in the past... but I still want to try. Do not throw your life away so easily, pup. Live for yourself, and live for those that care for you."

Wolf thought on his words for a minute, and then watched as Kazaa sighed and rose back to his feet. Only now did she notice he had changed into a guard's uniform with a white apron on over it, and his arms were entirely bare. They were littered with scars, some quite deep. As he began to slice pieces of the apple into one of the pots, Wolf thought back to her dream. The figure was a specter in her mind, something she would always have to live with. Death would always be a part of her.

She suddenly said, "Okay..."

"What?" Kazaa asked in surprise.

"I'll try and live," she said miserably. It was the hardest thing she had ever said before.

"Do you mean it?" he asked her.

As daunting as it was to say, she answered, "Yes."

Kazaa smiled and placed the knife down then said, "We'll have a bowl for you in a few minutes. Soon we'll be on the move again... with company."

"Those two are coming?" Wolf asked as she looked between the dwarf and the woman.

"Rude lil lass," the dwarf quietly huffed.

"Leave her alone, she's half dead," the woman chided him.

"So was I," he retorted.

Kazaa chuckled and said, "No. All of them. I have proposed mercy killing those that were too weak to go but... the others refused. So we are all heading to Cairn."

"Why everyone?" Wolf asked.

The woman said, "We can't just stay here. The Empire will send someone to find out what happened sooner or later, then we're right fucked."

"In the ass," the dwarf agreed.

"What if we're attacked?" Wolf asked. "By soldiers or monsters?"

Kazaa exchanged a look with the woman then said, "Hopefully there won't be any. There are only small patrols to the east, from what I've heard, and Cairn only has small trolls to worry about. They also protect their border very well."

"How well?" she asked.

"They have not been invaded since the First Age," he answered.

"What was that?" Wolf asked as she sprawled herself across the table in a depressed and hungry heap.

"Do either of you want to…?" Kazaa asked.

"I will," the woman said as she exchanged places with him. "An Age is how we sort a great amount of time, somewhat like your own age."

"Twenty, I think," Wolf replied.

"Right. Each one of your years, or your age, is made up of twelve months. But a historic Age is generally a thousand years or so. The First Age is not literally the start of time, but rather when the first great deeds were recorded. During that time, there was an immense war between the heroes and the giants, who were said to be the greatest evil to have lived. The heroes battled the giants across the world, only a handful of them mind you, before at last vanquishing the giants in what would one day become Cairn."

"So that was the only time Cairn was attacked?" Wolf asked.

"It was," the woman nodded.

"What Age are we in now?" Wolf asked with mild curiosity.

"The Fifth Age," the woman answered. "Also known as The Age of The Empire. After the First Age, which some call The Age of

Myth, there was The Age of Magic. During this time many wizards and mages laid waste to the world, and then built it anew. In the new world, magic was weaker than it was before, but people were to be much safer. Instead came The Age of Strife, where the world was rocked by a great many wars as tyrants sought power. After came The Age of Prosperity, but of course it couldn't last..."

"Some twisted story ye got there," the dwarf spat, luckily away from the kettles.

"What's that supposed to mean?" the woman asked.

"Ye got all the parts mixed up!" the dwarf huffed.

"Have not!" the woman retorted.

"Age of Myth was the one with all the wars," he said with uttermost determination. "Age of Strife was just the one big war. Yer whole "Age of Prosperity" is a load of donkey shit too. There was no such thing!"

"Was too, you stone headed moron," she hissed at him.

"The Fourth Age was the Age of Silence!" he insisted. "On account everyone was friends with each other!"

Wolf cut in, "How do you know all this?"

"What do ye mean?" the dwarf asked.

"We were taught it," the woman answered.

"By who?" Wolf pressed.

"Our... teachers?" the woman asked. "Did you not have teachers?"

"The girl is a barbarian," Kazaa interjected. "They're not taught much more than how to survive and kill."

This made Wolf's face turn red, so she hid her head between her arms. The woman then said, "Ah of course. That makes sense; those new boys had no idea how to even cut an onion."

Wolf mustered up enough courage to ask, "What do I call you?"

"I am Mira," the woman pleasantly said.

"I'm Cutter Halfaxe," the dwarf grunted. "The second, not that it matters."

"I'm Wolf," said Wolf.

Mira moved over to her, and stuck out her hand. In it was the fang that she had last seen planted in the throat of the northern battle cat. The clasp had been repaired, restoring it to its previous function as a necklace, and the blood had all been wiped away. The woman said, "Your friend found this with that awful animal. He said it was yours, so I fixed it up as best as I could."

Wolf peered up over her arms, then quickly grabbed the necklace and gently pulled it over her neck. Satisfied that it wasn't damaged she said, "Thank you," then lowered her head once again.

Suddenly a wooden bowl was pressed against Wolf's arms, and she sat up to look at it. The broth was a cloudy white, and was filled with small white things and thin slices of apple and grey meat chunks. There was no spoon provided, so Wolf cautiously sipped it straight from the bowl. The liquid burned her lips, but it tasted better than anything she had eaten in months, and it dawned on her just how hungry she was, so she began to slurp it down dangerously fast. Once finished drinking, Wolf placed the bowl down, then began to spoon the rest of it into her mouth with her hand.

Once finished she asked, "Water?"

"The girl can eat," Mira snickered.

"There's a crank in the barracks," Cutter replied.

"The...?" she trailed off.

"The building you woke up in," Kazaa answered. "Ask someone there to show it to you. There's also a crank outside, but the water it spews is dirty."

"Savages," Mira grimaced. "I had forgotten how good clean water was until the other day."

"Ay," Cutter agreed with a single heavy nod. "Food too."

"Make sure to only eat one bowl an hour," Kazaa said.

"We know," Mira groaned. "You throw up ONE time and you never live it down..."

"At least your stomach didn't explode," Kazaa shrugged.

"That doesn't happen," Mira stated.

"It very much does," he said. "That's why I made sure to distribute the first round of rations myself."

Wolf pushed herself away from the table and climbed back to her feet. She had an easier time walking now, and made it back to the barracks without stumbling even once. She made the mistake of trying to push the door inwards, before quickly correcting herself, and pulled it open. Inside she now noticed the smell of blood and infection that had filled the building, but it did little to upset her. She had smelled far worse, after all.

A woman with tan skin not unlike her own asked Wolf, "Is the food ready?"

"I think so," she said.

"FOOD'S READY!" the woman called over her shoulder, earning a chorus of cheers.

People began to hurry out the door, pushing past Wolf and buffeting her around the room. Only a handful of people stayed inside, barring those who were immobilized. These seemed to be the families and lovers of the injured, who dared not leave their loved ones sides. Even most of those who had kept to the walls had gone to eat. The one obvious exception was Splitter, who had approached the door, then stopped when he saw Wolf looking around.

"What is it?" he asked her.

"Water," she replied.

"It's over here," he said as he stepped past her.

Splitter showed Wolf to a back room where a strange object rose out of the ground with a hole below it. The object had a small lever that Splitter repeatedly pulled on to allow a thin stream of water to spill out. Wolf pushed him aside and began to use the lever herself, sitting down on her knees and craning her neck to lap the precious liquid up. It was strangely far more delicious than the water had been in her canteen, though she had no idea why. Perhaps it was due to her several days without it, or perhaps the water in Moia was simply better.

Splitter began to speak, the Wolf barely paid attention. "You know, I think I got a crush on you after that day... what the chieftain did was horrible. Especially now that I know the tribe will never bare another son. If you knew to fight and hunt, you should have been rewarded. All of the women should have been taught just as you were. Perhaps then we wouldn't have been captured by these monsters..."

Wolf pulled away from the water, wiped her mouth with her arm and said, "It would have helped, probably."

"Yeah," he let out a small laugh. "You know, I didn't think it was you at first. But some of the older women recognized you. They said you looked just like they thought you'd turn out."

"Okay," she replied.

"You really saved me once when I was a kid, and again now," he said. "You have no idea what a hero you are, Wolf. And you're more beautiful than I would have expected after all these years. You're more beautiful than anyone."

He leaned forward then, and before Wolf could react, kissed her gently upon the lips. As he pulled back, she stared at him with wide eyes. Then she punched him square in the face. Wolf felt his nose break beneath her knuckles, and her fist was stained red as she jumped up to her feet, but she paid it no mind. She simply walked away, leaving Splitter holding his bloody face as he shouted in pain behind her.

Wolf rejoined Kazaa outside, who had moved to sitting position at the front of the small house as he ate. She sat down beside him and asked, "Whose home was this?"

"A bad man's," he replied.

"Did we kill him?" she asked.

"No," he smiled. "They did. Tore him apart."

"Good," she said.

"Did you hurt your hand?" he asked her.

Wolf looked down at her fingers, still coated in fresh blood, then answered honestly. "Someone kissed me, so I broke his nose."

"Ah, good," Kazaa replied. "Who was it?"

"Some boy," she replied simply. "I feel... different."

"Different how?" he looked over at her curiously.

"Sad, I think," she said as she struggled to articulate her feelings. "My body feels so heavy, and my chest aches but it doesn't hurt. It also feels so much harder to care about anything. Without revenge... what's the point?"

"The point is that you are alive," he replied. "I agree that finding a purpose can be hard. It's why I'm a sellsword and not a gravetender or a carpenter, after all. Maybe you'll find it if you keep looking, or maybe you're like me, and you won't. But that's okay. Because at least then you still get to enjoy the beauty of the world, meet new people, and even grow to like them."

"I don't like people," was all she said in response.

Kazaa sighed and said, "No, it doesn't seem like you do. Maybe one day you will find a person you do like though. I hope you will, you deserve it, pup. If not... I hope you can at least live happily in peace."

"Why do you call me that?" she asked.

"Call you what?" he quickly responded.

"Pup," she said. "It's not my name. I'm not an animal."

308EVE ROSE

"I meant no offense," he replied earnestly. "I call you it because of your name, and because that's what you are."

"I'm not-" she began, but was quickly cut off.

"You are a child, though you don't know it," he said. "You know so little of the world, of yourself. I am sure you have grown to resent me; after all, you have tried to kill me. Maybe I'm just growing soft, but I can't bring myself to feel the same. Travelling with you has made me... wistful. I just want to see this through to the end, with you standing tall afterwards."

"I see," came her answer.

"Is there anything else?" he asked.

She leaned back and thought for a moment before asking, "What happened to my clothes?"

He laughed at that then said, "I have them with my own belongings. I found your knife, but your clothes are looking worse for wear though."

"What about my bow?" she asked.

He replied, "Ruined. I have no idea how to craft a new one, but I took that ranger's bow. I'm sure it will suit you just fine."

"I bet it will," she replied. "And the arrows?"

"All those from her quiver," he said. "I wouldn't use them without knowing what they do though. You may end up blowing yourself up."

She nodded, then said, "Thank you."

He smiled and replied, "You're welcome, pup."

***

When Colstone and the other dwarves arrived at Fragrant Meadows, it scarcely resembled the thriving village it had once been not too long ago. When the Imperial army marched through, they had taken to claiming nearly all of the town's crops and burning the rest. The few homes that had been left outside of the wall had been ransacked; every valuable or interesting trinket pocketed by whichever soldier had first set their eyes upon it. From the nearby trees hung several bodies, each of which had been an elf. It was a sickening mockery of the wood elves' culture to kill them in such a way, and Colstone shuddered at the thought of what these humans may do to a dwarf.

"I don' like the looks of this," Limecrack said from his side.

Brock added on, "We could jus' peel out, take the long way around."

"I think yer right on that point," Colstone nodded.

Brock urged the goats to turn, taking them far to the side of the village so that they could pass it by without trouble. Soon their sled began to pass beneath the trees, far too close to the lifeless elven bodies for comfort. The sickening stench of rot began to wade its way into each of their nostrils, and Limecrack had to cover his nose as he wretched violently. This was no fate for any being, and not one of the dwarves doubted what they would do if they crossed paths with the humans responsible for it.

There came a strange snuffling sound from the underbrush nearby, and a moment later the goats began to scream. Brock asked, "What's gotten into 'em!?"

Marblekeeper, who had instantly moved to try and sooth the animals urgently replied, "There's some sort o' beast nearby spookin' 'em!"

The dwarves did not raise their hammers or picks, but instead each reached into their chest to produce the same type of weapon that Colstone and a few others had once used to threaten Tusk, though the barbarian hadn't known what they were. The dwarves called them hand cannons, for they were portable versions of a weapon that was rarely ever seen outside of Bastadon. Each one was narrow and long, fitting a single shot capable of immense damage, at the expense of no defense.

They waited in fear drenched anxiety as the wretched sounds of gasping and snuffling filled the area, accompanied by general movement from the surrounding trees and bushes. When at last the first creature made its appearance, they nearly shot it out of panic alone. Then they each considered shooting it for its appearance, which was equally as grotesque as the hanging bodies not far away.

The creature was humanoid, too human even, and stood a little over five feet tall. Its skin was a color of grey that on any other being, save maybe for an elf, would mark it as deeply sick. It was bald across its entire body, with a head that was just a little too tall. Growing from both its hands and feet were sharp claws not unlike that of a large cat, and they were longer on its hands. The creature was lipless, and it possessed a maw of sharp and crooked teeth that dripped with putrid saliva. Its eyes, as sunken into its skull as they were, were entirely black. As it took a frail yet surprisingly quick step forward, its grotesque hanging member swung between its legs.

"What the fuck is that?" Brock whispered in disgust.

The creature made a clicking sound as it looked at them, then lowered onto all fours. The dwarves expected it to attack, but instead it scampered towards the corpses. There it took hold of the leg of an elf and began to roughly pull, until at last the corpse's bloated neck peeled away from the noose and it fell to the ground, where the creature began to tear into it with its hands and claws. It bit the elf's face off then grabbed the corpe by its hair and began to pull, until it tore the scalp free from its skull. There it feasted upon the brain of the poor deceased elf, all while the dwarves watched in disgust.

Then the monster leaned back, placing each of its hands onto the chest and groin of the corpse respectfully, as it tilted its head as far back as it could go. It let out an ear-splitting cry that filled the air, making the dwarves wince and the goats resume their screaming. The cry was soon accompanied by maybe a dozen more from the surrounding forest, and the dwarves quickly realized just how dire their situation was.

Marblekeeper urged the goats to begin moving, while all around more creatures began to make their appearance. Most of them headed towards the corpses, starved for an easy meal. Some of the monsters though, perhaps invigorated by their numerical advantage, instead began to move towards the dwarves and their sled. One after the other, starting with Limecrack, the dwarves fired their hand cannons.

The four explosions that ripped through the air were nothing compared to the pained squeals of the monsters, so high pitched and dreadful that even the most stalwart of men would shudder before their cries. The dwarves recoiled from the horrible sounds, but this proved to be yet another tactical error. Even the monsters that had been ignoring them now turned to face the being who had dared to attack their brood. With a long reload time, the dwarves had no choice but to instead rely upon their melee weapons.

While the four dwarves prepared themselves for the two dozen monsters crowding them to attack, a trio stood off in the distance watching them. The group had remained passive at first, wanting only to see the dwarves leave before they made their own way through the area, but it seemed like there was no longer a chance of that happening. The dark elf in the center of the trio let out a sigh and drew his daggers, before taking a step forward.

Dancing-Lights said to the two women, "Ruby-Gem, Spring, light your torches and use them to press the ghouls to the west."

"What of you?" Ruby-Gem asked, reaching into her pack to produce a torch.

He replied, "I was a Shadow Stalker, once upon a time. A dozen men are no match for me, to say nothing of a dozen ghouls."

They moved forward, the elf quicker than his companions. It was just after Marblekeeper had swung his hammer into the skull of the first of the ghouls to rattle their cart that Dancing-Lights slipped one of his daggers across the throat of another ghoul. Hammers and pickaxes worked side by side, keeping the monsters at bay, while exotic daggers danced amongst tender flesh.

Soon they were joined by Spring and Ruby-Gem, who waved their aflame torches fiercely as they hollered at the ghouls. First the monsters' attention were drawn by the noise of the pair, before quickly the creatures bellowed in terror at the sight of the fire. Many of them turned and ran or scampered away, too terrified to stay and fight in the presence of flame. A few of them remained though, too stubborn or too hungry to back off.

Spring used the butt of her torch to strike one ghoul through the eye, while Ruby-Gem set the genitals of another on fire before punching it in the throat. She recoiled after, shaking her hand in pain, while the ghoul gasped and wailed, attempting to extinguish its burning member to no avail. A moment later its head was severed by Dancing-Lights, while the last two ghouls were struck down by Colstone and Limecrack.

Once they were dead, Colstone called out, "Funny running into ye out here."

"I could say the same, dwarf," Dancing-Lights grimaced as he cleaned the blood from his blades. "What are you doing here, so far from home?"

"Same thing we've been doin," he grunted. "Lookin fir the girl."

"He's telling the truth," Spring said to her companion.

"Silence, Cold-Reprieve," he ordered. "Are you truthfully still searching for this lost child?"

"I am," Colstone stated. "How about yerself?"

"Our business has never been, and never will be, yours," the elf coldly stated. "Move along, little dwarf. Before the ghouls come back."

"Goat's ass," Colstone grumbled, turning away from the trio. Then he announced, "Get ready boys, we're moving again!"

As the dwarves left, Dancing-Lights muttered more to himself than the women, "I do not like coincidences..."

"That's all it is though," Ruby-Gem stated. "A coincidence."

"For lowly things, perhaps," he nodded. Then he elaborated, "When it comes to encounters such as these, strangers who are improbably connected, coincidence is merely the excuse mortals come up with. The gods are manipulators, and I fear they may be trying to pull us together."

"Why should that matter?" Spring curiously asked.

"Because it means the threads of destiny may be tightening around our throats," he grimaced. "I do not like to not be in control of my own fate, to be blinded by the machinations of unknown beings."

The other two were not entirely sure what he meant, but Ruby-Gem said, "One's fate is in one's own hands, no matter what another does."

"An idyllic statement," Dancing-Lights lamented. "Once I may have agreed with you. But I have seen what happens when the noose of destiny is made taught for a great elf. No matter how independent you may be, no matter how courageous or strong, there is no running from the fate imposed by a god."

"And which god do you think may be doing this?" Spring asked, not believing for a moment anything he said.

"I do not know," he said. "Perhaps The Trickster, Zen-Khuit. Speculation means nothing now. Come, ladies, we still have places to be and people to kill."

He strode forward, leaving Spring and Ruby-Gem to follow after him. The half-orc turned to the half-elf and asked, "What do you make of all that?"

All Spring could say, with a shake of her head was, "Northerner nonsense."

Chapter 16

The end was now in clear sight, and the final battle would soon be held. Atop a small hill, the heroes stood taking in the sights of Vhodan's castle. It rose magnificently up into the air from its small island, black towers and walls overlooking its moat and the surrounding farmlands that had been trampled upon by the boots of soldiers. Vhodan's forces were clearly in the thousands, with far more soldiers marching across the surrounding lands than any of them had ever seen at one time.

Mixed into the ground troops were various monsters that could be easily controlled. Wargs, ogres, wyrms, even a handful of basilisks whose snouts were muzzled. Every so often a harpy or wyrm would fly overhead, and on more than one occasion did one of the wyrms spot the heroes. Despite this, neither the monster's nor the soldiers take any action against them.

"What are they waitin' fer?" Ironja asked.

"For all the players to be on the board," Zetine replied. "He's waiting for the Army of Hope to arrive."

"Do you think he'd grant us an audience?" Jubilatious cautiously asked.

"Not a chance," We-Will-Reach-Sanctuary stated. "If the soldiers don't kill you first, Vhodan would order your execution before you ever made it to the throne room."

"Worth a shot," he shrugged.

"I think it may be best for us to split up," Zetine said. "Some of us go through the sewers, while the rest of us take on The Unknowing King."

"But who goes where?" Jubilatious asked.

"Who indeed?" Came a husky voice from behind them.

They all spun at once, drawing their respective weapons, aside from We-Will-Reach-Sanctuary who stood around looking intimidating. Standing before them was a tall elf dressed in a red cowl and cloak, with a steel chest plate and twin broadswords. The elf calmly pulled his hood town to reveal stark white skin and violet eyes in an attempt to show he was no threat, though this dissuaded no fears amongst the group.

"My name is Kira," the elf said. "I have come to join you."

"A bit late for that," Jubilatious snarked.

"How do we know you're not working for Vhodan?" Zetine asked.

"I am not the one accompanied by The Butcher of The Reach," Kira simply replied.

They all turned to look at We-Will-Reach-Sanctuary who shrugged and said, "I had a change of heart. For what it's worth, I do not recognize this elf."

"I do," Mizt-Ied said, making her the center of attention. "He had wanted posters back in town. They said he was a serial killer!"

"Then my reputation precedes me," the elf chuckled. He then said, "I have killed people, yes. I have done what's needed to survive, and nothing more. Were you in my shoes, I am sure you would have made the choices I did."

"You wish to breach the castle with us?" Zetine asked.

"I do," Kira replied. "My blades hunger for the blood of a tyrant."

"Well that's not intimidating at all," Jubilatious quipped.

"My partner has gone to meet your allies," Kira stated. "They will take up the brunt of the conflict. I heard you refer to splitting up. Why?"

The group exchanged looks, but Zetine explained, "To give ourselves a better chance at success. Half of us sneak in through the sewers, the other half risk battle in order to force entry through The Unknowing King."

"Sounds useless," Kira grunted. "I'll go through the sewers."

"As will I," Ironja said, holding his axe upwards.

"I guess I will too," Mizt-Ied said as she clicked her knives together. "I just hope it's low tide."

"Then I guess it's just the three of us," Jubilatious said as he looked at Zetine and We-Will-Reach-Sanctuary. "Let's hope we can do this."

"I don't know how much use I'll be," We-Will-Reach-Sanctuary said. "But I'll do my best to guide you when needed. Provided I don't die, of course."

Jubilatious   sighed,   then   turned   and   said, "We-Will-Reach-Sanctuary. I, Jubilatious, free you from your bindings. You are now free to do as you please."

The cuffs on We-Will-Reach-Sanctuary's wrists clicked then fell away, dissolving away in the air. The elf looked down to his chuffed wrists in surprise, before gingerly rubbing them in relief. He was smiling as he looked up, but each and every one of the others was now staring at him with anticipation. Even Kira, whose mouth was still concealed by his cowl, seemed to be scowling at the elf.

The dark elf remarked, "What? It's not like I was going to betray you at the last moment. I'm here for the long run."

Zetine looked to Kira and asked, "How long do you think until the army arrives?"

Kira shrugged and said, "An hour. Maybe two."

"And how long does it take to navigate the sewers?" She asked.

We-Will-Reach-Sanctuary answered, A little upwards of a half hour, and it would take maybe ten minutes for them to reach the entrance."

"Then we rest and eat," Zetine said. "We need whatever energy we can muster before this begins."

"Oh thank the gods," Mizt-Ied squeaked. "I've been famished for the past hour but didn't want to say anything."

"Ay, I could eat," Ironja grunted in affirmation.

***

Ironja, Mizt-Ied, and Kira found the entrance to the sewers with relative ease. It had taken more than ten minutes of walking, but beneath an old dogwood tree they found a wooden hatch that led into darkness. Kira was the first to go, leaping into the hole without concern. Second went Mizt-Ied, who carefully climbed down the rickety ladder, and Ironja followed after her.

Kira landed upon flattened rock, and then quickly spun around as he drew his swords. Satisfied the area was secure he waited patiently for the other two to arrive. Soon they all stood upon a ledge that overlooked a flow of water and filth, with a drain wall only a few meters away. Their path continued seemingly straightforward in the opposite direction, from which strange sounds occasionally bounced off the walls.

"Looks like there's only one way to go," Mizt-Ied said.

"Looks like it," Ironja agreed as he lit a torch, while Kira simply strode forward.

As they continued onwards, the occasional side path would open, but Kira ignored these entirely in favor of their straightforward one. Soon the water grew steadily deeper, while more filth began to accumulate. Disturbingly, they would occasionally see a humanoid body floating downstream, and once they even watched the body get pulled under the water by some unseen creature.

It was halfway through their trek when a monster lunged out from the water, hoping to drag down an easy meal. It was humanoid and covered in brown-grey scales, while lacking any eyes. Its three webbed fingers ended in dirty claws, and its mouth was full of fangs.

Kira cut the monster's head off with a single stroke, not even slowing down to do so. Its body collided with the ledge and sank back into the water, while its head went sailing into the far wall before landing atop the opposite side's wall. Ironja and Mizt-Ied exchanged a look of mutual shock, before hurrying to keep up with the elf.

"What was that thing?" Mizt-Ied asked.

"Dunno," Kira replied.

"How did ye slice it down so fast, lad?" Ironja asked.

"It's what I do," Kira replied.

"Slice heads off?" He sarcastically asked.

"Sometimes," Kira earnestly confirmed. "But kill things. I've gotten quite good at it. Always hoped to test my skills against that Sanctuary cunt. But I guess fate had other ideas."

"Ay, that would be a fight to behold," Ironja said as he imagined the legendary duel.

"If he survives this little war," Kira mused. "I'll kill him a few weeks later. Give him time to get ready."

"And why do ye want to kill him?" Ironja asked.

"He's a monster," he pointedly stated.

"He's a changed elf," Ironja replied.

Kira said, "Once a monster, always a monster. No mercy, no regret. Kill them all."

Ironja leaned over to Mizt-Ied and whispered, "I agree with him in principle, but doesn't this lad seem a little... volatile?"

"Big time," she agreed.

From beneath the waters, various monsters began to rise up. Chief amongst them were two basilisks, but a number of the strange deformed humanoids were present as well. It dawned on

Mizt-Ied that these were likely the scale beasts We-Will-Reach-Sanctuary had referred to. That seemed hardly relevant though, because Kira had already lunged for the nearest basilisk.

***

The Army of Hope consisted of a thousand civilian volunteers, three thousand elven and human soldiers, three hundred dwarven soldiers, and twenty-two wizards. They marched towards Vhodan's castle in hundred person lines, watching as Vhodan's forces assembled into a defensive formation. In the distance, Jubilatious, We-Will-Reach-Sanctuary, and Zetine watched with great interest.

The high elf general Zeydas called out, "Archers, take aim!" And at his command a thousand arrows were notched. "FIRE!"

From their view, the heroes watched as the sky was blocked out by the arrows which rained down upon Vhodan's forces. Many of those soldier raised shields overhead to block the incoming attack, though not all had protection, and not all were lucky enough to block the arrows. At least a hundred bodies fell to the ground, several wargs among them, but not nearly enough to turn the favor towards the righteous.

The human general Carver called out, "Shield formation! Guardian formation!"

As the archers perched atop the castle walls began to take aim, the front row of the Army of Hope raised their shields overhead. Eight of the gathered wizards worked in conjunction to spread a magical shield overhead, while two green mages grew a wall of trees from behind the army that developed into a protective canopy.

Arrows were deflected off the magical barrier, shattered against shields, or embedded in the trees, and not a single person was slain. Carver called out, "Line A, sweeping formation! Line B, follow! Lines C and D, pincer!"

The front two rows of soldiers began to march forward, while the two behind them split up to flank the enemy from the right and left. Zeydas then called out, "Archers, focus upon your rivals! Take their eyes and their bows!"

Arrows flew from both directions, and it was obvious that The Army of Hope was taking more losses than Vhodan's forces. By the time the front line had reached their enemies, half of the pincer attack had already been wiped out. Many of Vhodan's own archers had fallen though, allowing for ground combat to prevail.

Carver ordered, "Squads Green and White remain with the archers! The rest of you, get in there and defend your home!"

There came a chorus of cheering and battle cries as the soldiers marched forward, leaving the archers and several wizards behind. Zeydas was quiet though as he asked Carver, "When will the cavalry arrive?"

"It should have been here already," he shook his head. "I can only hope they've been delayed..."

From their distant spot, We-Will-Reach-Sanctuary asked, "Shall we join them?"

"I suppose we should," Jubilatious sighed.

"But first," Zetine said as she withdrew the elf's daggers. "These belong to you."

We-Will-Reach-Sanctuary took them in silence, a smile spreading far along his cheeks. He said only, "You won't regret this," then turned to face his destiny.

He ran faster than either of the humans could keep up, and reached the battlefield in no time. The first soldier to encounter the elf found his head detached from his body before he even registered the movement. With every turn of his body, every slide and thrust and swipe, We-Will-Reach-Sanctuary claimed a life. His blades danced amongst the throats and guts of Vhodan's forces, not a single strike missing its target.

As they caught up with him, a red wyrm swooped down from above at Zetine. Jubilatious quickly cast a spell and pointed his staff at the reptile, hitting it with a beam of ice that spread across its wings and forced it to the ground. As he ran past, he regretted that the fall didn't kill it, for the beast wailed in pain from its shattered spine.

Zetine stuck to the edges of the skirmish, cutting down the occasional soldier who strayed too far from the pack. These were mostly the younger recruits who barely knew how to fight. Zetine felt some remorse over this, but not enough to slow her. She severed hands and legs, stabbed through throats, and kept moving.

The sky began to swirl as a great many spells were cast, bolts of lightning and balls of fire raining down upon the ground with careful accuracy. Pillars of ice and stone pierced upwards, impaling soldiers upon them before branching into crude and dangerous sculptures. Jubilatious joined in with a spell of his own, launching a wave of fire at a group of nearby shield bearers unlucky enough to have their backs turned to him.

Then from nowhere, Jubilatious heard a voice as clear as day. "What are you doing here, boy?"

"No..." was all Jubilatious gasped, before the ground itself shook.

***

Beneath the castle, Kira had claimed the lives of two dozen monsters and counting. Ironja and Mizt-Ied barely had to do anything save for following the elf, though occasionally he would leave them some dismembered beast to finish off. It seemed like every step they took would summon more monsters, creating an endless line of enemies.

As Ironja brought his axe into the skull of an armless scalebeast he said, "I'm sick o' these pests! How much longer till the end?"

"It can't be too much longer," Mizt-Ied said as she walked beside him. "I'm more concerned about this elf's skills..."

"Ay, it is concerning," Ironja nodded in agreement. "He reminds me o' Sanctuary."

"Do you think this is a trap?" She asked.

"Probably," he grunted. "But more's important is, is he part o' the trap er not?"

As they said this, Kira was in the process of battling a basilisk that seemed to possess a greater level of intelligence than its ally. It rested in the water at the opposite side of the canal, spitting acid at the elf. Whenever it seemed like Kira would make a move on it, the monster would dive underwater and resurface somewhere else. This aggravated Kira greatly, and he began to grow sloppy, making frantic leaping slices at the creature with little consideration for his own safety.

It was during one of these leaps that a set of black tentacles shot out of the water, wrapping around Kira's right arm and legs before pulling him into the water. Mizt-Ied cried out, "KIRA!" But it seemed too late for anything to be done.

They hurried towards the spot where he was pulled under, but the basilisk was quick to take advantage of this. Ironja barely managed to block its acid spit, while Mizt-Ied quickly threw one of her knives into its snout. The basilisk let out a hiss of pain then retreated into the water, its acidic blood burning away the topmost layer of filth.

Kira burst up from beneath the chest deep sludge, gasping for breath, with his left hand holding tight to three squirming tentacles. Another one shot out from below to wrap around his neck, but Kira ignored it in favor of slicing off the tendrils he had taken hold of. Almost instantly they began to regrow, spreading out into six tentacles which instantly began to lash out at him.

"What is that thing!?" Mizt-Ied asked as she drew another knife and threw it into the water where she thought its torso may be.

"Pseudohydra," Kira croaked as he attempted to pry the gripping tentacle from his neck. He then rasped out, "Oil! Give me!"

Ironja slung his pack onto the ground and quickly rummaged through it, before pulling out a small oil flask. He then threw it to Kira, who caught it in his left hand, before immediately pouring it over the tentacle, spilling a considerable amount into the water. Several more tentacles then attacked, binding each one of Kira's limbs and rendering him helpless as it strangled the life out of him.

"Torch!" He wheezed, his vision growing blurry.

Ironja threw the torch, which bounced off one of the pseudohydra's tentacles, before falling into the sludge. Flames quickly spread outwards from the floating torch, propelled by the spilled oil. It enveloped the tendrils, which retreated underwater, and even caught Kira's chest plate aflame. With his arms free, the elf quickly began to pat the flames out as he stepped backwards.

From behind, the basilisk lunged at him, sinking claws into Kira's side. Kira chucked the monster off, before quickly placing his arms around its throat. The wrestled in the filth together, blood seeping from each one, before at last Kira broke the monster's neck and allowed its corpse to fall beneath the water.

"Are you okay!?" Mizt-Ied asked in worry.

"I'll live," Kira lied as he looked down to the filth soaked wound below his right ribs. "We need to move-"

Kira was cut off as there came a great rumbling, and the entire sewer system began to shake. Kira was knocked backwards into the water while both Ironja and Mizt-Ied fell against the ledge, nearly falling into the water with Kira. From ahead, a wall caved in spilling more light into the tunnel, while small pieces of stone fell from the ceiling around them.

"I think that's our exit," Ironja grumbled as he pushed himself to his feet.

"Then let's not wait," Kira said as he approached the ledge and began to climb out.

"Hold up lad," the dwarf called, causing Kira to peer back over his shoulder. Ironja produced one of his potions and said, "Take this. It'll make ya feel better."

"...thank you," Kira cautiously said as he approached Ironja, then took the potion.

Kira popped the cork out then began to drink half of the bottle's contents. His wounds quickly closed over, leaving behind scar tissue where bloody holes had been. This restored Kira to full health in a sense, though it also sealed in the sewage that had crept into his wounds. He would live for awhile longer, but there was no escaping the death that had come for the elf. Still, he carried on as though he was uninjured.

The chamber that had been revealed to the group opened up into a large spacious dungeon that had been converted into a laboratory of sorts. Bubbling cauldrons and steaming beakers covered various tables and fires that vented up into smokestacks in the rafters. There were glass boxes of all shapes and sizes stacked in neat rows, most of which were filled with creatures of various species. Roughly every fifteen meters there was a hole ten meters wide that ran too deep for any of them to see into, but they could hear the various snarling and scratching sounds that came from within. The blood smeared across the ground, and the pile of corpses by a large spiraling staircase, told them what the monsters fed upon.

There was a single person standing amidst the laboratory, back turned to them as he hacked apart a warg with a large cleaver. The person was dressed in a direwolf fur cape stained with blood, while iron gauntlets were clamped tight against his wrists, and a leather apron blocked the gore from covering his skin. As he moved, the group could see he was an orc, though he hardly looked like one. His left hand was that of a bear, and most of his visible flesh was covered in what looked like rocks. His eyes were that of a cat's, while his breaths exhaled a subtle green vapor.

Torrn, The Lord of Beasts turned to look at them, his left hand ripping a wad of intestines out from the poor animal he had been operating on. The orc aid, "I have been expecting you... who are you?"

"The good guys?" Mizt-Ied suggested.

"Not you!" be barked, then pointed his bloody cleaver at Kira. "You. Elf. I was expecting an orc. A ranger. Not whatever you are."

"Disappointed?" Kira smugly spat.

"No matter..." Torrn sighed as he rubbed his cleaver against his apron. "You all fall the same way anyway. Animal's an animal. Meat's meat."

"I've got this," Kira stated.

"Are ye sure about that, lad?" Ironja asked.

Mizt-Ied added on, "We can help you!"

"I'll be fine," Kira said before drawing a dagger with his left hand. "Hurry and kill The Emperor while I handle his dog walker."

"I am more than a simple beast tamer," Torrn chuckled. "I have discovered the secrets of flesh and transcended it. You are nothing more than a mortal elf."

Kira cocked his head and asked, "Is that all?"

Torrn pursed his lips then growled, "I'm going to enjoy this."

**

The ground itself had been torn asunder, a great ravine carved into the earth close to the archers. Jubilatious looked to the ravine only for a moment, but it was more than long enough to see the hellish creatures pulling themselves out from beneath the ground. This momentary distraction nearly claimed his life, but then there was Zetine, slicing the arms out from a soldier who had sought to impale Jubilatious with a spear.

"Focus, Jubilatious!" She quickly commanded as she parried the strike of another soldier.

"Right, I'm on it," he said before focusing his staff on the soldier to deliver a blast of ice that froze his opponent's legs in place.

As Zetine separated the man's head from his shoulders she asked, "Have you seen Sanctuary?"

"I can only hope he's giving them hell," Jubilatious responded.

From beyond the castle walls, there came a great and mighty roar that rattled the bones of every man and woman on the battlefield. Jubilatious quickly erected a magical barrier around him and Zetine so they could watch the breathtaking sight. A wyvern with pale blue and grey scales flew overhead, the gusts of its wings knocking entire groups of people over.

The wyvern descended towards the battlefield, crushing some of its own allies as it landed. With a better view they could make out the sharp grey quills that gave the lizard the appearance of a beard, and the metal collar around its neck. Seated upon the mighty beast's shoulders was a wizard, dressed in robes the color of storm clouds, with a wide brimmed hat and hood concealing his face. The wizard held a white staff in his right hand, with which he used to call the storm.

The wyvern took in a deep breath, before unleashing a devastating cone of lightning upon a valiant group of human soldiers. When the sparks subsided, their armor rested cooked on the ground, their corpses charred beyond recognition. The Stormcaller pointed his staff unto the heavens, pulling the scattered clouds from across the land to a point directly overhead. As they swirled and combined into a single oppressing hurricane, rain began to pour over the battlefield, making quick work of every lit flame.

The archers and wizards wasted no time in retaliating upon the Stormcaller, but it was little use. The wyvern raised its right wing to block the incoming arrows, while the Stormcaller erected a wall of lightning that blocked the flame and ice spells sent his way. The wyvern turned and began to breathe its lightning onto the archers, whose formation broke as fear flooded through the elves. But no lightning harmed them, for their wizards had kept the protective barrier active.

"Useless," he said to them as the wyvern continued to channel its lightning.

Then the Stormcaller aimed his staff towards the same spot where his wyvern was attacking, and sent a spiraling beam of lightning into the barrier. The wizards focused with all their might to keep the shield up, while the archers launched volley after volley into the wyvern and lightning shield. Cracks began to appear upon the barrier, glowing with transcendent light, and it seemed as though their fates were sealed.

Just as the barrier shattered, the Stormcaller turned with wide eyes to block another attack. A ball of fire collided with his open hand and flames washed over the wizard. When he closed his fist he was nearly unharmed, though his clothes were singed and his hand was badly burned. He lowered his hand as he gazed across the battlefield to the one who had dared to hurt him.

All he said was, "Jubilatious."

Then the wyvern turned, leaving most of the archers and wizards alive. With a flap of its wings the beast raised high into the air, and then it soared across the battlefield. It dived in low and Jubilatious and Zetine turned to run, but it was no use. The Stormcaller reached down and grabbed Jubilatious by his caller, pulling him high up into the air with him. The wyvern began to circle the battlefield as the Stormcaller sat Jubilatious in front of him on the wyvern neck so they could talk face to face.

"You would really stand against your Emperor, boy?" The Stormcaller asked.

Jubilatious glared into his lightning filled eyes and said, "I would, father. He's evil."

"That's subjective," Tyruden replied with a dismissal wave of his hand. "He gave our kind purpose. Built a school for us to study, stopped our persecution by the idiotic masses. He gave us CULTURE."

"And how many lives did it cost to do so?" Jubilatious retorted. "How many ruined villages and towns are your responsibility? Entire regions reduced to ash, or populations decimated? What culture that could do such a thing is worth preserving!?"

"One of power," Tyruden coldly stated. "A culture of strength and passion and nobility, who will rebuild these lands into something meaningful."

From behind him appeared a skeletal figure dressed in hooded white robes. It reached forward and placed a dead hand upon Tyruden's shoulder as it said, "It is time, Stormcaller. Are you finished?"

"I am," he replied, causing the figure to vanish once more. Tyruden looked back to Jubilatious and said, "I ask of you, my son. Will you stand beside me, in service of our glorious Emperor Vhodan, so that we may make something beautiful of the world?"

"Go to hell," Jubilatious spat in his face.

Tyruden rubbed the spit from his cheek, and then sighed. Before Jubilatious could react, he grabbed the young wizard's staff and snapped it beneath his fist. He said, "You always were just a bastard. No real loss."

Jubilatious felt Tyruden's staff press against his chest, and he saw the crackle of sparks. But he couldn't figure out what had happened between there and the open air he was suddenly falling through, a smoking hole in his robes. Jubilatious looked to the quickly approaching ravine and suddenly understood exactly what had happened. He said a quick spell, and then was swallowed by the earth.

Zetine watched Jubilatious fall and screamed in fear for her friend, but she had little time to be afraid. The castle gate suddenly began to rise, and from it emerged a palanquin carried by four dwarves. Seated atop it was an androgynous figure in hooded white robes, which rose to their feet with strange inhuman motions. As they raised their skeletal arms overhead, Zetine realized just who and what she was looking at.

In that moment she realized Vhodan's forces had stopped fighting anyone they were not directly engaged with, and were all looking to Kerotin, The Bone Lord. Suddenly they were all driving their blades into their own bodies, swords and daggers slicing wrists while spears were buried in throats. Blood began to float through the air, combining with each and every source as it flowed into Kerotin. Zetine began to hurry forward, knocking over whoever she could as she rushed the necromancer.

Muscular tissue began to build up across the Bone Lord's skeleton, veins and arteries sprouting out to swallow up the sacrificed blood. Soon pale skin began to wrap across his muscles, and a pair of ethereal green eyes appeared in his once empty sockets. Still the blood flowed into Kerotin, even though nothing else was being created. He was hairless, but complete, and utterly terrifying.

The Bone Lord looked to the pharaoh of Exia, a smile curling upon his lips. He said one simple word that filled Zetine with unspeakable Dread. He said only, "Rise."

From across the battlefield, every corpse that had fallen began to sit up. Severed legs failed around, arms pulled themselves forward, and heads gnashed their teeth at nearby ankles. The resurrected dead drew whatever weapons they had, sometimes from their own corpses. All of them waited in anticipation as The Army of Hope slew their enemies, waited for the confirmation on the order they were created to follow.

As the last drop of blood entered him, The Bone Lord ordered, "Kill them all."

***

Ironja and Mizt-Ied had made it to the next floor of the dungeons, this one arranged into a neat and organized grid system. Every five meters was a cell, about half of which were filled. Of the filled ones, many of the occupants were already dead. The pair continued past them, Ironja doing his best to remain quiet.

"What do you think happened to them?" Mizt-Ied asked.

Ironja glanced into one of the cells, whose occupant was a shriveled up corpse curled into a ball on the ground. He said, "Well, I have two guesses. A vampire or a bad case of thirst."

"I'm gonna guess vampire," she replied.

"Ay, there is one lurkin' about somewhere," he nodded.

"No, she's right there," Mizt-Ied pointed above him.

With talons sunk into the ceiling, Barragu, Queen of Vampires slumbered above them. Her wings were wrapped around her naked body to conceal most of her form, though little was left to the imagination. She looked like a beautiful half-elf, with pointed ears and pale white skin. Her coal colored black hair fell downwards, while her blood red lips seemed almost to smile at them.

"Let's go VERY quietly," Mizt-Ied said as she crept forward, not making a sound.

Ironja followed after her, making fairly little sound despite his heavy armor. From above him, Barragu said, "I can hear you."

She fell from the ceiling, landing perfectly upon her feet on the cold ground. The vampire's wings retracted as she moved towards them, an uncanny walk that wasn't quite alive, but was also strangely seductive. Ironja had to remove his eyes for decency's sake; while Mizt-Ied let her own gaze wander.

"Two little mortals enter my room, and they don't even bring me a snack," she purred, though at no point did she open her mouth.

"We're here to kill your boss," Mizt-Ied politely informed.

"Mizt-Ied!" Ironja cried with surprise.

"What?" She asked. "She can read minds. No point in lying."

Barragu looked between the two then said, "Leave us, dwarf. Your destiny lies with another."

"Eh? Mizt-Ied?" he asked.

"I've got this," she replied as she held her knives up in a defensive posture.

Ironja placed his hand on her shoulder and said "Good luck lass," then hurried off.

The goblin and the vampire stared at one another for several moments. Mizt-Ied broke the silence by saying, "Nice bush."

"You are a curious thing," Barragu replied as she strolled forward. Mizt-Ied tried to move away, but the vampire easily stayed within an arm's length as she continued to speak. "Your heart is filled with such sorrow. Wouldn't it feel so nice to abandon it? To no longer hurt?"

"Listen, l-lady," she nervously replied. "I have a steadfast loosely defined moral code that I refuse to break."

"I expected you to stutter as you said that," the vampire giggled, a cold and menacing little laugh.

"I know, right?" Mizt-Ied confidentially said. "I've been waiting like five months to say that, and thought I would mess it up so bad!"

"Cute," Barragu said, before quickly grabbing Mizt-Ied by the throat and raising her into the air. "You cannot kill me, little goblin. I have lived since the dawn of time, and I will live long after the world dies."

"Aren't you already d-dead though?" She croaked out.

"Semantics," the vampire shrugged. "You have no hope of killing me, though you can certainly try."

She released Mizt-Ied who fell on her butt gasping for breath. Then she asked, "Wait... are you l-letting me go-go?"

"More or less," Barragu replied, taking a seat on the ground next to her. "Though I can't have you interfering with the others."

Mizt-Ied looked to her suspiciously as she asked, "Why?"

"I have lived for many thousands of years," the vampire sighed, which was odd as she didn't breath. "I have met many prophets and oracles. Travelers from across time, who sought to make futile changes. Do you know what they tell me of this era?"

"What?" Mizt-Ied asked, curiosity practically dragging her into the vampire's arms.

Barragu's smile spread so wide her sharp teeth were visible as she said, "Nothing. Because none of this truly matters, and I have grown quite bored. So there's no point in stopping you, since I probably was never supposed to anyway."

Mizt-Ied took this all in then asked, "So why can't I go join Ironja?"

"Because there are rules to follow," she explained. "In every age, there comes a time when a set of heroes must battle their villains one on one, overcoming them through strength or skill or wits. Only then can they truly become heroes."

"So our battle is... talking?" Mizt-Ied asked.

"Indeed," she stated. "It's quite nice to talk to someone, is it not?"

"It's not what I was expecting," she confessed.

"Nothing is ever what you expect," the vampire replied. "When I first heard of you, and I deduced that each of the others had a near perfect match, I understood that I was the villain of this Era, and you were the heroes."

"Wait... you know you're the bad guy?" The goblin quizzically asked, mind spinning."

"My yes," she giggled again. "It is the nature of our world. Good will always fight evil, but good will always become evil. Perhaps my corruption began when I slew the giants, so many millennia ago. Or it was only when I met a charismatic man with a dream for the world. Or maybe it was always in my nature, and the consuming of a life is an inherently evil thing. I do not know what, if any of these, is true. All I know is what side I have chosen, and that the future holds many mysteries for me."

Mizt-Ied asked, "How can you be so aware of what evil is, but still take part in it?"

"There are a thousand different answers for that question, little thing," she replied. "But I have made my choice, have I not? Perhaps this may be redemption, or perhaps not. It is only fate that can decide whether my inaction absolves me of what I have take part in."

"I don't think it will," Mizt-Ied said.

"No..." she sighed once more without breathing."Neither do I."

"But you still did something good!" Mizt-Ied tried to encourage her. "I mean sure, there's better ways to help, but not killing me is a start! Maybe after this is all over, you can do something proper good again? Try to be a hero."

"You poor little fool," Barragu said as she took hold of Mizt-Ied's cheeks and forced her to make eye contact. "I hope that you die young, because you are far too good for a hero. It is inevitable that you will fall should you succeed and live long. Even Death will not save you from corruption, should your deeds become legendary. It is a core part of our world. Good always becomes evil."

Mizt-Ied pulled herself away and said, "That's not true! Being good is a choice, and it's a choice everyone should make every day!"

The vampire laid down upon the ground, her bones popping as she stretched backwards. She said, "So naive, you sweet thing. Our time together is almost up, though I have one last confession."

"What is it?" Mizt-Ied asked as she rose back up to her feet.

Barragu said, "When I realized it was you I was destined to meet, I had many expectations of how our encounter would go. None of them included you staring at my chest the entire time."

Mizt-Ied blushed and looked away as she mumbled, "They're really pointy and fun looking..."

"Go forth, little goblin," the vampire said. "Go save this land, and make your mistakes."

***

Shortly after he had left Mizt-Ied to face the Vampire Queen, Ironja had stumbled across a large chamber with a spiral staircase, absolutely filled with stone statues. They were of all sorts of humanoid races, but most common were statues of dwarves. Most of the statues also seemed to be screaming, which would have been more mildly alarming if Ironja hadn't immediately deduced that this was the layer of Artessa the Gorgon Queen.

Ironja readied his shield and axe as he looked around the chamber, dwarven eyes scanning every crevice and shadow. He turned and nearly had a heart attack as crimson eyes stared into his soul, accompanied by a few dozen smaller sets of matching eyes.

The dwarf leapt back and raised his shield as he stared her down, which was quite hard for him to do.

Artessa was tall even for elven standards, though half of her height could be contributed to the serpent's tail that sprouted from her hips. The gorgon was covered in stark white scales, as were the snakes that made up her hair. She carried with her a bronze spear, though from the way she held it limply in her left hand, Ironja could tell she had little experience with it.

The Gorgon Queen hissed, "Youuu are not sssstone..."

"Ay, and yer dead," Ironja replied before rushing her.

Artessa flicked the dwarf with her tail, knocking him into one of the statues which shattered upon impact. As Ironja pulled himself free, Artesia was there, stabbing down with her spear. He barely managed to block the blow with his shield in time. Before he could get free though, the gorgon's tail wrapped around his throat and tossed him against a wall.

She slithered forward and thrust her spear, but this time Ironja was ready. He parried the blow then retaliated with a swing of his axe. Artessa screamed in pain as her severed hand went flying, acidic blood spraying over the room. Ironja then quickly pushed her away with his shield and moved away, trying desperately to avoid the small pools of acid that bubbled away on the ground.

Artessa spun around and hissed, "You dare hurt me!?"

"Ay, it's what I'm here to do," he replied.

The gorgon quickly slithered forward, and as Ironja attempted to strike her again, wacked the dwarf's right arm with her tail. Ironja's axe went flying before embedding in a wall too high for him to reach. Before he could react, she body slammed him, knocking the dwarf onto the ground. Her tail wrapped around his throat and began to choke Ironja, while she held her stump out to drip acid onto his chest.

Ironja desperately tried to push her off of him, or at least free his throat from her tail, but it was in vain. Instead he began to punch the gorgon in the face, which worked surprisingly well. On the third strike he broke her nose, and Artessa fell away from him. Ironja took the opportunity to hop back to his feet, and then drew his hammer.

"Jus' you and me, ol' lass..." he whispered to the craftsman's weapon.

"Kill youuuu," Artessa hissed.

"Heard that one before," Ironja grunted.

She lunged at him but Ironja quickly swung his hammer, hitting Artessa in the right hip. With a squeal of pain she fell to the ground, writhing around and lashing her tail out dangerously. Statues crumbled beneath the whip of her tail and she even rolled into puddles of her own blood as she cried in pain. Ironja hurried forward and raised his hammer into the air, taking one last look down at the agonized gorgon.

"Rip you apart," she wailed.

"Jus' shuddup and die already," he replied before bringing the hammer down over her skull with a sickening thud. He groaned and stepped away as he said, "That felt good. Gonna need to crack some more gorgon skulls after this."

Chapter 17

It was hard work moving the caravan across Moia, made even harder by the wounded. They had taken the bedding from the bunks and swaddled the worst of the wounded in the various sheets, then tied the sheets to spears so that they could be carried. A few of the freed slaves hobbled along with limping or broken feet, aided by makeshift crutches crafted from the bed frames of the bunks and repurposed swords. Those who were uninjured, or whose wounds were minor, carried whatever weapons they had managed to get their hands on.

Kazaa headed the group, marching them purposefully across the land. Wolf slunk behind him, keeping a consistent pace, but unable to bring herself to move with any confidence. The pain that stretched across her bones was one thing, but every day since she had awoken had only increased the pain over her heart. She kept her head down as she followed Kazaa, doing what was asked of her, but little else.

On more than one occasion, they met with patrols of Imperial soldiers. The first two times were met with violence, and several of the freed slaves were killed. During these conflicts, Wolf actually felt alive, reveling in the bloodshed as she cut through her enemies. But then after the adrenaline wore off, she was left with the same empty void that only seemed to keep growing.

By the third time they met with a patrol, there was no need for any violence. They had gathered up enough pieces of armor and uniforms that each of the slaves was able to dress like an Imperial. Wolf and Kazaa also dressed in their slain enemies clothes, and Kazaa had encouraged her to at least wear a chest plate, but she had refused. Kazaa had also been reluctant to wear their uniform, but made the sacrifice. He stripped his head of its covering to reveal short and messy black hair, and could pass for an Imperial soldier with a flair for foreign weaponry.

On their third encounter, the patrols captain waved them down and calmly approached. He asked Kazaa, "What happened to you? Your men look... decimated."

"We were ambushed by bandits," Kazaa casually lied, though his fake accent was slightly off.

"All the way out here?" The captain asked.

"It came as a shock to us as well, as you can see," he gestured behind him. "We're going to get patched up and send out the report."

"You're heading east," he said.

"We are," Kazaa nodded.

The captain pointed north and said, "The nearest outpost is a day's walk that way. There's almost nothing out east."

"We have a white mage only two days away," Kazaa replied. "My men need her more than they do a field doctor."

"Fair enough," the captain shrugged. "Safe travels, commander."

"You as well," Kazaa nodded before leading the caravan off.

The troops watched them leave, and the captain made a note to report it when they arrived back at their outpost. Otherwise, the journey went fairly smoothly. The group had to regularly raid the farms they passed through for produce in order to keep their supplies from running out, but otherwise ran into no more trouble.

The border between Cairn and Moia had always been vaguely defined. Most would say Cairn began where the Black Mountain was, though you try telling a necromancer where to build a house. The residents of Cairn would often say their domain stretched out to the edges of The Dark Forest. This was also quite hard to define, as patches of their pine trees would grow in what was undeniably Moia.

"Are we here?" One of the freed slaves asked as tall pine trees began to rise up around them.

"I think so," Kazaa said back to her.

"We still have a while more," Mira corrected. "We're still in Moia."

"How do you know that?" Kazaa curiously asked her.

"I grew up here," was all she said.

"And yet they made you a slave?" He asked.

She looked down at her feet and replied, "We all make mistakes."

"Are you up for telling a story?" He asked.

She looked to him in silence for a few moments before answering, "Fine. I have nothing to hide. As I said, I was born and raised in Moia. During the summer we would collect pinecones from the edge of the land so that we could decorate them for the upcoming harvest. I was always warned never to stray beyond the trees, for beyond lied the domain of death. It was there that I would be eaten by a troll, or kidnapped by some evil necromancer.

"When I got older, I met a boy. I still do not know how much love there actually was between us, though I cared for him greatly. I thought my feelings were returned, for he never said otherwise. He convinced me to move to Imperial Heart with him, where he was so sure he would become a luxurious merchant. Instead he found himself cutting the heads off fish all day, while I sewed clothes endlessly.

"Eventually he came to me with an idea, and the fool that I was, I followed him to see it through. Somehow, the poor idiot had gotten hold of some fairy flower seeds. We grew them in our home, clipped the petals, and then ground them in a pestle before packing them into little clothes bags he had me sew. He would take them out and sell the flower to all sorts of people, or so he told me. From the lowest of low class, to the real merchants of the city. Lies, I'm sure. He probably only sold it to his coworkers.

"One day though, he drops a bag out in the streets. A guard saw it, picked the bag up, and it spilled open. Fairy powder falls over him. Now maybe the guard was an idiot, or he got high particularly fast, or both. Regardless, my sweet boy convinced the guard that I had made it, and he had no idea where it came from. He convinced him that I was the mastermind in his own idiotic plan!

"My boy came back to me before a squad could arrive to arrest me, and confessed everything. So I stabbed him in the eye with a sewing needle. It felt good, though I quickly came to regret it. I ran before any guards arrived, and even made it out of the city. They caught me a day later though. I hadn't cleaned myself, and they found my dress was covered in blood and fairy powder. So they took me to Sanctuary, so that I may be put to use for the good of the Empire."

"A tragic tale," Kazaa said as she finished. Then he asked, "Did your lover survive?"

"Probably," she replied. "I only wanted to hurt him, not kill him. Maybe one day I'll see him again, and he'll understand why I did what I did."

"I doubt that," one of the other freed slaves mumbled.

"I've got a story," Cutter spoke up.

"Then tell us," Kazaa replied.

"I hail from the hills of Oshack, where many a dwarves called home. We all grew up hearing stories of how our ancestors had battled the tyranny of The Rizzen Empire. As children, we'd even carve little idols of our greatest heroes in the war. Across the Empire's entire existence, we were the only ones to ever beat them! O'course, no one else considers it a win. "Mutual ceasefire," is what I think The Empire called it.

"My ancestors had kicked their asses, cut them down with our axes and kicked them out of the region. The humans and elves helped, sure, but it was us DWARVES that beat The Empire. The old Emperor at the time, I think his name was Carnal or some shite, even paid us a visit. Made a big deal about how we were supposed to sign a peace treaty. Most of the stories spent a good while making fun of his stupid crown, but we signed, it was to last for a good few centuries. My favorite ancestor, Bootbuckle Halfaxe even got ol' Carnal to spit into his hand and shake on it.

"So then you get to my pa's time, and everyone's scared because the peace treaty ends. Everyone was expecting an attack, so they all gear up for war just like their ancestors did. Even sent the elves across the country to scout it out and see when they were gonna come. But nothing happened. The Empire was happy with what it had, and it was leaving us alone.

"So pa and everyone got drunk, banged each other, and had a bunch of kids. Like I said, we were brought up with stories of how we kicked The Empire's ass. But we were idiots. We didn't realize the Empire couldn't just be content. It waited until we felt safe and secure, until our people were no longer warriors. Then it attacked.

"The Empire learned from their mistake, that's for sure. Cut down or burned every tree in its path as it slowly swallowed the region. Boxed us all in, even the elves. Or rather, they funneled most of those cowards out. They dinnit attack all at once. They would capture a village, and then spend a few weeks clearing trees and gaining reinforcements before moving to the next one, laying waste to the forest. It didn't matter how hard you fought if ye couldn't breathe, if the very air was so full of smoke it was poison. They burned our homes and killed most of those who fought back. Some of them though, they took as slaves. Collared us like dogs and drug us across the country. They killed my home, but they dinnit kill me. Their mistake."

Once Cutter had finished, Kazaa said, "We saw Oshack."

"Ye did?" He asked, a hint of hope on his voice. "What was it like?"

"Nice for a time," he replied. "But then The Empire arrived. If it helps, I think most of the villagers where we were evacuated. They are still out there somewhere."

"I hope so," Cutter sighed.

"Anyone else have a tale to tell?" Kazaa asked. There was a bit of mumbling, but no one came forward. He sighed and said, "I suppose it is my turn then. I have many stories, most of them full of bloodshed. But this is not a story of violence. More important than any live I've claimed, is one I lost.

"When I was very young, I studied under a cruel old man. He made sure to charge me for my bed, for my meals, for every tool I used and quill I broke. He was old and bitter, but he was not without kindness. As much as I hated him, I learned to love him, for he was the only person I had in my life at that point. I learned much from him during those years, and I think in his own way, he was glad to have company. Even the naive company of a child.

"When I had finished my apprenticeship, I came home to see a family who I no longer recognized. My mother looked the same, my father too save for the grey in his hair. But I realized I knew nothing about them. My brothers and sisters, those who had not gone to study in my absence, were true strangers. Not only did I not know what they were like, they looked nothing like the siblings I had left. It is the way of our people to be surrounded by strangers, and only then was I beginning to understand.

"Soon after, I visited that hate filled old man to pay off some of my debts. He invited me in to talk, and it felt nice to talk to someone I actually knew something about. Each month when I would pay off some of my debt, as much as I still hated him, I had someone with who I could relate. Someone I could tell of my life, and who would actually understand. I could say the same about no one else.

"He took on one more apprentice in that time, and he was as hard on that boy as he was on me. I was kinder though, and made sure to stick around long enough that the boy didn't feel completely isolated. Maybe it was the right thing to do, maybe it wasn't. He eventually left to start working as an adult, just as I had done, and never came back.

"I stayed with the old man as his health worsened, as the priests stood over him and said their death prayers. None tried to save him, for he was elderly, and the noblest thing an elderly person can do is die. I stayed with him for those long few weeks, as his breathing grew shallow, as his limbs fell too weak to move. I held his hand as he died, the last thing he was ever able to see or touch, telling him of all the adventure I hoped to see.

"It is the way of our people to be entombed, surrounded by strangers. But it was not the way of my master. Against the customs of my people, I wrapped his body in ceremonial sheets and made my preparations. I purchased a sword, supplies, and clothes, everything I thought I would need. Then I hired a boat to ferry me to new lands. With my master's body held firmly in my arms I stepped onto that vessel, and abandoned everything I had come to know.

"As he had wished of me, I buried him in the ocean. The sailors seemed to know just what I wanted to do, and they helped me tie sand bags to his body. I watched as it sunk beneath the waves, swallowed by his watery tomb. I cried over a man who I had hated, and who I had loved as a father. I cried over the past that I was leaving behind, and of the boy who had died so many years ago when he first stepped foot in a dark and cold tomb. I was not the first to cry on that vessel, but the sailors made sure to make me feel like I was."

There were a few chuckles at that, but Kazaa continued, "I learned everything I could from the ship's crew, from their understanding of swordsmanship to how to steer a vessel during a storm. Eventually they let me out in new lands further up coast, and I set to work learning everything I could of the place. Their cultures, their fighting styles, what weapons they commonly used, everything. It was a cycle I would repeat in many lands over the years.

"By the time I had reached this land, I was an accomplished sellsword and had made quite the name for myself. Not that it mattered here. I learned of the land just as I did elsewhere, and my interest was most drawn to Cairn. It seemed as though it was a sister to my own homeland, cut off from the outside world and so close to death. I had to see it. On my way I met a girl whose destiny seemed tied to Cairn as well, and so we began to travel together."

Wolf looked over at Kazaa but said nothing. It was Mira who said, "Then you two found us, and freed us."

"We did, somehow," he replied. "Truthfully, I thought it was a pointless cause. We got lucky."

"You saved us," Mira insisted. "It had to have been fate that led you through Sanctuary, fate that rescued us from that miserable hellhole."

"Fate's a load of crap," Cutter grumbled.

"It is not," Mira glared down at him.

"Is too," he returned the glare.

"If there was no fate, there would be no point in living," she said.

"Course there is," he chided. "Ye make your own destiny."

Wolf said, "Destiny is real, but we all have the same one."

"And what's that, lass?" Cutter asked.

"We all die," she grimly informed.

With that uncomfortable note, no one quite wanted to talk for some time. They continued on in silence, stopping only to bury two of the wounded who had passed away during their journey. During this time, the group split up in pairs to empty their bowels and look for any forgeable food or water. There was little water, but more than a few elderberry bushes grew in wild patches.

It was soon after this, before they had reconvened with the others, that Wolf noticed something shrouded by withered grey trees and dark green vines. She slowly approached it, unsure entirely of what she was looking at. She ran her hand through a patch of moss, then grabbed hold of some vines and yanked hard. The vines tore free, revealing part of a large stone door.

She called out, "Kazaa! Come look at this."

The Exian headed towards her, then stopped and took in the sight of the impressive stone structure. Though nature had reclaimed it, Kazaa could still make out the general architecture. The walls were impressively carved, and the entirety of the building seemed so massive it could house a thousand people or more. The stone door was ten feet tall, allowing it to accommodate most of the taller races, though there was nothing that indicated who built it.

Wolf asked him, "What is it?"

"A fortress of some sort," he replied. "Come on; help me get the door open."

Wolf followed him and together they placed their hands on the edge of the door, pulling with all their might. After a few moments it cracked ever so slightly, but that was all they needed. They each got a better grip then pulled once more, and the door slowly slid open. Dirt was pushed aside and vines were broken, revealing a second door right next to the first that was still concealed by the plant growth.

The interior was dark and cold, and almost painfully dry. There was the faintest residue of ash on the ground and the walls, which clung to their boots as they walked inside. The pair stepped into a large atrium with some sort of stone judge's table set up so that three figures could address the entirety of the room. They looked to the three figures, whose bones littered the table and ground around it.

"No one must have been in this place for centuries," Kazaa mused, running his hand over the perfect stone wall. "Three hundred years at least..."

He walked towards the middle of the room, then recoiled after stepping on something. He looked down to see a most peculiar sight. Despite there being nothing else left in the room save for ash and bones, there was a hat placed neatly upon the ground. It was a wide brimmed pointed cap, dyed a lovely shade of purple. The sort of hat one would expect to see worn by a wizard.

As Kazaa reached down to pick it up, Wolf asked, "What is it?"

"Just a hat," he replied. "I have no idea how it's survived for so long... but it looks rather nice."

He put it on his head and Wolf said, "You look like an idiot."

"You're just jealous," he replied as he strolled away.

They rejoined the others and made sure everyone was prepared before telling them of the news. Kazaa announced, "We found an ancient structure nearby. It is more than large enough to accommodate you all. But there is no telling of how long it could sustain you for."

There was then several minutes of discussion as they figured out whether it was worth it to stay or not. Eventually Mira announced, "Most of us will stay and try to make a life here. If things seem too bad... we'll head to Cairn and join you there."

"Are you sure?" Kazaa asked. "I do not thing those stories you heard of trolls were untrue."

"I am sure," she nodded.

"Besides," Cutter chuckled as he placed his sword onto his shoulder. "What kind of dwarf can't kill a few little trolls?"

"Just make sure not to feed them," Kazaa smiled down at him.

"Who's coming with us?" Wolf asked.

"I will accompany you to the ends of the world," Splitter said, which caused her to groan.

Four others announced they would join them, though Wolf didn't recognize any of them from her home, and Kazaa had not made any real connection with them. They helped the others settle down in the abandoned fortress, which took more time than they would have thought. There were many chambers to catalogue, ranging from personal and communal bedrooms, to empty storage rooms and large meeting rooms. Though the stone beds would offer little comfort, it was better than sleeping outside.

Before they left, Kazaa pulled Splitter aside and said, "Wolf does not like you. Leave the pup alone."

"You don't know that," he so cleverly retorted with.

"Shut up and listen, boy," Kazaa coldly stated, which reminded Splitter deeply of Shank. He continued, "She broke your nose when you tried to kiss her. She has not talked to you since. She avoids any area you stand in. At your mere suggestion of accompanying us, she voiced her frustrations. Wolf does not like you. Leave her alone, or I'll make you leave her alone. Do you understand?"

Splitter shook his head and said, "I do. And I will."

"Very good," Kazaa replied, before turning to leave.

Once he was out of ear shot, Splitter mumbled, "Mind your own business, outsider."

The group took careful note of their stock, and found a large well near the back of the fortress so that they could refill their water skins. Once ready, they said their goodbyes to the others, and Wolf noticed that Mira hugged Kazaa for a long few moments. Then they set off, walking through the dark forest once again. A chill was beginning to settle in the air, and the wind froze the bones of everyone other than Wolf and Splitter. Even still, they carried on and did not slow for any reason.

***

The journey from the fortress to the Black Mountain was slow and steady, but not particularly long. Soon after they had made camp at nightfall, a buck had wandered by. Wolf had quickly sent an arrow into its throat, and within no time it was dressed. They all ate well, stored what little meat they could in a couple bags of salt someone had brought from the sanctuary, then buried the deer so its carcass wouldn't attract any more creatures. The following morning they awoke shortly after sunrise, and found that Splitter, who had been appointed their spotter for the second half of the night, had also fell asleep.

"You put all of our lives in danger!" Kazaa spat at him.

"I should cut you down right here," Wolf growled, though her heart wasn't in it.

"I'm sorry! Splitter had wailed, which only made the others all the angrier.

After several minutes of them all berating him, a troll crossed their path. It was about half the size of Wolf and completely covered in black fur. Its long grey nose poked out from the fur, and beady black eyes scanned the travelers eagerly. After a few moments it decided they weren't worth the hassle, and then wandered off. They watched it waddle away, an almost adorable sight, were trolls not known to be vicious killers.

"Let's just go," Kazaa said as he began to walk away.

It was another half day before the group would arrive at the base of the mountain. It was an impressive sight, almost artificially carved. The entirety of the mountain was a wall made of solid black stone, rising up several hundred feet. There were a few parts of the mountain that looked damage, though for no discernible reason, and the damage was entirely superficial. They could all fully understand how Cairn had never been invaded before.

"How do we past the mountain?" one of the others, an orc, asked.

"We'll have to climb," Kazaa replied.

That was far easier said than done. Though handholds could be found easily enough, gripping them hurt one's hands. Kazaa wrapped his own hands in bandages, and then passed them around to the others so they could do the same. With the first challenge overcome, they continued on. Hand over hand, foot over foot, it was slow work. Muscles grew tense, then heavy, and eventually it seemed impossible to reach the top. Even still, they had to keep going, even as their arms screamed with pain.

There came the sound of tumbling rocks, a scream, and one of the others fell as he lost his gripping. They all watched the elf go, desperately trying to grab hold of the mountain again, tearing his own hands apart in the process and leaving a red trail along the wall. He hit the ground far below, and they all knew there was no point in letting their minds dwell on him. The local wildlife would get a nice little meal out of him that night.

It was just passed sunset when Wolf reached the top of the mountain. As her hand scoured the ledge for something to grab onto, a skeletal hand grabbed her wrist. It pulled her upwards with surprising strength, and then laid her on the ground. Wolf took the moment to lie in a heap, her entire body to heavy to move. Slowly though, she began to move her head about and look around.

The light in Cairn was different. It was almost grey, but overwelmed by a green glow from somewhere nearby. To say they were at the top of the mountain was also false, for now she could see the entire region was built onto the mountain, with many more walls to climb. Standing by Wolf were three people and two skeletons whose flesh had been entirely disposed of, their eye sockets glowing green. Two of the gathered people were men, dressed in black shirts and pants, their forearms exposed to reveal many scars. They each carried with them a straightsword locked in scabbards, and ceremonial daggers.

The other person was a woman, much shorter than Wolf, though about average height. Her back was to Wolf as she said something to the men, so all Wolf could see was her black cloak and hood. When she turned around, the first thing Wolf saw were the same eyes as the Dead Woman. She even looked remarkably similar, but with pale brown skin instead of stark white skin. Her lips were pursed into what Wolf could tell was a permanent scowl, though she didn't seem particularly angry.

The woman said to her, "Sleep," and Wolf fell limp.

Then Wolf sat up, and her passenger said, "It is good to see you again."

"Do not start," the necromancer replied. "There are five more approaching. Should we let them fall?"

"I promised one of them hospitality, and the others by extension I suppose," Wolf's mouth said. "Let them up."

"Very well," the necromancer nodded, and then jerked her head to order the skeletons forward. Then she looked back to Wolf and said, "Wake."

The skeletons each moved with a surprising amount of grace, crouching down and extending their arms towards the abyss below, while Wolf's eyes fluttered open and closed several times. One by one they pulled up each of the others, Kazaa coming first and Splitter coming last. They were all too tired to move, and were at the complete mercy of the necromancer. To Wolf, she seemed entirely disinterested in the others, as though they were nothing more than an afterthought. Instead the necromancer focused entirely on her, ethereal green eyes burrowing into her soul.

After they had taken several moments to catch their breath, the necromancer said, "Girl. Come with us."

Wolf began to uncomfortably push herself up, but was caught off guard by Kazaa who declared, "Wherever she goes, I do too. It was ordered by your kin."

She looked to him curiously for a few seconds before saying, "Very well. The two of you, come with me. The rest of you... I don't care. Throw yourselves off or find something to do."

The necromancer turned and began to walk away, cloak flowing behind her. The guards and skeletons followed, leaving Kazaa and Wolf to struggle to their feet. They trailed slowly behind, pushing themselves to their limits just to walk. In the distance they could see the home that the residents of Cairn had made for themselves. Some lived in caverns that had formed naturally in the mountain. Others lived in huts made of carved stone or metal sheets. Then of course were the domiciles made from bone. Of these, some were large leather tents that only used the bones for structure, while others had been entirely constructed out of skeletons belonging to various animals.

The sound of a hammer banging upon steel soon filled the air, along with the haunting tunes of flutes echoing out from the caverns. As they passed through the town, they would see humanoid skeletons tending to crops that were planted atop artificial grow beds. Other skeletons tended to livestock, mainly cattle and sheep. Nearby the pens, the dead could be seen tanning hides or spinning wool. Eventually they passed the blacksmith's forge, and sure enough there stood a dwarven skeleton cooling a black straightsword in a barrel of oil. He turned to watch them pass, and Wolf was sure she saw some hint of sapience behind its glowing eye sockets.

Kazaa asked, "Do you use the dead for every job?"

"Most of them," the necromancer replied. "Most of our men serve as loyal guards and knights to our prestige wizards. Their duties could easily be replaced by a stuck cow though, for all they really contribute is their blood."

"I don't understand," Wolf quietly said by Kazaa's side.

He explained, "They drain the blood from their allies to cast spells."

"I have seen the Dead Woman cast spells without blood," she replied.

The necromancer cut in, "A necromantic spell can be cast without draining another, but it still requires a sacrifice. The more a wizard uses the magic, the more their bodies will deteriorate. In the end, they will be nothing more than a skeleton themselves. This is why a necromancer never leaves Cairn alone... for what good that did."

"Her hands," Wolf said. "The Dead Woman's hands were from the grave."

"Yes, that sounds like her," the necromancer said more to herself than Wolf.

"Where is the music coming from?" Kazaa asked.

"Some of the men are unfit for protective duties," she explained. "Instead they tend to become artists. Illustrators, poets, bards," she then grimaced and croaked out, "*Comedians.*"

"The music is quite beautiful," Kazaa said. "Yet so tragic."

"It is the first song to ever fill the land of Cairn," she explained. "When the giants died here, their hearts carried with them a lament so powerful that it was heard even by our ancestors. It called them to this land, begged of them to stay and nurture the corpses so that they wouldn't be alone. They would be the first necromancers, and in truth, the first school of magic."

"A fascinating story," he mused. "My own people have a much different idea for the origins of necromancy."

"And what is that?" she asked, a sly smile spreading across her face.

He explained, "Evil desires nothing more than to exist. When it is unable to be born naturally, it invades the world of the dead. It gathers up whatever souls were once legendary figures, be they mighty heroes or horrid villains. It corrupts and twists the souls into parodies of what they once were, before returning them to the bodies they once inhabited. There, in the halfway point between life and death, they sew terror. They kill and violate and cause chaos until once again they are killed.

"It was our creator god, Tehn, who gave a select few the gift of necromancy to prevent evil from finding its way into our world. If a corpse is reanimated, given a hollow soul so that no others can fill it, there is no risk of it coming back to wreak havoc. Whenever a notable person dies, our priests embalm the body and perform a ritual to fill it with a hollow soul. For eternity they will rest in their tombs, protecting the world from evil by simply existing."

"Your people have an interesting mythos," the necromancer said. "But we have truth."

They came across a river that flowed through a trench in the mountain, streaming down from somewhere far outside of the town. The water was the same ethereal green as the necromancer's eyes, and carried with it a copper smell that assaulted one' senses. Even just standing next to it, each of them could tell that the water was also freezing cold even for the already cool air. To Kazaa, it reminded him of a pool of noxious acid, only decidedly alkaline and seemingly safer.

As they followed the river out of town, an awe inspiring sight filled their eyes. A single skeleton lay atop the mountain, far more massive than any living thing could ever conceivably have been.

Its open palm had fallen down the slope of one of the mountain tips, while its elbow pointed up into the air. Its ribcage had been impaled through a massive spear that had been broken off, leaving only the spearhead embedded in the ground beneath. That was all any of them could see, for the rest of the skeleton was simply too large to make out any distinct details from where they stood.

With a smug tone the necromancer said, "As you can see, our history is more than just myth."

"It's... how could it have been so big?" Kazaa gasped.

"What *is* it?" Wolf asked.

"The giant Yrgrun," the necromancer informed. "One of many who fell in our lands. Their blood fills the trenches of Cairn, and leads on to the life after death."

"That's not possible," Kazaa stated.

"It is," she replied. "I have been there several times, as has every true necromancer. It is the final step of our training."

Kazaa looked between the river and the giant skeleton, before looking back to the necromancer. In utter confusion he asked, "If you have that type of power, why do you stay in Cairn? Why not explore the world? Why not change it in any way?"

She tilted her head and simply asked back, "Why would we?" then she turned her gaze to Wolf and said, "Girl. Step into the river."

"What?" Wolf asked in surprise. Then she asked suspiciously, "Why?"

The necromancer explained, "It is time for your passenger to be reborn. She has gone far too long without a body of her own. Has come too close to Our Black Lady. She must live again."

Wolf nodded and stepped forward, only for Kazaa's arm to shoot out and grab her wrist. He asked her, "Are you sure? You don't have to do this."

"I am," she said as she shook free.

Wolf stepped into the river, and icy pain quickly spread up over her leg. She brought her other leg in, and quickly her lower body grew numb. She approached the center of the trench, the water rising up to cover her stomach. Despite the pain, as the water flowed past her, Wolf's wounds began to close over and heal. Even her fatigue seemed to pass somewhat, though she could barely notice it. Then a splitting pain rocketed across her skull, and a small piece of bone was torn from the right side of her head from just next to her ear. She let out a cry of pain, and the bone fell into the water, while the wound quickly closed over.

"What was that!?" she growled out as she held the side of her head. She blinked a few times, and for the first time in months, her eyes were entirely brown.

"All that was needed to bring new life," the necromancer replied. "Rise anew, from the abyss of life and death. Let warm flesh envelop you, skeletal structure expand, and nervous system spread. See through eyes and hear through ears once more. You who have been taken from us, I command you to *live*."

A pale arm rose up from beneath the water, grasping blindly. When Wolf moved towards it the necromancer shouted, "NO! Do not disturb her. She must find life on her own."

The arm fell back into the depths of the water, but from beneath its surface they could see a steady stream of motion. Then the other arm surfaced, followed by the first, and then a whole body violently flung up. Its back was to Wolf, and it fell forward almost as soon as it rose up. But then it breached the surface once more, and slowly rose up to its full height, which was about equal to Kazaa's height. It wore pale skin close to the color of snow, and was completely hairless. There was not a single blemish across its entire body, be it wound or freckle, and was in almost perfect health. The only apparent illness was just how strikingly slender it was.

A single word quietly escaped from Wolf's lips, heard only by one other, and his heart broke for her. She asked, "Mama?"

The necromancer said, "Rise, Velena. Live, Velena. Firstborn daughter of Lokas, sister of my house and sharer of my mother's womb. Let the dark sky wash over you anew, and breathe through new lungs. I welcome you into my embrace, eldest sister."

The Dead Woman turned and looked to Wolf with dull green eyes, so devoid of magic that she seemed almost like a different person. Truthfully, Wolf did not even know who she was looking at. But that did not quell the rage that blossomed in her heart. The anger over being used. The sorrow of finding that her hope was meaningless. The disgust that her body had been host to a necromantic parasite for months. The Dead Woman, Velena, opened her mouth to speak. Before a single woman could be uttered, Wolf had turned and began to climb out from the river trench.

As she began to storm away, Kazaa called out, "Wolf! Wait, do not go. You need to-"

"Did you know?" she asked bluntly, her voice hoarse as she barely managed to suppress her overflowing emotions.

He looked her in the eyes and felt his shoulders fall as he said, "Yes. I did. But-"

Wolf swung her right fist at Kazaa but he caught it before it could make contact with his jaw. She swung with her left, and he caught her wrist easily. So she head butted him, and Kazaa fell back with a bloody nose. Wolf turned and quickly walked away, before breaking into a jog. She began to run as far as her freshly restored legs would take her.

Velena was pulled out from the river by the two skeletons, shivering from the cold. She smiled at her sister and said, "It's good to see you again, Helena."

Helena looked to her and said, "It has been many years. We thought you dead, and spent many moons searching for your spirit."

"I was only mostly dead," she replied. "That girl, that... barbarian. I glimpsed her destiny, dearest sister of my house."

She scoffed, "What destiny could a barbarian possibly have that would interest either of us, Velena?"

A wicked smile spread up her lips. She explained, "I was killed by servants of the Rizzen Empire. "I believe I was not the first of our kind they killed, for they knew just how to disable my skeletons and the nature of the First Spell. Though the Empire does home that accursed Arkvine Academy... They killed me, and I would have been done for, had I not gazed into the future the girl held. Her home tarnished by Rizzen boots, her people slain by them. You, and I, aiding her as one of our own. I sewed a piece of myself into her because I knew what was to come, absconded from my magic to ensure it happens."

With a serious expression, Helena asked, "What did you see, eldest sister?"

Velena took hold of her sister's shoulders and answered, "That barbarian will kill The Rizzen Emperor."

***

Colstone gasped as he took in the sight of sanctuary. It was obvious some great battle had besieged the land even from a distance. One of the buildings had endured quite a bit of superficial fire damage, and there were a great number of swords sticking out from one patch of land. This was to say nothing of the mass grave that filled his heart with such profound dread that he nearly vomited on the spot. With great care he managed to suppress his sickness, and then look back upon the sight. There were a handful of soldiers milling about, patrolling the area. To him, they seemed the last remnants of whatever defenses the place had once held.

"Come on," he said to the others. "We need ta see what's down there?"

"Are ye sure about that, Colstone?" Marblekeeper asked. "We can see quite well from here... it doesn't look good down there..."

"I have ta know," Colstone shook his head. "Ye don' need ta come with, but I'm goin' down there."

"We'll never leave a dwarf behind," Limecrack smiled reassuringly at him.

"Then let's get a movin," Colstone replied, turning to mush the goats forward.

They quickly pulled the sled across the road, quite the strange sight to behold in Moia. Even the group that had been following after them after their paths had crossed unexpectedly still found them to be a curious sight. In no time at all, the soldiers had all become alerted to the incoming dwarves and moved to meet them. Spears were held at the ready at the end of the path, their leader a few meters in front with arms crossed around a stave to show his authority. The sled slowed to a stop, and the dwarves looked to the half-elf captain expectantly.

"What is your business in Sanctuary?" he asked, his tone implying they better not have any business.

"Lookin fer a girl," Colstone said simply.

"This is not a slave market to barter at, nor is it still in operation," the captain firmly stated. "Now please move along, or I'll be forced to cast a binding spell on you and remove you myself."

The dwarves exchanged looks with one another, and then they all burst out laughing. Colstone said, "Ay, ye had me goin there for a second! I thought you was serious!"

"I AM serious," the captain growled, brandishing his stave.

"In that case," Colstone cheekily said, before all four dwarves brought up strange weapons the soldiers couldn't fathom. "We'll have to let ourselves in."

Loud explosions echoed throughout the area, and three of the soldiers, along with the captain, fell to the ground dead. The remaining three soldiers looked to one another in shock, before throwing their weapons down. One of them said, "We don't want any trouble! We've just been followin' orders!"

"No need to hurt us, we'll be good," another added.

"Shuddup and get on the ground," Brock grumbled, to which the soldiers quickly complied. "Colstone, go find yer kid. We'll watch these freaks."

Colstone threw his hand cannon aside and hopped off the sled, hurrying forward to look around the area. First he checked the barracks, and found signs it had been recently used as an infirmary, but there was nothing that clued him into Wolf's whereabouts. Next he checked the Warden's house, but found it ransacked and empty of anything aside from chains in a wall and some particularly nasty looking slaves. The one and only clue Colstone wound find came when he found the remains of a bonfire near where a makeshift kitchen had been set up with supplies raided from the barracks.

The other dwarves who had been milling about came to see what was taking Colstone so long. They found him kneeled over, pulling scorched fur and leather from the ashes of the bonfire. There was still some amount of blood left on what Colstone realized was a shirt, along with a hole likely made from an arrow. He clenched the scraps of clothing tight in his hands as he swept his fist through the ashes, but there was nothing more to be found in there. All that had survived, save for a few arrowheads and animal bones, was the piece of a shirt he now held tight against his chest.

"What do ye got there?" Marblekeeper curiously asked, approaching his friend.

"I have to know..." Ironja whispered more to himself than the other dwarf.

"What was that?" Marblekeeper asked, stepping up alongside Colstone.

"I HAVE TO KNOW!" the dwarf yelled, before he bolted away.

The dwarves followed him, unsure of where Colstone was going, but horrific realization set in far too quickly. Colstone jumped into the mass grave, where he began flipping over and pushing aside every body he could. He scanned the face of every single corpse, fresh and decayed alike. Tears streamed down his face and into his beard as the dwarf worked relentlessly, determined to find out what had happened to his friend's daughter. In that moment, all of the others' hearts truly broke for Colstone.

Brock and Limecrack jumped into the mass grave with him, each of them grabbing one of the dwarf's arms so that they could pull him away. All the while Colstone cried, "I have to know! Let me go! I have to know if she's here! Just let me go dammit!"

"She's not here, laddie!" Brock called, suppressing the urge to vomit as he tore his eyes away from the corpses. "Wherever she is, she's not here! Don't do this anymore, Colstone, please... yer killing yourself."

Colstone collapsed to his knees and the other two dwarves released their grip upon him. He rubbed some of the tears from his eyes and said, "I promised him... I said I'd look out for her... I ruined everything..."

***

Wolf collapsed at the edge of the mountain, falling onto her knees as she gazed out across the world. She struggled for anything to think of, for anything to do. In the end she just screamed and howled at the slowly rising moon. Then she began to weep, for the first time in her life. She cried deeply and passionately, violently so. Her heart felt like a stab wound, worse even, and her back burned. Her breaths came far too fast and ragged so that she could barely breathe, but still the tears flowed and the wails continued. She beat her fists into the ground because it was all she could do to distract from the pain inside of her, but the pain on the outside did not even come close to comparing.

At some point she had noticed that Kazaa had sat down next to her, but she did not address him. Once her crying had begun to peter out he asked, "Are you okay?"

She glared at him for just a moment, but then the heartbreak over took her once again. She choked out, "It was pointless... I shouldn't have left..."

He said, "No, it wasn't. You have saved lives, pup. You met me. You faced the world. None of that was pointless."

"I thought..." she struggled to find the words. "They said she was a part of me. Someone I had always known. I thought it was... mama."

"I know," he sighed. "I am so sorry you thought that. If I had known you would think so... I would have told you before we arrived. You didn't deserve that."

"Why did you take me here?" she asked, wiping away some of the tears from her nose.

He looked out over the abyss and said, "I was always coming here, one way or another. When I met you, I thought it was fate. Me on my way to Cairn, and a Cairnite so far from home. But you were not from Cairn, she was. As you slept she spoke to me, asked me to watch over you and ensure you made it here. I said yes, mostly because I knew I would be rewarded. As time passed, I truly grew to care for you, pup. I never wanted anything bad to happen to you. And as hard as it is to say, this was the best outcome."

"Why?" she asked. "Why not just leave me be if you cared?"

"Because she would have killed you," he explained. "Not intentionally, I don't think. But either she lived or you did, and she was quite determined to live. So I did my best to protect you and get you here, so that the both of you would live. I'm sorry, but I only wanted to help you."

Wolf stared at the moon in silence for quite some time before saying, "Kazaa."

"What is it, pup?" he asked.

She took a deep breath and said, "I miss papa."

"I know pup," he replied.

"I don't know how I can live without him," she said.

"The same way you've lived these past few months," he explained. "One day at a time. Live for yourself, keep going no matter how hard it seems. Set your mind to a task, and do everything you can to achieve it."

"I... I'll try," she said, and sat by him for the better part of an hour.

From behind them, Helena spoke. "Wolf of The Southern Reach, Kazaa of Exia. Each of you has proved yourself in service of Cairn. Rewards have been determined based on your services."

They turned to see her and Velena, accompanied by their guards and skeletons. Velena was now dressed in a black robe identical to her sister's. Wolf asked, "What could you ever give to me?"

Helena said, "The mercenary Kazaa has earned the wealth of a lowly baron, and the military position of general should he desire it. A home will also be prepared if you accept the role, Exian."

Velena said, "To the barbarian Wolf. We hold for you the title of Grave Warden, champion of Cairn. You will be gifted weaponry, education, culture, and more. You will receive a house, servants to tend to your needs, and all the training you need to perform your duties. But most importantly, you will receive revenge."

"I don't care anymore," she shook her head. "I don't care what happens to The Empire."

"This isn't about The Empire," Velena slyly smiled. "Shortly after your first encounter with The Empire, your path crossed with a ranger. He beat and impaled you, before leaving you for dead in the snow. We know of him."

Wolf's fists instinctively clenched, and all thoughts of living for herself fled her mind. She asked, "How?"

Helena said, "His father was once a knight of Cairn, though when his mistress died, he took their son to live in the forests below. Eventually the boy was recruited by The Empire, and many years later, crossed your path."

Velena continued, "Apparently, our little ranger has a ritual he holds every year. He returns to the forest once a year, for no more than a few days. He has already left this year, but will return again this following year. You will have your revenge for what he did to you."

Kazaa looked to Wolf with concern, but she had none. She said, "I'll kill him. I'll do whatever you want if it means I can kill him."

***

Dancing-Lights spit with vitriol, "How can they be here too!?"

"The girl, Wolf," Spring said. "She must have been here."

The dark elf shuddered at that and said, "I hope to never meet this child, for whom our fates seem to be intertwined."

"She was a strange girl," Spring commented. "Like a rabid animal, but for small moments just as sweet as any other."

"She was never sweet," Ruby-Gem stated. "A rabid animal is an insult to the beasts. She was a little monster dressed in hide."

"She was a child," Spring shot a cold glare at the half-orc. "Wolf had no way of knowing what she was like, of how much she hurt the tribe."

"Enough," Dancing-Lights ordered. "Ruby-Gem, what do you see?"

"Dead bodies," she said. "Many of them. I see the dwarves by some kind of pit. Burned buildings, a campsite of some kind... and a house."

"Do not assume all of them are dead," he said. "Come, let us greet the dwarves, and check the faces of the deceased. Someone may have done our job for us."

They made their way through the field they had stood in, first arriving by the corpses of the guards that the dwarves had shot to death. A quick examination of their faces and the trio were off. It was evident that many of those that were killed when the slave camp was attacked had been buried, which deeply worried Dancing-Lights. He would have liked anything other than to waste time digging up graves when imperial soldiers could find him with his guard down. They made their way past the graves, towards the pit they had seen from the distance.

Ruby-Gem gagged and nearly vomited from the stench alone, before emptying her stomach at the sight of the mass grave. Spring also felt ill, but managed to keep herself composed. Dancing-Lights was unphased, and made his way straight for the dwarves who were huddled by the pit's edge. Two of them looked up, and one of them whispered to the others, before all turned to face the elf.

Dancing-Lights took note that the one in the middle had been crying before he asked, "Did you find what you were looking for, dwarves?"

"You best stay away from us, elf," Brock grumbled.

"It's fine," Colstone said with a trembling voice. "No, we dinnit."

"A shame," Dancing-Lights murmured. "We have our own business to attend to here. I suggest you stay out of the way."

"Wouldn't dream of botherin ya," Limecrack stated.

"Very well," Dancing-Lights nodded, before stepping away.

After rejoining his companions, Ruby-Gem asked, "Are we going to look through all those bodies?"

"Not yet," he said. "First we need to examine the land, get an idea of exactly what happened."

Splitting up, the three of them began to scour the area, looking for any stray clue they could find. Dancing-Lights took note of an arrow carved with runes, embedded in the ground. He followed the direction it came from, and then after arriving at the spot he expected it to come from, looked around. He found another arrow, curiously placed, and realized it had been fired nearly directly into the air. Once more he began to move around, before at last noticing a small hill nearby.

He peered over it, and sure enough there laid two bodies that had been abandoned for whatever reason. Dancing-Lights made his way over to them, carefully inspecting the corpse of the human. A stab wound through the ankle, numerous lacerations and stab wounds across the rib cage, but none of these were fatal. Instead he found that the woman had been strangled to death, before her body was looted. Looking over, he could see that the large monstrous cat beside the human had had its throat slit.

As Dancing-Lights finished his examination, a chill crept down his spine. He quickly backed away in panic, looking around feverishly. Seeing nothing, he produced a collapsible mirror from his pocket and spun around. For just a fraction of a second, there was a dark shape visible behind him, and then it was gone.

Dancing-Lights pocketed the mirror and turned, running back towards his companions.

"What is it?" Spring asked when she saw the panicked state he was in.

"We're leaving," he said briskly.

"What about our target?" Ruby-Gem asked.

"Dead," he said. "Someone made sure of it." he then looked past them and called out to the dwarves, "You best leave this place! Head to Imperial Heart or your homeland. If you stay here, you will meet Death."

"Was it bad?" Ruby-Gem asked, not fully understanding the context for which he spoke.

He nodded and said grimly, "Worse than you can imagine. We must head to the city, where our contact awaits us. And this place... we do not want to stay here for even a moment longer than we already have."

The two women nodded and began to walk away with him. Behind them, Colstone asked, "Where are ye going?"

Dancing-Lights paused then said, "Imperial Heart. It is not a hospitable place for nonhumans, but it will provide shelter."

Colstone thought about it for a moment then said, "Perhaps we'll see each other there."

"Perhaps," the elf agreed, though he wished he hadn't.

Both groups then set off, each for the same destination. It would be quite some time before they properly crossed paths once again, and by then none of them would be the same people they had been in their last meeting.

Chapter 18

Kira drove the broadswords through Torrn's abdomen with all of his strength, forcing the orc back against a table. Beakers and potions fell over, spilling foul liquids that caught fire when combined. Acidic blood seeped out from Torrn' wounds, but the smile on his face showed it hadn't done him much harm. Kira ripped the blades out and instantly was struck across the side of his face by the orc's bear hand, knocking him to the ground.

"Don't you get it, elf?" Torrn asked as he threw his arms to the side to display his rapidly healing wounds. "I can't die! Nothing you do is going to be enough!"

He picked up the table that Kira had pressed him against, and then broke it over the elf's back. As Kira rolled away, Tornn grabbed his left arm and pulled hard, popping Kira's shoulder from its socket. Kira howled in pain and dropped his broadsword, but still pulled himself away. He placed the edge of his blade along his shoulder and stared down the Lord of The Beasts, left arm hanging loosely from his body and acid dripping from his blade.

"What kind of metal do you got there?" Torrn curiously asked. "Not much that can survive basilisk blood, let alone my own."

"Dwarven steel," Kira gasped for air.

"Impressive..." he murmured.

Kira flung himself at Torrn, swinging his sword downwards as he passed by. Blood sprayed through the air, and Torrn's right arm went flying, while Kira spun around behind him. The orc turned as Kira swung at his legs, cutting off Torrn's right leg and embedding the blade in his left. The orc fell to his one remaining leg and thrust his paw into Kira's gut, sinking his claws in deep. Kira continued to push until he cut Torrn's other leg out from underneath him.

Kira stood panting over Torrn's mutilated body, but the orc only laughed. He asked in a maniacal voice, "Do you really think that's enough!?"

Black tentacles emerged from within his bloody stumps, acid steaming off of them. Kira leapt back, narrowly avoiding a grab from one set, while the other two grabbed hold of his legs and began to pull Torrn back together. The orc rose up on his twisted fusion of legs and tendrils, smile still held tight on his face. The tentacles that emerged from his arm curled into an approximation of a fist, and Torrn lunged.

Kira fought back, but the hybrid monster was too much for him. For every useless strike he got in, Torrn would deliver a punch to the face or claw across the chest. Far too much of his blood was beginning to stain the ground. Torrn's blood loss didn't even seem to bother him. The orc slugged Kira in the gut, knocking the elf backwards, and he nearly fell into one of the chamber's many pits. Kira looked to it for just a moment, and saw the ravenous basilisks held within. He looked back to the approaching orc, and settled on a plan.

With a quick and decisive thrust, Kira drove his sword through where Torrn's heart should have been. The orc laughed once again and asked, "How haven't you gotten it!? You can't kill me!"

"Sure I can," Kira replied as he began to step forward, pushing his full weight against the blade.

"What are you doing!?" Torrn demanded, before he felt one of his feet slip out into open air before he quickly caught himself. "Stop it!"

"Fuck off," Kira growled in response.

Torrn attempted to free himself, but Kira used all his might to swing his body to the side. Torrn hovered over the open pit for just a moment, and then they were both falling into it. Torrn landed hard upon his back, and Kira's broadsword radiated through his chest after striking the stone beneath him. Before either of them could react, two dozen ravenous monsters leapt upon them. Sharp reptile jaw clamping tight around whatever flesh they could, be it elf or orc. Meat was torn from bones and blood was spilled.

***

The dead need not worry about pain or fear. They flung themselves at their enemy with no regard for their own bodies, impaling themselves upon spears and swords. Even then they continued to attack, thrashing madly and lashing out with whatever weapons they happened to be holding. Some of the undead even crowded around lone soldiers, dog piling them. From there they would pull at any exposed limbs, tearing arms and legs off, while sinking their teeth in to whatever they could. While the dead could be stopped through dismemberment or by the few wizards they had on their side, it did little to even the odds.

All the while The Lord of Bone stood upon his palanquin, blood continuously flowing through his stolen veins. He would simply raise a hand and summon forth a spear of bone that emerged from the ground, impaling all around it. He had little regard for the safety of his own forces, often claiming more of their lives than his enemies. After all, flesh is flesh. He didn't need a single living being to fight in his army. Only the dead mattered.

Zetine lunged at him, intending to cut his head from his shoulders before she hit the ground. Kerotin raised his hand and clenched his fist, causing a wall of bone to rise up in front of her. Zetine quickly brought her daggers up to ease the fall, but she still crashed hard against the wall. She pulled her blades free and fell to the ground, undead soldiers pooling around her. They outstretched their bloody hands, held up their hungry blades, and prepared to end the pharaoh of Exia's life.

But Zetine refused to die so easily. She focused on the weapons first, slicing off the hands that held them. She then proceeded to sever several heads, but their numbers were too great with her back literally against the wall. Were it not for the arrival of We-Will-Reach-Sanctuary, Zetine surely would have died. The elf quickly carved a path through the undead, allowing her to regain her footing and move through them. Together they danced a beautiful and deadly ballet, their blades slicing through flesh and bone at frightening speeds.

"Your scepter is magic, is it not?" We-Will-Reach-Sanctuary asked, cleaving the arms off an approaching zombie.

"But I am not!" she responded, slicing one of their legs off. "It belonged to my ancestor, but I have never learned any magic!"

We-Will-Reach-Sanctuary's face lit up at that and he quickly said, "You don't need to know any spells! Necromancy runs in your blood! Use the scepter, use your people's magic!"

Zetine quickly sheathed her daggers and pulled the scepter of Ama from her back. Hands clenched tight against the staff, she held it into the air as magical energy coursed throughout her body. It felt painfully cold, yet immensely invigorating. The head of the scepter began to glow with a transcendent white light, before emitting a pulse. White light spread out in a circular motion around Zetine, cleaving its way across the battlefield.

One by one the undead warriors fell to the ground in limp heaps, as dead as when they first rose again. Even the bone spears and wall that Kerotin had created began to lose their structure. Slowly, they began to dissolve back into brittle dust. Through the growing holes in the wall, Kerotin stared at her in disbelief. Disbelief and immense anger.

"What did you DO?" he asked with furious vitriol.

A pair of hands wrapped themselves around Zetine's hands, holding them tight. She felt the body pressed up against her own, several inches shorter and far less athletic. The alien hands guided her to sweep the scepter over the battlefield, most vitally in the direction of The Army of Hope. The stranger spoke into her words as clear as day, a spell seemingly as simple as a mere sentence. Then there was nobody there, leaving Zetine alone to turn the tides of the battle back in their favor.

She chanted, "Souls of the righteous, of those who gave their selves hoping for a better world, return to us and fight again. Souls of the righteous, of those who gave their selves hoping for a better world, return to us and fight again. Souls of the righteous, of those who gave themselves hoping for a better world, return to us and FIGHT AGAIN!"

A green light flashed out from her scepter, and for the first time in her life, Zetine could *see* the dead. Truly see them. There were thousands of souls gathered across the battlefield, and she watched as many of them found their bodies and returned to them. Their corpses began to sit up, invigorated beyond life's limits. They claimed whatever weapons they could, then began to brutally attack Vhodan's forces. None would be spared from the fury and hate of the dead.

She said, "Thank you, Ama. We will remember you for all days."

Kerotin conjured a spear of bone in his hand and threw it to Zetine, who turned just in time to see it sailing towards her. Before it could land, an arrow appeared to strike it at just the right angle to knock the weapon off course. While it was embedded in the back of a dead soldier, Kerotin looked furiously in the direction the attack had come from. Then he quickly twisted his body, receiving an arrow to the right shoulder. The Lord of Bone tore it from his flesh and snapped it in his fist, throwing the remains to the ground.

Zetine risked a glance over her shoulder and saw none other than Garr, seated upon the back of a direwolf. He quickly fired arrows into whatever soldiers were unfortunate enough to cross his line of sight, while his mount rapidly approached Zetine and We-Will-Reach-Sanctuary. The elf began to move towards Kerotin and Zetine followed after, drawing a dagger in her left hand just in case.

Kerotin began to perform a series of hand gestures, and then once again called out a single haunting word. This time he said only, "Die."

Zetine could have sworn her heart stopped, but she didn't stop moving. Neither did We-Will-Reach-Sanctuary, who didn't even seem disturbed. As she looked around, she was both confused and horrified by what she had seen. Only Vhodan's own ground troops, with the exceptions of the monsters, had simply keeled over. Some of them held their hearts and grasped at empty air, while others lay upon their backs with blood dripping from their noses. The strange attack had not extended to Tyruden though, who used the momentary confusion to rain lightning upon the Army of Hope. It also had not affected the slaves that carried their cruel master upon their shoulders.

Eyes back on Kerotin, she watched as The Bone Lord lived up to his name. Stark white bone spread out over his skin to form an exoskeleton, and Zetine could see the fuel that allowed him to do so. He ripped the very souls of his own men from the limbo between life and death. It was their existence which allowed him to bolster his own power, to push himself away from the inevitable march of death. White claws covered Kerotin's fingers, a bulky ribcage laid over the thin carapace protected his chest, and a hawk-like beak extended out from his head. He looked to them with his ethereal green eyes half hidden behind his skull-helm, and Zetine could truly see how nothing human was left in the man.

Once more he said, "Rise!" and Vhodan's forces once again rose up. He descended from his palanquin, approaching Zetine as he said, "Kill them! Kill them all!"

We-Will-Reach-Sanctuary said, "He is yours to face, Zetine. Do you have this?"

"I do," she responded and left the elf's side.

Kerotin reached forward, and from his grip appeared a menacing greatsword made of pure white bone. Barbed spines jutted out from it, nearly as dangerous as the sharp tip of the blade. He took hold of the dreaded weapon in both hands and raised it overhead, waiting for his fateful meeting. Zetine stepped up to him, and Kerotin wasted no time in swinging the blade down at her. She easily caught it with her dagger, but the pure weight of the blow was enough to rattle her insides and nearly lose her footing.

She twisted her blade and danced around Kerotin, strafing towards his backside. The Bone Lord spun around, swinging his sword madly through the air after her. Zetine worked hard to avoid his strikes, leaping out of the way or ducking underneath as she delivered probing thrusts and slashes against his carapace. Even where she expected weak spots to be, such as under Kerotin's ribs or his joints were expertly protected. Each attack she made against him harmlessly bounced off, leaving her open for a reprisal from the greatsword that seemed always a hair's breath away from her.

Zetine risked an experiment, and aimed her scepter at Kerotin's back. White light washed over him for just a moment, and the Bone Lord screamed. Smoke drifted into the air from his backside, while bone and carapace began to crack. Several large pieces fell from his body, landing on the ground where they began to crumble away into dust. Kerotin spun around, and in the surprise, sliced Zetine across the chest. She fell onto her back, air fleeing her lungs as a thick trail of blood began to form. She looked up with fearful eyes as Kerotin nonchalantly approached her, dragging his sword in the dirt behind him.

He laughed and said, "When they told me of you, I did my research. Nothing said you were a necromancer. Every little story I could find about you said you were a courageous little warrior with a heart for good. You were pathetic. But that resurrection spell... that was something interesting. I almost feel bad killing you. There's so much we could have learned together.

Kerotin raised his sword overhead with the intent of driving it through Zetine's heart, before he suddenly cried out in pain. An arrow had blossomed between his shoulder blades, and the necromancer grabbed for it feebly with his right hand, while his left loosely held the sword. Taking the moment's advantage, Zetine pointed her scepter and unleashed a blast of white light. It washed over the Bone Lord, who soon found himself devoid of any exoskeleton. His armor crumbled away, leaving him totally naked and exposed, even his sword turning to ash in his hand.

"NO!" he cried out, but was quickly silenced.

Zetine drove her dagger carefully through his ribs, impaling Kerotin through the heart. He gasped for air, but she only pushed her blade in deeper, until it pierced out through his back. Kerotin looked to her in fear, but when he looked behind her, there was pure terror. Desperately he attempted to pull himself free, frothy pink foam falling from his lips. Kerotin pushed Zetine off of himself, and she took her blade with her. He fell onto the ground, writhing for just a moment. Then he fell completely still in such a way that it was clear he would not move again.

Zetine sheathed her dagger and returned her scepter to her back so that she could uncork her healing potion. As she did so, she saw a truly disturbing sight. Two tall women stood over Kerotin's body, one dressed in black robes, the other in white. The one in black took hold of his soul and ripped it screaming from his body.

The one in white laid a hand upon his shoulder, and Zetine watched as all magic was stripped away from his soul. The woman in black took him, and then they were both simply gone.

The woman dressed in white turned to her, and Zetine saw that she was nothing more than a skeleton. The woman approached her, and her skin was grey and lifeless. With split lips the woman leaned forward and whispered in Zetine's ear. Then she leaned up, and turned her burned face away. Zetine watched in stunned silence as the woman left her side, shortly disappearing from sight. All that was left for Zetine to do was uncork her healing potion, and then drink it.

***

At the bottom of the ravine, Jubilatious held his chest. It burned, but more importantly it felt like his heart had just been skewered. He had truly believed his father would side with him, his son, but he hadn't even cared. His staff had been broken, discarded somewhere on the battlefield where he would never be able to find it again. He could still see and hear the lightning and thunder that marked the death of his allies, unable to do anything about it. All he could do was imagine the many ways Zetine may die, or the cruelty his father may inflict upon the Army of Hope.

Anger began to fill Jubilatious' veins. It quickly overwhelmed any amount of sorrow or pity he felt for himself. He was angry that he had been hurt. Angry that his father had cast him aside. Angry that so many people were senselessly dying. It all coalesced into a black hole of rage within his heart. From that rage, he found a new source of power. Magic began to radiate out from his fingertips, and without a staff he began to cast a spell.

As the Stormcaller watched the death of Kerotin The Bone Lord, Jubilatious rose out from the ravine. Many of the remaining soldiers watched as he flew upwards, robes flowing around him.

They whispered a great many things, to themselves and one another. All were in agreement that it was a legendary sight to see that the wizard had risen. He came to a stop ahead of the wyvern, whose every sense told it that something was horribly wrong.

Tyruden turned to see Jubilatious, and offered up a smug smile. "Have you reconsidered my offer, boy?" he asked.

"I have," he coldly replied. "I offer you only my hail."

"Your hail?" Tyruden curiously asked, before a look of surprise coveted his face.

Tyruden quickly cast a protection spell over himself as Jubilatious raised his hand above his head then violently brought it down. But Tyruden was not who Jubilatious had cast the spell against. A chariot sized chunk of ice descended from the hurricane, striking the wyvern over the head. It fell with the weight of the blow, tossing Tyruden from its saddle. As the Stormcaller fell through the air, he cast a flight spell of his own. It was a shame watching his favorite pet crash to the ground below, but it was replaceable.

He floated back up to Jubilatious and said, "That was quite impressive. Where were you hiding all that power?"

"In the storm," Jubilatious replied before pointing his finger towards his father.

A bolt of lightning shot out from his fingertip, but Tyruden harmlessly slapped it aside. He asked, "Do you really think that I, the Stormcaller, can be harmed by lightning?"

"Probably not," Jubilatious shrugged. "Really that was just to distract you."

Tyruden's face fell and he asked, "Distract me from what?"

With a smug smile of his own, Jubilatious pointed upwards. The hurricane that Tyruden had summoned was now filled with onyx black clouds. Occasionally they would flash orange, and were slowly mixing with Tyruden's own clouds like a disease. As the

Stormcaller set his storm filled eyes back on Jubilatious, the young wizard cracked his knuckles as though he had not a care in the world.

"What?" Jubilatious asked. "I can't let you have all the fun."

Fire began to rain down from the hurricane, centered upon Tyruden. Instinctively he threw up a magical barrier, causing balls of flame to bounce off it, but left himself open to attack from Jubilatious. The young wizard extended his hand in a throwing motion, and a small spear of ice blossomed in the air. It sailed forward, hitting Tyruden in the thigh. The Stormcaller cried out in pain and his barrier weakened, but not for long.

He waved his hands around his entire body, and the barrier quickly enveloped his entire being. Then Tyruden said, "Clever, boy. But you cannot hope to beat me. I have studied magic for decades, and you flunked out!"

At this he threw a lightning bolt, which Jubilatious parried with a wave of his hand. He replied, "You see, I would be inclined to believe that, if it weren't for the fact that I've already beaten you. Fire raining down, you with a bloody leg, your storm and army defeated. Face it old man, you picked the losing side."

Tyruden considered this for a moment then said, "He will never lose. Beneath the skin that conceals my soul, protected by all of my might. Nestled within my true heart, of all that is myself and all that is another. From first love to last hated, all the rage and passion I have ever felt. Of all that is myself I call upon you, held within the temple that is my body. May you finally be free. I release you, Magika Elektrica, Magika Aquera, and Magika Aera."

The very moment he had realized that Tyruden was reciting The First Spell, Jubilatious fled. He flew as fast and as far as he could, while also gradually lowering himself towards the ground. After Tyruden said his final word, all of the magic in his body exploded outwards. Lightning spread out in all directions, nearly striking Jubilatious mid-flight. Water poured out in thick buckets of rain. The air itself seemed to grow more powerful, though no one on the ground had any way to notice it. Raw magic energy, with nowhere to go, poured into the nearest wizard body. But most importantly, Tyruden fell from the air.

As the effects of the spell ended, Jubilatious changed directions and tried to meet Tyruden in the air. It was no use, and the former wizard hit the ground hard. Blood covered the ground around his body, and his form was barely recognizable. As Jubilatious landed by his side, he gazed upon the nearly undamaged face of his father. Despite the horrible state of the rest of his body, Tyruden had spent his final moment grinning. Jubilatious spat on him.

***

Nearby, Garr approached the fallen wyvern. It lashed out at some nearby soldiers with its tail, crushing two of them. Garr hopped off his direwolf mount and continued on foot, raising his arms to show he was no threat. As it saw him, the wyvern began to channel its elemental breath. Garr saw the gathering electricity in its opened maw, but he continued anyway. He could see that the wyvern needed his help, and he would be damned if he abandoned an intelligent animal that needed assistance.

"I am no threat to you," he said. "My name is Garr. What' your name?"

The wyvern did not respond at first, but slowly ceased its charge. Then it spoke into Garr's mind, "Paxsion. Great Scion of The Eternal Storm."

He replied, "My name is Garr, and I bare no titles. Your master, he who chained you and called himself Stormcaller, is no more. You are free now, Paxsion."

The wyvern let out a roar and then said, "I wish you luck, Garr who bares no titles. These beings deserve death, but not all of them are capable of it."

"What do you mean?" Garr asked, but he received no reply.

The wyvern beat its wings and wind flooded the area before it rose up into the air. Paxsion took his leave, abandoning the lands he had been bound to with great hurry. Garr watched him go, then turned back to look around the battlefield. The Army of Hope moved forward, many of them dead, but that did not stop them from fighting for freedom. The archers had lowered their bows and were moving forward with daggers and curved swords drawn, led by the wizards in their vibrant robes. He could see that Zetine was standing over the corpse of Kerotin, exhausted from the fight. Close to her was We-Will-Reach-Sanctuary, sharpening his daggers in anticipation.

The sky began to darken, and there came the sound of metal grinding against stone. Garr could tell every single person there, living and dead, all turned to face the castle gate. Hundreds of soldiers began to pour out from the castle walls, more fresh faced than those they had already fought, but well fed and without any fatigue. Garr quickly readied his bow and began to launch arrows into the newly arrived army, while Zetine began an expeditors retreat. We-Will-Reach-Sanctuary disappeared into the crowd, and Garr was unable to tell if he was still fighting, if he had been taken down, or if he had joined his true allies.

Bolts of lightning and fire barraged the army, wiping them out as soon as they emerged from beyond the castle wall. Very few amongst them noticed what was happening in the sky. Only the purple mage Vrias, general Carver, and We-Will-Reach-Sanctuary witnessed the impossible. As the moon began to eclipse the sun, a single eye opened, and there had never been any moon. It gazed down upon them with its great and terrible golden stare, and there was nothing that it did not see. There was nothing the collective mortal beings could do but scream, and cry, and dream.

"Eye see an orc. Far from home, displaced from its rightful place. The orc prides itself on its kinship with nature, calls itself a ranger. Yet it stands here, allied with humans and elves, fighting against a power it has no business facing. The orc tries to focus, to draw its bowstring back, but there is no bowstring. There is no enemy. There is an orc, alone in the forest, the smell of blood in the air. The orc is running, it calls out for its mother, for its father, for anyone. It cries because it knows what it will soon find. Eye watch as the orc faces the monster from its nightmares, a monster that it has no recollection of ever defeating. The monster smiles, and the orc flees... the orc sees someone- who? It is gone, and there was never an orc.

"Upon the battlefield eye see a woman of great renowned. She has conjured the dead to fight for her. But there are no more souls here to follow you, there are only corpses. They fall to the ground once again, and the girl is terrified. There is a girl surrounded by priests. They lead her into the deep dark tomb of her ancestors. The girl is afraid of the dark. She begs them not to leave her, to at least provide a torch so that she can see. They do not reply, and leave her to be buried alive. There is a girl and there is only darkness. Only eye see her. A hand places itself on the girl's shoulder, and then she disappears into the dark never to be seen again.

"There is a wizard, yet he is really just a boy. Vain and arrogant, hiding behind an illusion of power and intelligence. The boy is not upon a battlefield, but a field of green by the riverside. His mother calls to him, and he goes to her with nothing more than relief nestled inside of his heart. I watch as they embrace, and all is right with the world. A voice calls out to the wizard, but he ignores it. The wizard is no more than a boy, and he is home.

"Side by side, a dwarf and a goblin walk together. The goblin notices me first, and it screams. It begs the dwarf to kill it, but there is no dwarf, and there never has been. There is only a child watching as the salamanders approach, burning the land and leaving only ash in their wake. Eye see the fear in her eyes, as she holds her human parents tight. The goblin thinks to herself, "At least this time we will die together," but what does that mean?

"The dwarf falls away, grasping at his own head. A protective charm placed around his fat little neck, warding away what is and what is not. But the charm was never meant for me. Eye look beyond it, and there never was a charm, and there never was an adventure. The dwarf tended to the mines, day in and day out, making perfectly sized tunnels that would go on forever. There is not even a monster to worry about. The dwarf wishes it had some reason to live.

"There is an elf, and it has been eaten alive. Little remains of the elf, yet it clings to life, cutting down its enemies with one remaining arm. The elf- wait. This is not the one eye search for...

"Eye see an elf, dressed in purple, trying with all of its might to defend against the reality that is myself. You are not who I seek, little elf, yet you seem to be a thorn. I witness you for what you are, in love with someone that lives only to die, devoid of any real purpose, pathetic and alone. Where has your lover gone, little elf? You are truly alone, but eye see you. You fall to your knees and you cry, and you have always been crying.

"There was an orc, but it is no more. There once was an orc who was surrounded by beasts, beasts who had once taken the orc in as their own. Now the orc is the head of the pack, and those who had rejected it feel its fury. A great being comes to the orc one day with an offer. He has uncovered a monster unlike any the world has ever seen, one that can change the flesh, and would like the orc to become its master.

"Eye see the vampire, so far from home, refusing to fulfill its duties. The vampire stands at the edge of the living world with two others, looking over an abyss of graves. For just a moment, it feels regret. Now, eye watch as that regret finally blossoms. There is a vampire, and it is screaming as it feels its flesh burn, deep down in the darkness.

"Eye watch as a clutch of eggs hatch. Green and brown creatures pull themselves out of their shells, slithering away into the swamp. The final egg hatches, and a white arm lands upon the ground. An albino gorgon should not survive, yet eye watch as again and again it cuts down and petrifies those that would harm it. Then one day arrives a great person, bearing it the gift of a true home and those who will respect it. The gorgon accepts, and in the coming months, would be declared queen of its kind.

"There is a man, half elf, with eyes of the storm. Eye watch the man's affair, not so far from home. Eye see when he returns so many years later, claiming the son who never knew his name. Eye watch the fear in the boy's eyes blossom into hate and fury. The seeds of a betrayal are already planted, yet the half-elf cannot see past himself to notice.

"Eye do not see you. Where are you? Eye see broken childhoods, memories of horrible monsters, of abuse and strife and tragedy and peace. Eye see everything there has ever been, and everything there has never been. In all of what is and is not, eye do not see you. Where are you, little elf? Magnificent traitor? Where are you, We-Will-Reach-Sanctuary?"

"Right behind you," came the tranquil response.

There was a flash of a dagger, and then the Unknowing King screamed. His pained wails echoed across the battlefield, leaving the golden eye to shatter, revealing the true moon still in place over the sun. The Army of Hope's senses were returned to them, and though the dead had fought valiantly, their defenseless forces had been decimated in the few minutes that they were unaware of their surroundings. Missing from the battlefield were Zetine, Garr, and We-Will-Reach-Sanctuary. Instead they now stood amidst the Unknowing King's personal chamber, surrounded by ancient tomes and strange projects.

The Unknowing King was a few inches shorter than any of them would have expected. He draped himself in black robes that entirely concealed his features, black sleeves falling over whatever hands may have been hidden. A gash had blossomed across The Unknowing King's chest, dripping blood that was every color at once. It was impossible to tell where one color ended and another began, hues fading into one another and tones changing every time someone's eyes lost focus. With each motion, no matter how subtle, the Unknowing King's body became an indecipherable blur before resettling into a coherent shape.

"What in the world..." Zetine muttered as she shook her head.

The Unknowing King cried out, "Traitor! Renegade! Betrayer! You were nothing more than an orphan- WE took you in! We gave you purpose!"

"You clearly didn't give me enough," We-Will-Reach-Sanctuary replied, a sentence that caused horrific realization in The Unknowing King, and only uncertainty in the other two.

As We-Will-Reach-Sanctuary strode forward, The Unknowing King leapt back, and the walls themselves reached out to grab at them all. Zetine deftly dodged out of the way of outstretched black stone hands while Garr was taken by surprise. The orc was pulled to the ground before the arms began to drag him back towards the wall, all the while more and more arms seemed to be appearing to grasp at Zetine. We-Will-Reach-Sanctuary did not let the warped reality slow him; deftly dodging out of the way of his opponent's many arms. Even as The Unknowing King's blood solidified into writhing, lashing tentacles, We-Will-Sanctuary merely sliced through them and pressed onwards.

He had taken a hundred steps in a room that at most could fit twenty steps before hitting a wall, and the end of the chamber seemed to be miles upon miles away. Behind the elf, Garr hit the wall and let out a frightened scream as he felt the coldness of the stone begin to swallow him. We-Will-Reach-Sanctuary tossed one of his daggers into the air then caught it by the blade, before throwing the weapon forward. It hit the Unknowing King in the head, and for just a moment they saw beneath his hood. There were only eyes, a thousand golden orbs staring in every direction. Then there came a screech unlike anything any of them had ever heard in their lives, before The Unknowing King fell to the ground.

There were no outstretched arms. There were no tendrils made of blood. There was just a dark elf, a human, and an orc. Around them were bookshelves with ancient tomes, a few alchemical experiments, and some decent artwork. Sprawled across the wooden floorboards was an empty black cloak, pinned to the ground by a straight dagger. We-Will-Reach-Sanctuary calmly reclaimed his weapon, twirling it between his fingers.

"I felt myself becoming stone..." Garr mumbled as he shook himself free of rock dust.

"Sanctuary, what was that?" Zetine asked before adding, "And why did it stop?"

"I told you all," he said. "The Unknowing King could make reality what he wanted, with few exceptions. It was power granted by some being he kept quite secret, though undeniably some type of dark god. When he died, all that power went with him."

"Where is his body?" Garr asked as he looked to the black cloak.

"I suppose his god took it," the elf shrugged.

"I shudder to think what would happen if we met him again," Zetine said.

"Then let's hope he has enough sense to stay dead," We-Will-Reach-Sanctuary replied. "Come along, we have to get to the throne room."

***

Jubilatious stood with arms outstretched, still held in his false hug. Around him there was screaming, and bloodshed, and chaos. A hand gripped his shoulder and pulled him backwards, and then suddenly he was face to face with Vrias. The high elf looked deep into his piercing blue eyes as he called his name, shaking him violently. Vrias even slapped him across the face, which pissed Jubilatious off just enough just enough to snap back to reality. He delivered a retaliatory slap to Vrias' cheek almost out of instinct.

"What in the hell!?" he asked with barely suppressed anger.

"You were still stuck in the trance," Vrias replied. "We need every mage we can get; most of our frontline soldiers are dead!"

Jubilatious looked back to the carnage around them then said, "Get word to the white mages. I need them to focus their power on me."

"What!?" he was utterly shocked. "Why? We need them to keep healing!"

"The Stormcaller did The First Spell," Jubilatious explained. "I think I got some of that excess power in the aftermath."

"You're mad," Vrias replied with a shake of his head.

"Mad or not, I imagine I can work quite the spell with a few white mages backing me," he smiled sincerely.

"Fine. I'm on it," Vrias nodded before hurrying off.

While he waited, there came the galloping of over a hundred horses. Jubilatious looked to the south, where he stared with dreadful eyes. The army that appeared from beyond the hills, riding magnificent steeds and carrying lances, were none other than the final platoon to join The Army of Hope. Their lances were stained with blood, and some of the horses had already received injuries. In that moment he knew the battle could have been far worse, had whatever forces yet to return to the castle been able to make it back. Jubilatious began to grin as he watched the cavalry charge into the battle, lances driven through chests and backs. Horses neighed and men cried, all while the odds fell into The Army of Hope's favor.

Vrias delivered Jubilatious' words well, and soon the four white mages worked in tandem while Vrias held up a shield around them. Two poured strength into Jubilatious' magic, another worked to maintain his stamina, and the fourth cast a continuous healing spell to keep aiding the wounded soldiers. Jubilatious walked forward, practically overflowing with power. In a voice as soft as a dove's dreams, he spoke the spells he wished to conjure forth. Lightning crackled between his fingertips, chaining together to form a thick mesh of electricity. Jubilatious then thrust his hands forward, shooting lightning out at Vhodan's forces. Screams of pain were quickly silenced as he bathed them in enough electricity to fry them instantly, causing dozens of people to combust in the middle of combat.

Then Jubilatious changed his chant, channeling forth a completely different spell. Water began to pool in the lungs of a handful of soldiers, drowning them far from any body of water. He switched to another chant yet again, and spears of ice burst from their bodies, impaling their nearby allies while leaving The Army of Hope unharmed. He then tore the icicles from their corpses, launching them at even more enemies. The cries of battle were soon replaced with a chorus of cheers that drowned out even the cries of the dying and afraid.

Jubilatious called out, "Army of Hope! Now is your chance! Charge the entrance!"

From further along the battlefield came Carver's shocked, "What!?"

With newfound zealotry the army surged forward, cutting down Vhodan's now retreating forces. Jubilatious focused his outstretched hand on the drawbridge gate, and then tore the wall down entirely. He set the loose bricks down into the moat, providing extra if uneven footing for his allies to cross into the courtyard where the last of the soldiers began to gather. They watched as Jubilatious walked towards them, lightning streaking off his body, and at their thousands of fallen enemies. They looked to the two hundred encroaching warriors, then collectively threw down their weapons and surrendered.

Zeydas appeared at Jubilatious' side, his one arm clenched tight to his straightsword. A few serious looking wounds littered his body, but still the dark elf fought. He said, "We have this out here, risen one. Your final battle lies inside."

"Good luck," Jubilatious nodded before heading off towards the castle entrance.

"You as well," Zeydas called after him.

***

Mizt-Ied and Ironja were the first to reach Vhodan's throne room, finding their way up to a balcony that overlooked the room's entirety with a staircase to their left. Six archers remained on the balcony, while six more resided on a balcony on the opposite end of the hall. Down below, Vhodan sat upon his throne as though nothing was wrong. At his feet rested a great and mighty black hammer, with a shaft nearly as tall as an average sized person. To the Emperor's left side was the Tree Gate, or its remains. It seemed as though Vhodan had seen fit to burn the gate before the battle began, eliminating its use as a point of entry.

Mizt-Ied moved forward without Ironja, carefully positioning herself behind two of the archers. She stabbed into the both of their ankles at once, causing them to cry out in pain and fall to the ground. Ironja then rushed forward to cave one of their heads in, while Mizt-Ied attacked the other four. She sliced the calves of the next archer in line, slid under the legs of the following one while cutting his heels, before pouncing on shoulders of the fifth and stabbing him in the throat. As he fell, she leapt towards the last soldier and stabbed him in the eye. She fell to the ground, leaving Ironja to quickly finish off the other soldiers while she recovered.

The last archer grasped his bloody eye as he cried out in pain, before kicking Mizt-Ied in the chest. He cried out, "You little cunt! I'm gonna rip yer fuckin' eyes out!"

"Not if I have anything to say about it," Ironja grunted before barreling into the man, sending him falling off of the balcony.

He hit the ground with a sickening splat, but still laid sputtering below. Before words could be exchanged between the dwarf and the goblin, a volley of arrows hit the wall behind them. They took cover behind the stone balcony, pinned in place by the occasional blind arrow. They waited together like that for several minutes, each arrow a sign that their deaths were imminent. But then suddenly there came the sound of violence, and when Mizt-Ied peaked over the balcony wall, she saw her friends and ally slicing down the rest of the archers.

Mizt-Ied and Ironja then hurried down the stairs, where they were soon met by the other three. Mizt-Ied was first to say, "It's so good to see you guys again! I was worried some of you might not have made it..."

"Not a chance on it," Zetine smiled down at her.

"Where's Jubilatious?" she asked, looking past them as though he may be standing there.

We-Will-Reach-Sanctuary answered, "He did not want to come. He was too attached to his delusion."

Zetine spoke, "We are going to have to do this without him. Whatever happens, the hope of the world lies upon our shoulders."

Ironja mumbled, "I guess this belongs to you. Never really liked swords anyway," and handed the elf back his falcata.

"Thank you," We-Will-Reach-Sanctuary smiled, sheathing his straight dagger to claim the weapon.

Then Zetine said, "Come on. It's time we finish this."

They walked together, shoulder to shoulder, each brandishing their preferred weapons. Each footstep carried them closer and closer to the Emperor, the being of evil that had awaited them all of this time. He did nothing save for stare at them from behind his accursed black visor. Slowly they began to notice a strange semi-rhythmic sound emanating from beneath Vhodan's armor. Mizt-Ied was the first to realize just what they were hearing.

She asked, "Is that... snoring?"

"The bastard's asleep," We-Will-Reach-Sanctuary shook his head.

"Makes it easier to end this then," Zetine replied.

Before any of them could react, she ran forward and leapt into the air. Zetine raised her daggers, intent on spearing them straight through Vhodan's eyes. Instead, mere heartbeats before she would have brought her arms down, The Emperor raised his hand and froze her in the air. He tilted his helmed head, then tossed his hand back and threw Zetine harshly to the ground. Vhodan took hold of his hammer with his left hand, lifting it like it was nothing, and then scanned the gathered heroes that sought to kill him.

"I was expecting you much earlier," he said with uttermost boredom in his voice.

Zetine rolled away from Vhodan and got back to her feet saying, "We're going to stop you, Vhodan! Your subjugation of these lands, the lives you've taken, the slavery you've upheld! It all ends tonight! In chains or in a coffin, you can choose how we pull you from this castle!"

Vhodan tilted his head and said, "That's cute. It has been quite some time since I was subjected to one of your speeches. You terrorists just love your speeches. But I have one of my own. I have gathered the dispossessed, the hungry, and the beaten. I have granted them homes and lands and purpose. Within the confines of my kingdom there has been prosperity unlike any you could hope to achieve. What kind of monsters are you that you would seek to deprive so many people of this life? What change could you possibly hope to enact, that is not simply the eradication of the life so many people have come to cherish? If you truly think you are worthy, that you have cause, that your wants are greater than the needs of my people, then come at me. I will not hold back, but I, Emperor Vhodan The Eternal of The Signet Empire, will face you as an equal so that you may prove your entitlement."

The doors at the end of the hall flung open, and Jubilatious made his entrance. He walked forward, raising his arms overhead as the dagger of Ahk-Zul was centered just above his reach. Jubilatious quietly chanted a spell, and then thrust his arms down to his sides. Just below each set of his fingertips, there was the dagger. Two golden hilts, two sharp and magnificent blades. Each dagger then floated up beside his head, waiting for when he would need it in the fight to come.

Jubilatious came to a stop beside Ironja and asked, "What did I miss?"

"He gave a big ol' speech about how we're the evil ones, and how he'll fight for his people," the dwarf informed.

"Ah, so nothing important then," he smirked.

"Enough of this prattle," Vhodan growled, before taking his hammer into both hands.

Vhodan swung at Zetine, who dropped to her knees and sliced at the Dark Lord's thighs to no avail. Garr quickly fired his last three arrows into Vhodan's side, all three breaking against his armor. Ironja charged forward, swinging his own hammer against Vhodan's leg. The Emperor fell to his knee, giving Mizt-Ied the opening to leap onto his shoulders and stab at where his neck ought to have been. Jubilatious sent forth a wave of magical fire into Vhodan's chest, but it seemed to do nothing.

The Emperor grabbed Mizt-Ied by her hair and threw her across the hall, before rising back up to his feet. He swung his hammer down into the ground between himself and Ironja, cracking the stone ground so greatly that the dwarf was knocked onto his chest. As Zetine slashed at his sides, Vhodan then smacked her across the face with his iron gauntlet and knocked her backwards. Then he turned to Jubilatious, and with both hands, threw his hammer at the wizard.

Jubilatious barely managed to erect the magical shield, barely managed to will his daggers in front of his face. The wizard still went soaring backwards, landing roughly on the ground. Garr dropped his bow and drew his Scimitar, charging the Dark Lord. Vhodan parried each of Garr's strikes with his gauntlets, flashes of fire dancing along them with each blow. Then Vhodan reached forward and grabbed Garr by the throat, before tossing him back into a recovering Zetine.

Then there was We-Will-Reach-Sanctuary, driving his falcata into the back plate of Vhodan's left leg. He quickly shouted, "Peel the armor off! It's the only way!"

Just as the plate bent away, Vhodan spun around and delivered a harsh uppercut to the elf's jaw. As We-Will-Reach-Sanctuary rose into the air, Vhodan grabbed him by the legs and swung him back into the ground. He then took hold of Ironja's skull and pulled the dwarf up to eye level, grabbing his right arm. Ironja screamed a true wail of agony that seemed so horrifyingly out of place for the dwarf's voice. Tendons split apart, skin stretched, bones snapped, and Vhodan tore Ironja's arm from his body. Then he simply tossed the dwarf aside like a broken toy, fit only to be discarded.

Jubilatious flung a ball of fire at the Dark Lord, who merely caught it in the palm of his hand. He took a step forward, then another, and then there was Zetine. She drove her daggers into the gap We-Will-Reach-Sanctuary had created, creating a small cut on Vhodan's leg. He turned on her, right fist in full motion, and Zetine barely managed to leap backwards. As she landed, Vhodan thrust his left fist forward, hitting her in the chest. By the time Zetine had landed on the ground, Jubilatious had created a small tornado centered on Vhodan. The wind tore at his armor, making incremental progress in removing it.

But then just as quickly as the tornado had appeared, it vanished. While Jubilatious looked on in shock, Vhodan extended his left hand. The hammer levitated off the ground and flew towards its master, knocking Jubilatious off his feet. Reunited once more, Vhodan raised his hammer up over Zetine who looked on with wide eyes. Then Mizt-Ied was upon him, pulling at his helmet. As Vhodan grabbed at her, Garr was working on prying his chest plate off with his scimitar. We-Will-Reach-Sanctuary returned to his feet as well, driving his falcata under Vhodan's back plate.

As the plates fell away, and Vhodan's helmet began to loosen, he yelled out, "ENOUGH!"

The Emperor dropped his hammer to the ground then held out his hands and the three of them, along with Zetine and Ironja, were thrown across the hall in all directions. Jubilatious cast a spell upon Vhodan, freezing his legs in place with a thick patch of ice that rose off the floor and up his thighs. Garr was first off his feet after this, returning to slash at Vhodan's chest. The Emperor blocked Garr's strikes, and found the orc left him with no openings to retaliate.

Each blow he blocked sent a small burning sensation along his arms, and it was only a matter of time before either Garr got lucky, or someone else attacked. So Vhodan removed the orc from the equation.

Quickly, Vhodan made a series of hand motions of which only Jubilatious was able to decipher half. For just a moment, Garr let out a scream, and then would never make a sound again. His flesh was torn from his bones and burned away to ash, before his skeleton fell to the ground before the Dark Lord. There was screaming from many sources in that moment, names called and orders shouted.

The only one that truly mattered was Jubilatious' instructions of, "Bind his hands! Don't let his fingers move!"

Zetine pinned three of Vhodan's fingers together by driving her daggers between the plates of his gauntlet, then held onto the Emperor's arm for dear life. We-Will-Reach-Sanctuary dropped his falcata and grabbed Vhodan's hand, pulling his fingers back with all of his might. Mizt-Ied returned to her previous task, dutifully leaping onto Vhodan's shoulders. This time she was victorious, and pulled the Emperor's dark helmet from his head. She dropped it upon the ground and drew two of her knives.

Vhodan's appearance was rather attractive. He was of elven descent, though with primarily human traits. His eyes were a magnificent golden color that seemed to almost glow. His brown hair was kept short, and he possessed a small amount of stubble since he hadn't shaved that day. He was not at all what any of them would have expected Vhodan The Eternal to look like, save for the one amongst them that had known him personally.

The Dark Lord freed his right hand from We-Will-Reach-Sanctuary, tearing his arm free from his gauntlet. He reached up and grabbed Mizt-Ied by the leg, before slamming her into We-Will-Reach-Sanctuary like a club. Even as Jubilatious pelted Vhodan with fire ball after fire ball, he then reached for Zetine and grabbed both of her wrists in his fist. He squeezed down and she screamed in pain, before spitting in his face. During this exchange, none of them noticed a stout and thick little hand taking hold of the discarded falcata. Vhodan turned his gaze just in time to see the blade brought down over his exposed forearm.

He let out a cry of pain as blood sprayed from his newly formed stump, while Ironja grinned up at him and said, "Never cross a dwarf."

As though that small act of vengeance was all that kept the blood loss at bay, Ironja then fell to the ground unconscious. Zetine stepped backwards; wrestling Vhodan's severed hand free from her wrists. She watched as he tore his legs free from the ice, and then stomped down harshly upon We-Will-Reach-Sanctuary's back. He took hold of the hammer in his left hand once again, and then spun around to strike Zetine with it, sending her skidding across the ground with a broken rib. He turned back to finish off We-Will-Reach-Sanctuary only to see Mizt-Ied glaring up at him with uttermost contempt.

"What do you hope to do against me, goblin?" he asked with a cruel smile.

"Not much," she replied. "Buy a little bit of time, maybe."

Vhodan raised his hammer up, but Mizt-Ied quickly pulled a smoke bomb from her chest and threw it directly at his face. The bomb exploded, enveloping the three of them in dark smoke. The Emperor coughed as he stumbled away, half blind. By the time he had emerged from the smoke cloud, Jubilatious was there. The two looked to each other for just a moment with quiet understanding. Then Vhodan raised his hammer overhead.

Jubilatious delivered a lightning bolt directly to Vhodan's face, scorching it and knocking the hammer from his hands. This barely even slowed the Emperor though, who then began to punch in

Jubilatious' direction. Then wizard quickly back stepped, letting one of his daggers parry each of Vhodan's blows. During this exchange, Jubilatious watched Vhodan quickly move his hand in a familiar pattern, before rain began to fall throughout the enclosed room. Vhodan blocked the dagger a few more times, made a stranger pattern, and then thrust his wide hand towards the ground.

The wizard quickly cast a levitation spell on himself and floated up in the air by a few feet, though not even an entire inch was required. He watched as Vhodan sent electricity streaking across the water, electrocuting all of Jubilatious' allies. Then the Dark Lord was upon him, delivering punch after punch, each of which was only just barely parried by Jubilatious' dagger. Jubilatious quickly verbalized his own spells, casting concentrated magic, ice, fire, whatever he could muster at Vhodan without taking too long. It all seemed to just bounce off whatever magical protection the Emperor had upon him though.

Suddenly Vhodan grabbed the dagger from the air, and then thrust it into the ground, trapping it amidst the stone floor. Jubilatious attempted to pour water into Vhodan's lungs, but he lacked the power from the white mages to perform such a spell. Vhodan was then upon him in an instant, grabbing Jubilatious by the throat. He lifted the wizard up into the air, slowly squeezing the life out of him. Jubilatious could feel the absolute joy resonating from Vhodan as he suffocated his enemy, the last who was still on their feet.

"You... forgot... something..." Jubilatious gasped.

"And what's that," Vhodan purred, taking great pleasure in hearing his victim's last words.

"You forgot... I had two..." he slowly sputtered, before Vhodan's eyes went wide and his grip slackened. Jubilatious took in a deep breath then finished, "Daggers."

Vhodan dropped the wizard and fell to his knees, a golden blade sticking out from his chest. Jubilatious landed on his feet, now a little above eye level with the Emperor. Vhodan abruptly reached out again, grabbing hold of Jubilatious' throat to finish the job. He felt iron claws pricking against his flesh, intent on claiming one final life. Jubilatious put both of his hands upon the hilt of the dagger, pushing it deep through Vhodan's chest. The tip of the blade poked out through his back, and Vhodan coughed up blood onto Jubilatious' face.

He looked up to the wizard with a sick smile on his face as he said, "Be seeing you soon..."

Then he died. Jubilatious watched as Vhodan's body fell to the side, nearly pulling him down with it, had his hand not gone entirely limp. He lay there, unmoving, blood pooling around his lifeless corpse. Jubilatious stumbled away, throat burning, as the others slowly pushed themselves up. They focused upon Vhodan's body, their attention turning to Jubilatious only after hearing a soft thud. He had fallen into the Emperor's throne, taking a seat to unwind from the excitement, pain, and exhaustion of the battle. From the Emperor's throne, he looked down at all of them.

Chapter 19

The past several months had not been unkind to Wolf, though it had not been a time of particularly fond memories. The necromancers had taken her title quite seriously, and intended on indoctrinating Wolf into their culture as thoroughly as possible in a relatively short time frame. Even if she couldn't learn the art of necromancy, for she had no substantial magic in her blood, Wolf was still expected to learn how to read and write, as well as how to behave. All of this education angered Wolf, made her feel belittled, but she did not have the energy left to fight over it. Instead she just sat back and passively listened to whatever she was told.

She was awoken early in the mornings by the cawing of a creature she had never seen, but was quite sure had been dead for decades. From there she would head down the stairs of her two-story house, careful not to trip over the stairs that always seemed just slightly out of line. On the ground floor, she would be treated to breakfast by one of the servants that had been appointed to tend to her needs. They were all men, and would change every few days, but a few weeks in she realized it was a rotation of five people. None of the five men ever said much to her, even if she attempted conversation, and this left Wolf feeling exceptionally alone when she was within the confines of her own home.

Most breakfasts at Cairn had consisted of boiled vegetables and occasionally eggs fried in a pan over the fireplace. Today Wolf was treated to boiled turnips that had been mashed into a paste. She actually rather liked the turnips, though she would have much rather mixed them with egg to give them some amount of a savory flavor. Wolf sat by herself at a table that could easily fit eight people, and waited as the servant laid a spoon made from polished bone atop a cloth for her. He returned only a moment later with a bowl of mashed turnips, which he placed next to the spoon and cloth before turning to leave.

"Thanks," she called to him as he left.

The servant paused and bowed as he said, "Of course, mistress," before he took his leave.

Wolf picked up the spoon and gave it a probing lick before sighing. Despite the necromancers' use of bones for their utensils, they had been entirely removed of marrow and anything else that might give her food some more flavor. Wolf slowly fed herself spoonfuls of turnips, holding the food in her mouth for only a second before swallowing. The servant returned to place a glass by her side and filled it with a jug of milk, which Wolf happily gulped down. In her time there she had discovered that only about a third of the necromancers were treated to the drink, and none of the men. As such, she reveled in the small delicacy that reminded her softly of her youth.

Once her meal was finished, Wolf rose to her feet, wiped her mouth with her sleeve, and went back upstairs to change. The clothing that the Cairnites had provided for her seemed insulting, for it was never the sort of thing she would willingly wear otherwise. There was a black skirt that fell to her ankles, a long sleeve shirt that exposed much of her back, and a scarf she refused to wear that was meant to cover her head. They had provided other clothes for her as well, but they all showed far too much skin for her liking, or were simply cloaks, so she left them in a pile in the corner of her room. Every few days a servant would come to take her clothing away, leaving her naked save for whatever she had stashed away under her pillow. As the weeks progressed into months, she had learned to hide whole shifts beneath her head.

Once dressed, Wolf headed downstairs once more and left the house. Cool mountain air immediately washed over her as she held the door open, before stepping out for the day. Her first lesson each day was letters, which was held in a cave that had several chairs, boards, and scrolls of parchment in it. It had been explained to Wolf that the class was meant for children, much to her horror, but they gave her a private lesson before any of the children were even awake so she had nothing to worry about. She absolutely hated letters, and struggled with forming them into properly arranged words.

"If it sounds the same, why is it wrong?" is a question she frequently asked, usually shouting in frustration.

Her teacher, Mistress Varia, an elderly woman with short grey hair and more wrinkles than she could count explained each time, "Because words are spelled a certain way. Try again, and remember what I've told you."

It had been slow progress for many months, but as the year came to an end Wolf felt confident that she at least had a basic grasp of reading and writing. She could at the very least read through most of the scrolls her teacher provided. The fact that the scrolls detailed myths intended for children was not lost on Wolf, but she found a small amount of comfort in the stories, so she didn't mind as much as other parts of her lessons. By the time she was able to recite some of those scrolls as she read them, her teacher had seemed to become quite proud of her. As proud as she could get, anyway.

Varia worded her compliments in such a way they always felt just slightly like an insult. Chief amongst them was, "You have learned so well for a girl from The Southern Reach."

After letters, Wolf would go to her first sword fighting lesson of the day. She had protested at first, after all, why should she take sword lesson when she used an axe? The necromancers wouldn't hear it though, and instead she faced a man that wore dark leather armor over his black shift. He carried with him a thin black straightsword, a duplicate of which he would always give Wolf at the start of their lessons together. This teacher, of all the Cairnites, was possibly her favorite. It came down sheer to the fact that he didn't seem to care about anything that wasn't directly connected to his blade.

Mikelle as he was called often told her, "Come at me and let me see what you're made of."

So Wolf would charge at him, sword held overhead. He would easily parry her every time, and then usually deliver a strike with the butt of his hilt. Again and again he would have her attack him, and again and again he would deflect her blow. Eventually Wolf began to wise up to his actions, and move in more carefully. Still he would beat her without much effort, but it was at least taking more time than before. The downside of Mikelle was that due to his lack of a care, he didn't explain what Wolf was meant to do. This frequently caused her to feel like she was expected to overcome a solid stone wall.

On this particular day, Mikelle felt generous. He offered up the wisdom, "Focus on my sword, mistress. I cannot parry you if I do not have it."

Wolf took his words to heart, and began her attack once more. She held the hilt between her two hands and focused on the end of his sword, striking at it with all of her might. Her teacher continued to hold his own weapon with just one hand, and still didn't seem particularly concerned by her actions. He attempted to pull his blade away a few times, but soon realized she swung her weapon with a greater speed than he could match. Instead he resorted to another parrying technique, quickly twisting his sword before her own made contact. Their blades clashed, Wolf's bounced away, and Mikelle gently laid the tip of his blade against her throat.

He said, "That is my win once again, mistress."

After sword fighting with Mikelle, there was the grave lesson. Despite a lack of necromantic training, or even the ability to cast a spell, Wolf was to be taught of the undead. Most commonly, this was in the form of skeletal anatomy. Her teacher, another old little necromancer named Mistress Varsh, would point to a part of a skeleton and explain what it was and what it did. Sometimes these parts were obvious, other times it actually was somewhat interesting to hear. Later on, Wolf would be expected to recite back everything she had been taught that day, though she got very little right most days. For whatever it was worth, the anatomy skeleton seemed quite delighted to hear what Wolf had to say about it.

Varsh would say things such as, "This is the joint between the hip and the thigh. It is one of the connecting points that binds a skeleton together while animated. Should you strike here, you could potentially cause the entire skeleton to crumble. While more specialized undead will keep moving even after a joint is taken out, typically you will find mass reanimated who do not have these protections. Simply removing a leg, or both, will cause it to revert to its dormant state. It is crucial you hit the skeleton at just the right angle though, for if you miss, you would do nothing more than knock it down."

Later on Wolf would repeat the message as, "If you hit the skeleton between the hip and the thigh, you kill it. Sometimes this doesn't kill it, so hit it a few more times in the same spots. If you miss, you won't kill it."

After grave lesson, Wolf would eat lunch back at her home. It was almost always waiting for her on the table, only slightly cooled. This day she had roasted turnips instead of mashed like in the morning, and there was even a few small pieces of cured meat on her plate. She took the fork she had been supplied and eagerly bit into the meat, delighting in its taste. After she had devoured the first piece of meat, Wolf made sure to take a bite of the turnips before swallowing her next bite of meat. This way the two tastes intermingled, and it felt more like real food than the turnips would on their own. A glass of wine had also been supplied, though Wolf didn't much care for the drink.

As the servant passed her by she asked him, "Can I have some water?"

"Of course mistress," he replied with a small bow. "I boiled some just an hour ago. I will have it for you in a moment."

When he returned with a glass and a jug of water, Wolf feared the refreshing fluids would be too warm to be enjoyable. To her relief it had cooled fairly nicely, and while not as cold as she would have liked, it was more than enough to satisfy her. After eating, Wolf rose to her feet and returned outside to continue her lessons. She only had two left in the day, then a meeting with Velena and Helena afterwards.

Wolf's next lesson was maths. She hated maths most of all. The first few lessons had been deceptively easy, and so Wolf grew confident. The teacher, a skeletal old lady who Wolf was convinced actually was a skeleton in a veil by the name of Mistress Piety, was the most callous person Wolf had ever meant. After those first few lessons, she had grown to understand that Wolf knew how to add and subtract. So she switched lessons suddenly, and expected Wolf to be able to keep up just as well as she had before.

Frequently Wolf would cry things like, "But I don't know how to multiply!"

Every single time Mistress Piety would respond in her thick Cairn accent, "I won't be having any of that attitude. If you can add ten plus ten, you can multiply ten times ten."

Then Wolf would say something along the lines of, "But that's different!"

To which Mistress Piety would always chide her with, "It's the same basic principle. Just try harder, and eventually you will get it."

After maths, she normally would have another sparring lesson with Kazaa where she got to use her axe. On that particular evening though, when she entered the cave they normally fought, she found Cutter was also there. Over the course of the past year, the young man had taken to Cairn culture quite well. He looked remarkably similar to one of the native Cairnites, especially dressed in one of their black shifts. He held in his hand a bone flute, and sat cross legged against one of the walls.

He said, "I hope you don't mind I've come to watch..."

Wolf remembered her manners and said, "It's fine... just stay quiet."

"I can do that," he replied with a grin that Wolf did not return.

Kazaa arrived soon after, tightening the bandages around his knuckles. Wolf drew her axe once she saw him, and the Exian drew each of his own weapons. Then he said, "Come at me."

Wolf let out a battle cry and charged him, doing her best to outmaneuver Kazaa. She managed to keep him on his feet, which she took as a sign of her progress. She swept her axe at Kazaa's feet, which he deftly stepped away from. She then brought the axe up and jabbed at him with the shaft, but Kazaa ducked underneath and retaliated with a strike to her stomach. Wolf resisted the urge to keel over and instead swung her axe at him, but Kazaa ducked and placed the groove of his dagger over the backend of her axe. He pushed it along with Wolf's own momentum, and then sent the axe falling out of her reach.

Wolf quickly punched Kazaa and the blow actually landed, nearly knocking him off of his feet. But then he was back, a whirl of blades that Wolf had no way to defend against. She stepped backwards, narrowly avoiding each slash and stab, before her back hit the wall. Wolf looked on in faux terror as Kazaa thrust his dagger forward, landing the tip gently against Wolf's neck.

The faintest drop of blood began to blossom as he said, "Match. You have not been working on your steps, pup."

"They're boring," Wolf replied. "It doesn't feel right doing it with a skeleton."

Kazaa sheathed his blades and took a few steps back as he said, "Then do it with me."

"Do what with you?" Cutter asked, though no one paid him much mind.

Wolf asked him, "Are you sure?"

"I am," he nodded. "Stop an inch away from hitting me."

"Alright," Wolf huffed as she went to retrieve her axe.

Step one, the right arm. Wolf swung her blade just an inch from Kazaa's shoulder. Step two, the left arm. Wolf swung her blade to his other shoulder. Step three, the right leg. Wolf stopped herself just before his knee. Step four, the left leg. She swung towards his knee but stopped before even touching his garments. Step five, the head. She swung her axe overhead but stopped it before it could kill her friend. Repeat.

Step one, step two, step three, step four, step five. Repeat. Again and again she swung her blade; again and again she did not hit Kazaa. He had her repeat the steps monotonous for the better part of an hour, looking Wolf directly in the eye as she fainted attacks against him. By the time she had even noticed Kazaa had begun deflecting her blows with his dagger, she had been completely consumed by the repetition.

Realizing the lesson had shifted, she pressed the attack more seriously, pushing Kazaa back. He continued to deflect her blows but she increased her speed and ferocity, before abruptly changing her tactics. Step three, step one, step four, step three, step two, step one. Piourrette, parry, back step, back step, parry, parry. The two were engaging in a delicate dance that could easily end in Kazaa's death, though he didn't seem particularly worried.

The match ended abruptly as Kazaa drew his khopesh, placing the curved sword across Wolf's throat between her blows. With a grin he said, "Match once again, pup."

After Kazaa had taken his leave, Cutter rose to his feet and approached Wolf. He said, "You did really well out there! It was nice watching yo-"

"Don't talk to me," came Wolf's cold reply.

"A-alright then," he winced at her.

Like the repetition of her steps, Cutter had continuously tried to follow her around and grow close with her. Wolf was disgusted by him, and had either told him off or ignored him every time the whelp showed his face. That did little to dissuade Cutter though, for every several days or so he would muster up some new bit of courage and try to talk to Wolf once again. At first she had wondered if some of the Cairnites were giving him bad advice, but seeing just how meek the men were in front of the women, she doubted that was it. No, the boy was just as stubborn as a mule and couldn't be turned away from his pursuit.

He had tried to follow her to her meeting, but even Cutter knew better than to step foot into The Pale Temple. It was one of two religious buildings Wolf had seen in Cairn, the other being The Black Temple. While the latter was constructed with ash infused brick, this one was made entirely from human bones. They were so well polished that an outsider may not even realize what they were sitting on for some time inside, though the realization would inevitably set in. With ten rows of pews laid out beside a central walkway and hanging ivory chandeliers, the inside was almost beautiful.

Wolf pushed open the twin doors to see Helena and Velena standing in front of a chalice at the end of the walkway, their backs to the ornate sculpture depicting The Pale Lady. Seated throughout the pews were each of Wolf's teachers, even Kazaa. They looked to

Wolf in silence, filled with anticipation. She did her best to ignore them and walked forward, each foot step echoing throughout the hall. The doors slowly shut behind her, creaking steadily before the thud of their closing rung out with finality.

She asked, "You wanted to see me, mistresses?"

"You have done well, Grave Warden Wolf, said Helena.

Velena said, "Your studies have progressed acceptably, if slowly."

Helena continued, "And your skills with a blade are passable for your title. The time has come."

"The time for your final trial," Velena took hold of the goblet and passed it to Wolf. "Drink deep; consume the essence of life and death. Go forth and slay the demon that consumes you. May it be wiped clean from this mortal realm, and embrace death just as you have."

Wolf stared down into the sickly green liquid, a thick red swirl blended into it. The drink bubbled ominously, and it let off a stench that made Wolf gag. Still, she held her held back and gulped down every single drop from the chalice. It was the foulest thing she had ever tasted, like rotten eggs and old cabbage, accompanied by a burning sensation all the way down to her stomach. Wolf had to gasp for air after finishing, her head pounding and heart drumming so fast it felt as though it would tear itself free from her chest.

She managed to rasp out the words, "What was that!?"

Helena's lips contorted into a subtle smile as she answered, "Drugs. Quite a lot of them, too."

Wolf stumbled backwards, her vision swirling just like the drink. Great twisting colors began to seep into her vision, suffocating out all the normal colors Wolf should have been seeing. Kazaa reached out a hand to her, but Wolf recoiled as it twisted and twisted and twisted into an impossible shape. Someone was saying something to her, but Wolf couldn't make out what the words meant, they were all nonsense.

She made it to the doors and pulled them open before falling out of the Pale Temple into the evening. The air didn't feel right outside, far too thick and heavy. Wolf continued onwards, moving in some random direction. She passed by a few people, but she couldn't tell if they were skeletons or humans, and their bodies had distorted into such impossible shape that there was no point in talking to them.

It was hard work to stay on her feet, for each step carried with it the risk of falling into a heap on the ground or tripping over some errant rock. Still, Wolf pushed herself forward, and eventually found herself out in the barren wastes of Cairn. She had no idea how much time passed, but the green river had come to meet her as it had once before. She fell to her knees before it, humbled by the blood of the giants slain so long ago.

From beneath the river rose a great and mighty beast, the thing of nightmares. It placed skeletal hands onto the ground on either side of Wolf, and then pushed its bulking frame up out of the water. It looked much like a dire wolf, but somehow even larger, with jet-black fur and eyes of ethereal green. Arrows and swords jutted out of the monster's hide, trophies from the many that had attempted in vain to kill it before.

The undead wolf moved forward, causing Wolf to fall onto her back as she looked up at the horrible thing. It snarled at her, showing off a mouth of sharp and crooked teeth save for a single missing fang. Something clicked in Wolf's head, and she awkwardly moved her hand to her chest. Her fingers danced along skin and cloth as she looked for it, but what felt like an eternity was no more than a second. Her thumb hooked into the thread of her necklace, and she raised it up for the beast to see.

She asked it, "Is this yours?"

The wolf's empty green gaze bore down on her, burrowing into her very soul. Abruptly its head lurched forward, mere centimeters from Wolf's face. Its snout traced across her hand, soft fur a euphoric sensation against her fingers. The dire wolf opened its mouth and enveloped the entirety of Wolf's hand, practically swallowing her arm up to the elbow. Then it pulled away, releasing Wolf's arm unscathed, and taking the necklace with it. It slowly stepped back away from her, then turned to re-enter the water.

Before it left, it spoke in a familiar voice that cut through Wolf more harshly than any blade ever could. It said, "Thank you, Wolf. You will not be forgotten."

Its body slumped forward, cold fluid rising up to meet it. Wolf watched in awe as it was swallowed by the river, falling into impossible deepness. The dire wolf quickly disappeared, leaving Wolf alone in the oppressive night. She laid there for quite some time, sprawled out beneath the stars, luminescent green glow the only thing keeping her company.

She watched as the stars took on a great many shapes. A hunter and a bear, a ruler, two people of small size, and a wizard though she had no frame of reference for that one. A hunter alone and a hunter with a cub. A woodsman, and a warrior, a figure she could not make out. The woodsman and a different warrior, another wizard and that same indecipherable figure. Then at last all of the stars parted so that a single figure could exist in supreme glory, its head flanked by six curved lines of stars.

But then the stars all twirled together, and though Wolf looked to the sky, her vision was one of the ground. A figure stood there, draped in a tattered black cape and clutching a bloody straightsword. Around the figure were trees and corpses, though not all of the corpses were dead. The figure turned and Wolf saw that their face had been painted to resemble a skull. The figure walked forward, and from beyond Wolf's vision came a great many warriors. They wore patchwork leather armor, and seemed to be mostly orcs with a few humans mixed in.

The figure- the first Grave Warden, slew them with ease. Their sword severed limbs as easily as one slices through a stick of warm butter, and thrust through every gap in the enemies' armor. Though the dead fought beside the Grave Warden, they were little more than cannon fodder to keep the enemy warriors busy as the Warden made their way through the army. Not a single blow would land upon the Grave Warden, while every strike proved lethal.

One of the raiders ran to the Grave Warden's side, intent on driving a handaxe into their skull. Instead the Warden caught the axe and tore it from the orc's grip, before flipping it around in their hand. Just as the orc intended to do, the Grave Warden planted the axe into the orc's skull. It fell to the ground dead, just as dozens more had fallen in the Grave Warden's wake. Just as many more still would.

At some point, Wolf had risen to her feet. She had no idea when, only that she was walking back in the direction of town. The haze had begun to fall away from her, and Wolf realized just how horribly drenched in sweat she was. Everything ached too, and the time of day was now early morning. Wolf was left unsure of where to go, and so she returned to The Pale Temple, hoping there would be someone there to give her direction.

After pushing those twin doors open once again, she found three people inside. Kazaa had fallen asleep on one of the pews, his legs lifted onto the bench so that he could lie down. At the sound of the doors creaking he had stirred, looking groggily to Wolf. At the end of the walkway, as though they had not moved an inch, were Helena and Velena. The both of them looked to Wolf eagerly, their ethereal green eyes so horribly similar to the glow of the river.

Velena said, "And so the Grave Warden returns! Have you slain your demon, Grave Warden Wolf?"

Wolf's hand went to her necklace, but there was nothing there to take hold of. So she said, "Yes. I did."

Velena's smile was much broader than her sister's as she said, "Well done! The ritual is completed, and as all previous Grave Wardens have, you have slain the beast that haunts you. Your status is now cemented, Wolf who was of The Southern Reach, and is now of Cairn. You are the latest to bare the title of Grave Warden, and it will be you who carries the burden of striking at the heart of our enemy."

Helena said, "While you prepare for your journey into the mouth of the beast, we will prepare for our war. Together, we will strike at the Empire, with blade and with magic. Our enemies stand no chance against the might of Cairn. We will storm Imperial Heart, and hang the Rizzen Emperor in the streets for all to see!"

Wolf hated the way Helena spoke, for it always seemed far too overly stated for what were fairly simple concepts. Still, she let the woman have her little speech then said, "I will do whatever you want. My axe is yours, body too. Whoever you want dead, Emperor or hunter, they will die."

Helena grinned at her words then said, "Go home, honored Grave Warden. You deserve your rest. Your lessons will continue tomorrow, but soon the day will come when the vengeance we have promised you comes to fruition. Go home, and let sleep take you."

Wolf turned and began to walk away, but not before Kazaa said, "Well done, pup. I'm proud of you."

"Thanks," was all she said in response before sauntering off.

She returned to her home, as hauntingly beautiful and seemingly empty as always. As she passed into the kitchen, there stood one of the servants, arranging a plate of bread and boiled chicken. Upon noticing her he said, "Welcome home, mistress. I hope your ritual went well."

"It went fine," Wolf grunted as she sat down at the table.

The servant placed the plate in front of her along with a glass of red wine then asked, "Shall I draw a bath for you, mistress?"

Wolf picked up on the not so subtle clue that she stank then said, "Please do. Cold water."

"Of course, mistress," he said before taking his leave.

Wolf ate quickly, not realizing how hungry she was until the first bite of bread passed through her lips. She proceeded to devour the bread in its entirety, using the wine to moisten it in her mouth so she could swallow faster. Then without using the fork and knife to her side, she picked up the chicken breast and tore into it. As flavorless as it was, the meat came as a great relief to her. It was gone even faster than the bread, and then Wolf finished off the rest of the wine and was left alone.

She rubbed her hands on her shirt then rose to her feet, moving towards the washroom. Inside there was the servant, cranking the faucet to spill cold water into a metal tub. Once it was filled high enough he turned, he almost leapt back in surprise as he saw Wolf standing there. He said, "I will be back with a towel, mistress. The bath is ready for you."

Wolf nodded and stepped out of the way so the servant could leave the room, then approached the tub. She stripped down completely, leaving her clothes in a pile at her feet, and then climbed into the tub. Icy cold water rushed to meet her, but it came as a great relief. Wolf lowered herself into the tub, submerging herself up to her chin. In that bath she found true relief, the world melting away from her in a way that still left her senses intact.

The servant returned just as he promised, and was careful not to look at her in the tub. With his eyes on the floor he placed the towel on the ground beside Wolf, and then picked up her clothes. She watched as he turned and left, disappearing to go wash her clothes wherever it was that servants washed clothes. Once he had gone, she allowed herself to be taken away entirely by the cold water.

All that was Wolf was washed away.

***

The suit of armor that harbored Donovan's soul had neatly pieced itself back together, but had been unable to repair the dents and cuts that had been left by Wolf. It awaited, sword at the ready, as yet another person approached it. This one did not appear to be a warrior; instead the man was clad in a hooded black robe and used a simple wooden staff as a walking stick. Even still, he dared to approach, and Donovan was ready to end the man's life just like anyone else that dared to face him.

"You are not Lady Selena," Donovan said, his distorted voice subtly lined with anger.

"I am not," The Black Mage spoke. "Was she your master?"

"As fine a mistress as has ever lived," he solemnly stated.

"And just who are you, little soul?" The Black Mage asked, his words filled with pity.

If Donovan still possessed a body he would have puffed his chest out as he said, "I am Sir Donovan, Lost Soul of Cairn, and Prized Thrall of her Lady Selena the Third. I have slain warrior and necromancer alike, and do not fear you, wizard."

"I am no more a wizard than you are," he lamented. "But I can still offer you peace."

"If it is my destiny to fall to you, then so be it," Donovan said with what was almost a growl. "Have at you!"

The animated suit of armor lumbered forward, raising its sword overhead with the intent of cleaving his opponent in two. Instead The Black Mage placed his left hand calmly upon the face of Donovan's helmet, and the entire suit of armor was blown away. With his hand still clutching the helmet, The Black Mage locked eyes with Donovan, his own golden eyes staring into the swirls of green that served as Donovan's.

He said, "Sir Donovan, Prized Thrall of her Lady Selena The Third. I release you from this mortal coil. Go forth and be free. Find your afterlife."

The lights faded from behind the helmet's visor, and The Black Mage dropped the helmet to the ground. For just a moment he ruminated on an imprint that had been placed upon the armor. He didn't quite recall what the familiar pattern was, but it soon came to him. A soft smile crept across the mage's lips as he considered the implication.

Speaking to himself he said, "So the girl made it all the way out here and survived... by now I imagine she's reached Cairn, and found whatever fate destiny has led her to. I hope it is one she can be happy with."

The Black Mage placed both hands upon his staff and closed his eyes, beginning a subtle meditation. Several minutes would come and go, before at last he opened his golden eyes. He had reached a conclusion on a topic he had debated with himself for many months now, and the answer was something he had feared having to do.

"Yes, I will go home," he said to himself. "Whatever has become of it, I must at least pay my respects and face those I have left behind."

He turned to the east and began to walk, a sly smile crossing his lips. Just as he had spoken to himself before he said, "I too wonder what they have made of themselves. Powerful wizards, I imagine. Let us hope they have made the right decisions."

Chapter 20

"We need to do something about Sanctuary," Jubilatious' words rung through the air like a funeral bell.

The past several hours had been a proverbial hell. One of the white mages had appeared to tend to their wounds, and while no one save for Garr in the group was fatally injured, Ironja had been taken away for a more continuous healing along with the other amputees from the battle. Soldiers had roughly pushed past the heroes as they entered the throne room, clamoring to take in the sight of the castle's interior, then to get hold of Vhodan's body. They were relentless in the mutilation of the body, using their bare hands to tear his limbs from his torso. In the end they impaled each severed body part on a separate spear, then brought them to the outside of the castle to plant in the ground. There, the limbs would serve as a haunting reminder to the prisoners that even their leader had been laid to waste by The Army of Hope.

Soon after, one of the human soldiers had opened a door he believed would lead to a food store room. Instead it opened up into a pit of starved wargs, who quickly tore the man apart and devoured him. Had it not been for the several witnesses gathered around, many more may have made the mistake throughout the night. Word travelled fast, and soon exploration of the castle was forbidden for the entire army. This did not stop several other soldiers from falling into spike pits left inside the castle's outer wall, or the gathered prisoners growing restless and causing great aggravation to their jailors.

Soon after the battle had ended, Vrias came to the heroes. He said, "I have looked all over, and have yet to find Kira. He was last with you; do you have any idea where he might have wandered off to?"

Jubilatious and Zetine looked to Mizt-Ied, who was not entirely sure of Kira's fate herself. She said, "The last we saw, your friend went to fight Torrn The Beast Lord. We haven't seen 'im since. But I'm sure he's fine! I've never seen anyone fight as well as him!"

"Oh, I see," Vrias quietly said more to himself than her. "Very well, take care, Heroes of Castle Take. May the moon take you well."

He left them, and as soon as he was out of earshot Zetine asked, "Do you know what actually happened to him?"

Mizt-Ied answered, "He got hurt, but me and Ironja saw him use a healing potion! After that... we went our separate ways. I suppose he could have died, but he was such a good fighter! Just like We-Will-Reach-Sanctuary!"

The elf had mused over that and said, "If so, I would have liked to fight him. I hope I see him again one day."

"I'm sure you will," Jubilatious shook his head.

We-Will-Reach-Sanctuary had looked agitated since the battle ended, restless and filled with some unexplainable anxiety. He was constantly pacing throughout the throne room, or fiddling with his daggers much to the anxiety of his allies. Eventually he walked towards them and said, "I am going to head towards my old quarters. I suppose I will see the three of you tomorrow, and then we can get started on whatever comes next."

"Of course," Zetine had said.

Mizt-Ied piped in with, "Have a good night!"

While Jubilatious only said, "Be seeing you."

It was after he left through one of the room's back doors that Jubilatious made his declaration. Mizt-Ied was quick to say, "But he's our friend!"

"He's a monster," Jubilatious retorted. "An assassin that served the most ruthless tyrant Valael has ever seen. Whatever reason he changed his mind on serving Vhodan, it wasn't out of the goodness of his heart. No, if anything he did it to take Vhodan's place. He used us to whittle the bastard down, so that he could kill us in our sleep and take the title of emperor for himself. We can't let that happen."

"You're mad," Mizt-Ied gasped up at him.

"He's right," Zetine sighed with a tone of bitter defeat. "You have heard the way he talks, the clues he has left us... Sanctuary has never been our friend. We cannot trust him, and we have to do something sooner rather than later."

"We won't kill him," Jubilatious said. "Whatever reason he had, he still helped us kill Vhodan. We take him as a prisoner, so that he can't hurt anyone ever again, but we won't make him suffer."

Mizt-Ied suppressed tears and rubbed her eyes before she asked, "When do we do this?"

Jubilatious looked down at her and said only, "Now."

They quickly found the dark elf walking through a stone corridor lit by torches. To We-Will-Reach-Sanctuary's left were several stained glass windows that let in just a little bit of sunlight, and obscured the sight of the castle's inner-court garden. The elf had reached the halfway mark in the hall, when he turned around to see Jubilatious and Zetine standing at the entrance he had come from. They stood silently, watching him.

We-Will-Reach-Sanctuary smiled and called out, "Hello again, friends! Have you come to join me? I suppose I can stick you in one of the other rooms, but there will be some surprises there I need to..." then his eyes settled upon Zetine's drawn daggers. He asked them, "Please don't do this. I don't want to do this."

Mizt-Ied leapt from behind, and We-Will-Reach-Sanctuary spun to knock her from the air before one of her knives could breach his skin. She hit the wall, but then there was Zetine, who We-Will-Reach-Sanctuary evaded easily enough. While she was fast, he was far faster. Mizt-Ied got to her feet and joined in, the pair of them slowly pushing We-Will-Reach-Sanctuary towards one of the walls. As fast as he was, he refused to fight back, and only dodged their strikes. Mizt-Ied couldn't help but feel that this was all too wrong, and while Zetine felt similarly, her mind landed in a much different reason for why.

All the while, Jubilatious chanted a spell. With his hands following We-Will-Reach-Sanctuary's movements he said, "We-Will-Reach-Sanctuary, I bind your hands until the time that you are of use to me. Your hands will never raise a weapon again so long that I, Jubilatious, will it. Your legs will be bound just as your hands, and never will you walk, until I Jubilatious command it. For as long as it takes, you will remain stationary and helpless, a prisoner in your own body. In the event of my death, your hands and legs will be removed from your body. You are mine."

Cold crept up We-Will-Reach-Sanctuary's wrists and ankles, but there was nothing he could do as chilling realization hit him. A heavy weight grew across all four of his limbs as twin sets of manacles were conjured forth. Then his arms were forced together, followed by his legs. We-Will-Reach-Sanctuary fell to the ground hard, bruising his cheek against the stone floor. He began to writhe around like a fish out of water, but there was nothing more he could do, so he quickly fell motionless. Both Mizt-Ied and Zetine stood over him, while Jubilatious soon joined their sides.

We-Will-Reach-Sanctuary meekly said, "Please, don't. Not now... you can't do this to me now... I thought we were friends..."

"We were never friends," Jubilatious coldly stated. "You're just another monster we had to rid this world of."

We-Will-Reach-Sanctuary twisted around so he could look Jubilatious in the eyes, and it was there he saw a familiar expression.

With his lips twisted into a scowl he asked, "If I, despite every effort I took to redeem myself am a monster, what does that make you?"

Jubilatious turned and said, "Zetine, take him to the other prisoners... no, not there. We don't want him stirring a revolt."

"I saw the dungeons on my way in," Mizt-Ied squeaked. "I don't know about keys to lock up, but there are absolutely places to put him!"

"Then go with her," Jubilatious said. "I'm going to scout the quarters, make sure our assassin doesn't have any traps waiting for us."

Zetine hoisted We-Will-Reach-Sanctuary onto her shoulder then set off with Mizt-Ied as a guide. The goblin led her dutifully to the dungeons she had arrived in the central castle from, and all the while their prisoner offered little resistance. It was as though his spirit had broken entirely from his capture, though neither of them was quite sure why. They began to walk down the spiral staircase, overlooking the corpse of the Gorgon Queen down below.

Suddenly Mizt-Ied squeaked and she asked, "What if Jubilatious runs into trouble?"

"What do you mean?" Zetine asked her, looking down towards her ally.

"He said there were traps, right?" she asked.

Zetine nodded and said, "Yes..."

She continued, "Well there's definitely none this way, but there may be a lot up there! And I'm the only one good at spotting them!"

Zetine offered a weak chuckle then said, "Go forth then, Mizt-Ied. I will take it from here."

Mizt-Ied thanked her and began to hurry back up the stairs, running as fast as she could to meet Jubilatious. Unbeknownst to her, he had not run into a single trap. The wizard had walked past several sets of thick wooden doors, each carved with the name of whoever had been intended to reside within. Most of the names were unfamiliar, belonging to some previous commanders or allies of Vhodan. Soon though he came across the doors that belonged to the quarters of Vhodan himself, and pulled them open.

The interior was quite spacious, and was not at all what Jubilatious would have expected. To the left wall was a fine bed, along with a modestly sized bookshelf. At the front wall was a round window overlooking the courtyard, and below it a chest. To the right wall was a set of bunk beds and by them some parchment and chalk. But most importantly, directly in front of Jubilatious, were two children. Their skin was pale, and each had ears with the faintest of sharp tips. One child was brown haired, and his older brother possessed blond hair. The younger child's eyes were an orange-gold, while the older brother's eyes were the same magnificent gold as his father's had been.

The older brother stared up at Jubilatious defiantly, staring daggers up into the wizard's piercing blue eyes. Cold and detached understanding filled Jubilatious, and he did not find himself at any fault for what he did next. From his robes he produced one of his daggers, then stepped foot into the bedroom. The older brother was first, then the younger brother, and neither of them screamed. They didn't scream, but their eyes bored into his the entire time. He stood over their lifeless and bloody bodies in a trance, reasoning with himself that what he had done was the right thing.

Though he was barely even able to notice it in the thick of the trance, the moment he killed the younger brother, the castle itself died. Stone cracked throughout the entire structure, and a few small rooms even caved in. The most notable damage came when the Unknowing King's tower came crashing down, taking a large chunk of the outer wall with it. This Jubilatious heard, and he knew he made the right decision.

From behind Jubilatious a voiced gasped out, "You killed them... they were children and you- you killed them!"

Jubilatious let out a sigh to himself and then said, "You never did know when to shut up."

He spun around and grasped at Mizt-Ied, grabbing her by the hair before she was able to move away in time. She cried out in pain as he yanked her forward and crouched down, tearing a few hairs from her scrap. Mizt-Ied's eyes filled with water, and tears of both pain and fear began to trail down her cheeks. Jubilatious pressed the tip of his blade against her lips, sliding the dagger into her mouth even as she beat against his leg.

He commanded, "Don't struggle. This will keep you from mouthing off to anyone."

Mizt-Ied felt the blade slice her tongue open, and she screamed as loud as she could, but there was no one to come to her aid. Jubilatious pulled the dagger away, and she wretched up the tip of her tongue which he had cut off. The wizard looked down at her with sick satisfaction, and then released his grip upon her hair. Whatever he had expected to happen next, it wasn't for Mizt-Ied to grab his wrist and chomp down tightly upon it.

He cried out, "You bitch!" and flung her off him, growling in pain as he dropped his dagger to clench his bloody wrist.

Mizt-Ied watched as the dagger floated back up in the air, then was joined by its twin. The man she had called her friend was going to kill her, and there was nothing she could do to stop him. As fast as she could, she grabbed hold of one of the smoke bombs on her belt and threw it to the ground. Thick black smoke enveloped the area as Jubilatious' daggers pierced her veil, each one entering and exiting the smoke as he guided them to try and impale Mizt-Ied. By the time the smoke thinned out though, there was no sign of the goblin.

"MIZT-IED!" he called out at the top of his lungs, his words echoing off the walls. "PRAY I NEVER FIND YOU AGAIN!"

Still clenching his wrist, Jubilatious pushed closed the doors to Vhodan's quarters and took his leave. He considered checking over the other rooms, but decided against it. Instead he left the castle's interior, seeking out a white mage to heal his wound. From there, he would reunite with Zetine in the throne room. Whatever would happen next, he didn't know, but he had plans that he hoped to see pay off.

***

It was shortly after the battle that a single hand reached up from the basilisk pit that Torrn and Kira had fallen into. The hand was missing three of its fingers and was severely burned, but it slowly pulled itself forward. In the pit behind it, there were only corpses. Soon Kira pulled his entire body out of the pit, or what was left of it. He was missing most of his left leg, and his right hand had been bitten off, to say nothing of the many chunks that had been torn out of his body. The elf dragged himself forward, leaving a steady trail of blood behind him.

Then the high elf heard a voice, grand and otherworldly. It said to him, "Your suffering is not without reward. Join me. Embrace flesh. Let it consume you. Consume it. Be reborn. The body that has failed you will become a relic of the past. You will rise again, new and replenished, greater than you ever were before."

Kira had no idea what the voice was, or even if it was real. He watched as a wall cracked open ahead of him, opening up a chamber of flesh and organs that waited patiently for him. This too he had no idea if it was real or simply a death induced illusion. Either way, Kira dragged his failing body forward, refusing to give up. The moment his hand fell upon the sickly wet flesh, he was pulled inside entirely, and the crack closed up behind him.

***

When Zetine returned to Jubilatious, he was relieved to see her. He had spent the past several minutes meticulously going over the throne room, sealing each door aside from the one that led to the dungeons. As an extra level of precaution, Jubilatious had even placed several wards along the ground by each entrance. They wouldn't do much, but would at least stall any would be intruder for a few seconds, and alert him to their presence. The various cracks and fractures that had appeared in the stonework were another problem he didn't have a solution for, and it seemed as though eventually even the ceiling would cave in. It would be a problem Jubilatious would need to remedy in the near future.

He said to her, "I don't think I have had a chance to say it yet. Zetine, I am filled with relief the likes of which only the gods could know, seeing that you have made it through everything with me."

She gently smiled and replied, "I am relieved to have you here with me too, Jubilatious. My heart breaks for Garr, and all those that we lost taking the castle..."

He took a step closer, so close he was practically on top of her and said, "Zetine, my feelings are more than that of seeing a comrade has survived. I am glad *you* are here. I have stayed silent as we travelled together, because I did not know what the future held in store for us. Now that we have completed our quest, now that evil is defeated and we are both safe... Zetine, I love you, and I would like for nothing more than to spend the rest of my days with you."

Zetine stood in silence for a moment before she said, "I think I feel the same way, though love is a mystery. If my feelings are anything more than a crush or simple infatuation, I do not know. But I would like to find out."

She placed her hand upon Jubilatious' cheek, and then the two of them laid their lips upon one another. They kissed gently at first, then passionately. Soon they began to pull at each other's clothes until each of them were naked, taking in the sight of each other's skin and scars. They quickly returned to kissing, before slowly falling to the ground. It was not comfortable lovemaking, nor was it the most thrilling, but in the moment it was all that mattered. After everything that had happened, there was no greater relief than the sensations Jubilatious and Zetine shared with one another.

After what seemed like a divine hour, the pair laid embraced in one another's arms, wanting nothing more for the moment to end. However, there soon came the sound of the main doors being rattled, before urgent knocking came. The pair quickly began to redress as best as they could, which was far easier for Jubilatious than Zetine. She ended up forgoing most of her bandages, and instead pulled on Jubilatious' robe while he wore only his shirt and trousers. He placed his hat upon his head for a moment, then decided against it, and instead dropped it to the ground beside the throne.

Zetine said, "I think it will be obvious what we were doing."

Jubilatious ran his hands over his face, flinching at the sensation of his beard then said, "Head through the door to the quarters. I'll see what they want, and then meet you back there. Just... stay by the door, just in case."

"Of course," she smiled before kissing him upon the nose.

Jubilatious watched her go, and then moved towards the doors. He pulled the wooden beam off the latch that sealed them, and then opened up one of the doors. There stood Carver, Zeydas, and three humans that he did not recognize. Carver and Zeydas each still wore their armor, along with the scars of victory. The other three however came dressed in expensive white robes, hemmed with mud around the bottom. They were also much older than Jubilatious would have expected for anyone on the battlefield, save for a wizard, which they clearly weren't.

He asked them, "What do you want?"

"May we come in?" Zeydas asked.

"If you answer my question," he replied.

Carver said, "We have come to discuss what happens now that Vhodan is dead."

Jubilatious stared at him for a few seconds then said, "Very well. Come in."

He began to walk back towards the throne, taking a seat upon it while one of the humans spoke. He said, "Risen one, my name is Charon. I and each of my friends, Ryu and Harris, once served as advisors to Vhodan in the earliest days of his campaign."

"Bold of you to show your face here then," Jubilatious said.

"Humble, is what we are," Ryu retorted.

Charon continued, "Vhodan no longer had need of us when his plans turned to violent conquest for the sake of violent conquest. In the beginning, we were excellent aids, and held his empire together with our knowledge and wisdom. We are crucial assets, and once again seek service."

Zeydas said, "Amongst the surviving troops, you are a beacon of hope and might. They watched as you fell, before rising again to slay The Stormcaller. Before slaying Vhodan The Eternal. Tales of your quest have spread across the land as well, and many have called you a hero before the news will even reach them of your final actions in the battle. There are few that would refuse to follow you."

Carver wrapped it up with, "If we want a new governance, it should be you upon the throne. No one else has as much respect or awe as you do at the moment."

Jubilatious leaned back in the throne and thought about it for a moment before answering, a smile upon his face. He said, "I will lead this Risen Empire, and I will take you as my advisors as well. I will not repeat the mistakes nor the horrors of the Signet Empire. We will care for the people, ensure they are protected and treated well. Where Vodan ruled with might, I will rule with hope. Together, we will reforge Valael into a unified and powerful country."

"We are proud to serve you, Jubilatious the Risen Emperor," Carver said as he took a knee. Behind him, each of the others took a knee as well.

Jubilatious said, "I need to step away for a moment, gentlemen. I will be back soon."

"As you wish, emperor," Harris said.

***

Against Jubilatious' instructions, Zetine had begun to wander. She passed by where they had captured We-Will-Reach-Sanctuary, then into the hall where each of the personal quarters was clustered. It took no time at all for her to spot the small puddle of blood with some small chunk of flesh amidst it, though she had no idea what the source was. Zetine's attention was instead drawn to the door inscribed with We-Will-Reach-Sanctuary's name, curious as to what reason he possibly had to hurry to his room so soon after the battle.

She pulled the door open, her eyes glancing over each feature. A round window, a bookshelf perched beneath it, a few chairs, a weapon rack, a modest bed with a blue blanket, and a slightly smaller bed with a red blanket. Seated upon that second bed was an elven girl in her late teens, who looked to Zetine with terror in her emerald eyes. Her pink skin was mostly covered up by a yellow shift, and she held in her hands a doll that looked like it had been rescued from a fire.

The girl cried out, "Who are you!? Where's my father!?"

Zetine raised her hands to show she wasn't a threat and said, "I'm not going to hurt you. My name is Zetine. Who is your... father?"

The girl pushed herself back along the bed and answered, "We-Will-Reach-Sanctuary..."

Cold brutal realization hit Zetine, along with a wave of regret. She said, "I know your father. Come on, I can take you to him," and held out her hand. When the girl meagerly took it she asked, "What's your name?"

The girl cautiously took Zetine's hand and answered, "Wind-Through-The-Valley."

She pulled Wind-Through-The-Valley to her feet and began to lead the elf back towards the throne room, but by the time they made it back to the first corridor, Jubilatious stood there waiting for them. His arms were crossed, and his piercing blue eyes quickly scanned over the elf. He hardly seemed surprised to see her, though Zetine wasn't sure if it was because he knew of her existence, or if he simply hid his shock well.

"And who do we have here?" he asked casually.

"She is Sanctuary's daughter," Zetine told him. "We have made a terrible mistake."

"There have been no mistakes made today," Jubilatious shook his head. "We have done what is necessary to bring peace to the land. Vhodan, Sanctuary, Tyruden, they were all the same. They were threats to order, and now they're gone."

Zetine's eyes burrowed into him as she asked, "Whose order?"

"You're one of the first to know," Jubilatious smiled at her, genuinely happy to share the news. "Some of the others have decided that I should be the one to lead a new empire, risen from the ashes of what came before."

"So you're just another despot like Vhodan," she spat.

"I am nothing like him!" Jubilatious barked at her. "We have ended the suffering of a million people! We can have proper order now, without the threat of some other tyrant rising up to try and take over the land."

"Because you would be the tyrant," she shook her head. "I can't believe you."

"I would not be a tyrant, but you have no room to speak," he stated. "Pharaoh of Exia, so far from home. You and I are the same, Zetine. The leaders of two nations, two great heroes who vanquished evil together. But we could be more. If we ruled together, Valael and Exia could be one and the same. We would be unmatched throughout the world, a mighty and unified empire that was respected throughout every land."

"Just answer me one thing," she requested.

"Anything for you," he offered.

She asked, "Where is Mizt-Ied?" when he didn't answer she followed her question up with, "Was she a threat to your new empire? Did she see something she wasn't supposed to, or refuse to side with you? What did you do to her, Jubilatious? Where is our friend?"

"I don't know where she is," he growled, clenching his fist. "Maybe she's somewhere in the castle, maybe she's not, and I don't care. This isn't about her. It's about you and me, Zetine. Will you rule by my side or not?"

She said only, "Go fuck yourself."

Zetine quickly pulled the scepter from her back, and before Jubilatious could cast a spell of his own, fired a blast of white light at the wizard. It sent him flying back, colliding with the doors of the hall before passing through them. Jubilatious landed in a roll before rising to his feet, bruised but relatively unharmed. He pushed himself to his feet as his newly elected aids came rushing over, Carver and Zeydas drawing their swords to defend The Emperor from his attacker.

"Leave us," Jubilatious ordered. "This is a private matter."

"But my lord, Carver began before he was swiftly cut off.

Jubilatious harshly said, "That's an order, Carver."

"Very well, my lord," the general said as he sheathed his sword.

All five of them began to walk away, eyes on Zetine as she marched forward, Wind-Through-The-Valley waiting by the doorway. She raised her scepter while Jubilatious extended his hands, and this time the white light was stopped by a magic shield. Zetine focused intently, pushing as much as she could to will the magic forth, but it wasn't enough. By the time the light dissipated, he had been pushed back several feet, but his shield hadn't even cracked. The most she had to show for her efforts was that Jubilatious had begun to sweat and pant.

She placed the scepter upon her back and instead drew her daggers. Zetine ran at Jubilatious, and he immediately understood that she was intent upon killing him. He backed away, narrowly avoiding the first of her slices. Then Jubilatious' own daggers were parrying her blows, each blade glancing off of another, sparks flying through the air. Jubilatious kept retreating, far too unmatched to face Zetine in a close quarters battle. It was all he could do to keep from being impaled on the end of one of her blades.

The pair performed a dance so intricate and dangerous that the rest of the world began to fade away. Step after step; turn after turn, thrust after slice after thrust, a continuous stream of parries. At first Jubilatious' focus was entirely placed upon keeping Zetine's daggers from hitting him, but the rhythm soon took over. It felt as second nature to predict where she would strike, and he no longer needed his full attention to block her attacks. He spoke his spell quickly, as Zetine hastened her efforts.

She fainted with her right blade while she sliced with her left, causing one of Jubilatious' daggers to miss a parry, then quickly thrust forward. She felt his hand upon her chest, and then just before her blade pierced his throat, a bolt of lightning sent Zetine flying towards the main doors. She landed in a heap, gasping and writhing from the pain and loss of air, hands still clenched tightly to her daggers. Zetine dropped them to begin pawing at her chest, looking down with the expectation of seeing a mortal wound, but instead found it to be a superficial burn and nothing more.

Jubilatious fell into his throne, watching Zetine as she painfully pushed herself to her feet. He simply said, "Get the hell out of my country."

Zetine looked back at him with bewildered and pained eyes, but nodded and said, "Very well. Come, Wind-Through-The-Valley. We are leaving."

The elf hurried across the hall to meet her, while Zetine reclaimed her blades and sheathed them. She asked, "What about him? You said he killed Vhodan? And what of my father?"

"I will tell you on the way," Zetine groaned from the pain in her chest. "This is not a fight we can win."

Jubilatious watched as they left, complete apathy in his cold eyes. Once Zetine had passed beyond his line of sight though, Jubilatious' heart broke, and he felt himself as empty as he had ever been. Outside, his aids would watch the pair leave as well, but none of them would stand in Zetine's way. They then entered the throne room, once again joining their emperor.

"What happened, my lord?" Harris asked.

"A minor argument," Jubilatious sighed, doing his best to sound impartial. "I do not believe Exia will be an ally in the near future, but I do not fear any conflict between us either. Now what do you want?"

Charon said, "There are a number of matters regarding to your rule we must go over. First of all, what to do about the slaves."

"Isn't that simple?" Jubilatious asked. "We free them."

The aids exchanged looks between one another then Ryu said, "That is unwise, emperor. Following your proclamation, your empire will be starved of resources and wealth. Slaves provide both a massive boon to the economy, as well as cheap labor to rebuild infrastructure and tend to farms. Without them, the newly born empire would die within three years."

Jubilatious thought about that for several moments then said, "Very well. We do not nullify the slave trade, but we will not allow it to be as rampant as it once was. Criminals only, and the slaves should be treated with basic decency.

Ryu said, "Very well, my lord..."

***

Zetine found Ironja inside one of the hastily constructed medical tents outside the castle. The dwarf was much paler than she had ever seen him, and had been stripped of his armor so that the white mages could tend to him. There had been no saving his arm, and so there was only an empty spot on his shoulder where an arm should go. The white mages had done an excellent job in healing it, to the point there was only about an inch of noticeable scar tissue, but that did the dwarf little peace of mind. He looked truly miserable.

"Good to see ye, lass," he grumbled as they approached. "Who's this ye've got with ye?"

"My name is Wind-Through-The-Valley," she nodded to him.

"She is Sanctuary's daughter," Zetine explained.

"Yer shittin me," Ironja said in disbelief. "I can't believe he had a family. Where is he, anyhow?"

Zetine said, "Jubilatious tricked us, Ironja. While you healed, he convinced me and Mizt-Ied to help arrest Sanctuary. When

I found Wind and confronted him, Jubilatious told me he had declared himself the new emperor. Now I don't know where Mizt-Ied is, or what Jubilatious plans to do."

"Ye don't trust him?" Ironja asked.

"I... what?" Zetine asked right back.

"Jubilatious," he elaborated. "Sure, he's a bit of an ass, but he's a good lad. He wouldn't do nothin' bad without a good reason."

"You have to be kidding me," Zetine shook her head. "We just fought a war, Ironja! Do you really want to join with someone that wants to stand for the very principles we fought against!"

"It can't be like that," Ironja replied. "If he seems truly bad, of course I won't stand with him. But an empire on its own- there's nothin' wrong with that. An I know Jubilatious only wants to help people, just like ye or me."

Zetine began to walk away from him as she said, "You disappoint me, Ironja. I had hoped you would understand just how evil he has shown himself to be."

Outside, Jubilatious stood atop a balcony to address all who were gathered throughout the castle courtyard. He said, "My friends, my countrymen, those who risked their lives and have lost those they loved. We stand now, free people towering over the ruins of our enemies. Tyranny has been stopped, and evil vanquished. The rumors you have heard are true. I, Jubilatious who rose from the abyss, have slain Vhodan The Eternal. I drove my blade through his heart, and watched his body fall lifeless before me. Were there any doubt now to those amongst you when the body was presented, may it be dashed now. That body indeed belonged to Vhodan, and now it rests in pieces impaled upon your spears.

"We now rest in a state of unbalance. Vhodan had conquered most of Valael, fracturing our nation and abusing it. Were we to leave now we would still be free, but our nation would fall to chaos. There would be no governance, no one to keep the peace, no one to distribute food to the people. Several of you have come to me, including the great heroes Carver and Zeydas, with a request. You have requested that I take up the title of emperor so that I may lead Valael into a new age, away from the brutality of what Vhodan once stood for.

"Valael, I promise you a chance at a new life! We have saved our homeland from tyranny, and now we have a chance to restore it to its former glory! Together, with myself at the throne serving the people, we shall ensure Valael prospers. I ask of you all, you who have shed your blood to save our home, to accept me as your emperor, so that we can save Valael together!"

The crowd of soldiers began to chant, "Risen! Risen! Risen! Rizen! Rizzen! Rizzen!"

As Zetine made her way through the crowd, hand held tight around Wind-Through-The-Valley's wrist she said, "They don't even realize they're cheering for their own subjugation. They welcome the boot of a fascist just as quickly as they overthrow the last despot."

The elf asked, "Are we going to do anything about it?"

"What can we do?" Zetine asked her. "He's already won."

***

Jubilatious was dressed in an ornate and shimmering golden robe, with his purple hat still held proudly on his head. He had taken care to remain cleanly shaved, not a single strand of hair on his face. Jubilatious was flanked by six of his elite guards, each dressed in iron platemail with uncanny golden masks that resembled weeping faces. They each carried a spear in their right hand, while a dagger was sheathed at each of their left hips. They made their way to the Citadel of Remembrance.

Two of the guards pushed open the doors to the citadel, while Jubilatious stepped foot inside alone. The three sages were still seated at their stone pedestal, as though they hadn't moved over the past three years. Apos said, "Ah, if it isn't The Rizzen Emperor. Have you come to seek our services, Jubiliatious?"

Jubilatious stood still at the entrance as he said, "I have been through the archives at the academy."

"Have you?" Brindus asked, stroking his beard. "I would think the great emperor had more important things to do than go through student records and spell tomes."

The Emperor cast his cold gaze upon each of them as he said, "Tyruden kept special notes about me, outside of those he shared with you. He included an interesting one about my mother..."

"We had no other choice!" Valedict abruptly shouted out.

"Valedict!" Apos attempted to hush him too late.

"So you admit it?" Jubilatious asked, his words cutting through the air like a guillotine.

Apos attempted to explain, "Jubilatious, we had no other choice!"

"Save it," he growled. "I don't want to hear it."

"Hear it you will, boy!" Brindus barked. "To understand history, you need context!"

Apos continued, "We don't know how, but your mother somehow acquired the Sword of Vesh-Aku! By the time she had made it to Arkvine, she was no longer aware that she was even human. That cursed sword had taken her over entirely, using her body to wreak senseless violence upon the land. If left alone she would have killed every single being she came across, including you."

Jubilatious said, "Tyruden's notes were vague. He only said that you stopped her."

Valedict told him, "We did only what we had to. For the greater good."

Jubilatious asked, "You killed her?"

There was an uncomfortable silence, broken only by Brindus flatly saying, "We did."

Jubilatious let out a sigh then said, "Then I will avenge her death."

From the palms of both of his hands, balls of fire began to manifest. Valedict cried out in shock and fear, "How are you doing that without speaking, boy!?"

With a smile Jubilatious said, "Tyruden wasn't the only one that kept notes. You would be amazed at what Vhodan realized he could do with magic."

He brought his hands forward, merging both balls into one. The fire began to grow wider and taller, eating the air out from around everyone gathered there. Once it had grown so large it took up nearly half the chamber, Jubilatious sent it flying towards the three sages. For what good it did them, they accepted their deaths quietly. Jubilatious stood amidst the ashes, looking to their skeletons in disappointment. Then he pulled his hat from his head and tossed it to the floor before walking away.

He told his guards, "Seal the doors. I don't want anyone every stepping foot in here again."

"As you wish, my lord," one of them said.

After a brief moment's consideration, Jubilatious then said, "When we get home, strike it from the maps, and have their names stricken from the books. I want no record that any of this ever happened, and that there was ever anything here to harm."

Chapter 21

Wolf sat patiently as the servant painted her face, having grown used to it by now. Once a week she would sit on a stool as one of the servants carefully cloaked Wolf in a mask of white. Then they would move onto her eyes, enshrouding them in black. Then her cheekbones and lips too would be rendered black, until her face looked like a skull. There was no point in protesting the face painting, as much as Wolf detested it. Helena had drilled it into her head that it was a required element of her title. Having the sentence reduced to once a week instead of daily was the best compromise Wolf had been able to reach, with much yelling involved.

This was the second day that week she had her face painted however. The news had been delivered to her that morning that a ranger had entered the Dark Forest. So she sat having her face painted and her blades sharpened so that she could face him. Kazaa stood pacing around the room behind her, mumbling his own protests against the idea of sending Wolf out alone. She had tuned him out entirely, and was instead ruminating on the events that had played out a year before.

She remembered how fast he was, and his skill with a bow. She also remembered that he hadn't seemed interested in using any other weapons. Then she recalled the birds, and knew that they would provide an unfair advantage for the ranger. Her mind soon drifted away from the man she had made her sworn enemy however, and instead came to the events that had occurred before she met him. She remembered carrying Tusk's body through the snow, weighed down so heavily, and fighting back the urge to cry. She remembered the Dead Woman, Velena, and how there was nothing the necromancer could do for her. Nothing save for fusing her own bone to Wolf's skull without her consent.

Her mind trailed back even further, to the last moments that she had spent with her father. Her head had laid upon his chest, listening to his ragged breaths and slow heartbeats. He had grown too ill to speak, and Wolf hadn't entirely been sure if he was even conscious for those last few hours. She had held tight and hoped that somehow he would get better, but that is not how the world works. Tusk had been the first person she had ever truly lost, and his death was the only one that had truly broken her.

Wolf thought about the journey she had embarked on, chasing the elusive seduction of revenge. It had very nearly killed her many times, and she had nothing substantial to show for it. There were scars and bitter memories and little else. But then Wolf's mind drifted to Kazaa. He had not been a part of her revenge, and had in fact opposed her wishes to whatever extent she had allowed, and she somehow felt thankful for him. Without Kazaa, she never would have made it to Cairn; she never would have survived as long as she did. Wolf couldn't think of him as a father, as much as she knew he wanted her to, but somehow the mercenary had carved out a spot in her heart she never would have thought to possess.

"The paint is done, mistress," the servant said to her.

"Thank you," Wolf simply said to him as she rose to her feet.

Kazaa approached her as she turned around, and placed a hand gently upon her shoulder. He said, "You don't have to do this, pup. It won't bring you any satisfaction."

"What else do I have?" she asked him, and Kazaa found himself at a loss for words.

"Your axe, mistress," one of the servants said as he presented it for Wolf.

She took hold of the axe and placed it upon her back as she said, "Thank you as well. Where is my bow?"

The servant replied, "Waiting for you by the front door."

"Then I'll be going," she said, beginning to walk away.

"Wolf," Kazaa called after her. "If you go this far for revenge, imagine how far someone may come after *you* as well."

"I'm fine with that," Wolf nonchalantly replied.

She found her bow and quiver placed upon a chair next to the door, and carefully strung the quiver to her waist before pulling the bow over her shoulder. Wolf then pushed open the door and headed outside into the cool winter evening. A thick blanket of snow had encompassed the village, rendering the once black and dismal place with a somewhat welcoming tone. It also served to remind Wolf of her own home, something that she was both grateful for and sickened by, for each small reminder broke her heart just a little bit more.

As Wolf walked through the village, various Cairnites bowed and voiced their appreciation for Wolf. It was something she had grown used to, but had not come to enjoy. There were also a greater number of skeleton out than usual, doing their best to shovel the snow out of the walkways. What undead she did not see out in the streets, Wolf had to assume were working hard to cure and preserve the stockpiled food until the end of winter. The only one still out doing its normal menial labor was the blacksmith, who worked around the clock to forge black swords and daggers for the coming war.

As she passed by the forge, the blacksmith called out to here, "Come 'ere, lass. I have somethin' for ye..."

She made her way up to the forge and said, "You did not call me Grave Warden, or mistress."

"I never much cared for that fancy shit," the dwarven skeleton shrugged. "Hard to learn new rules when you're dead."

"Why can you talk, when the others can't?" she curiously asked.

"Because the others are just bones," he said. "I'm still me, jus' no skin. I died a few centuries back, and they needed someone who could work the forge. Lucky me, my soul was still around when they found my body sticking out of a pile'o rocks. Now I make whatever those bastard necromancers want, and in return I get to make whatever those pricks want."

"You said you had a gift for me?" Wolf asked.

"Ye really know how to show you care about an old dwarf's life, ey? Ay, I have somethin' for ye." he reached for something obscured by his anvil, then handed Wolf a rather nice hunting knife with a black blade. He said, "I hope it suits ye. I didn't think ye'd care for that fancy shit either."

Wolf took the dagger, feeling the weight and passing her thumb along the blade. She then said, "Thank you. It seems perfect."

"Yer welcome," the skeleton replied. "An good luck with your purpose, lass."

"What's your name?" she asked.

"They called me Ironmaw, once upon a time," he said. "Now I'm just the blacksmith."

"I am Wolf. Good luck then, Ironmaw," Wolf nodded before turning to walk away.

She slid the knife into her belt and carried on, heading for the mountain's edge. When she arrived, Helena and Velena were waiting for her there, along with a sight that she once would have considered strange and threatening. It was a black carriage pulled by two skeletal horses, each of which seemed inpatient in waiting for her. Driving the carriage was a figure dressed like most of the men in Cairn, with the addition of a cape and trousers. However, the man's head was tied to his belt by a piece of rope, and his ethereal green eyes watched Wolf with great interest.

Helena said, "Honored Grave Warden, we are glad to see that you are ready. Is all business taken care of?"

"It is," Wolf grumbled as she crossed her arms. "What is that?" she asked as she tilted her head towards the carriage.

"That is how you will get to the forest and back," Helena stated.

Velena elaborated, "The driver is a dullohan. Half dead, half alive, it travels the worlds of both the living and the dead. It will ensure you reach your destination safely."

"Is there anything else?" Wolf asked.

"Nothing more," Helena said. "You may go, Grave Warden, and claim the life that we owed you."

Wolf moved past them, and then said to the dullohan, "Hello. You're taking me down to the forest?"

"I am," the severed head said from the creature's hip. "Climb inside. Keep the door closed; you won't like what's outside."

Wolf followed his instructions and climbed into the carriage, pulling the door shut behind her. The inside was rather nice, with comfortable cushions to sit upon. Each door held a small window not unlike a porthole on a ship, though Wolf did not know that. She watched as the carriage lurched forward, and then began to steadily move. She watched in panicked fear as the horses pulled the carriage over the ledge, but they did not fall. Instead the world outside became entirely white as though the snow had consumed truly everything.

Just as suddenly as the world had disappeared, it began to return. Wolf watched in awe as single trees began to pop into the empty space, accompanied by small boulders and snow. Then they were suddenly in the forest proper, where the carriage came to a stop. There came three knocks from the front of the carriage, which Wolf took to mean it was time for her to get out. She pushed the door open and hopped out into the snow, then closed the door behind her before walking towards the front of the carriage.

The dullohan spoke from its severed head, "I will be waiting for you. Finish your business, then we return."

"I will," Wolf nodded to it, and then set off into the forest.

***

Whistler stood over a patch of land that would be meaningless to most people. The snow had covered up the stone slab he had placed there, and despite his best effort at brushing it away, it was still relatively obscured. High above him, three white birds circled, while two more rested in the trees nearby. He had draped himself in a thick white fox fur cloak, but even still the winter caused him to shiver frequently. As harsh as the cold was for him, he refused to leave until his words were said.

To the ground he spoke, "I'm sorry it took so long for me to come here this time. These past few years have been so hard for me. I know you always told me to do the right thing no matter what, but it's been getting harder and harder to do so. I've tried my best, the gods know I have tried, but it all seems pointless. The Empire has reduced my rank, stripped me of most of my privileges. I find it so hard to do good when I no longer have the power that was once afforded to me. Bardan certainly doesn't think so. He hasn't asked me to do anything since, not even grunt work. That pet guard of his, Erika, gets more responsibility than I do.

"I just don't know what to do anymore... part of me just wants to walk away, to find a place here to live out the rest of my days. The Empire wouldn't let me do that though, and I would be abandoning so many... but then if I stay, I would have to stay my hand. I would have to witness atrocity and horror and do nothing, save for the few opportunities to do something truly good that may not even be offered to me. Does that good outweigh the evil I take part in? Does one great deed make up for a thousand more small ones?

"I have asked Bardan again and again for guidance, for something I can do to help, to make up for my inactions now that my rank had been taken from me. Again and again he turns me down, tells me he has nothing for me to do, that he has nothing to tell me. When they took me from you, Bardan was the closest thing to a father I had. He took care of me, and taught me so much about the rest of the world. It hurt so much when they took me away from him too, because he was the only person left that had cared about me. He was the only person that cared about me for every year that has come since.

"It hurt so much to lose you, more than anything has ever hurt me in my entire life. I don't know if I'm losing Bardan, but I fear so much that I am. That I'm not good enough for him. That he has a new child to love. I don't know if I could take that. If losing you was the worst pain in the world, I cannot fathom the pain that would come from losing my second father. I don't know how to talk to him anymore, how to prove that I'm still worthy of being his son, to just make him look at me once more with the pride that he used to look at me with.

"This past year, I have thought about killing myself... it seems so much better than what my life has been becoming. I keep thinking about how I wouldn't have to beg for Bardan's attention anymore, that I wouldn't have to take part in the slavery or the murder, that I wouldn't be surrounded by the psychopaths of the army. That I could just be free, and be nothing, because it would all just end. I would love nothing more than for my suffering to just end, then I wouldn't have to hurt anymore. And who knows, maybe I would see you again...

"But then I think about how Bardan would feel. He's disappointed in me, and we've drawn so far away from one another, but how would he feel if I died? Worse, if I killed myself because of him? How could I possibly do that to my father? I can't, so I'm still alive. I don't know if that's better or worse. Maybe I should just tie a piece of rope around my neck and leap off a tree, or slit my throat, feed myself to a pack of wolves. But if that's the worse decision, then there was no point in doing it.

"I don't know what to do anymore, dad... it hurts so much to keep going, but it hurts even more thinking about ending it. I had so much potential and ruined it all, and now there's nothing I can do to make up for it! I just want... I just... I want... I don't know. A reason to keep going, I guess. I don't want to die, but I don't want to be alive either. I don't have you, and I don't have Bardan anymore. When I go back, I don't know what will happen, but I know it won't be worth it. I'll just want to die even more.

"I'll see how Bardan praises and trains with Erika, of how he gives her tasks that once would have been mine to perform. I'll probably be demoted again. Even if I'm not, I'll have to put up with the new CO day in and day out. I'll watch the slaves expanding the city, or waiting on their masters hand and foot. I'll be ordered to kill someone at some point, someone that probably doesn't deserve it, and I'll have to do it because that's my job.

"I don't want to do this anymore, dad. I just want to lie down. I can't join you, but I don't know what else to do. I must be such a disappointment to you to. I'm sorry... I wish I could have been better."

A bird cawed overhead and Whistler spun around, drawing his bow and an arrow as his eyes scanned the forest around him. Then his eyes became a solid white as he took on the sight of his birds. Whatever they had seen out there had moved beyond their vision, filling Whistler with dread. He willed them all to fly out over the surrounding area, using them as scouts to weed out his enemy. In the form of a bird he watched his own death as an arrow tore through the bird's ribcage. He took on the sight of another bird, only for that one too to be taken out by an arrow that seemed far too powerful for its thin frame.

Whoever his attacker was, it seemed like they knew he was a ranger, and was intentionally taking out his bird first. The loss of two of his pets had at least served to narrow down the location of his enemy though. Whistler notched an arrow and took aim, scanning the brush with pinpoint accurate eyes. There was a rustle in a large bush, which Whistler instantly fired at. He heard the telltale splat of the arrow finding flesh, and then hurried forward to see what he had hit.

To his dismay, he found himself looking at a white fox now stained with red. Suddenly Whistler's birds began cawing, and he took on each of their sights just to witness the end. Two arrows, then a black dagger that impaled the final bird to a tree. It was a horrible sight to look down at the blade sticking out of his chest, but Whistler dispelled the image and returned to his human senses. As horrible as it was to see, some good had come out of the vision.

"Gotchu," he whispered as he notched another arrow and took aim.

The arrow sailed through the air, and without a doubt found its mark. Whistler hurried forward, hopping over a fallen log to reach the location of his enemy. Just as he landed upon the ground however, a thick green vine wrapped around his leg and pulled him to the ground. Whistler spun around to see a series of vines growing out from an arrow that had been left beneath the log as a trap. Each vine was grasping out for him, intent on enveloping the ranger. Before another vine could grab him, he delivered a swift kick to the arrow shaft, breaking it in half. The vines all withered and died, allowing him to move out of the way.

Whistler rose back to his feet and began to move forward, but he now had to exercise caution over more traps. He managed to spot a few suspicious patches of leaves, along with two arrows that had claimed the lives of his birds. Not trusting what may happen if he touched them; Whistler ignored the arrows and carried on. He ended up jumping down into a small trench with melted snow at the bottom, so his boots sloshed in the water.

From above, an arrow fell, something Whistler noticed before it even entered his line of sight. He dived out of the way and was more than relieved he had, for the arrow exploded into a ball of fire mere inches from where he had been standing. As dangerous as it would be to retaliate, the attack had once again narrowed down the location of his opponent, and he wouldn't let the opportunity pass him by.

The ranger notched three arrows at once, pointed his bow towards the sky, and then released his grip upon the drawstring. A moment before he expected the arrows to land, Whistler leapt out from the trench and charged forward, notching another arrow. His enemy sent another arrow at him, but this allowed Whistler to shoot it out of the air long before it would have hit him. The arrow erupted in another burst of flames, but it was too far to do him any harm. Whistler cleared the distance, and then broke into the tree line that his enemy hid behind.

Whistler slowly moved forward, looking over everything as he hunted whoever had attacked him. Whoever they were, they left little signs. He would almost think that they their self were a ranger, but the lack of any animal aid and the callous destruction told him otherwise. Finding himself unsure of where the person had gone, Whistler placed his back against a tree trunk and took a moment to get his bearings on the area.

There came a deafening crack from behind Whistler, and then the tree began to fall to his right. He spun around, raising his bow to look into the eyes of his enemy. There she stood, draped in black fur with a mask of death glaring into him. She held a greataxe in her hands, and had felled the tree with a single strike. Whistler released the arrow, hitting the woman in her shoulder, but it didn't even slow her down.

She came at him fast, swinging her axe with deadly precision and unbridled anger. Whistler began to backpedal, notching another arrow as he took in her tactics. There was an air of familiarity about the woman, but he had no idea why. He ducked down as she swung the axe at his head, and then released an arrow into her thigh. The mad woman growled out in pain but kept coming after him, just as relentless as before.

As he back stepped, Whistler tripped over a rock, and while he caught himself, it left him open for attack from the woman. She reached forward with her left hand, intent on grabbing him by the hair. Whistler fired an arrow at her hand, severing her middle finger at the base of her hand. She let out a roar of pain and grasped at her bloody hand, allowing Whistler to turn and run. Almost instantly he cursed himself, because he had just broken the first rule that Bardan had ever taught him.

Never turn your back on an enemy.

The woman threw her axe forward, a precise and calculated throw for someone who seemed so full of rage. As Whistler turned he saw it coming, and only had half a second to tract. He tried to leap to the side, but the edge of the blade clipped his foot, taking off about a centimeter of his heel. He fell to the ground cursing, before readying another arrow as he looked to the woman.

She drew her dagger and moved forward, looking far more like a monster than a person. Whistler took aim at her heart and fired, expecting to kill the woman before she could make it any closer. Instead he watched as she deflected the arrow with the blade of her dagger, and then threw it at him just as she had thrown the axe. Whistler raised up both of his arms in an X shape to block his chest and face, and then cried out in pain as the blade embedded in his right arm. He dropped his bow so that he could try and remove it, but he didn't have the time.

The woman was atop him, delivering a right hook that sunk Whistler into the snow. She fell onto his stomach, delivering punch after punch to his face. Whistler attempted to push her away, placing his hands over her face to gouge her eyes or even just disorient her. This backfired when she bit two of his fingers off and spat them back in his face. Then the woman took hold of the dagger still embedded in Whistler's arm and began to push down.

Whistler fought back with all of his strength, reinforcing his bloody arm with his left hand, but it was no use. The woman's raw strength was overpowering him, and soon it would mark his death. Whistler's left hand fell away, and then grasped at his belt. He pulled his own knife from it and stabbed the woman in the side, but she ignored his attack. Even as he stabbed her again and again, the woman continued to push the knife down, until the tip pressed against his chest. With one final rush of strength, the woman forced the blade through Whistler.

He stared up at her in shock, feeling the blood slowly fill his lungs. He managed to rasp out, "Why? What did I do... to you?"

Wolf looked down at him, her eyes entirely empty as she said, "You got in the way. You hurt me. You couldn't just let me be alone. You couldn't just let me bury papa."

Whistler lacked any context for what she was talking about, only recalling the vague memories of how once he had let a barbarian live. He died in the snow beneath Wolf, who fell to the ground beside him. Her breaths were heavy as she writhed there, body aching and wounds bloody, still full of arrows. Her hands clenched fistfuls of snow, crushing and releasing it as she moved in senseless pain.

Then Wolf did something she did not think herself capable of, certainly not anymore. As she lay upon crimson snow, body so full of pain and longing, she began to cry. Violently, passionately, she wailed for the entire forest to hear. It wouldn't be long before her wails were joined by the howling of the wolves who normally called the forest home. In her own way, she too was singing just as the wolves did. She sang all of the pain and sorrow that had built up in her, and let it finally wash away.

When at last Wolf stopped crying, she felt better than she had for so long. But there was something else there with her. As she looked over to Whistler's corpse, there was just the smallest trace of a feeling Wolf was all but alien to. She felt regret, and that hurt almost as much as her sorrow had.

***

"I really hate these speeches," Val groaned.

"They're your duty, my lord," Brelos said as he rubbed his eyes. "Besides, you make one what, once every three years? What's the worst that could happen anyway?"

"I could accidentally spurn the ire of a dragon," he joked.

"Nothing is going to go wrong," Brelos sighed. "Just go up on stage, give your rousing speech, and then we can go home."

Val began to stretch as he said, "Tell me you don't enjoy all of this. I mean, we get to take in the lovely Oshack scenery... or what's left of it, anyway. Not to mention we've met so many interesting people!"

"I can't stand being out of Imperial Heart," Brelos shook his head. "It's far too dangerous, and you're far too reckless away from home."

"You just need to learn to live a little," Val chuckled. "Besides, I am not worried about anything out here. It has been generations since monsters plagued these woods, and there isn't a man alive that can kill me."

"As far as you know," Brelos said as he folded his arms over his chest. "All it takes is one lucky arrow or unfair condition for you to be felled. I don't want to lose you out here, my lord."

"That's very kind of you Brelos, but I-" he began for being cut off.

Brelos added, "It would be far too hard to ship your body back to Imperial Heart."

"You're a real rat bastard," Val chuckled.

"Don't forget your crown, my lord," Brelos said as he motioned toward a trunk at the back of their carriage.

"How could I forget," Val sighed as he approached the trunk. "I hate this thing. It's far too heavy to be comfortable, and even with padding it digs into my skull."

"Then you best give your speech fast," Brelos told him.

Val produced from the trunk an object that was more of a helmet than a crown, and more resplendent than anything most people would ever even see in their lifetimes. It was made from solid gold, and held six blades that rose out from behind like the rays of the sun. Val pulled it down over his head, transforming his majestic appearance into something truly deified. He then began to walk forward, white robes flowing behind him as he made his way towards the stage that had been erected for just this occasion.

He walked towards the center of the stage where a small podium awaited with a few pieces of parchment that served as notes. He didn't need them, but they were useful to have anyway. Spread out in front of the stage, kept in check by several dozen soldiers, were approximately a thousand Oshack villagers. None of them were elderly, and some were even children. All of them were either humans or dwarves. They all looked to Val in fear and awe, having never seen such a beautiful and ornately dressed man for as long as they had lived.

When he spoke, every being there heard him loud and clear. Each and every one of them, no matter how they had previously wanted to resist, found themselves captivated by Val's words. He said, "Centuries ago, Oshack was a proud part of The Rizzen

Empire. Your ancestors watched over the barbarians from The Southern Reach, ensuring they would not raid our divine Empire. They tended to orchards that kept all of the citizens of The Empire well-fed and happy. The Empire provided protection and jobs for them and ensured they could lead their best possible lives. It was a beautiful and peaceful time, and my heart breaks thinking of how that time had to come to an end.

"It was not any of your faults, and I will never blame you for that. So long ago that I am sure even the elves you may know would struggle to remember, there came a horrible act of betrayal towards the people of Oshack. Insurgents from your homeland, terrorists that sought the destruction of this glorious Empire, burned your orchards and killed many Imperial soldiers, many of which were native to Oshack. They severed all ties with The Rizzen Empire, declaring war on us and forced many of your ancestors to serve as warrior slaves against our Empire. They even sent children into battle, using them as shields if it meant claiming just one more Imperial life. It was truly the darkest of times in our shared histories.

"Emperor Caelus made the decision for peace talks so that no more Oshack blood had to be spilled. It was a difficult compromise, for the bloodthirsty savages that had taken over your home wanted something that very well may have, and did, lead to your people's suffering. They demanded that Oshack be separated from The Empire, so that your ancestors would have to fend for themselves with little food and no support. To make matters worse, this compromise came at the start of direwolf season, a time when Oshack needed the Empire more than ever. But because he knew it would mean the ultimate safety of your people, the wise Emperor Caelus in his infinite mercy agreed. Oshack was no longer a part of the Empire, and your ancestors were left to suffer.

"In the centuries since, the Empire has only blossomed and grown more powerful. Our reach has spread out to envelop the entire country, unifying Valael as one single and strong nation. We have purged the monsters from across the land, and work towards building a paradise where all are welcome. It has been hard but important work, for nothing is more important than the protection of our people. All of our people be they the humblest of workers, or the highest of nobility.

"Now after all these years, I, Emperor Valatious Rizzen stand before you humbly and without ill will. The time has come for Oshack to once again become a part of The Empire. You, as a region and as a people, will be welcomed with open arms into our glorious Empire once more. I have come here personally to see that each and every one of you here has been freed from your metaphorical chains. To see that all of you now have the opportunities denied to you by those savages from times passed. To ensure that you find happiness in The Empire that has missed you for so very long.

"No matter how much time has passed, no matter what has transpired between us and you, be it personal or familiar, it does not matter. You are all citizens of The Empire now, children beneath my rule that I have sworn to protect and nurture. Whatever lives you choose to live now will be under The Empire. Should you wish to return to the humble lives you lived before, tending to orchards and cattle, you are welcome to do so. Imperial soldiers will remain to watch over you, ensuring that your work is appreciated and that no harm comes to you. If you wish to join the army or find a new calling in Imperial Heart, you may join us in our travels back home. It is there you may take part in the highest of training awarded to the Imperial army, and serve as our noble guard against the enemies that would seek to besiege us.

"No matter what happens now, we, I, am rejoiced to have you. For too long has Oshack been separated from The Empire. Too long have you been left to suffer and toil away so far from those that truly care for you. Now that we are one again, the Empire will ensure that there is never any trouble in Oshack again. I leave you in the capable hands of my soldiers, the loyal hands of The Empire. They will take care of your needs and get you started on your new lives in The Empire."

Val turned and walked away, leaving any questions that the people of Oshack may have had unanswered. After stepping off the stage and disappearing behind it, Val stripped the crown from his head and held it awkwardly as he approached his personal carriage once more. Brelos was there waiting for him, checking over a scroll of parchment.

"Your speech went well, my lord," Brelos said. "Your amplification spell will have you heard for a mile out, at least."

"How was it?" he asked. "I hope I didn't sound too authoritative. I want them to want this, not to view us as invaders."

Brelos thought about it for a moment then said, "Some of the older ones certainly will view us as so. However, I think ultimately most of them will just go along with it, and the children will believe everything you said. I don't expect we'll have any problems from Oshack for awhile, at least nothing more than the usual menial problems."

"Then I did well," Val smirked. "Go fetch us a driver, I'm tired of standing in this field. I need better scenery before I pass out from boredom."

"Of course, my lord," Brelos bowed before hurrying off.

Val watched him go with his piercing blue eyes, then turned away. He placed the crown back into the trunk and strapped it tight against the carriage, before climbing inside of the cart. He closed the door, then allowed himself some peace and quiet. In the darkness of the carriage, lit only by the small window, his mind began to drift back to a time so long ago he had nearly forgotten it so many years later.

It is the nature of time to change the world, and though Val was sure he had once stood in this very field with his closest friends, he could not with any confidence say the field looked remotely similar. Time changes the world, the land, transforming it gradually with every single moment that passes by. But people almost never change, and that was a fact that Val knew more than anything. They never change in any way that matters.

He looked towards the stage and thought about how many people had been killed to reclaim Oshack. He thought about how many people he had personally killed, whether for defense or conquest. Then his mind drifted back towards his friends. They were all long dead now, as people are want to do. They had left him all alone with nothing save for The Empire. With nothing more than The Empire to care for, Val would ensure it prospered until the end of time, and well beyond his mortal death.

The End